TEXAS SHORT FICTION
A WORLD IN ITSELF

Spencer
I Am really going To
Miss you! I Admire
you And respect you
More Then you will
Ever Realize. As a
Football coach, There is
no one Better!
Just TAKE Some Time
To play your great
Music, read a Book, And
Smell The Roses. Life just
goes by Too damn FAST!!
I hope you Enjoy This
Brief insight To The
Real Texas Culture.

II

EDITED BY   *Mike Hennech*
5-21-2001

MIKE HENNECH & BILLY BOB HILL

2001 **Mike Hennech**
P.O. Box 1396
Alto, NM 88312-1396

For information address: ALE Publishing Co., P. O. Box 2348, Redmond, WA 98073-2348.

For information about *Texas Short Fiction III* submissions, write to:
Billy Bob Hill
P. O. Box 823521
Dallas, TX 75382

Cover: Dana Adams

Editing and Design: Jane L. Tanner & Chris Kibbie

Library of Congress Catalog: 94-73039

ISBN 1-881301-05-2

Texas Short Fiction
A World in Itself II

CONTENTS

vi

PREFACE

To begin with, the editors would like to thank all the writers who sent in their short stories for consideration for *Texas Short Fiction: A World in Itself, II*. We hope that this final mix, distilled from the many publishable submissions, manages to say something about what Texas is and about who Texans are. We also hope that this mix, to a slight extent, contributes to the rich literary tradition of our state.

All works in *Texas Short Fiction II* are previously unpublished. They were posted to us from Fort Worth, Fritch, Fredricksburg, and from points scattered across the Lone Star State. From a look at the table of contents, a reader might recognize the names of several of our most popular authors. Importantly, the editors of this anthology are pleased to present selections from a number of Texans who have never before had their fiction appear in print.

One step further, our editorial intent is for these thirty-one narratives to fit together into a readable, meaningful whole, or at least, fit together as well as the geographical, linguistic, and cultural pieces of the mind-boggling puzzle of Texas.

Finally, besides hoping that you enjoy this year's collection, the editors encourage you, the reader, to send us your best short stories—the best of your Texas—for consideration for inclusion in *Texas Short Fiction III*.

Mike Hennech and Billy Bob Hill

OLADEAN'S DIARY

NANCY R. BELL

Labor Day, September 7

My name is Oladean Davis, and I am in the eighth grade. My mother's name is Natasha Rambova Weatherford Davis which Grandma Weatherford says was the name of one of Rudolph Valentino's wives. Everybody just calls her *Tashy*. My Aunt Pola is named for a Mrs. Valentino, too. Grandma was in love with Rudolph Valentino and took a train all the way to Hollywood just to visit his grave.

We live in Houston, me and Mama and our cat, Estelle. I go to Jacinto City Junior High. Mama waitresses at the Autotel Ballroom which is near the ship channel.

Mama says her only prayer is that someday we can move to a little place in the country and get away from Crime in the Streets and Town Niggers and Whores.

Sunday, 9/13

Mama is really steamed at me. Here's what happened. Yesterday, I am at the mall with my two best friends in the whole world, Foxy Ungermann and LaTresha Patterson.

Foxy goes, "I'm getting a nose ring."

Well, me and LaTresha think that's just the coolest thing going, but we know our moms would kill us if we came home with any extra holes in our bodies. Foxy is **only** the luckiest human alive. Her dad is raising her. He's a pilot for a big oil company and is away a lot, so he gives Foxy money and lets her do whatever she pleases. I really like that in a parent. I wish Mama could

1

be more like Foxy's dad but she can't because, frankly, I think she's the kind of person that never learned how to stay out of other people's business.

Foxy has something I would kill for—an I.D. bracelet tattooed around her right ankle. It is so cool!!! The only bad thing is, she says she wishes she hadn't had Charlie King's initials put on right after hers just because she had the hots for him in the seventh grade. Now she's going to have to go through life with FUCK tattooed on her ankle.

So we're all sitting around the Piercing Pagoda waiting for Foxy's nose to get pierced, and LaTresha and I are bitching because our moms won't let us express ourselves stylistically the way Foxy does when Foxy comes up with a plan.

"How about if I give you a make over? You know, update your hairstyles."

LaTresha is black, and her mother makes her go to the Bronze House of hair to have her curl relaxed. My hair used to be down to my waist—and blonde.

Mama about had a cow when she came home and saw what Foxy had done. She had styled my hair with her dad's electric razor so it was shaved up one side and in back then left long on top. We colored it coal black with Rit dye. I wanted magenta, but Foxy said black was much more sophisticated.

Well, I am grounded for practically the rest of my life, and so is LaTresha. We bleached her hair and gave her dreadlocks.

Now, all Mama talks about is getting me out of the city. I'm like, Ohmygod! don't let her do it. I like it here.

TFIG, Sept. 18

Mama says we are going to the Channelview Full Gospel Church every Sunday and pray for a way out of here. She bought me a blonde wig to wear when we go there. Oh, brother!

Saturday Nite, 11:00, 9/19

My hand is shaking like a leaf as I write this. The cop cars and ambulance just left. We had a real murder right here at Gulf Gate Apartments.

Channel Thirteen Eye-Witness News was here for a minute but they left because, I guess, it wasn't a very *interesting* murder—just Skinny Minchew who was nothing but an old wino that got his rent free here for cleaning out the pool and cutting the grass. Skinny was coming home from the Space City Ice House with a bottle of Thunderbird in a sack when a bunch of gang guys rolled him and took away his bottle. They beat him up and left him for dead, which, in actual fact, he was. Mama says more than likely, he was scared to death as anybody would be if they saw a bunch of drugged-up Mexican teenagers coming at them.

Mama says for sure we're getting out of this town. She just don't know how yet.

Monday, Sept. 21

It's spooky the way that woman gets everything she wants. Today, a letter came from a lawyer in the town of Harmony where Mama grew up and Grandma Weatherford still lives. It's 'way up in Northeast Texas. It seems Mama's Uncle Papa died. Uncle Papa never had a wife and kids and, since Mama was his favorite niece, he left his house and lot in Harmony to her.

Green Acres, here I come!!!

Oct. 9

I haven't written much lately because it's depressing. O.K.? Mama's already quit her job at the Autotel Ballroom and is packing and humming all day. Barf!!!

October 10

Things are looking up. Mama got a check in the mail from the lawyer. The first thing we did was, me and her went down to Weiner's and stocked up on jeans and sweaters and tennies. We both got genuine sueded jackets with six-inch fringe and imitation silver concha buckles. She made me get some cowboy boots which I wouldn't be caught dead in only she said they'd love them in Harmony.

3

November 1, Harmony-the-end-of-the-world, Texas

Well, here we are in the Valley of the Dead.

The house is O.K. I have my own bedroom with lots of windows and a big closet. Estelle likes it because the only cafe in town, Sonny Boy's Cafe, is close by, and the cook throws scraps out the back door for her. Mama is applying for a job there.

I wore my new cowboy boots to school the first day—the ones Mama was so sure they'd love. Yeah! Right! These kids out here are more clothes conscious than they ever were in Jacinto City. Except for the kickers, who are real nerdy, everybody else wears Girbaud jeans and Nikes.

And, get this, their idea of a good time is to go down to WalMart and drive around the parking lot. No kidding!

Sun. Nite, 11/8

The best thing about this place is my Grandma. She is cool even if she does have wrinkles all over her face. I have never seen a person with so many wrinkles. She says it's from working like a man all her life. Grandma is very old, but she's tough—not like Mama. She wouldn't let a little crime and dope run her out of a place, I bet.

Today, she picked me up in her car to go to the Church of God of Prophecy. We tried to get Mama to go, but she said the Lord wanted her to stay home and preserve her strength so she could earn a living for herself and her little girl. It is not easy having a mother who has a direct line to The Almighty—and Him always telling her to do exactly what she was going to do anyway. One of these days God's going to speak to me, and He's going to tell me to get the hell out of here.

Actually, it's not too bad down at Grandma's church. After a while, the grownups get to singing and waving their arms in the air. Pretty soon they get the Gifts of the Spirit and start jerking and talking in tongues. That's when us kids sneak out back to smoke cigarettes and tell dirty jokes.

Mama wrote a poem and put it up on the refrigerator. It went:

"Off to church goes my Oladean,

The cutest girl you've ever seen,

She thinks that making her go is mean,
But someday, she'll thank me and call me a queen."
Mama said it just came to her while she was watching Brother Copeland on TV.

Monday, Nov. 21

Mama went to work at Sonny Boy's and, of course, he started hitting on her right away. Mama looks pretty good when she's fixed up. Mama says it doesn't matter because, after those clowns at the Autotel Ballroom, Sonny Boy Pearson is a cream puff. Besides, she says with that big old belly of his he's probably all blow and no go.

Grandma says he sells dope—grows pot out behind the cafe. Mama says that's silly and those are just old castor bean plants back there. Sonny Boy told her so.

Tuesday, November 22

We had macaroni and cheese, tater tots, and imitation chicken-fried steak in the cafeteria today.

I am now a woman. I "started" last night. I am wearing one of those mini-pads Mama has been saving for this blessed event. You would of thought I had sprouted wings or something.

Saturday (again!)

This morning Grandma came over just as me and Mama were sitting down to breakfast. She had just come from the beauty shop, and her hair was tall with little curlicues and ringlets hanging down.

"Praise the Lord!" she said. "You two still in your nightgowns?" She sat down with a grunt. "Pour me some coffee, Oladean, and shove that ashtray over here."

"Well, good morning to you too, Mother," Mama said.

"How's the job?" Grandma said.

"Fine," Mama said.

"Had any trouble with Sonny Boy?"

"No, why?"

"Just askin'."

Mama shifted her chair so she could look straight at Grandma. "What's up, Ma?"

"Oh, nothin'."

"Mother!"

Grandma put out her cigarette. "O.K. Tash, I know what you're thinking. You're thinking just because you're in the country with the grass growing and the birds singing nothing bad can happen. Well, the devil works in the sticks same as he works in the city—and don't you forget it." She looked over at me. "Want to come help me sort some record albums?"

I said, "Sure!"

Grandma is a junktique dealer, which means her whole house and yard are one big garage sale. I love it! I wound up spending the whole day over there helping her sort and price things. She gave me a china lady that has a hoop skirt that's a pincushion and a Jim Beam bottle in the shape of a jolly sea captain. Grandma and I are a lot alike in that we both like nice things.

Wed. 11/23

Today, I will write about LaVon Overstreet who bags groceries at the U-Sac-Um. He lives with his mother even though he is probably at least forty years old. He has a pricing gun which he is very proud of and wears in his belt all times—even at the bowling alley. Even at church!!!

Old LaVon is dynamite when it comes to marking groceries. Oscar, the manger says if a truck comes in at seven, Lavon will have the whole load marked and shelved by noon.

He comes in the cafe every Saturday after he gets paid and sits on the third stool from the end. Mama says, you can bet on it, he is going to order the chicken-fried steak basket with gravy on the side, a large milk and Dutch apple pie *à la mode*. He cuts his meat in perfect little squares and chews each one exactly ten times. When he finishes he takes the paper liner out of his basket, folds it four ways and puts it back in the basket. I mean, this guy is Weird!!

6

Even though LaVon's mother is old, she keeps him very neat. His shirts are starched and ironed—ditto his jeans and even the aprons he wears sacking groceries. Every third Saturday, she gives him seven dollars out of his pay and sends him to Jimmy's Barber Shop to get a dorky old-man's haircut.

I feel sorry for LaVon, but you can't be nice to him or he will follow you around wanting to talk to you and be your friend. I imagine he is probably lonesome.

11/30

Something weird is going on in Kemp County. Personally, I think it is UFO's doing it. I am investigating the whole thing for the F.B.I. men who will be coming soon I know. For sure, Sheriff Earl Dean Stacy is too old and stupid to do it right.

HERE IS WHAT HAPPENED:

8:05 A.M. The school bus passes Ode Farley's pasture and, lying right by the road is a dead cow, or what is left of her. Here is what she looked like: she was slit right down the belly and gutted. Her head was cut off and stuck on a fence post, and she looked like she was grinning but, under the circumstances, I doubt if she was. Her whole bag had been sliced off slicker than a whistle.

8:15 A.M. A lot of the kids on the bus get sick and stuff.

4:05 P.M. The bus lets me off at home.

4:19 P.M. I am on my bike headed for Ode's place. Arrive at 4:23. Investigation of the scene turns up no dead cow. Grass in the ditch mashed down a lot. A whole bunch of blood and some cow s——.

4:31 P.M. Am about to leave when I discover something spray-painted on the road. It is a clue! It is a drawing of a five-pointed star with a circle around it.

4:45 P.M. Back at home, I quickly draw a picture of the thing somebody painted on the road. THIS IS IMPORTANT!!!!

I didn't have to tell Mama about it because it was all anybody talked about down at the cafe today.

"Sheriff Stacy says he knows darn well it was wolves," Mama said. "I told him I hear them all the time howling down in the creek bottom."

"Mama," I had to say, "that sheriff is nine ways dumb."

7

Mama's face shut up tight. I could see her mind was made up so I didn't tell her it was a sharp knife that cut old Bossy's bag off. No wolf did that. She wouldn't believe it anyway. Mama is determined to believe the country is like the safest place in the whole world.

November 30

All anybody talks about anymore is the big cow murder. You wouldn't understand that unless you lived in a town so boring the Little League scores are front-page news.

Dec.5, Midnight

Forget what I said about the country being boring. We had EXCITEMENT tonight, and I was INVOLVED!! COOL!!!

Here is what happened. I'm over at the cafe. It's about six P.M. and I'm waiting for Mama to get off so we can go to WalMart and get me some sneakers. LaVon's in there chowing down on his steak basket, and Sonny Boy is wiping off the counter with a dirty rag when three biker guys come in and sit down at the counter. They are dressed in black leather and have on these big heavy boots with spikes! No kidding! These guys are BAD! Sonny Boy has quit wiping the counter and is staring at them with this totally wigged-out expression on his face. Mama goes over with her little green pad to take their orders like they get bikers in there every day. One of them says something I can't hear then pulls her across the counter and plants a big old stinky kiss right on her lips. By now, I am totally grossed out—and scared, too.

They don't want anything," Sonny Boy says. "Go back in the kitchen and take the girl with you."

Mama grabs my arm and we get in there fast. Lavon is sitting on his stool cutting his chicken fried steak in little squares.

Me and Mama watch through the pass-through, but we can't hear a word because Randy Travis is on the jukebox singing his little hayseed heart out.

It is obvious that these guys are plenty steamed at Sonny Boy. The one with the blonde beard has got him around the waist while the one with a swastika earring keeps punching him hard in his big old jelly-belly.

LaVon is sitting there eating his pie like nothing unusual is happening.

Then I notice something very strange. They all have really neat tattoos of like snakes and daggers and stuff, but (and this is weird!) everyone has the same thing on their right hand. It is a sign I have seen before and will never forget. A FIVE-POINTED STAR IN A CIRCLE!!!! My clue!

By now, LaVon has finished his pie and is folding his paper basket liner.

I am starting to feel a little sorry for Sonny Boy because one of them is holding a knife at his throat. Sonny Boy looks like he is going to pass out from fear.

Just then, the door opens and here comes Mrs. Overstreet looking for LaVon because he didn't get home at precisely 6:28 like he always does. Mama sees her and hollers, "Help!"

The three bikers are distracted just long enough for Sonny Boy to grab a gun from under the counter and start shooting. He gets three shots off, and one of them hits poor old LaVon in the shoulder. Naturally, he misses all three bad guys.

I don't know what happens next because Mama grabs me and pulls me to the floor, but we hear one more shot, then Mrs. Overstreet screaming her head off. Mama isn't doing anything but lying there asking the Lord Jesus to save us, which I think is a long shot, so I crawl to the back door and tear across the vacant lot to Grandma's house.

As soon as I get her to understand what is happening, Grandma grabs her old shotgun and we race back to the cafe.

"Stay still," Grandma whispers, and I do, but not too far. Grandma tip-toes around front and peeps in the window.

I hear Mama scream, "Help me Jesus!" and I run to the back door. Those three guys have her down on the kitchen table and are pulling her dress up.

Suddenly, the barrel of Grandma's old shotgun pokes through the pass-through window and BOOM! BOOM! Two shots.

Two of the bad guys hit the floor and the third almost knocks me over running out the back door. Then, VAROOM, him and his bike are outa there.

I run past Mama into the front room before anybody can stop me. LaVon is still on his stool looking down at the blood running all over his clean shirt and kind of whimpering. Mrs. Overstreet has her arms around him. And that last shot we heard?

Sonny Boy had forgotten he had a gun in his hand and shot himself in the foot.

December 6

The sheriff just left. Sonny Boy is in jail. Sheriff Stacy said Grandma was right—that stuff growing out back was pot. Grandma said only someone as miff-minded as Tash would believe marijuana plants were castor bean plants in the first place and if the sheriff had been doing his job he would have investigated it long ago. Anyway, Sonny Boy had been selling his pot crop to that bunch of weirded-out, Satan worshiping bikers. The sheriff said Sonny Boy never would say what he did to get them so mad at him, but Grandma says, knowing Sonny Boy, he might have short-changed them. She says Sonny Boy Pearson would steal pennies off a dead man's eyes. I don't know what that means, but if Grandma said it, I believe it.

Dallas, Texas February 12

Well, you know my mama. She can't leave well enough alone. Just when things were looking up in Harmony, she packs us up and moves us to Big D.

I am now a freshman at Frederick Douglass High in Oak Cliff. Mama has a day job in a pants factory so she can be home at night to keep an eye on me. The pay's not so good but she says it's worth it for the peace of mind.

We sold Uncle Papa's house and bought this duplex on Ricter Street. Mama rented out the other half to a couple who fight all the time, but that's O.K. because it helps pay the bills.

Only half a mile away is a big mall which is where I hang out on weekends. What I say is, you've seen one mall, you've seen them all. Still, it sure beats hell out of WalMart.

The only bad part is, I don't get to see Grandma anymore, but she says I can come to Harmony next summer and help her out in her business.

Oh, yeah, I have a new friend. Her name is Bambi. She gave me a tube of black lipstick and is teaching me to apply makeup. COOL!!!

THE PINK PETTICOAT

JAMES WARD LEE

At 6:30 on a cold, blue, drizzling East Texas Monday morning, Grady Dell pulled into his parking space beside the Bodark Springs Post Office. He wanted to be early so Melvin Spruille, the postmaster, and Charley Little, the window clerk, would be so busy working the weekend mail that they wouldn't have any time to notice how hungover he was. Charley was a deacon in the Primitive Baptist Church, and Melvin preached every third Sunday at the Campbellite Church over in Dodd City in Fannin County. They both hated whiskey. They also hated other people's sin.

Grady hoped to get his weekend mail sorted so he could run across the square to the Busy Bee for a quick cup of coffee and a piece of dry toast before the morning mail came in on Number 31. Grady had his mail sorted and sacked and was headed out the side door when Melvin called to him, "You might as well take your time, Grady. Number 31 is going to be an hour late according to Max over at the T&P. Maybe you ought to try eating a little something."

"Yeah, I guess I might as well."

Damn, Grady thought, I hoped he wouldn't notice. If my job wasn't Civil Service, Melvin would've got rid of me the day Hoover left office and Melvin took over as postmaster from Jack Hurst. Not a one of them Spruilles ever took a drink. I guess that's what makes 'em so damned mean. I guess I could stay as sober as Melvin and Charley if I didn't need a little something to steady my nerves once in a while. I'd probably be a heap better off if I didn't, but hell, I might wind up as sour as old Melvin. Damn, if Franklin D. runs for a third term in 1940, I may be working for Melvin till I retire.

Grady held Friday's copy of the *Dallas Morning News* over his head as he crossed the square to the Busy Bee. He tried to see who was inside, but the windows were all fogged, so he squared his shoulders, opened the door,

11

and went in. He walked the length of the counter to sit on the end stool and be away from the early regulars up at the front. He nodded and spoke to six or seven people, but kept moving to avoid small talk.

He sat on the last stool in front of the window that opened into the kitchen and nodded to Modell Floyd, the cook. Modell grinned and said, "How you, Mr. Grady?"

"Fine, Modell, how's your mamma?"

"She about to get well. Dr. Clayton first said she gonna have to have that gall bladder took out. But Mamma say she ain't lettin' nobody at her with a knife without he slip up on her. Then Dr. Clayton decide Mamma just have some kind of infection. She gonna be fine, I guess. How's Miss Mamie? She still sick all the time?"

"Most of the time. If it ain't one thing, it's another."

Modell sighed, "Yeah, ain't that the way everything is?"

Bernice Mayes, the waitress, slid a cup of coffee in front of Grady and said, "You look like you could use some of this. Want anything to eat?"

"I guess so. You reckon you got anything I can keep down?" Grady had known Bernice a long time—some people even thought he might know her a little better than he was supposed to."

Bernice looked sympathetic and said, "I'll have Modell scramble you a couple of hen eggs and fix you a slice of dry toast." She turned around and gave the order to Modell. Then she leaned over the counter toward Grady and said, "You feel as bad as you look?"

Grady, with a Lucky Strike in one hand and his chin cupped in the other, said, "I don't know how bad I look, Bernice, but I'd have to get better to die."

Bernice laughed, but she kept it low so as not to add a jolt to Grady's throbbing head. "You looked like you felt good Saturday night when I seen you and Mamie up at the Briar Patch. I thought Mamie had sick headaches all the time, but you and her was dancing every dance."

Grady gave a weak grin and said, "She usually gets well on the weekend—and during the week if I mention going up to the Moon River Beach or somewhere."

Bernice looked disgusted at the thought of Mamie's famous illnesses and said, "You must mention honky tonking a good deal. I see you all every time I go out."

"Well, it's better to go out than to stay home and have to call the doctor. 'Course sometimes she gets sick when we get in, and then I have to walk over to Cooter Poe's house and wake them up and call old Clayton. You know how he cusses when you call him late, but he usually comes out and gives her a shot."

"Mamie don't drink, does she?"

"Oh, Lord, no! Mamie can smell a shot of whiskey over the telephone. She says she hates for me to take a drink, but she'll put up with it to get to go honky-tonking. Maybe that's why I'm always ready to go up to the Red River as soon as it gets dark."

Bernice blushed and lowered her voice, "You ever think about going by yourself? Or maybe taking somebody else?"

"I guess I've thought about it, but somehow it never works out that way."

Bernice hesitated till she got her nerve up. Then she blurted it out in a hoarse whisper, "Did you ever think about coming by my house when you get off from work? Like maybe today about 4:30? You might could use a drink of that Four Roses that Burl Weems left at my house last week. I'll even give you some ice and a Co-Cola to go with it. I may even have some 7-Up." She didn't wait for Grady to answer but kept talking, getting redder the more she said. "Old Charley Fite calls 7-Up 'a chaser.' Did you know that? When he comes in here to order one, he never says, 'Bernice, give me a 7-Up'; he always says, 'Bernice, give me a chaser.' Old Charlie always—"

Grady held up his hand to cut her off. And then he whispered, "I've thought about coming by a lot, but I don't know. Somehow, it don't seem right. I don't know. I guess as small as Bodark Springs is—"

Bernice was suddenly furious, "Hell, don't nothing seem right. Not a damned thing. Not anymore. They say they are gonna have another war and that that crazy damned Hitler is gonna to take over the world. That damned Roosevelt says the Depression is over, but I ain't seen no sign of it. All I see is that I am working my ass off in this damned cafe and—"

Grady was half way off the stool and was shaking his hand back and forth in front of him trying to get Bernice to quieten down. "Hush, Bernice, everybody in here can hear you. You know how they talk in a town like this."

Bernice lowered her voice, but she didn't end her litany. "The whole damned world is crazy. Remember this spring—when was it, May?—that old man claiming he was Jesse James come to town to the American Theater and nearly caused Lark and Hammaker to fall out for good. And in the summer that fool Edna Earl Morris claimed that Jesus Christ his ownself just waltzed into her house one evening about 3:00, come right through a locked screen door where she was ironing. And her not wearing nothing but a pink petticoat. And Jesus started telling her some crap about how him and her was going to save Bodark from sin. I mean, can you believe that fool girl? And can you believe that half the people in Eastis County thought she was telling the truth? And now that damned hussy is missing." Bernice put her hands on her hips and turned away; then she wheeled back toward Grady and said—loud this time—"And now you are worried because somebody might see *you*. And what about me? What if somebody sees me? Nobody gives a damn if somebody sees me. I don't give a shit—"

Bernice sobbed and ran out through the kitchen.

Bear Higgins, the owner of the Busy Bee, came down the counter toward Grady. Bear never smiled and hardly ever spoke. Mostly he just grunted at his customers. He approached Grady looking even sourer than usual and said, "What in the hell did you do to Bernice?"

"Nothing."

"Then why in the hell did she fall in to crying and run out of here? Did you day something out of the way to her?"

Grady, one of the best-humored men in the county, suddenly felt a fury come over him. He half rose from the stool and gritted his teeth at Bear Higgins, "Did you ever hear me say anything out of the way to her or any other woman? Well, did you? Hell no, you never did. And I didn't say nothing to Bernice. Now am I going to get anything to eat in this goddamned cafe or not?"

Grady's headache pounded so much that his anger drained away instantly and he sat back on the stool. Bear, apparently satisfied, didn't speak but turned and lumbered back to the front of the cafe. Modell, seeing and hearing everything, waited till Bear was back at the cash register; then she came out the swinging door from the kitchen bringing Grady's eggs and toast in one hand and a glass of tomato juice in the other.

"Here, Mr. Grady, drink this and eat them eggs and you may make it 'til dinner. But I'll tell you this, if you don't eat something, you may plumb shake yourself to death." She laughed silently and turned to the urn to get him another cup of coffee.

"Thank you, Modell, I'm much obliged."

"Aw, it ain't nothing, Mr. Grady."

Everybody in Eastis County knew Grady Dell—and liked him. He was always polite, and he never grumbled when people on his route asked him to bring them something from Bodark—a few groceries, medicine from the drugstore, even a few yards of cloth from H. Goldberg's Department Store. All Grady asked was that the women on his route send a note telling Harry Goldberg exactly what kind of yard goods they wanted and what color. Every day the mail ran, Grady delivered two nickel packages of Speedo Headache Powders to Warsaw Bryant's wife. If she didn't have a dime, Grady took her the powders anyway. Warsaw was serving a year and a day in prison for making bootleg whiskey, and Grady figured that Ola May Bryant had a good reason to have a headache. Most people in town knew that Grady had been drinking for the past five or six years, but they put it down to his having to take a mortgage on the house when he couldn't pay Mamie's doctor bills, and then losing the house when he couldn't make the payments. And then there was Mamie's sickness, which Dr. Clayton said was all in her head. Grady never complained to Mamie about being sick, and he never failed to call the doctor when she had one of her "jumping headaches" in the middle of the night. Lindley Fadley at the drugstore once told Grady, "You are getting most too many prescriptions for Dilaudin filled," so Grady started getting some filled at Fadley's and some at Doc Miller's. But he knew he wasn't fooling either Lindley or Doc Miller. He thought, I'd rather have a tooth pulled than to go into either one of them damn drugstores with a prescription in my hand, but he never complained to Mamie. It wouldn't have done any good because Mamie complained enough for both of them. She always had a lot to say about his drinking. He always said the same thing back to her, "I could quit if I wanted to. I just drink a little something ever once in a while to settle my nerves." And he thought that was all it amounted to.

Grady sat nursing his hangover and waiting to hear Number 31 blow its whistle. By the time he had finished eating his breakfast, Bernice had come back from outside looking as if she had never shed a tear in her life. She went up and down the counter pouring coffee and joking with the customers. Grady ate the eggs and toast that Modell brought him and thought he might keep the food down after all. Maybe Modell's breakfast had saved his life, he thought. He lit his eighth cigarette of the day as Tarp Davidson came in the front door.

Tarp, the city mail carrier, loved carrying the mail. It was pure fun for Tarp to walk all over Bodark and go in all the stores with the day's mail. He stopped to visit people sitting out on their porches, and if nobody was out, Tarp took his pleasure in reading people's post cards as he walked along between houses. When Buck Lawson wrote cards home to his folks from Idaho where he was in the CCC camp he always wrote at the bottom, "Hello Tarp!" Estelle Lawrence, who was always out in her yard working in her flower bed or feeding her chickens or sweeping the yard when Tarp came by, got most of her mail read to her. Tarp would open the gate and walk up the walk, and, while Mrs. Lawrence was wiping off her hands on her apron to take her letters, would announce the news from her daughter in Dallas. "Well, let's see. You got a card here from Inez. Says she likes her new job. Says she may be coming home week after next." Tarp didn't seem to worry about the privacy guaranteed by the U.S. Mail. Tarp thought if you had a secret you didn't want told, you ought to put it in a letter and not on a penny post card.

He was all smiles as he came down the counter, nodding and speaking and pausing to dispense a bit of gossip here or a wisecrack there. When he got to the end of the counter, he slid onto the stool and said, "Hidy, Grady, you gonna live after all? Melvin said we might have to bury you."

Grady winced, "I guess I'm good for another day. I hate it that old Melvin noticed I was hungover."

Tarp could hardly wait to pass beyond pleasantries and get to the real news, so he just made a pouring motion in Bernice's direction and said to Grady, "Well, I guess you heard that Edna Earl Morris is missing?" Without waiting for a reply, Tarp began whispering his version of her disappearance.

About three months before, Edna Earl had had a visit from Jesus. The way Tarp told the story, she was standing in the kitchen of the little shotgun house down on Star Street that she and Roy Gene rented from Bill McLaughlin. She was ironing. She looked up to find Jesus standing beside her looking tall and blond like Wayne Morris in the movies. He called her by name and sat down at her kitchen table with her for an hour talking about Heaven and sin and the Baptist church that Edna Earl grew up in over in Honey Grove. He took one of her forks and with a tine drew a picture of the throne of God on her oilcloth tablecloth. Then he just disappeared. Everybody in Bodark who knew Edna Earl came to look at the picture that Jesus drew on her tablecloth. Some said it was a inspired representation from the hand of God, but some said a third grader at the William Barrett Travis Grammar School could have made a better picture of a throne. Mamie Dell made Tommy Earl go down to Star Street one afternoon after school just to talk to Edna Earl Morris. He came home half scared and half hypnotized. He was scared of being so close to the presence of the Lord, but was struck dumb by Edna Earl's beauty. When Mamie asked him what Edna Earl had told him, he said he didn't exactly remember. He just kept humming, "How Beautiful Heaven Must Be." Mamie thought the boy was overwhelmed by Jesus's effect on Edna Earl and that the humming was in preparation for declaring himself for Christ when Mt. Hebron Church had its next revival. Grady figured the boy had been addled by being so close to Edna Earl and that the hymn humming was a sign that puberty might be around the corner.

All the men in town talked about how pretty Edna Earl was. But most of them said something like, "She ain't got much brains, but Lord God is she pretty!"

Grady was thinking about how mad he had been when Mamie sent Tommy Earl down there to hear about Jesus while Tarp was telling his story.

"Did you hear what I just said?," Tarp asked Grady.

"Yeah, you said Edna Earl Morris was missing."

"Hell, you wasn't listening. You was thinking about how pretty that girl was."

Grady caught Tarp's use of the past tense, "Why did you say 'was?' Do you think she's dead or something?"

Tarp looked pained. "Of course she's dead. You didn't hear a word I said did you? Sheriff Wells has looked all over the county for her body. Now they have brought in that Texas Ranger from over at Bonham, one of the ones that killed Clyde Barrow. They plan to start dragging the creeks around town and then branch out from there."

Grady looked down at the counter while he tried to decide whether to tell Tarp where Edna Earl was. It would all come out sooner or later anyhow, so he figured he might as well tell Tarp now and get it over with.

"Now, Tarp, don't you fall into hollering when I tell you what I'm gonna tell you. Do You hear?"

"Yeah, I hear. What you gonna tell me?"

"Well, Edna Earle ain't dead. She was—"

"Ain't dead! How the hell—"

Grady said, "Will you shut up? You said you wouldn't yell and take on if I told you something. Now are you gonna do what you said you was?"

Tarp leaned close and whispered, "Yeah. Of course I am. Now go on. How do you know she ain't dead?"

"Cause she's out at my house asleep right now," Grady said.

"Out at your—" Tarp jumped up off the stool, but Grady pushed him down and said, "Will you shut the hell up?"

"Yeah, yeah, o.k., but how come? Where's Mamie? Did you and Edna Earl—"

"No, me and Edna Earl didn't do nothing. Nothing like that. Sunday night me and Mamie went up to the Briar Patch. You know that little joint that Ed Butts just opened up on the Red River?"

"Yeah, yeah," Tarp said, "What about it?"

"Well, on the way home, just when we was coming up the bluff where the road bends to the right, I saw something red laying in the road. I slammed on the brakes and run off in the ditch to miss it. When I got out and went back up on the road, I seen a woman laying right in the middle of the road wearing nothing but a slip. It was Edna Earl. She said she wanted to get run over and killed. She commenced to crying and hollering and saying how she had been betrayed and how she wanted to die and join her Lord and how she—"

Tarp couldn't wait to hear more. He broke in with, "Betrayed. By who? Jesus? Is that what she meant? Did she think the Lord should have took her with him when he was—"

Now is was Grady who cut in. "No it wasn't Jesus. It was that sorry damned Chick Bailey. Her and Chick run off and went to Oklahoma and stayed in a tourist court in Durant until Chick told her he wasn't gonna take her to California with him after all. Then he brought her back across the river on the ferry and put her out. That's when she decided to take off her good dress and lay it beside the road and get herself killed in that pink petticoat. She wanted to save her good dress that Roy Gene had bought her after Jesus come. She wanted to be buried in it. I guess Chick went on to California like he planned to."

Tarp said, "Well, I'll be a son of a bitch. What you gonna do with her?"

"I don't know. When I get in this evening, I guess I'll take her out to her daddy's place. He lives out close to Savoy. Then it won't be my problem. I hate to have to go up to the sheriff's office and tell what I know, but I guess Herman Wells needs to send that Ranger on back to Bonham or wherever he come from."

Grady got up to go pay Bear for his breakfast, but Tarp called him back and said, "Hey, Grady, who do you think it was that come to Edna Earl's last summer? You know when she was ironing and wearing nothing but that petticoat?"

Grady came back and stared a Tarp a minute. "What? I don't know but I 'spect it was Jesus, Tarp."

Grady turned and walked away quickly to hide his laughter.

Tarp sat in front of Modell's window with his mouth hanging open. He couldn't believe that Grady Dell had swallowed Edna Earl's looney story about Jesus.

Telling Tarp it was Jesus put a spring in Grady's walk that had been missing for three months. Outside, he began whistling "I Come to the Garden Alone" and suddenly changed to "How Beautiful Heaven Must Be." The rain had stopped and the sun was trying to break through. Hell, he thought, I may make it through the day. Maybe even the week. Shoot, if it keeps on being this much fun around here, I may live to see 1939.

Inmate 93274

Talibah F. Modupe

For six long and laborious years, I was referred to as Inmate 93274. Very few guards knew or cared to know my real name. I now realize I have no one to blame but myself. I still can't believe what I put myself and my family through. With the help of God and a good man, I was able to reclaim the victory and get my dignity back.

Trevor was all any woman could ever ask for. I often felt I did not deserve him—partly because of the way that I treated him. He tolerated the lying, stealing, hitting, hot checks and, cheating for over five years. I guess he really does love me.

My story began the summer of 1984. I awoke on a Wednesday morning from a night of reckless drinking and partying with the wrong crowd. The way I behaved no one would have guessed I was the mother of three lovely daughters and had a wonderful, supportive husband. I guess you could say I was not decent enough to recognize it at the time. Trevor begged me to seek professional counseling and threatened to leave me several times if I didn't. I knew him better than he knew himself. There was no way he was going to walk out on me.

That particular morning really wasn't any different from the other mornings. As usual, Trevor prepared breakfast for himself and the girls, assisted them with getting dressed and driving them to school while I was still asleep. While practically stumbling downstairs and trying to make my way into the kitchen for a fresh cup of brewed coffee (I knew Trevor had prepared for me), I was disturbed by several hard knocks on the front door. I remember wondering why didn't they bother to use the doorbell. Casually walking to the front door, I looked out of the peephole and observed two men in dark suits. When I asked who was it, one of them held up a badge to the peephole and responded, "Police. Open up!" I struggled to finish tying the belt on my flimsy housecoat and fluffing my hair before opening the door to the strangers. They introduced themselves while still showing their badges. I asked, "Is there a problem?" Then one of them asked, "Are you Patricia Weller?" I replied, "Yes. Is there something wrong?" The officer responded, "Ms. Weller you are under arrest for prostitution and forgery of unauthorized checks. I'm sorry Ma'am, but we're going to have to ask you to get dressed and come with us." I nearly fainted directly in front of them. For the life of me, I could not remember forging anything, and all the men I slept with, not one of them ever paid me. Surely there must be some mistake.

The officers entered my house and stood in the foyer. They allowed me to get dressed before hauling me off to jail. I cried all the way to the station and wondered how was I going to explain this to Trevor. I knew this would surely destroy him. And what about the girls. I realize I had not been a good mother to them, but girls need their mothers.

When we arrived at the police station, I was fingerprinted and searched by a female officer. Once she finished invading every part of my body I asked if I could make a phone call. She hastily escorted me down a long and narrow corridor and pointed to the pay telephone attached to a dingy wall. I told her I didn't have any money with me and she responded, "Call collect." I could hardly remember Trevor's office number as I slowly gave it to the operator and contemplated what and how I was going to tell him about the mess I had unknowingly gotten myself into.

The phone rang three times before Melissa, Trevor's cute young secretary, decided to answer. The operator asked her if she would accept a collect call for Trevor Weller and she hesitantly responded, "Yes, I guess so." I asked Melissa if I could speak with him and she cheerfully responded, "He's in a meeting with his boss." Telling her it was an emergency did not register at all nor did it help. I envisioned her filing and blowing her long fake nails as she responded, "Sorry, Mrs. Weller, I was told not to interrupt the meeting even if it was the Pope." She asked, "Do you want me to take your number and have Trevor get back with you later on?" I didn't realize they were on a first name basis. I'll have to mention this inappropriate behavior to him later. But first, I've got to try and get past his overly protective secretary and speak with him directly. I was attuned by now to her behavior and decided to give the impression I was playing into her hands. I didn't want the situation to become worse. Drifting back from my daze, I heard her ask again, "Do you want me to have him call you?" I hurriedly responded, "No. I'll have to call him back. When do you expect the meeting to end?" Melissa answered, "I'm not certain, but I expect it to last at least a good two to three more hours." Biting my bottom lip, I reluctantly thanked her and hung up the phone.

The female officer escorted me to my cell and locked it behind me. As she started to walk away I said, "Excuse me Ma'am, but I was not able to reach my husband. I'm told he's in a meeting for a few hours. Is it possible to try my call again later?" She gave me a pathetic look and responded, "Yeah, I guess so. I'll come get ya in a coupla hours." I sat on my musty, filthy cot and begin weeping and wondering how was I going to concoct a reasonable and believable lie to tell Trevor.

As promised, the female officer returned to my cell and escorted me to the phone. She leaned up against the opposite wall and pretended not to be interested in my conversation, but I'm sure she was planted there to listen. I nervously counted each ring before Melissa answered the phone. The operator asked if she'd accept a collect call for Trevor Weller. This time Melissa asked, "From where?" Before the operator had a chance to respond I butted in and said, "Melissa, it's Pat, I mean, Mrs. Weller again. Is Trevor out of his meeting?" She responded, "Yes." I thought she was going to hand the phone to him, but after several moments of dead silence I asked, "Well, Melissa, may I please speak with him?" She responded, "He's not here." It took all I had not to scream at her. I asked, "Melissa, do you know where he is and did you tell him I called earlier?" She replied, "I believe he's at lunch and no, I didn't tell him you called. You didn't ask me to. If you'd like, I can have him call you when he returns from lunch." "No! Just tell him I called and I'll try and call back in approximately one hour and that it is extremely important. Would you please tell him that, Melissa?" I said. "Got it," she responded.

Slowly walking back to my cell with my unfriendly guard dog, I explained to her that my husband was still out of the office and asked if I could try him once more. She responded, "Dear, you are really pressing your luck here. We'll see." One hour later the officer returned to my cell to escort me once again down the long and narrow corridor to use the phone. This time when the operator dialed, Trevor answered the phone. She asked if he would accept a collect call and he responded, "Yes." I explained to Trevor that I had been mistakenly arrested and needed him to come quickly. He asked me for what and I told him I could not discuss it over the phone, but needed to tell him in person.

Trevor arrived at the police station approximately thirty minutes later. The female officer escorted him to my cell advising us he had only ten minutes to visit. We embraced and he asked me if I was all right. I asked him to have a seat on the soiled cot as I began telling him about my arrest. Trevor always knew when I was lying because he said I wrung my hands. I looked down and that's exactly what I was doing. So for once, I decided to tell the truth and deal with the consequences later. Trevor was sickened by what I told him. He stumbled out of my cell without saying a word and headed away to the privacy of our home or the nearest bar for comfort.

A few hours later, a new female officer appeared at my cell. She unlocked the cell door and advised me I had a phone call and to follow her. I swiftly walked behind her until we reached the wall phone. In an almost inaudible voice I said, "Hello." It was Trevor. I guess he had finally digested what I told him earlier. He responded in a low monotone voice, "Yeah it's me." I determined by the tone of his voice he was acutely unhappy. He was not very coherent. His speech was slurred as he cried out, "Why Pat? Why? Baby, don't you know I need you? I love you, Pat. I'd do anything for you!" We both started crying.

To try and defuse the conversation a little, I asked, "How are the girls? Did you tell them where I am?" He replied, "I phoned Mom and asked if she'd pick up the girls from school and sit with them. I spoke with her a few minutes before phoning you, and she said the girls were fine and getting ready for bed. I asked her to spend the night with them, and she had no problem. Mom said the girls asked about you. I told her to tell them you were visiting with a sick friend for the night. I didn't tell her anything else. It's too late to try and raise bail money, so you'll have to spend the night in that hell-hole. I'm sorry. I promise to get you out first thing in the morning. Try and get some rest." He paused, "Pat, I do love you," as he hung up the phone before hearing my reply. I held the phone to my ear wishing that the conversation would not have to end. The female officer apparently heard the click on the other end of the receiver because she said, "Okay, let's go." I said nothing as she escorted me back to my little ratty cell. I lay down on that filthy cot and cried myself to sleep.

Early the next morning I was rudely awakened by a sassy-looking, well-groomed, middle-aged brunette in a charcoal pinstriped suit. She repeatedly banged her attache case up against the cell bars, while glancing down at her expensive-looking watch and shouting my name. I sluggishly sat up on the cot and asked, "Who the hell are you and what do you want?" She responded, "Mrs. Weller, my name is Jacqueline Reese, attorney at law. I've been retained by your husband to represent you." I butted in, "Represent me for what!" She responded, "Hopefully, you're aware that you have been charged with forgery and prostitution. Were you not read your rights and informed of that?" I scratched my head and walked over to retrieve a business card she had so graciously extended through my bars. Slightly jerking the card from the finger tips of her well-manicured nails, I looked over it front and back then asked, "So, where's my husband?" She responded, "Honey, that should be the least of your worries right now. Besides, I really don't know nor do I care. Oh, your husband has posted bond and I'm here to schedule a meeting with you for this evening. Since your bail has been paid, you're free to go. However, I'd like to see you in my office today at 3:30 sharp. And please try and be on time." As my shrewd attorney bid me goodbye, I hurriedly put on my shoes and left a few minutes behind her.

Trevor was waiting for me at the front desk. He looked as if he had slept in his clothes and appeared extremely fatigued. After signing for my personal belongings from the locker room attendant, we departed from the police station. Trevor asked if I was hungry, and before I could respond he stated that he was and headed toward Sarah's Cafe. Once we arrived we placed our food order and both casually sat and stared out of the diner's window. I didn't know what to say, so I waited for Trevor to initiate the conversation. We continued silently eating our meal. I was so nervous; I didn't know what he was thinking or if he was waiting for me to initiate the conversation, so I remained silent. After paying for our meal we returned to our car and drove home without saying a word.

Trevor pulled up in the driveway, parked the car then turned to me and said, "Remember, Mom knows nothing about what's going on, so please don't blow it. Tell her your friend is better, tell her anything, but please, please don't blow it. We'll talk later after I've calmed down." I felt my body tense as I slowly exited the car.

Mother Weller must have heard us pull up because she greeted us on the front porch. She had the strangest look on her face as she looked at Trevor then back at me. I greeted and hugged her lightly (not wanting her to smell the odor from my jail cot) and rushed into the house, leaving Trevor to explain the situation. After taking a much needed shower, I exited the bathroom and could hear Mother Weller questioning Trevor. I pretended to be sleepy and lay across the bed, leaving him to defend me.

Twenty minutes later, Trevor walked into our bedroom, sat on the bed and touched me gently on my back. He said, "I think it's time for us to talk." I turned over on my back and looked up at him with tears in my eyes and replied, "Honey, you're right. Where do you want me to begin."

Trevor looked me straight in the eyes. I looked past his grim look and into his beautiful light brown eyes. I didn't want to hurt him any more than I had, but I knew in order for us both to heal, I had to be honest with myself and with him. I recounted my last three lovers, telling him they meant absolutely nothing to me and that I could hardly remember their names, let alone the affairs. I swore to him I never touched their wallets and neither of them volunteered any money. I paused for a few seconds and Trevor reluctantly asked that I continue. Swallowing hard I continued with all the sordid details of each affair which brought me up to the current one.

"My very best friend, Sheila, hooked us up with a couple of live ones from Tennessee. They wined and dined us through the night. We hopped around to three different clubs and briefly snorted coke at the last establishment. I was becoming extremely high so Sheila's trick . . . I mean her friend, Leslie, suggested we go back to their hotel room and finish our party there. I think Leslie's friend's name was Jasper or Jarrett . . . something like that." Trevor interrupted at this point and shouted, "For Christ's sake Pat, you don't know the man you f——!" I cut him off before he could finish his sentence. I did not want to hear that word. It constantly reminded me of how the last fellow talked. He kept referring to me as a good piece and to fuck him harder. Lord, I didn't want to hear that word again!

After drying my eyes I asked Trevor what was our next step. He got up off the bed, balled his left fist and hit the wall. I jumped and screamed telling him how sorry I was and that it was over. He grabbed his wounded hand and folded over a little bit while rushing to the bathroom. He told me to get dressed so he could drive me to my 3:30 meeting with Jacqueline Reese.

When we exited our bedroom, I was expecting to be accosted by Trevor's Mom. Thankfully, she got the message and left us a note pinned to the refrigerator that she had left, hoped all was well, and that she'd speak with us later. I asked Trevor if he wanted me to drive because of his injured fist and he replied, "No, I can handle it." Silence is sometimes golden. Neither of us spoke a word while driving to Ms. Reese's office.

Ms. Reese was really a class act. She courteously greeted us (nothing like what I had earlier experienced). She asked if she could get us something to drink and Trevor declined for both of us. He leaned over toward me and sternly told me to sit up straight. As long as we've been together that is something he has never done. However, considering the situation, I did not fault him.

Ms. Reese started by saying, "Mr. and Mrs. Weller, I'd like to thank you both for coming in. I know the situation sounds bleak, but I will do everything in my power to get all charges against Mrs. Weller dropped. Do you mind if I call you Pat?" I looked into her steel gray eyes and responded, "No. Please."

"Fine. Pat, I need to know if you've ever been arrested before?" she asked.

I responded, "No."

She inquired, "How long have you been on the streets?"

I was very offended by her line of questioning and looked at Trevor for intervention. He acted totally dejected from the conversation and continued to look at his injured fist. I responded, "Well, see . . . I really don't work the streets. I entertain . . . use to entertain them."

She cut me off by asking, "When you say them whom are you referring to . . . men or what?"

I looked at Trevor again, who was now looking directly at me. He was about to find out another side of me he didn't know. I replied, "Well. Most of the time they were men. On a few occasions we entertained women."

Ms. Reese cut me off again by asking, "We. Who's we?"

I responded, "My best friend, Sheila. She's the one who got me started in all of this. I don't consider myself gay or bisexual or anything like that, you see." I glanced over at Trevor as he bowed his head and began stroking the top of his nose. I was thinking that if the case ever went to trial I didn't want him to find out then, so I decided to be honest and tell everything now. Besides, I always heard you are never to lie to your doctor or attorney. Right now I was wishing for another attorney.

The line of questioning soon turned toward the alleged forgery of checks. Ms. Reese came out and directly asked, "Pat, are you a thief?"

I shouted, "No!"—then corrected myself by saying, "Well, I've stolen from Trevor and on occasion from nice department stores, but I've never been caught. It was usually something petty I thought I just had to have. Sheila and I would play this game sometimes, called steal it if you can. Half the time we didn't need it—it was the thrill of stealing and not getting caught." I wanted to stop the questioning so desperately because I knew it was tearing Trevor up inside hearing about his darling little wife.

Ms. Reese then asked, "Pat, did you steal checks from any of your victims?"

I shouted, "Victims! Hell I am the victim here. I never charged their ass one damn penny, and now I'm being accused of stealing some checks and don't even know who my accusers are. I promise you—I haven't stolen from any of them."

After about an hour Ms. Reese was finally finished interrogating me and tearing me to shreds in front of my husband. I saw how she looked at Trevor when I responded to several of her questions. She tried to pretend she was helping me. Yeah, she's helping all right . . . right into our bed while she sends my ass straight to jail.

While riding home I apologized to Trevor for what he had earlier found out about me. I expressed my displeasure with Ms. Reese and asked if it were possible to secure another attorney. His response was, "She's all you've got. Ms. Reese is a cunning and monstrously clever attorney, who has yet to lose a case. She'll stop at nothing to win. She's the kind of attorney you want on your side, so don't blow it." I remained silent the duration of our trip home and felt so helpless.

Two days later, I phoned Ms. Reese's office and gave her Sheila's home phone number and address. She promised she'd call Sheila and try to determine what transpired with several of our ex-lovers. She said hopefully she'd be able to determine if there had been a mistaken identity with regard to who actually stole the checks and possibly get the solicitation charge thrown out. After three days of biting my nails and waiting to hear back from Ms. Reese, I phoned her office again. I asked her about the outcome of her conversation with Sheila and she asked, "Are you sure you gave me the correct phone number and address? No one lives at 3723 Bluffman, the number has been disconnected, and no one seems to know of your friend, Sheila Sims." Sheila apparently had skipped town, never to be heard from again.

She was my only hope. It never dawned on me to call her after my release from jail. Besides, Trevor constantly watched my every move after returning home from jail. I realized I was left alone to defend my honor against my invisible accusers.

For two months our household was in a fever of anticipation as we awaited my trial date. Each time the phone rang, anxiety of the worst kind built up inside of me. Trevor had decided to take an extended vacation leave from his job and was fearful of his boss and peers finding out about the case. He asked Mother Weller if the girls could come and stay with her for a while until we worked out a few problems at home. He never told me if he ever got around to telling her her daughter-in-law is a whore and thief and might go to prison for it. Fortunately, Ms. Reese managed to keep it out of the newspapers.

Finally the day arrived. We were scheduled to appear in Judge Harry Faltzwater's court at 10:15 A.M. According to Ms. Reese, she had an excellent relationship with the judge and felt he would be fair. When we initially walked into the courtroom there was only a handful of people present. Ms. Reese instructed me to sit next to her and keep quiet. She placed a No. 2 pencil and a yellow legal tablet in front of me and told me I could write or doodle. I turned and stared at her. She ignored my stare and turned in the direction of the opposing counsel, greeted the two men with a friendly smile and nodded her head as if she were blushing. I was wondering why was she being so nice to these guys who were about to fry my ass. I looked back at Trevor and he winked at me. Feeling the tension grow inside of me, I wanted so desperately to get up and run out of the courtroom into the safety of my home. I just couldn't believe my past had finally caught up with me.

The courtroom starting filling up quickly. Seven women and five men entered the jury box, took their seats, and looked sedately in my direction. The same people who would later determine if I went to prison or would release me to the custody of my loving family. The bailiff stepped forward and asked everyone to stand. A door opened and an elderly gentleman with silver hair, wearing a long black robe emerged. He seated himself at the front of the room, banged his gavel, and declared order. The bailiff instructed everyone to be seated. He walked over to the judge and handed him several files. The judge briefly reviewed each then stated, "The City of Dallas vs. Patricia Weller, (a/k/a Pat, Patty, and Love Joy)." I could have fainted when he read off my aliases. I had no idea the district attorney's office would dig that deep into my past and actually interview several of my ex-lovers.

After three full days of hearing testimony, the jury was finally issued instructions. They retired to another room directly behind the jury box for deliberation of my future. The remainder of us stood outside the courtroom and anxiously awaited their findings. Two grueling hours went by. I began wringing my hands and pacing the floor. Ms. Reese walked over, grabbed my right hand and told me to calm down. She stated, "Usually when it takes the jury a long time to reach a verdict, that's a good sign for the defense." She asked to speak in private with Trevor and excused herself. I thought it was damn rude of her and totally out of the ordinary, seeing how I was supposed to be her client. Occasionally, Trevor would look in my direction, but he never once smiled.

The bailiff signaled for us to return to the courtroom. Apparently, the jurors had finally reached a verdict. The silver-haired judge returned to his position along with the twelve jurors. The foreman handed the bailiff a folded piece of paper who in turn delivered it to the judge. I looked over at the jurors to try and read their faces. None of them would look at me. I felt a sickening feeling and became short of breath. I asked Ms. Reese what did she think and she responded, "Honey, we'll both know soon enough."

The judge looked in my direction and asked me to stand. He asked, "Is there anything you wish to say before sentencing, Mrs. Weller?"

I nervously replied, "Yes Sir, Your Honor. I vehemently deny that I forged any checks. While I'll admit to sleeping around on my husband, I swear I never charged any of my accusers one dime. I swear to you. In fact, Sir, where are my accusers? Not one of them is here today to look me in the face!"

Dear Ms. Reese cut me off in a low voice, "Pat, I think you've made your point; that's enough!"

The judge read the verdict, "Mrs. Weller, you have been found guilty of prostitution and forgery by a jury of your peers. You are hereby sentenced to twelve years in prison at the Mountain View Women's Correctional Facilities in Gatesville, Texas, whereby you will commence serving your term immediately. You are hereby remanded to the custody of the bailiff." My legs went from under me and I fainted. When I came to, I was in a holding cell inside the court facility. I looked over at Trevor who was stroking my hand. Out of the goodness of her heart, Ms. Reese had decided to join him. She pretended to be just as upset with my guilty verdict as I was, or perhaps it was the fact of losing her first case. I'm certain it was the latter. Perhaps now she could join the fine array of women waiting impatiently to steal my husband from me. Why not; after all, I'd be hidden from view for twelve years. I really didn't expect Trevor to wait for me.

After several months of keeping the situation hidden from Mother Weller and my daughters, Trevor said he had no choice but to tell them the truth. I asked if they could come and visit me before being transferred to the women's correctional facilities, but he felt it wasn't a good idea. He promised to try and explain the situation to them and felt it was best that I did not try and contact them for a while. I allowed Trevor to handle everything.

After sentencing, I remained in the county jail for four more days. The food was lousy and the jail was over-crowded. Fights regularly occurred over sleeping spaces, food, and smelly cots and blankets. Most of the time I fell asleep in a corner on the bare floor, just to keep the peace. The day arrived and I was finally transferred to a prison hospital in Galveston, Texas, along with twenty-three other women. I was treated for substance abuse and was released in about a month. Antoinette S. Moten, warden of that facility, paid me several visits and told me I was a model prisoner. She told me to stay strong and to avoid trouble—it would make my prison term a lot easier. The day I left the prison hospital, Warden Moten paid her last visit, hugged me, and wished me well.

A few hours later I arrived at the Gatesville Unit. I was introduced to Warden Susan C. Cranford and several members of her staff. For some reason, she appeared to take a special liking to me. Warden Cranford also instructed me to keep my nose clean and abide by the rules. She stated that by doing so, I could possibly qualify for an early release. That gave me all the motivation I needed.

I was allowed to bring small pictures of my daughters with me, which I posted on my new cell walls. Each day I'd talk to the pictures of my girls as if they could talk back, letting them know how much I loved and missed them. I reassured them that once I got out of prison I'd try my best to make it up to them. I prayed daily and asked God to protect them and Trevor and not to let them forget about me. I tried as best I could to stay out of trouble, but it was extremely difficult. I promised myself that whatever it was I had to do to survive, I'd do it. I adhered to all prison rules and followed through with steady, persistent labor of all assigned tasks.

I'll tell anyone—this is not the kind of place you want to end up. I witnessed several prisoners being raped by other prisoners, and two women were strangled to death with their own panties. I tried to remain pretty much to myself and pretended to be tough. I only had one encounter with one of the other prisoners, Adrian. She slapped me once for not answering her quick enough. When I found her off by herself away from her other goonies, I approached her and told her my game plan. I did not wish to cause her harm or embarrassment. I asked her if she had children and she said yes. I told her surely she understood where I was coming from. I told her I was never a good mother to my children and that I was trying to get an early release in order to make up for it before my girls got too old and would no longer need me. It worked! Adrian not only backed off, but she told all the other prisoners to leave me alone.

My efforts were eventually recognized and appreciated by Warden Cranford. After six grueling years, my case came up for parole. I was interviewed by twelve people who would determine whether I had paid my debt to society. Prior to the hearing I met with Warden Cranford, who told me to act natural and be honest. I thought it was going to be difficult watching them jot down notes as they hinged on every word I said. Gratefully, I passed! My parole was granted and I was released in two weeks. Before my departure I met with Adrian and thanked her because I knew she could have made my life a living hell. I promised her that I would stay in touch. I said thank you and goodbye to Warden Cranford. She told me my strong will and desire to change were two of the determining factors in my early release.

It is scarcely surprising that my family decided to wait for me. Trevor and the girls greeted me outside the prison gate. I found out, a few years after my incarceration, that Trevor had informed the girls about me. He told them I had been falsely accused of a crime and was poorly represented. Trevor apologized to them for my not being allowed to write or contact them. He sheltered the full blame. It is amazing the love of children for their parents. My flagrant behavior had inflicted pain on my family. How could they still love me, I questioned. Not only that, I repeatedly flaunted this inexcusable behavior in front of our neighbors, yet none of my daughters held it against me. Instead, they gave me a long hug as we stood outside the prison facilities. As we rode home, they sat in the back seat and each explained what they had been doing over the course of six years. Trevor and I rode up front in silence.

When we arrived home two hours later, we were greeted by Mother Weller. She grabbed me and told me how much she loved and missed me. She said she enjoyed helping Trevor raise our daughters, and now it was time for me to take over. She pulled me aside and whispered, "Pat, God has given you another chance. Be good to yourself and your family. Trevor and the girls really do love you." I stood there crying and holding my mother-in-law, praying that I'd be half the woman she was.

It feels strange being back in my old house and in my old bed with my husband. We have yet to make love, but I'm sure in due time. I won't rush him. After all . . . it's been six long years.

31

THE DOG

PAUL RUFFIN

Buddy's about six feet tall or so, maybe a little over, but he weighs enough that if he was stretched out to fit those insurance weight tables he'd be something just over eight feet. Heavy. He's heavy. But he's not really fat. Just big, big bones and muscles, shoulders and legs and all, neck like a bull. And when you see him lumbering down the aisle of the church and dropping back on the bench and you hear the way it complains when he settles onto it, you know that you have just seen a whole lot of man go past you, and you're glad you're not that bench.

But what you notice most is the way everybody looks at him when he comes in, the way they quit their little whispering and giggling and turn the minute he darkens the doorway and watch him step by step as he walks down to his spot, where he just drops down like a big storm cloud and fills in his portion of what used to be a bench taken up by him and his family. A gloom settles on the congregation, and you know that what they're thinking has got nothing to do with the fact that old Buddy has finally found his way back to church on Sunday morning or that his wife has left him, taking the three kids with her, but that Buddy Winters hasn't got a nose.

They don't stare, mind you, maybe because if he *did* get sore about his appearance and thought they were making fun of him, he just might go out and turn their truck over in the caliche parking lot. They sort of corner their eyes, look in his general direction, then sweep across his face, just as casual as if they were looking at the sky for clouds. But they always, by God, *look*, like maybe they figure his nose has grown back since last Sunday or something or he's lost an eye to go with the nose.

Everything will be humming along for half an hour before the service is supposed to begin, that soft little twittering and chirping, with here and there someone turning and craning toward the main doors, and suddenly a

32

hush will fall over the congregation and you know Buddy has arrived. He is a *presence*, almost as good, I'd figure, as some sort of miracle Brother Barclay might summon up each Sunday to astound and perplex and keep people coming back for more and inviting their friends, swelling the rank and file until there's barely a seat left. And maybe that's what he is, a miracle. At least for Brother Barclay, who must fall on his knees every day and give thanks to God for Buddy and his monstrous body and face. And the dog.

That dog. Well, hell, of course. The dog is what this is all about. Not about how big Buddy is or that he's lost his family or started coming back to church, not even about the fact that he ain't got a nose, which is probably enough to draw your attention all right. But about the dog.

It's one of those things that you can't quite put your finger on as the cause of. If we hadn't been on the river that particular morning or that old trotline hadn't been there, or the dog, or if the dog had decided not to cross the river at that point or had dodged the trotline or got hooked but tore loose from it on his own, or Buddy hadn't been along with us or had just said, "Fuck that dog, keep going." I mean, anything could have happened that would have made things turn out different. Just like if Mr. and Mrs. Hitler hadn't decided to mess around that night, World War II might not have happened. You know. Little things.

But it happened. It all came together. And Buddy lost his nose and his family, but he found the church again and Brother Barclay doubled his gate.

Oh yeah. The dog.

We were on the Trinity, early one Sunday, running the lines we'd set the night before, when it happened, just like a story you might read somewhere, one of those lessons for living, you might say—not exactly what you're thrashing around on the river for, but it happens. As they say, shit happens. And you witness it. And you have to testify. And this is the way it happened.

It was me and Buddy and Jim Eliot—Ramblin' Jim, we called him, after Ramblin' Jack Eliot, because he was into rodeos and bull-riding and all that stuff that normal people don't even talk much about, and he stayed drunk most of the time he wasn't trying to balance on some kind of animal that didn't particularly want him on their back.

Running lines, like I said, checking sethooks that hung from limbs out far enough that assholes walking along the bank couldn't just lean out and haul in the fish that was bowing them into the water. People do that, you know, just walking along the river bank. They see a willow limb jerking down into the water just so, and they know somebody's got a line on it and a fish on the end of the line, so they just reach out there and curl the limb around and take the fish off like it was theirs. I've seen it. It makes you glad you don't have a gun along—sometimes you wish real hard that you did.

And running trotlines, which we'd tie off on snags or stumps on each side of the river with lengths of brown parachute line that you can't see shining in the water. You know where they are tied off, but you wouldn't tell your own mother where they're at. No sir. If you think folks'll take fish off a drop line, think what they'll do to a trotline that might have a dozen damn channels or blues or yellows tugging away on it. Shit, they'll rob you blind. The minute you reach down and touch that trotline and you don't feel more than the thrum of the current on it, you know some sonofabitch has been at it during the night. So you keep it hid and you keep it quiet, just like you would the location of your dope stash. Don't nobody know but you and the one or two people running lines with you, and they wouldn't say a word about it if you was to put a big-caliber gun to their heads and say, "Tell me where that line's at or you're dead." Shit, they'd rather die than tell. That's how it is when you got a code. Besides, they know that if they do tell and the others find out, they gon' die anyway. Like I say, that's the way it is when you got a code.

We come out from Huntsville early, the three of us, in Jim's truck, towing the little bass boat behind, which is a joke to call it that, because we'd rather set and run lines any day than rip around whipping the water for bass. Buddy used to say that nobody catches enough bass to *eat*, much less to sell, unless they got somebody just outside the edge of the camera frame hooking a bass on for you when you cast. He asked us once whether we'd ever noticed how much the sun moved in them sportsman shows where people are dragging in bass every other cast.

"Watch it sometimes," he said. "That sun'll be on one side of the boat when they catch a fish and on the other when they catch the next one, and they'll let on that it's the very next cast. Shit. Give me catfish any day. I want to measure my fish by the boatload."

And that's pretty much the way all three of us looked at it. When we came in from running lines, there wasn't a scale in the county that wouldn't groan with what we hung on'm. I mean, it was a rare weekend when we didn't haul in a coupla hundred pounds of channels and blues and yellows.

We'd keep what we wanted to eat, which usually wasn't all that much, since when you spend as much time with catfish as we did you don't always want to be looking at'm on your plate, even when the women have learned a thousand different ways to fix'm, from fried to pâté. We'd take the rest into town and sell'm at a buck a pound, on the hoof, as Ramblin' Jim put it.

On Friday after work, just about every decent day that came around, we taken off for the Trinity with plenty of bait and lines and enough beer and junk food to hold us a week, work till well after dark setting our hooks out and baiting up the trots, which we just left in the water week after week. After we got through on the river we'd set up camp beside the truck and drink beer and play cards or just bullshit around until it got late; then we'd run the lines and come back to the truck and ice the fish down and camp for the night or go on home. Usually we went home. Ain't any of us real young anymore, and that damp, hard ground just plays absolute hell with your bones.

Saturday morning we'd be out on the river just as soon as we figured we could see how to run—sometimes the mist hangs in real low and tight and you can't see your hand in front of your face until the sun burns it off. But soon as we could we'd run the lines, ice the fish down, and take'm back to town and sell'm. By noon we were already back home and up to other things. Late Saturday afternoon we'd bait up again and go through the whole process, usually going in late that night and coming back early Sunday.

Our women—we were all three married, with eight children altogether—put up with this week in and week out until hunting season came along each fall and changed the routine just a little, but not much. They just planned their lives without counting Friday and Saturday nights and Saturday and Sunday mornings. They didn't have them *to* count. They belonged to us, the days *and* the women. And it worked pretty damned well for a long time.

Trouble was, the Sundays. The women, like they always do, got kinda itchy about things when the kids got up big enough to sit through church without making everybody miserable, and they started putting pressure on us to either not run the lines on Sundays or wait until afternoon. Well, hell, like Buddy said, you might as well not run at all if you ain't gon' run on Sunday mornings. By Saturday morning the word has just got out good among the fish that you're serving fresh bait, so your haul is usually about half it'll be on Sunday mornings. And if you wait until Sunday afternoon, when every fool in the world is on the river, you ain't gon' find the time to run the lines in privacy. You might as well just plant a red flag at every stump your trots are tied onto. And once people find out where your lines are at, they treat that river like free range: they get there first, the fish are theirs. We just drew the line—there wasn't going to be any giving up Sunday mornings.

So we were running the lines that particular Sunday morning, late in March, when the trees had already leafed out pretty well and the water had that nice bright-green tint to it from the reflected early leaves. Buddy was sitting in the middle seat, facing forward, his body so wide that Jim, who was driving, since it was his boat, had to lean out to see around him—not that he needed to, since me or Jim either one could have run that mile of river in the *dark* without hitting anything that hadn't just floated down. I was the lightest, so I was on the front seat facing backward except when we got close to the hooks; then I'd turn around and kneel on the seat and pull up the line and check it, taking off the fish if there was one on it, drop it in the bottom of the boat, and pass the line back to Buddy for baiting. He'd scoop his hand down in the bait bucket for little perch or silver-sides, run the hook through just behind the dorsal and drop the line back in the water.

When we got to the trots, we'd turn the boat sideways and ease across the river, with Jim holding the main line at the rear and me at the front. Again, I'd take off the fish, then pass the little drop lines back to Buddy, who'd hook on a perch or silver-side, then chicken liver, then a ball of that smelly catfish bait you buy in little plastic tubs, like butter. There's about thirty hooks on a full trotline, so by alternating baits like that we'd have about ten servings of all three kinds of bait. That way, no matter how finicky a catfish happened to be swimming up or down the channel, he'd have something dangling in front of him that he just couldn't resist. As Buddy used to say, anything swimming down there that didn't like one of the three, you probably didn't want to take back home with you anyway.

That particular Sunday we had worked upriver about half our run, maybe half a mile, when Buddy, who was looking forward past me, saw something strange in the water and told me to turn around and see what I thought it was. Which I did.

It wasn't anything strange, at least not then, just a dog swimming along under a willow limb, maybe five or six feet out from the bank, churning his front feet like he was heading for shore in a big hurry. We didn't have any lines on that particular limb, so we just watched him slide past as we worked our way upriver on the other side.

After a while, Buddy turned and looked back down toward the dog, who was still about the same distance out, his head poked up out of the water like a white snag. "Boys, that dog's a mighty slow swimmer, or he's done hung up on a old trotline."

I squinted and shook my head. "Yep. He's caught on somebody's old line."

"We'll get him loose when we come back down," Ramblin' Jim said, revving to gain on the current, which picked up in the shallow water we were running through.

It took us nearly two hours to check all the sethooks and trots upriver, so that by the time we headed back down, the sun was getting on up in the sky and we were loaded with catfish, all colors and sizes, but mostly big blues. We drifted along and drank a couple of beers in celebration before Jim turned the bow south and started idling along the shore that the dog was closest to.

Jim hadn't forgotten about him, and neither had me and Buddy, but none of us said anything until we saw his head in that brown rush beneath the willows. He hadn't gained an inch, naturally, since it was obvious that he'd hung himself on somebody's old line that probably ran up underneath the overhanging limbs and dead-ended around one of the roots that curled down into the water.

"Yessir," Buddy said, "he's hung or he's a mighty slow swimmer."

"What you reckon, Jim?" I asked.

Jim swung out toward the middle of the river. "I 'spect the best thing to do, if we're gon' fool with him, is go down and ease back up."

"What you mean, *fool* with him?" Buddy asked. "We can't leave that goddamned dog on that line. I don't know why he was crossing here, what he figured was worth swimming all this distance for, but he never counted on nobody's trotline. It ain't his fault."

"Settle down," Jim said. "I'll curl around and come up beside him."

"Hell," Buddy went on, "it could have been one of our lines, you know, only we never had one in that particular spot." He hawked and spat into the water, then slugged down the rest of the beer he had just opened. "Could have been, I'm saying."

Jim idled on down past the dog and turned upstream. "Buddy," he said, "you and me're gon' steady things with the paddles when we get up to him. Let Earl cut him loose."

Buddy shifted his massive weight and turned to look at him. "Bullshit. I seen him first. I'm the one's gon' cut him loose." He raised one of his big hairy arms and pointed at the dog.

Jim shrugged. I shrugged. "So who gives a shit who does it?" Jim said. "Fine. Earl, get your paddle ready."

"Go on past him and cut your engine," Buddy instructed. "Drift back to him and he'll be easier to handle. Just lay into the paddles to hold the boat until I get him cut loose." He sounded like he'd done this kind of rescue work all his life.

"Yessir," I said saluting. "Too bad we ain't got a movie camera up there in a helicopter to get this on the news."

As we puttered up past the dog, he turned his head and rolled his eyes to follow us, his feet clawing toward the bank. I couldn't hear anything for the motor, but it looked like he was growling. Jim cut the power and grabbed his paddle, I shoved mine in deep, and we drifted back alongside the dog, then held the boat dead still against the flow while Buddy leaned out over him.

"Arright, dog," he said, "ol' Buddy will save you in a second. Just calm down. Easy now."

He leaned forward, thrusting his arm deep into the water behind the dog, then slipped his knife hand down, his head dropping over the side of the boat. His big butt stuck up and his jeans and shirt parted and his hairy cleavage glowed in the early sun, just the way fat men's asses always do, no matter what.

"It'd be a real good time to kick his ass," Jim said.

"You just hold the goddamned boat steady," Buddy grunted. His voice sounded like it was coming from the woods.

Then it happened. Buddy was humped way over, both arms down almost to his armpits in the water, his face right beside the dog's, with the two of us leaning the opposite way to keep the boat from rolling over, which with his weight it could have done even with that ballast of catfish in the bottom. He yelled something, kind of sputtering, and tried to yank his head back, but only his shoulders heaved, like his head was tied down. Then he jerked his arms out of the water and braced his hands against the side of the boat and shoved up until the boat rolled our way, almost dumping us, when his head came up from the water, the dog still clinging to it for a brief instant until he dropped off like a poorly hooked fish. He plopped into the water and, feet churning, struck out for the bank without looking back.

Buddy was kneeling down in the bottom of the boat in the catfish, boiling blood like a stuck hog through his fingers, which he had clasped to his face like someone who's just seen something so terrible he has to cover his face to keep from looking again. The catfish had to be jabbing spines all in his legs, but he seemed not to notice them.

"Oh, boys, oh, boys," he whimpered, "that sonofabitch bit me. Oh, boys, he bit me bad." He took his hands away briefly and blew and slung his head over the water. Me and Jim turned away when he did that.

"Where at, Buddy?" Jim asked. He had steadied the boat and eased forward behind Buddy.

"My nose, my nose." Only he was saying it, "By *doze*, by *doze*."

Jim tried to pull his hands away from his face. "Lemme see, Buddy, lemme see how bad."

"It's bad. Jesus Christ. Jesus Christ," Buddy slobbered, blood frothing through his fingers and around his palms. "Just head for the truck!" He was bowed over on his knees in the fish. "Jesus Christ," he kept saying.

We didn't get to see his nose, or what was left of what used to be his nose, till a lot later, after they got through with him at the ER. They let me and Jim come in when they were salving it up for the bandage that he had to wear for weeks afterwards. There was nothing to sew back on—the dog had got the nose—so all they could do at the hospital was clean it and trim it up some and bandage it. By the time they got through with Buddy's face, it looked a lot like somebody had come straight down with a sword or axe and just lopped the nose right off, clean as a whistle. You could see right into his adenoids and sinuses and stuff. *Gross* is what it was. They give ol' Buddy a tetanus shot and arranged for him to come back in for the rabies series, which at first Buddy said he wasn't going through; but a young doctor told him what he could expect if the dog did have rabies and Buddy rethought it and said OK, he'd be in the next day.

We took him home and then went back out to get the boat, which we'd just tied up to a tree in our haste to get Buddy to the ER. Of course, some sonofabitch had come along and stole every catfish we had piled in it. They'll do it every time. They probably didn't even know that all the blood in the bottom of the boat was from Buddy and not from the fish.

"It looks like to me," Ramblin' Jim said as we bounced out onto the highway, "that the rules was broke this morning." He shook his head. "There's an old saying that a dog won't bite the hand that feeds him."

"Buddy wasn't feeding him," I pointed out. "And he went for the nose, not the hand."

"Yeah, but it looks like the rule would apply."

"Sometimes things are different," I said.

We drove on in silence for a few minutes. Then Jim turned to me. "Did you see the dog when he got on the bank?"

"No. I was watching Buddy."

"Damndest thing," Jim said. "I just happened to turn around and look back to see where he'd got off to, and he was just standing there in the sun— he was a big old skinny white, black-spotted hound of some sort, maybe a bluetick—shaking like somebody had just give him a bath. Just standing there shaking, the way dogs do." He reached over and tapped my leg. "And do you know, that sonofabitch made a *rainbow*."

"A rainbow?"

"Yeah. A rainbow. With the water he was shaking off. In the sun, you know. A goddamned *rainbow*."

"Maybe it was a sign," I said, and we didn't say anything else the whole trip home.

I guess maybe it was a sign, at least to Buddy, who didn't even see the rainbow. All I know is that the next time we saw him, later in the week, after he'd started his rabies shots, he talked to us quietly in his living room about how bad a person he'd been most of his life and about how he was ready to turn it all around, start living right, and get back into the church. He said something strange, sort of mumbled it, about understanding how Christ must have felt about trying to save people and what they did to him for trying. We didn't make much of it. But it did sound strange.

We didn't see him again until we went over to his place a few weeks later, after the bandages came off, and I swear, I wish we hadn't seen him then. You talking about weird looking. Folks talk about how ugly noses are, but you see a man without one, and you realize that whether they're long or hooked or laid over or pugged, they're a damned sight better looking than what they cover up. And we just up and asked him whether he was going to have plastic surgery, you know, have part of his ass cut off and sewn on up front there and shaped like a nose—which me and Ramblin' Jim thought was a funny idea—but he just shook his head sadly and said no, he was going to leave things the way they were. That he reckoned God intended it that way.

And that was that. His face healed up all right and the rabies shots worked, but Buddy was never the same again. His wife stayed on a few months, but one day she loaded the children into her old Pinto and left—told Mabel Kitchens down at the beauty shop she couldn't spend the rest of her life with a man so deformed that the kids wouldn't even look at him. Said Buddy hadn't even tried to touch her since the *event*, as she called it. Said she was glad. Didn't know how it'd be looking right up into his head through those two holes.

Buddy turned to the church, never missed another Wednesday night or Sunday morning or Sunday night. Never says a word, just comes in real quiet and takes his seat on the bench that his family used to fill, and closes his eyes during prayer. Kept on working at the welding shop, where he's got a mask on most of the time anyway, and won't have any-thing to do with us. Like we had something to do with what happened to him. Sometimes me and Jim will go to church too, with our families, even on Sunday mornings, and much as we hate to admit it, we find ourselves turning and looking when we see his shadow darken the doorway and hear his heavy steps bearing down on us. I won't look at his face, though, not even in a glance, as he moves past me, huge and dark, like some kind of old remembered or imagined sin.

THE SEPTEMBER BABIES BIRTHDAY PARTY
(OR "SANS PEUR")*

LIN SUTHERLAND

Four of us seven sisters and Mama and Daddy were born in September so we decided years ago it'd be easier to hold the September Babies Birthday Party for all of us on one day and get it over with. This year the date to have the party fell on my birthday so it fell upon me to have it at my house, or rather, in my front yard, since there are too many of us to fit in any one room of my house. We're the kind of family that doesn't divide into separate rooms well—we like to all be packed into one room, all talking at once. As a matter of fact, we can't seem to divide at all. Even though Mama and Daddy got divorced several years back, the bond of forty-five years of marriage refuses to die. They still get together most mornings of the week for six A.M. coffee to poke and prod and outwit each other. There's a lot of mutual admiration there.

The party took exhaustive arranging. It always does with a family our size. Gayle had to drive up from Houston and then we had to change the party from Saturday to Sunday because Beth couldn't make it on Saturday. She got on one of her high-horse huffs because no one consulted her about her schedule. It took three sisters and several phone calls to placate her enough to come.

❖   ❖   ❖

I asked Daddy to get the cake, which he did, only he got it on Thursday so by Sunday it was soggy and crestfallen. He had "Sans Peur" inscribed on it, our family motto. That's French for Without Fear. It's true we're a fearless family, but that cake gave us trepidation. I'll tell you why.

---

*The author dedicates this story to her late father, Thomas Sutherland.

From long experience we have learned that anything Daddy fixes to eat should be approached with great caution. He has a cast-iron stomach, false teeth, his vision is not too good, and his tastebuds were burned out long ago by jalapeños and picante sauce. So he has no way to distinguish fresh versus spoiled. He brought to one family gathering a suspicious-looking green ham and butter beans that quivered. For years he has had no sense of inedible food. I'm not sure he cares. After all, with no tastebuds, teeth, or vision, what's inedible?

Beth brought red fruit jello that matched the color of her fire-engine lips; Carol, the richest of all of us, brought an economy box of snack sticks; and Barbara, the poorest, spent a lot on cantaloupes and grapes. We had a regular feast set out by noon on the cedar table. We arranged the lawn chairs in a circle and sipped iced tea and began warming up to the real purpose of these get-togethers, telling stories. But first we had to find a chair that would hold Daddy. He is as big in size as he is big in presence and chairs seem to collapse at the sight of him. It's not that he's fat. He's just BIG. He says whenever he goes over to any of our houses we run around pulling chairs from behind him just as he's going to sit down, yelling, "No, Daddy, not that one!" We've all lost some perfectly good chairs to him.

We finally got Daddy situated in one that would hold him, knowing he'd stay there for a good while. Once he gets to sitting down, you don't see a lot of action from him. He occasionally makes the effort, grunting and thrusting forward. These are all false starts. We have often talked of inventing a special ejection chair for him, but no one in the family is mechanically gifted enough. Although his immobility means we have to serve him everything he wants, this is better than the alternative, which is watching him try to get up for ten minutes. Then if he actually succeeds we have to watch him wander around picking at food until he returns, inevitably, to the wrong chair and we have to scream, "No, Daddy, not that one!" That annoys him because it interrupts his story. See, the only time he can actually lift himself

43

out of a chair is at the highpoint of a story he's telling, when he gets the Storyteller's Adrenalin Rush. Right at some crucial highpoint, he will suddenly pop up out of the chair, startling us all. It makes us lose our concentration and we can't get it back as he wanders around because we are anticipating the moment he will return to the wrong chair and we have to scream at him or lose another chair. It has developed in us sisters a certain ability to concentrate on several things at once.

Now that we had Daddy ensconced in the big metal lawn chair that had proven itself through time, we relaxed. The dogs curled up under us as we settled down with our ice tea for conversation and story telling. Or so we thought.

Beth began by announcing she'd decided to start a match-making service. She'd gotten the idea because Verner, her husband's brother, was now divorced and on the prowl. Daddy pointed out she hadn't done too well finding a potential mate for me. We all hooted at this understatement of the year. She set me up on dates with three of the Champion Losers of the Western World. She replied she'd figured out the problem there: she was trying to find men for women. Now that she realized that wasn't her forte, she was limiting herself to women for men. She knew what men wanted, she said confidently.

Verner, her first client, had stated his mate's requirements. They were: she couldn't be fat, she had to be cheerful and well-adjusted and not mind his smoking, and she had to have an independent income.

I asked the obvious: "Why would a woman like THAT want to marry Verner?"

"Verner's a great catch," Beth insisted.

"Verner's a loser," Carol stated flatly.

"What?" Daddy shouted. His hearing is terrible, too.

"A LOSER." Carol repeated loudly in his direction.

"A boozer!" Daddy looked shocked. "I didn't know Verner drank to excess."

"No, A LOO-ZER," Beth enunciated, her large mobile red lips inches from his face. Beth's lips have a life of their own. He focused on them, fascinated.

"Oh, a loser . . . yes, absolutely." he agreed.

"Hey, I've got a name for your dating service, Beth," I said. "Why don't you call it Hopeless Cases?"

Everyone cackled ruthlessly.

"Because he's not," Beth continued seriously. "He's got a great job as a courier with a pharmaceutical company."

"Oh, sure." I said, priming my voice to drip sarcasm. "Remember all his failed projects? Remember the land deal in Costa Rica? And then the Worm Ranch that was going to make him a millionaire?"

"Verner's Vorm Ranch," Mama laughed, recalling our moniker for it.

"WHAT?" Daddy shouted.

Out of patience with Daddy interrupting the flow of our gossip, Mama leaned over Carol toward him and bellowed, "VERNER'S VORM RANCH!!"

Unfortunately she yelled it nano-meters from Carol's ear. Carol reeled backwards, the shocked look of eardrum damage on her face. When she did, the flimsy lawn chair kept going backwards and she fell, feet straight up in the air, and landed directly on top of my dog Alfie. He had been sleeping peacefully in the shade behind the chair, but now, thinking he was being ambushed by Kay's beagle Max, his arch rival, he leapt up and attacked the snoring hound.

Instantly, the air was filled with the horrible howling and thrashing of a male dog fight. We all bailed out of our chairs and out of the way. Except for me, the family bleeding-heart-animal-lover. I threw himself into the fray, grabbed Max and jerked him away from Alfie by the forearms, exposing his pink belly. Not the thing to do. Alfie instantly defied all Geneva Conventions of Dog War and buried his teeth into the protruding fleshy knob on Max's belly. A deafening banshee dog scream suddenly emitted from the beagle and continued issuing forth for what seemed an eternity. In the midst of the chaos, Beth screamed, "Lin—Max's penis! Max's penis!" Briefly, I wondered what my neighbors thought. We finally got the dogs separated, but by then my hand was bleeding.

I watched Daddy clean his fingernails with a Bowie knife while Kay poured alcohol on my hand.

Still shaken, we all sat down again and looked over at Daddy. He had never moved an inch during the fight. However, we noticed he'd lost his teeth. They were gone from his mouth and nowhere in sight. We began an involved search of the area of yard around him. No teeth. It was a mystery. How far can teeth jump? Mama wondered out loud. Finally, I noticed a lump in the plate of cake in his lap. There they were, buried in the P of Sans Peur. We got Daddy's teeth back in and settled down for the umpteenth time.

"I need a cup of coffee," Daddy announced, glancing hopefully from one to the other of us. We all froze.

The benefit of siring seven female children is that at any given time the odds are at least one will be willing to serve you. Daddy has had two burning goals his entire life: to be served constantly, and to have interesting, thought-provoking conversations. Ideally at the same time. In terms of these ambitions, his life is a great success. He has the capacity to generate endless, original, fascinating conversation. He is a scholar and a poet and a thinker, so no matter what idle question comes up, he is able to speak knowledgeably and eloquently on it.

I remember once when I was 14 years old I took a five-day car trip through Mexico with my parents. It was long and unbearable. The last thing I wanted was to be stuck in a car with my parents. I was in that unpleasable teenager stage. Eventually I whined that I was bored, bored, bored. I was *dying* of boredom.

My father got his Black Look and replied shortly, "If you are bored, it's your own damn fault." A simple statement, and the profound truth of it hit me on the head like a sledgehammer, penetrating my current state of pubescent obliviousness. That's true, I thought. The second revelation that occurred to me was that I had *never seen* my father bored.

So I asked him, "Daddy, have you ever been bored?"

"Never," he answered, with certainty. "Now, how about a game of chance with our wealth of silver pesos?"

For the duration of the drive through Mexico we entertained ourselves with the mountains of silver pesos we'd gotten in exchange for five dollars at the border. We invented hundreds of money games. One moment I was rich, rich, rich, gloating and powerful, lording it over my peso-less papa; the next game he'd make up the rules and I'd be plunged into poverty. We explored this to the hilt, imagining what we'd do if we were millionaires, then what we'd do if we were zero-naires. I realized that my mindless flirtation with boredom had been exposed for what it was and dispatched with imagination and insight.

A direct result of this gift of my father's is that he knows its value and that he can get a lot of mileage out of it for being served. Being wily as well as book-learned, Daddy figured out the one thing that will elicit service from us—great conversation. If you're in the middle of listening to an elaborate, eloquent exposition on Shakespeare's sonnet form and the speaker breaks to ask for a bowl of vanilla ice cream, you're likely to go get it without even noticing the speaker could have gotten it himself. Or caring. More profound things are at hand.

However, it gets more complicated because Daddy wants to be served in every way all the time. I was eighteen before I realized I didn't need to tie his shoelaces anymore. When I went on strike, he simply got slip-on loafers, but he kept asking me to fetch them when he wanted them.

On the other hand, it is a just and wonderful irony that a man who spent his entire life planning how to get seven daughters to wait on him also ensured, through that same intelligence, that those daughters were independent, educated, and stubbornly individualistic. That was his undoing. Now in his autumn years, just when he wants to sit around and play Patriarch of the Family, obeyed and pampered as such—instead, what does he have? Seven sassy, quick-thinking, articulate, self-confident, liberated grown women who wouldn't serve the Pope if he were paraplegic.

It has been hard for Daddy to accept.

So, when he glanced around after announcing his desire for a cup of coffee, he noticed he got the usual response—none. That's because we were involved in the kind of discussion seven sassy, quick-thinking, articulate, etc. etc. sisters have when they get together–i.e., gossip. We had returned to the pre-dog-fight topic, Beth's Hopeless Cases Dating Service, ignoring Daddy's request. He knew he would need a great story.

Beth was saying that if the clients didn't adhere to her Rules, she wouldn't set them up on a date with each other.

I asked her what rules was she talking about.

"My Rules for A Good Relationship," she said. "See, I give them advice on relationships AS WELL AS a potential mate, so they have a chance to succeed at this one. I'm not going to have any back-sliders."

"You want a low rate of recidivism in your dating service?"

"Exactly," she nodded.

"What are your Rules?" Carol asked, genuinely interested. Carol's always interested to know if anyone's Rules can beat hers. She's got Rules for Everything, including which way you're supposed to unwind toilet paper.

"First, respect," Beth stated. "They've got to behave with respect toward each other. Second, communication. 'Don't let the sun set on your anger' the old saying goes. Third–"

"Wait, wait, wait," I interrupted. "How are you going to make sure they adhere to your Rules on the date? Are you going to hide behind the plant at the restaurant and monitor them?"

During the second it took Beth to consider the solution to this hitch in her operating plan, Daddy, who had been biding his time waiting for the right opportunity, saw the opening he'd been waiting.

"I discovered a middle-aged woman hiding in my clothes closet this morning," he said.

We wheeled our heads at him in one synchronized movement.

"Who was she?" three of us asked at once.

"Ellen Blockett."

"Why was she in your closet?"

"I don't know. She was dressed in my clothes, standing in the dark in the closet when I opened the door."

"Good God!" Carol exclaimed with delight. "What was she wearing?"

"My Duncan brush pants, brown shirt, and the gaucho belt Kay brought me from Paraguay."

"But they're huge," Carol said. "How could she wear your clothes when they're ten sizes too big for her?"

"They did seem to envelope her," Daddy allowed.

"I think I'd have to have them sign a contract first," Beth finally decided. "Or maybe I could use the Honor System and have them fill out a form before the date."

Needless to say, none of us gave her conclusion a moment's attention.

"Daddy," Carol continued. "Why was Ellen Blockett hiding in your closet at—when did you find her?"

"Five A.M.," he said matter-of-factly.

"Five A.M.!" Carol shrieked. "That's not even seven or eight A.M."

"Why?" I turned to her. "Would it be normal for her to be hiding in there at seven or eight A.M.?"

"Well, it's not like FIVE A.M. that's for sure. That means she could have been in the closet all night."

We all looked at Daddy for information on this new All-Night Hypothesis.

"Well, she'd been there a while," he said slowly.

"How do you know?" we snapped.

"She told me—"

"Right there? Standing in your closet at five A.M.?"

"No. Later."

"What do you mean, later?" we persisted.

"After she stole my car and brought it back."

"What!!" we whooped.

This was definitely shaping up into a great story. It was outrageous, it was original, and it was gripping. Just the kind we thrive on.

And Daddy knew it. With Machiavellian timing, he said, "I sure could use a cup of coffee."

Four of us leapt toward the kitchen.

"I'll get it. I'll get it," I said, waving them off. "Just don't say another word 'til I get back."

I raced into the kitchen and in one continuous motion sloshed coffee all over the drainboard, filled the cup, hit the sugar bowl, stirred and ran back out with it.

"Record time." Mama observed as I handed the cup to Daddy.

He took his Patriarchal time savoring the coffee and service.

After a moment, Carol couldn't stand it anymore. "She stole your car . . ." she prompted him.

"Oh, yes," he looked up. "She leapt out of the closet in my clothes, startling me, ran around the house several times and then left in the Buick."

"Why didn't you stop her?" Beth persisted.

"Common sense told me not to," he replied.

We nodded in agreement to this.

"How did you get the car back?"

"I waited a while then I called her at her house."

"That's where she went?"

"Directly. 'Bring back my car right now, Ellen,' I said."

"And she did?" I asked.

"Yes. Unfortunately, then she was back at my house."

"Daddy, do you think she's stopped taking her medication?" Barbara offered.

"That is precisely what happened, I found out later. Apparently, she was having a psychotic episode. In my clothes closet."

"Well, who wouldn't if they stood in your closet all night?" Mama snorted. "Was your gun collection locked up?"

"Yes, it was. Lucky thing, too . . ."

"You mean your trunks of guns were in there too?" Mama asked incredulously.

"Only one of them."

"What? The one with the war replicas?"

"No," I interjected. "The one with the psychotic-proof twist-off lid, Mama."

There was another well-timed pause. Daddy looked in his lap.

"I wouldn't mind another piece of birthday cake," he said.

Beth picked up the whole pan of cake and thrust it under his face. "Here you are."

"Oh—" he took a piece—"thank you."

"Well, is she nuts?" Carol asked with finality.

Daddy bit into the soggy, fallen cake with relish. "Mmmmmm. Good cake," he mouthed.

We all turned to look at something else.

Beth leapt out of her chair. "Of course she's nuts. She's nuttier than a ten pound fruitcake."

"THAT'S what we should bring to the next September Birthday Party," Mama said suddenly, lighting up. "A fruitcake. That would be real good."

That would be real appropriate, I thought. Yet I couldn't help savoring a vision of the fruitcake fit for the next September Babies Birthday Party.

NINE HUNDRED AND THIRTY ACRES

PAT CARR

"It's rightfully mine," her grandmother said while her lacquered fingertips caught the scowl before it imprinted her nose, and she reshaped her face into an expression of astonishment, which a beautician had once assured her would tighten the muscles and retard aging. "I can't help it if old Faye Dunlap fell in love and cut them two fat stupid sons a' his out a' his will."

"Billy Todd ain't fat." Carlotta slouched on a sewing rocker, in which no woman had sat and sewn since 1859, and pointed the toes of her unlaced hightops.

"His kind a' twenty-year-old pork will turn into the same barrel a' lard as J. D. when he gets to forty." She posed, examined her size seven lavender suit in the pier glass, which she insisted on calling it, and tapped her brick pink curls. "Nobody'd guess I was forty-eight, would they? You got to admit Faye had good taste."

"I heard Wilhamena wasn't much of a prize," Carlotta said.

"Wilhamena Dunlap died the year before you was born, Miss Sass." But her tone was indifferent. "She was suppose to be a real beauty in her day."

"They called anybody a beauty that didn't have a face full a' smallpox scars."

"That something you got out a' one a' them books?" It wasn't a question, however, and she went on at once. "It ain't my fault either that Faye wasn't in tip-top shape after all that wedding fuss—"

"Does that mean 'after all that sex'?"

"—and that his old heart just give out six weeks after we got married."

51

The air was an oily mix of absorbed tobacco fumes laced with linseed polish, and the courtroom spectators wore the pinched expression of people who had swallowed the capacity of their lungs for the past two hours. Although most of them probably remained curious about the disposition of the land, most of them also surreptitiously squinted from the judge to their watches.

Carlotta lounged directly behind her grandmother's lilac suit at the defendant's table, pressed her bony legs tight against the banister, and crossed her arms. The irreverent curve of her shoulders indicated to those in the back rows that she was one of the few people in the room who didn't give a damn who got the nine hundred and thirty acres.

The bulbous giant of a man in the witness box was repeating, "—in less than six weeks. If there ain't something suspicious in a man hearty as a bull keeling over into his breakfast eggs—"

Judge Harlan lifted his hand, palm vertical as though shoving back the stale air. "That ain't in the considering, J. D. This is a case to decide if the new Mrs. Dunlap is entitled to old Faye's land."

"It's been our land since before I was born." His huge face, its cheeks and chins so distended with flesh that the skull was undiscernible, seemed to be trying to register anger. His bloated fingers clenched.

"The question is whose land it's gonna be tomorrow, J. D.," the judge said, and when someone in the courtroom tried to bite back a laugh, he added, as if to the crowd as well as to the witness, "That'll do."

"I'd hope so," a woman's voice whispered near Carlotta's ear, but she didn't glance around.

The judge called Boland Ames, old Faye's lawyer, who at seventy-three was the most articulate witness of the morning.

"Faye wanted them acres connecting Corbitt land to his deeded to Prin. He won it fair from her daddy, but he always felt guilty keeping it. He'd have signed them all over to Hughleen before she died if she'd ever give him the time a day." Boland paused to cough into a handkerchief so white it dazzled. "So when him and Prin got married, he just naturally done what he aimed to do for forty years."

He paused again, and the judge looked down at a deposition, or perhaps his thumbnail, and the spectators shifted on the wooden benches. Only Carlotta didn't unfold her arms or unfavor a hip.

"And he called you to make that change in his will? Signing over the house and that adjoining nine hundred and thirty acres to Prin?"

"Hell, no. You know how Faye hated to use the phone. He just wrote it on the tag end of the will sheets. He was one for saving paper when he could."

Judge Harlan sighed. "J. D. and Billy Todd say that ain't Faye's handwriting."

"When would they've studied old Faye's handwriting? Neither a' them ever got far enough out a town for a letter. Big Bill would be the one to ask if he wasn't dead."

The judge sighed again. Everyone knew that William Custer Dunlap's name was eight feet high up on the Vietnam Memorial and that old Faye'd had to climb a ladder to make the rubbing that still hung on his living room wall. "I suppose you're right, Boland."

Then Ed Bunch from the bank was called to agree that it was old Faye's signature, Doc Wilson to argue that it probably wasn't because of the old man's arthritis, and finally the judge stared across his bench at the two men and their lawyer on the left and Carlotta's grandmother with her lawyer on the right. "Anything else?"

When neither lawyer jumped immediately to his feet, the judge's mouth framed, "The court will take ten minutes" while he banged the gavel across every word but 'minutes.'

Prin stood up and glanced at her granddaughter while she made her eyes wide as if in surprise to stretch the tendons and prevent crow's feet. The startled eyes held a question about how the case had gone, but when Carlotta kept her arms crossed and her chin down, Prin smiled at her Palestine lawyer instead.

The only other people who hadn't moved before the judge's black robe flapped through he side door again were J. D. and Billy Todd Dunlap, and they, too, had to struggle out of their chairs and sink back into them when the judge began to crack his wooden hammer on the wooden desk.

"Well, since nobody seems about to concur on whether old Faye wrote that note himself before he died, I guess it's up to me to decide." He glowered at the courtroom. "And I don't want any disturbance about what I say. I know some a' you can get hot-headed at times." He may have been referring to the occasion a few years earlier when J. D. drowned half a dozen spur-fitted roosters in a stock tank because their owner had accused him of cheating at the cock fights. "I'll throw the book at anybody I hear making threats—since I'm going to rule in favor of Princess Lynn Corbitt Wagner Bates Dunlap." And he charged on before anyone snickered, as people occasionally did when they heard Prin's string of names, the first of which Hughleen Corbitt had chosen from the label of a maternity dress. "I'm awarding them acres to her as the widow of Faye Dunlap whether or not old Faye wrote that note. You boys can keep the house." And he pounded the mallet. "Court's adjourned." Prin turned back to her granddaughter, and this time Carlotta unwound and stood up. She lankily topped the dainty woman in the pink-red, almost fuchsia, wig, and didn't look toward the Dunlap table.

"All right, Granny, let's go," she said.

"Not that I think she did spoon something in his coffee or over his egg yolks," Carlotta said to the horse's eye as she cinched on the saddle. "But she's sure fire capable."

She adjusted the bridle on the nose too blunt to classify as Arabian even though that was half the gene pool, and put her foot in the stirrup. "Oh, hell." She halted her leg swing halfway across the tooled saddle. "There's March snakes out."

She dropped to the ground again and latched the reins around a fence shaft before she loped across the yard to the house.

As she flung open the kitchen door, her grandmother came from the front of the house snugging another wig, this one a jet black page boy cut, over her forehead.

"I thought you left already," she said.

"I'm getting the pistol. After Smokey got bit by that blind snake, I ain't taking chances."

"Don't shoot yourself in the foot."

"You say that every time." Carlotta took down the heavy gun, dug the shells from the spice rack drawer, and loaded the cylinder.

"Well, then don't." Prin opened the refrigerator door onto which clung magnets in the plastic forms of Oreo cookies, chocolate drops, pink bonbons, and various slices of pie with cherry and blueberry fillings. "Shit, we're out of pound cake."

"Cake's fattening." She clicked the safety catch.

"It don't seem to blimp you out."

"I'm thirty years younger than you, Granny."

"And still a spinster. I had your mama when I was fifteen, and your mama had you—"

Carlotta let the door slam on Prin's words.

"I had your mama when I was fifteen, and she had you at fifteen." She opened her eyes very wide and mimicked for the horse. "And you never had a date yet." Then her voice lowered as if to avoid shocking the brown velvet ears. "Big fucking deal."

She touched the horse's sides with her heels and they cantered down the dirt road. She paused to climb off once more and unfasten the barbed wire loop that held the gate shut. But instead of laying the wooden posts and their stranded barbed wire carefully in the weeds as she usually did, she looked at the gate a moment, then kicked it into a tangle of wood and wire.

"Since it's Granny's land now I guess we don't have to fence you out, do we?"

The horse watched her and hummed a modulated trill.

"And I guess we can look it over some." She turned the not-quite-Arabian head uphill, and the horse began to pick its way through brittle fescue and waist-high yellow milkweed.

At the edge of the cedar and oak woods, the ground cover changed to leaf mulch and shards of limestone, and Carlotta watched beside the hooves for rattlers shedding skin that might hood their eyes.

"They don't care to fang you and use up a month's worth of venom when they damn well can't swallow you whole, but if they don't see you coming, they get spooked," she explained to the horse whose ears alternately flattened and straightened.

"Ain't that a sign you're going nuts? Talking to yourself?"

Carlotta's knees clamped the saddle and her head jerked alert.

Billy Todd Dunlap hunkered on a six-foot limestone outcropping and stared down at her.

"I was talking to Blaze."

"Same thing," he said. His eyes were the blue of the freshly beading juniper berries. "I guess you're out exploring your new land?"

Her chin came up. "It's Granny's. I ain't involved."

He slid off the jagged ledge of rock and stepped next to the horse. "Well, it's a damned nice piece a' land."

"Like I say, it ain't got anything to do with me."

He reached out to stroke the horse's neck and his jacket sleeve brushed her knee. He didn't seem to notice. "There's something on it I bet you never seen before."

"I don't bet," she said, her lips stiffening.

He laughed. "I didn't mean that literally, lunkhead."

His teeth were very straight and white. "Come on, I'll show you." He tugged the lead away from her fingers. "Blaze can stay here if you can walk in them shoes."

She hesitated, then jumped down while he strung the reins around a pole-clean sapling.

"Of course I can." She stooped to tie the laces and her eyes swept his fitted jeans. "At least you ain't fat like J. D. "

"Nobody's fat like J. D." He gestured beyond the jut of limestone. "That way."

"Well, hell, you go ahead. I don't know where we're suppose to be going."

"You're sure mouthy to your elders, ain't you?"

She snorted. "You're two years older than me."

"Three."

Their feet crackled dead oak leaves, kicked up loose chips of stone. Once he swung back a cedar branch that might have slapped across her cheek if he hadn't been holding it.

"How far is this sight I never seen before?"

Up by the bluff." He glanced back at her over his shoulder. "Your granny earned herself a lot a' land this morning."

She stopped. "Oh, hell."

"Hey, I was just joshing you. Come on."

"Well, knock off that guilt trip shit." She frowned but followed him as he started again.

A few minutes later he put his hand on her arm. "It's through them trees, but move over this way."

She stiffened slightly and glanced at him. "This better be good."

His fingers fell away from her sleeve to come to rest on her hand. "Okay, now walk here beside me."

He led her along a narrow path into a small meadow.

Centered in the clearing were two massive cubes of limestone, one balanced over the other on what appeared to be a cone of rock no larger than a fist.

"Well, I'll be damned." Carlotta looked from the tons of perfectly balanced stone to his face. "There really was something up here."

"I told you, didn't I?" He straightened the open zipper of his jacket. "You could charge admission to see this."

"And I told you this is Granny's land."

"I didn't mean you personally." He took her hand again and pulled her down beside him. "Sit here on this flat rock. It's the best view."

"I'll be damned."

They sat in silence a moment.

"How come you got the name Carlotta?"

"Not everybody's got a dead war hero brother to be named after."

"Hey, I just wondered."

She studied him, then shrugged. "Granny thought when I was born I'd grow a head full a black hair, but it all wore off and came in dishwater blond."

"It ain't a bad color."

He stood up abruptly and looked down soberly at her for a few seconds before he turned and started back the way they'd come.

That evening the phone rang half a dozen times, but each time Prin answered it, only deliberate silence came across the line.

Her query "Who is this?" progressed to "Who the hell do you think you are?" but still no one answered.

"We're shutting off the damned bell," Prin yelled the final time as she slammed the receiver into its cradle.

"You think it's J. D.?" Carlotta asked.

"Or that piss-ant Billy Todd." She fumbled with the back of the telephone. "I could tell both a them was mad as hornets this morning."

"I didn't think so."

"What do you know? You was living here with Mel for the six weeks I was over there seeing the two a' them every damned day."

Carlotta scooted forward until the back of her neck rested on the edge of the rocker and then she raised herself upright without touching her hand to the floor. "I'm going to bed."

Prin scratched under the wig with her index finger. "Shut off that cater-wauling TV on your way out. This damned phone shit got me too nervous to watch." She was unstacking the freezer compartment to reach a carton of strawberry ice cream.

Carlotta kicked her bedroom door shut as she pulled off her jacket. The pistol she'd forgotten to put away banged her hip.

"Oh, hell." She took it from the pocket and laid it on the night table beside the hobnailed milk glass lamp.

The gun barrel and the symmetrical porcelain bubbles reflected aching filament dots of brightness, and she snapped off the lamp before she re-moved her shirt and jeans and put on the checkered cotton pajamas with the frayed collar. She didn't close the curtains but looked out onto the dirt yard that was almost white in the moonlight.

"Shit," she said softly before she left the window and turned back to the bed quilt.

She stretched out under the sheets and stared at the ceiling where the moon trailed a rope-thin bar of light toward the angle of the wall.

Her grandmother was shelving enameled pans or tossing jar lids into a drawer in the kitchen, and Carlotta closed her eyes.

She opened them suddenly in complete blackness.

A rasp of labored breathing filled the room, and the window rectangle was blocked with the dark silhouette of a man.

"What—?" She sat up.

The man's leg that had been inside the window ledge drew back with a scrape, and the thud of boots hit the ground.

"What the hell—?"

As she flung back the covers, her hand came down on the night table and the pistol. She swept up the gun and sprang to the window.

"Is that you, Billy Todd?"

She swung across the sill and threw herself feet first into the yard.

The shadow of the man was already merging with the dark of the near-est cedars, and she couldn't distinguish size or shape. She sprinted after it. The stock of the revolver was tallow-smooth in her palm as she raced to-ward the woods.

Her bare feet skimmed the crisp leaves and snapping twigs. Her breath puffed out, a moon cloud mist, in the cold air, and the thrash of heavy running came from just ahead.

She gained the tree line but she didn't slow her run. And she didn't pause to aim in the darkness as she raised the gun toward the clumsy booted sounds and pulled the trigger.

The crack of the shot bounded and rebounded against the black tree trunks. What might have been a scream or the shriek of an owl shrilled upward and then echoed in circles of black sound.

She stopped abruptly.

Now there was only silence, and the white moon caught motionless in the bare ribs of an oak.

"You stupid fool!"

The darkness obscured the cry that might have been meant for the man or for herself as she hurled the pistol as hard as she could into the black underbrush. "It's a fucking piece of land!"

A NIGHT FOR MYSTERY

RICHARD CLINTON

It was a cool, clear evening during spring break as Jeff and his dad drove east along US 90 in far West Texas, between Marfa and Alpine. They had come down from his granddad's ranch north of Fort Davis to see the mysterious Marfa Lights. Jeff's dad told him that people had driven out there for years to see these strange dancing lights, although you could never be sure to see them. Jeff was hoping they would appear this night, and that maybe he could see them up close through the new telescope his granddad had given him last Christmas.

There were several cars and a tour bus already parked at the viewing area, about nine miles east of Marfa, when they arrived just as it was getting dark. Jeff and his dad proceeded to set up the telescope, pointing it southwest, toward the Chinati Mountains, in the direction most people reported seeing the lights. Jeff's dog, Raffles, who had come along for the ride, was busy running around the parking area, sniffing out his own adventure.

"Do you think we'll see any lights tonight?" Jeff asked.

"There's no telling," his dad replied. "The lights are very unpredictable."

"What are they, anyway?" Jeff asked.

"No one knows for sure," his dad said. "There are lots of theories. Some people think they are caused by an electrical discharge of some kind. A group of mining people thought at one time that the lights were radiation caused by large deposits of uranium in the area, but they never found any. Others think it's no more than a reflection of car headlights somewhere off in the distance."

Jeff and his dad had been sitting on the hood of their car for nearly an hour, scanning the wide expanse of West Texas plains, when someone called out: "I think I see some. There, toward the base of the mountains, down to the right, see them?" Jeff looked where the people next to him were pointing. Yes, there they were. First two lights, then none, then one, then three. The flickering red, bluish-white, sometimes yellow lights seemed to dance around in no particular pattern. "No telling just how big or far away they are," said Jeff's dad. "They're bouncing around so fast." Jeff jumped down from the car, and pointed his telescope in the direction he had seen the lights. But almost as suddenly as they had appeared, they were gone.

Jeff and his dad continued to stare for a while into the darkness, but there were no more lights to be seen. The tour bus and some of the cars began to drive off. "Let's take some time while we're here to look at the stars, and see if we can find any of the planets through your telescope," said Jeff's dad. "With the air so clear and no moon yet tonight, we ought to be able to see Saturn's rings pretty well."

Later, as Jeff was trying to count the rings around the planet Saturn, something even brighter blocked his view. At the same time, Jeff's dog came up close to him and began to growl. Jeff looked up and saw a cluster of flashing lights moving across the sky, sort of like the others, but in a way different. "Look, Dad," exclaimed Jeff. "I see some of those lights up in the sky. Maybe it's a UFO." But almost as he spoke, the lights seemed to zip over his head and were gone. Jeff's dad looked up. "I don't see anything," he said. "Perhaps you've been staring through that telescope too long. I think maybe it's time we were getting back." "No," said Jeff. "I'm sure I saw something. And I think Raffles saw it, too. Can we stay just a little longer? Maybe they will come back." They watched for a few more minutes, then Jeff sadly helped his dad load the telescope back into the trunk of the car. With Raffles curled up on the back seat, they headed for the ranch.

It was nearly an hour's drive back to the ranch, and by then Jeff was ready for bed. It had, after all, been a long night for him and he was tired, but at least he had seen the mysterious Marfa Lights, and maybe something even more mysterious. He would always wonder about that. As they walked up to the ranch house, Raffles stopped and cocked his head to better hear a sound that neither Jeff nor his dad could hear. And they also didn't see the flashing lights that were coming lower over the hills behind them as they closed the ranch house door.

RIGHT FIELD BLUES

CLAY REYNOLDS

 Being thirteen in my hometown during the summertime was a lot like being in purgatory. I was too old to ride a bike, too young to drive, old enough to like girls, too young to admit it, old enough to "act like a man," too young to be "trusted alone," so I looked forward with a nagging sense of loathing to the one thing that might make the summer pass and bring my birthday and an end to West Texas August around more quickly—Little League Baseball.

Being a Little Leaguer then wasn't like being a Little Leaguer now, at least not in my hometown. In West Texas, it never was. We didn't have fancy uniforms or even brightly lettered tee-shirts. We just wore the same colored caps with the team name stitched on them, and if we were lucky, we all got the same colored shirts to wear over our jeans. There was no national hookup, no "world series" to hope for, no goal at all beyond winning the city championship in early August. And there were no girls. Little League was serious business in West Texas, as serious as football was in the fall.

Each team in each of the three divisions—Pee Wee, Jack Rabbit, and Pony—would play a ten-game season, and the winners got a free hamburger dinner with any dessert they wanted at the Dairy Mart after their final game. Outside of that, there wasn't much more to it than hours and hours of hot, windy, dusty practice on some school yard, and the weekly game, which was played in a dilapidated old stadium that the WPA had built for an A semi-pro team back during the Depression.

My thirteenth summer I was finally graduated to the Pony Division. I was supposed to be fourteen to play in it, but I was big for my age, and my birthday came in September, so I had always played with kids who were ahead of me in school and ability as well. But we had the same coach I had always had, Mr. Kruickshank, so I felt pretty comfortable even if I was the youngest member of the Cubs—our name that season—and even if Ol' Kruck, as we called him, knew that I probably wouldn't do any better than I usually did.

I had been a Little Leaguer since my seventh summer when my old man decided that playing baseball would keep my mind off the .22 rifle I had wanted since the day I was born. Sports, he assured my mother, would be good for me. He didn't know what he was doing.

First of all he had to buy me a glove. I remember him piling me into our old 1952 Ford and driving me down to the hardware store where the only sporting goods in town were sold. Knowing that he would never permit me to have the rifle and that my hanging around the firearms display in the store made him angry, I had already spent a couple of centuries in front of the baseball equipment lusting after a Joe Dimaggio Fielder's Mitt every time my parents took me shopping with them, and I was excited that at last the golden glove was going to be mine.

"Remember," I told my old man as he fiddled around with the cigarette lighter than never worked in the Ford, "I'm right-handed. I want a right-handed glove."

"You want a left-handed glove!" he snapped me as he searched his pockets for his Zippo. "You catch with your left and throw with your right. Don't you know anything?"

I didn't believe him, but I was too abashed to say anything, and my feelings of inadequacy were in no way relieved when I was brought home without the Joe Dimaggio mitt—which had proved too costly—but instead carrying an unautographed fielder's glove that was in no way an imitation of the hand-tooled, pre-pocketed, double-stitched beauty I had dreamed of for so long.

The fingers on the monstrosity my old man bought me at the urging of Harold Goodnight, the hardware store clerk, weren't laced together, and there was no webbing at all. In spite of the fact that my old man had announced to my mother as we walked in with this major disappointment in my life that it was "one damned expensive toy," it looked cheap. It was about five times too large for my hands, and when I tried to close it over a ball, the fingers flopped in five different directions and let it fall out from a million holes. There was no pocket at all. But the worst thing was that instead of getting a golden, tanned leather, it was sort of orange with bright yellow stitches on the seams. It was big, it was ugly, it was embarrassing.

But since my old man had bought it, I knew that more than anything else, it was mine.

I worried a lot about what my future teammates would say when they saw this grotesque imitation of real baseball equipment dangling from my left hand—at least my old man had been right about that—but that was really a minor concern when I faced the hard question: How was I supposed to catch balls with this thing? The answer came during my first practice: I wasn't.

Line drives passed through the splayed fingers without touching one of them. Flies rolled right off the palm. Grounders bent the glove back in two, and I found that unless I could get my bare right hand on the ball and use the mitt as a kind of backstop, I couldn't even work up a passable game of catch. The cowhide disaster my old man had given me condemned me to chasing more balls than I would ever catch, and I quickly developed a reputation as someone who couldn't catch a cold, let along a hard hit ball from as close in as third base, the position of my dreams. But when I would carry the bane of my athletic existence to my old man every spring and present it to him for inspection and, I prayed, a decision that I needed a real glove this year, he would only turn it over and note that it was hardly worn out at all—not surprising considering how few balls had actually touched it—and I would face yet another season with a major handicap on my left hand.

I did develop some ability with a bat, however. My nearsightedness hadn't been detected yet, and in order to see the ball better when the pitcher threw it, I had to stand at a slight angle to the plate. The result was that I accidentally managed to slice the ball to right field when I hit it—something that only a few batters in our Little League could do on purpose—and it confused the dickens out of the defense, since they always adjusted to left whenever a right-handed batter came up to the plate. And because I was a chubby kid and big for my age, I could also get some weight behind my hits—which was a good thing, as I ran like a ruptured walrus—or so Ol' Kruck was fond of reminding me whenever I got a hit and managed to be thrown out—but if the pitch was just right, I could usually line one out over the first baseman's head and sometimes stumble into second before their right fielder could make it to the ball.

But this knack of mine presented Ol' Kruck with a problem: I could hit, but I couldn't field. So he did what most coaches do when they have a batter who can't play defense—he put me in right field where I wouldn't have to.

Right Field is the West Texas Little League version of hell.

In spite of the fact that *I* and maybe a handful of other kids could hit out that way on purpose, it was the one position in Little League where a kid could play all season and not have to worry about fielding more than two or three balls. Being sentenced there is more or less permanent, since when a ball does finally roll out toward right, the fielder is so bored that he's fallen asleep on his feet and isn't even aware that a game is going on, so he has no chance of proving that he might be better than the coach originally thought he was, which he probably isn't.

I spent the better part of my childhood's summers standing out in right, waiting for something–*anything*–to happen to relieve my torture. Once, I remember, I counted the number of stickers on a goathead weed fifty times before practice was over, and when I came in, Ol' Kruck apologized for forgetting to hit anything out my way. But I knew if he did, I probably would have missed it, so intent was I on counting those stickers. Other times I worked on poems we had to memorize for school, or I concentrated on my multiplication tables. Once I was all the way up to twelve times eleven is one-thirty-two when Ol' Kruck woke me up by yelling, "Move, damnit!" and I blinked in time to see a nice grounder hissing through the weeks right past me. I dove down into the dirt to stop it, but I knew I was too late. Sure enough, the useless glove's fingers sprayed around in the dusty goatheads and milkweed, and the ball slid right through them. I knew then that I was in right field for good. Nothing could save me.

So even though Ol' Kruck batted me in cleanup position and would scream with laughter when I'd lay one out in the very place nobody was supposed to and earn us a couple of runs, he kept me out in right field to watch the weeds burn up while the rest of the kids played ball. I didn't know what I was supposed to do about it, and my playing Little League made my old man happy, even if I was stuck out in right, so I endured it summer after summer and prayed uselessly for rain on practice days.

When practice sessions began my thirteenth summer, I had no hopes of anything changing. I had managed to save up my allowance and to mow some lawns, and I finally bought myself a genuine big league glove–autographed by the whole '55 Dodgers team across the deep pocket–but my habit of missing balls was so ingrained in me, that goofing around in a vacant lot with a bunch of the guys proved to me that I was doomed never to make a decent catch in my life, new glove or not. When a ball came my way, I automatically started turning to chase it down even before it got to me. Nobody laughed at me anymore. Everyone knew I couldn't catch a baseball, even a pop fly, new glove or not.

While that goofing around was going on, however, my kid brother used my old mitt, even though I told him not to try it. Sure enough, the ball came down and passed right through the fingers and smashed out two teeth. My mother committed it to the trash barrel that very afternoon, pronouncing the worst of maternal curses over it as the flames consumed it. Even though it had doomed me to right field forever, I was sort of sad to see it go.

But one Wednesday afternoon, mid-way through that season, things did change in a way I never would have imagined possible. That was the afternoon Teddy Thompson came out for Little League.

Theodore Thompson III, Teddy, was what later generations would call a "nerd." We all just called him a "square." What he was was a *brain*—and he knew it. His old man was a big shot lawyer and his mother was an artist, and even though my old man said they could "buy and sell everybody in town," they were, as my mother said, "tighter than Dick's hatband." They drove new cars all the time, but Teddy never could get money to go on field trips or school outings that weren't free. They had a grand piano and a houseful of books—miles of books, bookcases in every room of the house, including the bathroom—but they didn't own a TV, and poor Teddy—who was already about six-five, even though he wasn't but fourteen—never had pants that were long enough or shirts with cuffs he could button. His hair was always shaggy and too long, and he was so farsighted that he couldn't see the ground he was standing on. He wore these thick, old-fashioned glasses that made him look as smart as he was, but they also made him look fuzzy, and he had to squint half the time to see who he was talking to.

So Teddy wasn't like most of us, and lots of kids made fun of him all the time. But even so, he was sort of popular. He got elected to student council and was usually on most of the class committees, and he was the first kid in our class to bring a girl to a school party. But the one thing he could never be was an athlete. He just didn't have the moves, and I strongly suspected that he didn't have the desire either. He was too awkward and tall for football, and he didn't have enough coordination for basketball, and he had tried out for the junior high teams for both and caused more laughter than a Jerry Lewis movie. He claimed he could play tennis pretty well—he learned how at church camp—but no one else in town could play, and the only courts were concrete affairs with chain-link nets and more grass growing up through the cracks than most people had on their lawns. In those days we all thought tennis was sort of a sissy sport anyway, and his demand that someone learn the game and play with him did nothing to sell him as a real athlete. Mostly, the guys said, Teddy played chess, and, we laughed, we heard he was a real killer at Monopoly.

So jaws hit the ground when we saw him show up for practice one afternoon on the junior high playground. He was wearing these high-topped basketball shoes and jeans that were falling down around his skinny waist but still didn't cover the tops of his socks. His cap was too big for him, and it was pulled down to his ears and made his hair stick out in a hundred directions at once. He had a beatup old first baseman's mitt with torn webbing for a glove—one I knew had belonged to his big brother, who, to hear Teddy tell it, had been varsity everything when he was graduated five years ago—and he had it on the wrong hand. You would never know his folks had any money at all to look at him. He was pathetic and outlandish at the same time, and if Ol' Kruck hadn't yelled at us, we would have burst out laughing as soon as he turned the corner and started toward the playground.

But the oddest thing about him wasn't visible until he came up close, and then nothing Kruck could do or say could stop us from breaking up. We were all rolling around in the dirt around homeplate and giggling uncontrollably when we saw his glasses.

His usual horn-rimmed jobs were gone, and in their place were these "sportsman's glasses," as he called them. He announced to us when he realized we were laughing at them that they cost his old man a hundred dollars, and they were especially designed for athletes, particularly baseball players. But expensive or not, especially designed or not, they were ridiculous, and they looked even funnier on poor Teddy.

If anything, they were thicker than his regular glasses. Instead of plastic frames, they had these wires that stretched around behind his ears, and all the way around the lenses was this yellow, spongy-looking stuff that made them look like welder's goggles. They sat up on his nose on these pink pads that caused the lenses to stick out like huge insect eyes, and I could tell that he couldn't see too well out of them, since he kept turning his head from side to side to see who was standing next to him. In ten minutes, we were all falling down and running into each other, groping around like a team of blind men trying to find the exit from a burning building. It seemed enormously funny at the time, and only one or two of us noticed that Teddy was taking it as well as he could, standing there and smiling at our antics and trying to focus on who was doing what.

Ol' Kruck cussed us out and made us shut up, though, and practice started. I dragged myself out to right field as usual and began wishing as usual that things would change and I might catch something. I had this dream of moving to third base, and my favorite fantasy was that Ralph Pearson would catch mono or something, or his parents would suddenly decide to take him away for a long vacation, and I might inherit the envied third bag. I had no hopes of the new mitt making much difference, but miracles do happen—my mother always told me that anyway—and I was long overdue.

Right field was the biggest part of the problem in the first place. Just being stuck out there was so demoralizing that I *had* to mess up just to prove Ol' Kruck right in putting me there. I decided that it didn't help having to stand around and wait for something to happen for so long. The longer I had to think about messing up, I knew, the more likely I was to mess up. But as practice went on and the heat of the outfield was coming up through the soles of my sneakers so much that I was having to balance on one foot at a time while I counted all the rocks in my immediate area that were bigger than golf balls, I found myself watching Teddy and wondering again why in the world he wanted to play Little League ball.

He obviously would never make any sort of ball player. Ol' Kruck moved him around a lot, trying him at different positions, even *my* third base, which caused me a moment or two of anxiety, but it was only a moment or two. It would have been clear to the mentally disturbed that Teddy would never master the fundamentals of the game. I couldn't catch, I knew, but I had sense enough to at least *look* like I knew what I was doing. Poor Teddy couldn't even do that. He stood up straight wherever Ol' Kruck told him to play, and he just waited. He didn't get down in a crouch the way we all did, and he didn't move on the grounders, try to get under the flies, or even stick out his glove for the line drives Ol' Kruck kept hitting his way. He just stood there and sort of opened and closed the worn out old glove in the general direction of the ball and waited until it slid past him. Then he'd run after it.

That was when things became funny.

He had these long, long legs, and he'd pump them up and down when he ran until he got the ball underneath him, then he'd bend down like a giant stork and pick it up. By this time, most of us were giggling pretty loud, but it got better yet. He'd turn around with the ball in his right hand, cock his arm back, and throw it about six feet in front of him, right into the dirt.

When he'd let go of it, he'd sort of raise his right leg in a hopping motion and dance around a little bit. At this point bedlam swept the whole field, and we all collapsed on the ground howling in painful peals of laughter.

It wasn't so much that he threw like a girl. A lot of guys did that until they learned to plant their feet and really peg the ball in on target. It was something else. Maybe it was because he was so tall and skinny that he looked so funny, or maybe it was because of the little dance he did. But probably what made the whole thing so appealingly hilarious was Ol' Kruck's reaction. Every time Teddy tried to throw it, Ol' Kruck would stand there with his mouth hanging open like he couldn't believe what his eyes were telling him. Then he would turn as red as an inflamed boil and start cussing poor Teddy and then turn around and start yelling at us for laughing and then throw his hands up over his head and cuss the clouds because baseball in general and Little League in particular even existed. But whatever it was that made it so funny didn't diminish with any attempt Ol' Kruck made to teach Teddy how to throw a baseball, and it destroyed field practice that afternoon. Ol' Kruck gave up and called us in to bat.

Teddy couldn't bat any better than he could field. Tall as he was, his strike zone was about a mile high, and Phil Ledbetter, our pitcher, had no trouble buzzing in strike after strike while Teddy just stood there, his bat uncertainly waving over his right shoulder, peering through those thick, silly glasses at the ball as it zipped past him. Ol' Kruck yelled at Phil to "ease up a little," and then he would scream "Swing, damnit!" at Teddy every time Phil tossed one over the plate. Teddy would stick the bat out when Ol' Kruck yelled, but he was choked up so high that even if he got it out there in time to hit a pitch, the ball would probably have crushed his fingers. We were all laughing so hard by this time that Ol' Kruck called off batting practice and made us all sit on the playground's jungle gym while he yelled at us and stomped around until the veins on his forehead were standing out like huge purple worms. I was sure he was going to have a stroke or something, but before he collapsed into a pile of sputtering swear words, he sent us away with a wave of his hand and stomped off to his pickup where, we all knew, he kept some beer on ice.

The next afternoon was no better. Teddy tried to swing the bat a little more often, but by the time he got it around in front of him, Larry Whitehead had already caught it and was throwing it back to Phil for the next pitch. Teddy tried all the positions again, and Ol' Kruck screamed at him until he went hoarse and finally lost his voice. Our lexicons of vulgar words trebled that afternoon as Ol' Kruck reached new heights of obscenity in an attempt to inspire his newest player. Teddy tried to imitate a sort of crouch and to look, at least, like he might be interested in fielding a ball, but he never caught one or managed to throw it back, no matter how hard he tried or how red and angry Ol' Kruck became or how loud he yelled. He just couldn't get the hang of putting his glove out in front of the ball, and practice ended with him catching nothing more than enough sun to burn the end of his nose.

I wasn't doing much better, I knew, but at least I could hit. And when I missed a ball in the field, I knew how to run it down and heave it back to the cut-off man or even into the infield to stop the runner. I was thrilled to death to have Teddy on the team. Not only did it mean that for the first time in my Little League career I wasn't the worst player on the field, and I really felt like part of the group, but it also meant that there was something to do while I stood around kicking gravel and the tops off weeds and waiting for practice to end. Teddy was putting on the best show in town, and I never knew my time on the griddle of the playground's right field to pass so quickly.

Teddy's presence also meant that there was someone else on the team to take all the abuse the older guys felt like dishing out. I suddenly began to like playing Little League for the first time in my life. I actually found myself whispering to Joe Hogan, our center fielder and best all around player, that we could carry ol' Teddy—that is, if he ever got to play, which we were sure he wouldn't, not unless we were ahead about a hundred to nothing in the bottom of the ninth. He didn't even seem to understand enough about the game to keep the stats on the opposing team's pitchers and batters. He was absolutely useless to the team, and one thing any of us would have bet on was that Teddy's permanent position was going to be left bench.

But we were wrong about that.

After batting practice—when Teddy proved that Phil was possibly the most sensational strike-out artist in the league and that Ol' Kruck's screams could bring people out of their houses from as far as a block and a half away—we were called together for the usual pre-game pep talk and assignments. We were to take on the Pirates the following night, and it was an important game. We hadn't won but two of our first six outings, and if we lost on Friday, we'd be out of the running for good. Ol' Kruck went on and on, and I was studying the worn-out laces in my sneakers and wondering what was on TV that night when I suddenly heard him say that Teddy would take over right field.

I snapped to attention, broke out in a sweat, and felt a lump form in the pit of my stomach. That was *my* job! I almost said it out loud. I waited for Ol' Kruck to look at me, to see how devastated I was, but he was talking to Phil about something he just remembered, and I could feel everybody on the team nervously shifting around. As much as I hated right field, as much as I felt it was the cause of two-thirds of the entire misery in my life, it was *mine*. I had had it for the last six seasons, and I had *made* it mine. No one had more right to it than I. But what was really eating at me was the knowledge that there was no place to go from there. Once you were demoted from right field, I knew, there was only the bench, and I felt confusion and anger swarming around my head like a bunch of wasps.

Ol' Kruck relieved my worry, however, by telling Eddy Franklin that he had missed too many practices—which he had—and by telling him that since he was scheduled to go into the hospital to have his tonsils out and would miss the rest of the season anyway, he would have to warm the bench tomorrow night. Meanwhile, he said while Eddy turned red and shot dirty looks in my direction, I would take over left field.

LEFT FIELD! My heart soared. That was where all the action was in the outfield—usually—and if I couldn't have third base, I would be more than content with left. I felt tremendous, and I almost choked when I said, "You can count on me, Coach!" But he looked at me and shook his head. He knew—and I suspected—that I couldn't catch any better in left than I could in right, but for some reason none of us could understand—especially Eddy and his old man who, I heard, called up the Little League office and demanded that Ol' Kruck be fired and didn't back off until they said if Ol' Kruck went then he would have to take over the team—Teddy was going to start in right.

My old man cleared it up for me that night over supper. Teddy's old man had bought the whole team matching tee-shirts with our names sewn on the backs. He also promised Ol' Kruck that if he would play Teddy and we could finish in at least second place in our division, he would take us down to Fort Worth to see the Cleveland Indians who were scheduled to put on an exhibition game against the Fort Worth Cats in August. Ol' Kruck wasn't going to let a chance like that get by him, so Teddy was going to play, whether he could field and bat or not.

Now one thing about Little League in West Texas small towns was that it was literally the only game in town in the summer. It was all there was to do. Also, since our high school couldn't afford to maintain a baseball team, any player who wanted to try for a college scholarship or to go for the majors had to come up through the Little League. There hadn't even been a minor league team in town since before I was born, so the kids' games took on a very special meaning and were played five nights a week. They started about five-thirty when the Pee Wee Division took the diamond, and they went right on through the Jack Rabbit and Pony Divisions which sometimes didn't finish until after ten. Nobody would have tolerated a time limit or a maximum run rule or a tie. This was baseball, Small Town, West Texas, America-style.

The stadium was ancient, and the splintery bleachers backed an enormous press box, protected by a rusty chicken-wire backstop. The outfield was bordered by a barbed-wire fence which separated it from the nastiest mesquite thicket in the world. No one ever went in there after dark, no matter how many runs were at stake, so anything hit over the barbed-wire was a homer. But in Little League, not that many kids could get it out of the infield, so nobody worried too much about it.

There was no grass anywhere in the infield or the outfield, just a bunch of skinny weeds, and the ground was pounded down so hard that it felt like concrete. It would soak up sun all day and give it back through the players' sneakers, cooking the soles of their feet and making their lives generally miserable, especially in a pitching contest where there weren't a lot of hits to run down. When we did run around on the field, dust came up in great clouds, so after a couple of innings the baselines had to be re-lined. A grounder could go for miles on the well-packed surface, and a high fly that missed a fielder's glove sometimes just hit the ground and buried itself in the dirt.

But poor as the park was, it was where everybody in town came every summer's night but Sunday. There was nothing on TV but reruns anyway, and in a small town, almost everyone has a son, a nephew, a grandson, or a neighbor's kid out there sometime during the evening. It was a chance for folks to get out of the house, eat a snowcone or two, and gossip between screaming themselves insane at their kids, the umpires and coaches, and the other sides' fans, all of whom were people they knew well and, under other circumstances, liked a lot. Much as I always hated it, the thought of quitting never entered my mind. *Everybody*—at least every male body—my age played Little League, or almost, and my parents would never have understood if I weren't out there at least until I was old enough to drive and date or find more mature and dangerous ways to waste my youth.

I guess that was why Teddy finally came out. He managed to avoid it longer than anyone else, but I suppose his old man finally put the pressure on him, and he decided to try. It was better to be a bad player than no player at all, I guess, but even if his being on our team meant I was saved from right field, I had serious doubts that he would ever work his way up even to the level of amusingly awful. He just had no knack for sports at all.

That Friday night we didn't take the field until nearly nine-thirty, but no one had gone home. The Jack Rabbit teams had played out a twelve-inning tie, and it had been a big hitting contest—the sort of game that has a lot of back and forth and keeps people yelling until their throats are sore. The crowd was pretty large when we went out to warm up, and they were ready for more action.

The Pirates were a mean team. We'd been dreading this game all season, especially since the local paper had picked them as favorites for the division championship. They were the oldest team in the division, too. While our team averaged kids around fifteen with some a lot younger, like me, the Pirates ranged all the way up to seventeen, and they had some hard hitters and crackerjack fielders who already had their hopes set on scholarships or tryouts with the majors. Ol' Kruck had been telling us all along that we could run faster than they could, and he was still giving us a pep talk that no one was listening to when we left the dugout and took the field.

I really didn't much care whether we won or not. I trotted out to left field proudly waving my glove at my old man who was grinning like I had done something special, and I began to think that maybe I might have a chance of doing some good this night. I might even catch the winning out, peg second for a double play, save an error, or something. Since the number of balls coming my way would be increased by about a thousand times, I figured I had the law of averages on my side, and I set my jaw and got down in my best fielder's crouch, determined to do the very best I could as soon as I got my chance. I even let myself think that if I succeeded here, Ol' Kruck might move me to third base. It was a new beginning, and even though I suspected deeply in my heart that there was no way I would do anything more than mess up as I usually did, I refused to let my doubts ruin this small triumph in my Little League career. This was my night, I told myself, and we were the best team in the division.

They got five runs off of us in the first inning.

It wasn't Phil's fault, really. The Pirates were a physically big team, and they were intimidating. One of them almost knocked him down with a line drive right by his head, and after that, it seemed that anything he threw at them they tried to hit right back at him as if they were deliberately trying to hurt him. I thought Ol' Kruck was going to have a stroke, though. He yelled so much at Phil that Nolan Quisenberry, the umpire, threatened to eject him from the game.

Two hits came my way. One tipped off Ralph Pearson's glove at third and dribbled right to my feet, and the second was a sort of bouncer that died before it really got to the outfield. I scooped up both of them easily and managed to throw the runners out at second. I felt great! A foul tip wound up in Larry's glove before he knew what happened, and that retired the side. We came in to bat.

We had two outs by the time I came to the plate, and I fanned away the third. I was overanxious, I guess, but with cries of "It's Awwriiight" coming from Ol' Kruck and assurances that I would "get 'em next time" shouted from my old man who was chain smoking and smiling too much, I grabbed my glove and headed out to left feeling okay. Little League, I decided, could be fun if you looked at it right.

By the bottom of the fifth, we were still down by five, but it had turned into a pretty good game. They had ten runs, but we'd managed to get some decent hits and actually to settle down and play some fairly solid defense. A couple of balls had come out my way each inning, but they had been well hit, and I managed to chase them down and get them into the infield to save extra bases without looking too foolish. I even stopped one from rolling into the mesquite thicket by kicking sideways it when I got to it. I was charged with an error, but Ol' Kruck knew what I had done, and he gave me a pat on the butt when I came back to the dugout. I really felt special.

The Pirate coach was really mad because we were getting so many hits off of his pitcher, Jack Allsen, and he was taking it out on his own players, yelling at them every time they swung and didn't connect. He even yelled when they hit a foul. The umpire took both coaches off to one side and talked to them after the Baptist and Church of Christ preachers protested at the language they were using.

Teddy had been to the plate and struck out three times. Actually, he didn't strike out at all. He never moved. Even though Ol' Kruck had gotten him to crouch down a little bit, he still had a strike zone the worst pitcher in the Pee Wee Division could hit, and Allsen had no trouble burning them right in there. Each time Teddy walked up to the plate, sort of bent those stork-like legs of his and squinted through those idiotic glasses out toward the mound, the Pirates' fans would go crazy. I spotted Teddy's old man sitting proudly behind our dugout and ignoring all the cat calls and laughter that were coming from the Pirates' bench. He would yell something at his son, but if Teddy heard it, he never showed it. He would just stand there and stare, and he'd still be staring when Mike Goodhue, their catcher, would receive the ball and the umpire would yell "Steerike!" After a while, Goodhue got the notion that Teddy was just nervous, and he'd start a chant of "No Battah! No Battah!" which their infield and bench would pick up. Teddy's knees would actually start to shake. I could see that he was so relieved when the third strike was called that he almost collapsed, and when he ran to the dugout, he was grimly grinning, happy the ordeal was over.

I hadn't done much better at the plate. I struck out twice more and walked once, and Ol' Kruck told me I'd better start paying attention. But I wasn't too worried, not with Teddy making such a fool of himself. Besides, Allsen had pitched to me for years. He knew better than to give me anything but low and inside fast balls and maybe a curve or two. And he had trouble throwing those particular pitches, especially to a chubby, right-hander.

After his fourth straight strike-out, Teddy's old man came down and talked to him, and the poor kid actually started trying to get a hit after that. But his swing was too slow, and his next time up, he swung at two pitches that were nowhere near the plate. On the third pitch, he stuck his bat out in front of him in time, and the ball hit it. It popped straight up, and Goodhue almost knocked Teddy down trying to get to it. Teddy just stood there, holding his bat and trying to focus through his glasses. He didn't know enough to run after he got a hit—even a pop-up—since Ol' Kruck hadn't gotten that far with him in practice. Goodhue dropped the ball, but Teddy still didn't move, and all Goodhue had to do was turn around and tag him. Things were so confused with both sides of the stadium yelling and cussing at Teddy and Mike and the gods of baseball, that our runner stopped between second and third and tried to find out what he should do from Ol' Kruck, who was on his knees begging at the top of his lungs for Teddy to run. Goodhue threw our man out, and Ol' Kruck's blood vessels popped up on his forehead like a huge blue river delta while he protested the play with Nolan Quisenberry. I don't know when I've seen Ol' Kruck so mad.

By the top of the eighth, I discovered that left field was no better than right. I hadn't had more than a dozen hits come out my way, and two of those had been outright homers into the weeds and mesquite beyond the fence. I hadn't missed anything other than the ball I ran down and kicked, but I hadn't really caught anything either except a couple of dribblers and some low hoppers. All the action was going to center, where Joe Hogan was having a wonderful night. The Pirates seem to have practiced hitting right over the pitcher and second baseman's heads, and this late in the game, Joe was about worn out.

The usual outfield boredom was setting in pretty heavily, and I found myself watching poor Teddy. He was down in the crouch Ol' Kruck had taught him, and he looked about as tense as anyone could be. Not one ball had been hit his way except a hard grounder to right-center, which Joe scampered over and scooped up before Teddy realized a play was going on, and I couldn't understand how anyone could be so tense with all that boredom around. But he looked ready, even though I knew he wasn't. I found myself wondering what he was really doing there, and then I shocked myself by wondering why I was there. There really wasn't an answer to either question.

We came into bat the bottom of the eighth knowing that we had to get ahead or it was all over. We were down fourteen to nine, and the Pirates smelled victory. Then Phil got a homer on errors. After he dribbled one out to their short stop, who booted it when he bent over to pick it up, Phil turned on his speed and rounded first just as the short recovered and threw wild over their first baseman's head. By the time the Pirate right fielder woke up to what was going on, their first baseman reached the overthrow, and the two of them argued over who was going to try to throw it just as Phil crossed the second bag and dug in for number three. The right fielder won the debate and threw the ball hard toward their third baseman, and just as it slapped into his mitt, Phil put on a final burst of speed and ran right under him on his way home. The throw to their catcher beaned umpire Nolan Quisenberry right on the top of his head, and Phil slid in safe. Their coach came out and started yelling at Nolan about how it should be ruled a ground-rule triple since he got in the way. The Pirate's third baseman, Hank Martinez, also got into it by saying that it was all Phil's fault for sliding into home and making "such a fat slob" as was Quisenberry bend over so far to make the call. After about ten minutes, Quisenberry threw Martinez out of the game and warned their coach and yelled "Play Ball." Hank's old man and entire family screamed at Nolan Quisenberry from the chicken wire.

Now we had the momentum, and the Pirates began to fall apart.

The next two batters walked, and then Fred Simmons put down a bunt and moved everybody around one base. Then Joe walked when he got hit in the foot by a wild pitch, and I was up.

"Hit away," Ol' Kruck whispered to me loud enough to make my ear ring as I left the on-deck circle and stepped into the box. I felt good, and I tried hard not to turn around and look at my old man. This was really his moment, I thought. I hadn't had a single hit all night, but I could feel the tension in the stadium, and I was confident that this was *my* moment too. The crowd's roar seemed to shake the ground I stood on.

The first pitch was like everything Allsen had thrown to me all night, low and inside. But the umpire called it a strike, I guess to make up to the Pirates for throwing Martinez out of the game, and the crowd was scream- ing at him so loud I could hardly hear myself think. My old man was cussing worse than anybody, and I hoped no one would notice and get me thrown out before I had a chance to hit something.

The next pitch was a high curve that started outside and then brushed me back and almost knocked me down. That was it for the crowd. Ol' Kruck even marched out and demanded that Allsen be thrown out for deliberately trying to bean a batter. Joe took advantage of the time out to limp around the first base bag a little and study his injured foot to lend weight to Ol' Kruck's argument, but Quisenberry wasn't impressed, and he yelled for us to get back to play or he'd call the game and go home and watch Jack Paar. Everybody settled down a little bit, then, and Allsen went into his wind-up.

It was just the kind of pitch I like—a breaking ball, just a little outside but not too much and at the top of the strike zone. It wasn't too fast, either, and I felt it was perfect the second Allsen let go of it. I took a little backswing and laid into it with a solid arching swing that met it right on the stitching.

I knew it was gone before I even connected with it.

I lifted my cap and watched the ball sail up into the outfield lights and over the right fielder's head into the mesquite thicket well beyond the barbed wire. *A GRAND SLAM!* I almost shouted as I jogged toward first and around the baseline to second, holding my cap like a flag and waving it to the crowd. I could see my old man jumping up and down and Ol' Kruck laughing and whipping his legs with his cap as he danced a little jig in front of our dugout. I was a real hero, even if I couldn't catch a ball. When I crossed the plate Ol' Kruck grabbed me in a bear hug that took my breath away and almost cracked my ribs. Pandemonium reigned. The score was tied.

We picked up two more runs after that, and then Teddy came up and shook around until he was struck out and we went into the ninth. We were ahead by two, and the Pirate coach was giving his team a verbal blistering for letting us come back on them. The crowd was wild, and I felt like Mickey Mantle as I jogged out to left field. I was sure Ol' Kruck would be putting me at third next week. He wouldn't be able to say no to anything I asked now. I also noted that Ralph Pearson hadn't gotten a hit at all that night.

They started the top of their order, and right off they managed a double to center. It was a well-hit ball and would have been an easy triple, except Joe managed to catch it on a high hop and peg third from way out. Phil struck out the next batter, and then he walked one, and the cleanup man popped one up just out of the infield where Joe could run in and pick it off.

Phil burned in two strikes on the next batter, and things began to look grim for the Pirates. One more out and it was over. I was glad. I didn't want to bat again that night. I figured I had done something too special to match, and I wanted to go home and enjoy it during the week before our next game when, I was afraid, I might do something really stupid, like try to catch something.

The crowd was about used up. Every voice that came from the bleachers seemed hoarse and raw, and I figured that more than one breakfast conversation would be whispered the next morning. Their coach called a time out just as Phil was going into his pre-windup, and he came out to talk to their batter, Leslie Johnson. I could see them looking out to right field, and they were grinning and pointing. I wondered if anyone else was watching them. Ol' Kruck was strutting around and shoving his chest out. He thought we already had it sewn up, but he had forgotten about right field. He had forgotten about Teddy. I was trying to get his attention when Quisenberry yelled "Play Ball!" and Johnson stepped back into the box.

I looked over toward Teddy who was still down in his crouch, staring through those dusty goggles toward the infield like he had some notion of what was going on. He hadn't moved a muscle, but Joe had shifted over toward left a bit since Johnson was a righty and had pulled his last hit right over the gap between short and second. I yelled at Joe, but the crowd got a second wind somewhere and was screaming for either a hit or a strike, depending on which side of the bleachers they sat on, and Joe couldn't hear me. Then Phil let loose a fast ball.

Johnson shifted his feet a bit and adjusted his swing. He smashed the pitch high, but it wasn't a solid hit. It popped up in a high curve and was falling directly out of the field lights toward Teddy. I could see their lead runners were already gone, and their coach was waving his arms like he was signaling a freight train.

Teddy had seen the hit and was now peering up into the lights, his glove stuck out in the air in some wild hope that the ball would land in it. The lenses of his glasses caught the lights, and he kept moving his head left and right trying to find the ball, but it was hopeless. I saw Joe hauling over toward him, but he'd never make it. Our right fielder was going to make us or break us, and our right fielder was Theodore Thompson III. We were broken.

Johnson hit first before the ball fell, and Teddy was holding his right hand up, trying to shield the light away from his eyes and get a bead on the ball, but I could see that even if he spotted it, the ancient mitt on his hand would never catch it, and Johnson was already digging for second base. Teddy was shuffling his feet around and causing little puffs of dust to rise beneath him and gaping into the lights, his gloved hand waving around over his head, his right hand trying to block the glare of the field lights out of those thick lenses.

The ball landed in the dirt five feet behind him. It didn't even bounce.

From somewhere the crowd found the voice to raise an oral hurricane. About half were yelling "Run! Run!!" to the Pirate players while their lead runner crossed home. About half were hollering all sorts of obscene things at poor Teddy—some encouraging, some questioning his intelligence, his legitimacy, his humanity—as he was still standing there, his glove stuck up into the lights, his glasses bouncing reflected beams all over the place, his feet helplessly shuffling around in a miniature dust storm.

Leslie Johnson hit second, stumbled, and then looked around before he started for third, while their next runner crossed the plate. The score was tied, but there was still hope. It all rested on Teddy who still stood there like a statue helplessly awaiting the arrival of the ball in his glove. I could hear Ol' Kruck screaming above everyone else, "Pick it up! Pick it up! Pick the son of a bitch up, goddamnit!!!"

Johnson was almost to third, and our infielders were all lined up for a cut-off throw or a relay. It was textbook baseball, but it all depended on receiving the ball from the outfield. We still had a chance, and the crowd all of a sudden joined the team in yelling at our confused right fielder. It seemed that the whole world, including me, was yelling at Teddy, "BEHIND YOU! PICK THE SON OF A BITCH UP! BEHIND YOU!!"

Finally, he looked around, turned, and spotted the ball. He bent his knees in that odd, storklike way of his and spun around a little when he grabbed it. Joe was almost there, and we all had the same thought at the same time. If he would lateral the ball to Joe, we knew our center fielder could peg home plate with one throw.

Then Johnson rounded third too quickly and slid down on the hard-packed earth and knocked their coach over. They were totally tangled up in the third base coaching box, both working hard not to touch each other with their hands or arms, which would mean the runner was out. It was an act of God! Not even Teddy could screw this up. Joe was right on top of him, and all he had to do was underhand the ball to him, and the game would be over, we would win. But Teddy never saw Joe. He cocked his arm back and threw the all as hard as he could in the general direction of the infield. It sailed in a short, deliberate arch and hit the ground about ten feet in front of him. It was like he threw it down on purpose.

Joe overran the throw, crashed into Teddy's dancing figure, and both of them were down in the outfield.

Johnson escaped his coach's arms and legs without an illegal touch, got up, and walked across home plate.

The crowd went insane.

When I came off the field, I felt pretty low. Phil struck out the next batter, but we knew we had lost the momentum, and the game was over. They retired us one-two-three, no sweat, and the crowd began to drift off in a buzz of angry mutters.

Nobody talked to Teddy, not even Ol' Kruck who usually had something good to say to everybody when we lost. I saw Teddy sitting by himself in the dugout listening to the "Who Do We Appreciate?" chant from the Pirates. His glasses were cracked from his collision with Joe, and I could see that he was trying not to cry. It didn't help things when Ol' Kruck came up to me and slapped me on the butt and said in a voice loud enough for Teddy to hear, "Never should've moved you," and then he walked off toward his pickup and his beer.

I really didn't know what I felt. This had been the greatest night in my baseball life. I got out of right field at long last. I hit a Grand Slam Homer and almost saved the day. It was the kind of thing you read about in books about great athletes. But it hadn't mattered. We still lost. No one remembers a grand slam homer in a losing game. I could have been the talk of the town, a genuine hero. And this poor kid who never really wanted to play baseball in the first place had ruined it for me. I was disappointed, so was my old man. I could tell from the way he came up and patted me on the shoulder after the game. So was Ol' Kruck, and so was the team.

I felt sorry for Teddy, but I could sympathize with him. I had missed a lot of balls myself, but I never had just thrown one in the dirt, and we had never lost a game because of me. But at the same time, I was angry with him. He took away the only good thing that Little League had ever meant to me, and it pissed me off. Mostly, though, I felt confused.

The team broke up and moved off with their folks, and I saw Ol' Kruck out by his pickup with a beer in his hand. He was talking to Teddy's old man. They were gesturing a lot and their voices were pretty loud, but I guess they must have been too hoarse for me to hear, because I couldn't make out their words. But I really didn't have to. If Teddy stayed on the team, he'd be lucky to play bat boy, and I was absolutely sure that I was on my way back to right field.

That was when I decided that I wasn't going to go.

It could happen to me. It could happen to anyone, but I knew it could happen to me. I had had my great moment, but it was more or less an accident—the right pitch at the right time—and I could only send up a prayer of thanksgiving that no serious hit had come close enough to me during the game. I sat down on the bench in the dugout and waited while Teddy's old man followed Ol' Kruck around the infield and argued with him. And then I looked over at Teddy.

He was really hurting, I knew. He hadn't asked for this, and it really wasn't his fault. Still, he had let the whole team down, and he would never have a chance to make it up to them. He didn't have the ability to do so anyway, and he never would. He might make all A's for the rest of his life, and he might become a great scientist or scholar, but his career as a baseball player—even a right fielder—was over after nine innings.

I looked down at my almost new mitt and thought about the old one I had cursed for so many years, the one that had condemned me forever to right field. Baseball, I decided, wasn't worth it. Something about it just wasn't fair. And, I realized, I never liked it very much in the first place.

"Hey, Thompson," I called. He looked up through those absurd sportsman's glasses and squinted through the cracked lenses at me. He was ready, I knew, for another insult, but he wasn't going to back down. I liked that about him. I admired it more than I admired Joe Hogan's fielding. "You doin' anything next Friday night?"

He shook his head, uncertain what I might mean, wary of the coming jab at his ego. He knew we were supposed to play the Cardinals next Friday.

"Wanna go to the movies?" I asked him. "Double feature! John Wayne!"

He was startled. "Sure," he said hesitantly, "I guess, but—" he looked out onto the field. Ol' Kruck had collected all the base bags and stood openly drinking his beer while Teddy's old man continued to yell at him. The outfield lights suddenly went off.

"I'll ask my old man to pick us up after," I said. "Maybe you can come over and spend the night, and we can watch some late movies on TV or something. If we're lucky, Mary Jean Baker across the street'll have a slumber party and we can go peek in the windows."

He studied me again. "TV?" he asked. I knew it was a special treat for him. Then he started to grin, and I realized he was imitating me. He jumped up and went over to drag his old man away from Ol' Kruck who looked like he was getting fed up and might be about to hit him. I could see the veins in his forehead even from the dugout. "See you Friday," Teddy said with a short wave of the battered old glove.

Then I walked out to meet my old man who was waiting for me by the car. I didn't know what he would say when I told him I was quitting Little League, but I figured he could learn to live with it if I could, and I knew I could. You can learn to live with a lot when you're faced with right field.

PECOS

CAROL CULLAR

The woman had been paddling since eleven, past vertical desert cliffs, black and peach, old and new, worn and broken. Much of *Lechugilla* clung to steep angles of the Chihuahua landscape the last day of February. Two shelter caves with twelve-thousand-year-old rock art, a flock of spotted goats with spring kids (some belled, all bleating), a lesser blue heron, and a hawk drifted past. Sixty buzzards gyring in the perpetual updrafts of the canyon paced her. The air was still and hot.

Grey temples under flat straw hat ran perspiration into filthy twine that held beneath fleshy chin. The fine moustache on upper lip beaded with salty sweat, which she licked away—both hands locked about the wooden paddle. Progress was slow.

Glitter-flake twin engine power boats flatulated past at high speeds, the occupants stared, then waved good-naturedly as their wake sent tidal waves out to inundated the craft, forcing the woman to halt her forward crawl and face outward to the crest that would have swamped the fourteen-foot canoe had she ignored them; but that was impossible anyway, since the motors could be heard a mile away; their crass arrivals left ample time in which to prepare.

She paddled until she was tired, then paddled past weary and beyond collapse, through barriers of pain and endurance, but there were no accessible breaks in the canyon. Three times the woman stopped, gave up, rested, determined to hail the next boat and ask for a tow, but that next boat came, and she watched it pass, and the next. She paddled with her thighs, then her seat, then back; finally the only thing left was weak arm motions that moved her forward far slower than she could have walked; then the wind came up, cat's paws riffling the dappled surface of the afternoon, catching hat, chest, the sides of the canoe, pushing, slowing her advance to a stand-still.

She paddled for an hour in the same spot before the wind broke and allowed her to pull beneath the vertical, protective stone walls; then she praised what she had cursed, what had kept her confined to the canoe now sheltered her from the facing wind.

At five the woman could see the high bridge; the speed boats had all gone to supper; the silence was hers at last; she lay back in the canoe as she drifted beneath its arches at six. The buzzards had all come to rest on struts and under-pinnings three hundred feet above her fatigued body. They would not feast on her vacant bones this day. The wind died.

Progress across the mirrored surface was smooth, quiet. Fish jumped up into her world to see where the fishermen had gone, just as they had after the passage of each of the fast boats earlier in the day, their world, *her world*, unchanged by temporary interruptions.

The woman finished what she had started: the nose of her canoe thrust up onto the shore just as the canyon eclipsed the dying sun.

THE SEDUCTION

JOY-ELLIS MCLEMORE

Bright towels scattered around the pool provided the only brightness during the hottest part of the August afternoon. She studied the blue water, yellow furniture, and green of the astroturf and grass surrounding. Pretty. The chaise lounge stabbed her in the back every time she shifted her 110 pounds, but Susan had greased herself with some coconut oil and didn't intend to wash it all off by swimming again. The voices sounded like a tired herd speaking another language.

Sweat poured between her breasts, out her face, even behind her knees. She was tired of reading and feeling tragic. Here she was, facing the end of summer, and all she had to show for it was nine more hours of graduate credit and some vague restlessness she couldn't pinpoint. A soon-to-be-divorced forty-year-old ex-"Miss Tyler" should have probably done something this summer besides read books. Unless she counted coffee in the student union or study sessions, she hadn't even had a date. Robert had been in town every two weeks to see Robyn, but he was the last person she wanted to think about on this hot, slippery afternoon. Almost ready for final exams, she was fed up with *A Doll's House* anyway.

Everybody else at the pool was talking to another shiny brown twenty-year-old, or so it seemed to Susan. Often she'd sat in this chair and considered that she might be invisible for all the attention paid her by the daily convocation. Just now, however, across the pool she noticed a tall guy with eyebrows a little darker than his sun-bleached hair. A locally famous disc jockey named Paul. Older than the others, maybe thirty-three, he glanced in Susan's direction now and then. Through the summer he had mumbled hello a couple of times at the mailbox, but he wasn't at the pool much. Susan couldn't tell behind his sunglasses how much he was watching her. She shifted in her chair, let her long auburn hair out of its pony tail, then positioned herself on her stomach right beside the pool's edge. The astroturf tickled.

He was staring, and she smiled in his direction, occasionally dabbing a little oil on her legs. Glad she'd shaved her legs, washed her hair, and worn the bright blue bathing suit, Susan was happy with her sun-tanned, slender body. When the challenge rose, and headed for the coke machine, Susan left her towel at the pool's edge and walked toward him. She waved the quarter in the air so that her motivation would be clear. His barometric brown eyes studied her as she lost the quarter, hit the machine with her fist, jammed the coin return, and mumbled a couple of deliciously naughty words, words she usually repressed.

"You look like you could use some help." His voice was rich and deep, not at all like that of the drugstore cowboys in her classes. Being a disc jockey couldn't be an entirely bad thing. His large-lipped mouth and shaggy eyebrows weren't bad either.

"Of course I need help. Machines are all out to get me." She watched as he maneuvered the levers, doors, cans, and then handed her a Dr. Pepper.

"It's a conspiracy. You may have a Dr. Pepper or a Dr. Pepper. Here, let me open it for you so you don't break fingernails." She smiled at him.

"Your name is Susan Something, and you don't talk to anybody but books and machines. I'm Paul." He handed the cold can back to her and looked at her directly, which made her uncomfortable. His teeth were milk white.

"It's my favorite drink. Thanks a lot." She waited, and neither of them moved. "How did you know my name?"

"Everybody knows your name." He kept staring. "Don't you have a little girl?"

She nodded, grateful for something to talk about. "Yes, Robyn is nine, and she's at Wildwood every day until four. I'm taking courses toward a master's in comparative lit." She felt the old guilt about not being a conventional mother this summer. Paul seemed interested. "After I get her every day we swim, have picnics, and play Monopoly until eight. Then she goes to bed, and my true identity emerges." She grinned.

Paul smiled too. "Dare I ask?"

"I am a machine that ingests pages and pages full of words, then grinds them out into profound rearrangements on neatly typed papers."

"I'll bet you're good at it."

"I can't tell, but I get A-minuses. It's something to do."

"I meant I'll bet you're good at all of it, a four-point average and mothering—"

Susan laughed. Paul was nice, and she wanted to talk to him more. "You'll have to ask Robyn. She just thinks I'm weird because I don't act like all her friends' mothers." Susan shrugged. "If you ask her anything, I'd be afraid of what she might say."

"She's lucky. There are several things I'd like to ask her actually. She's a cutie pie—and a hell of a lot friendlier than her mother." How did he know Robyn?

Susan glared at him and decided to ignore the dig for the time being. Enjoying a man's company, she considered that defending herself never worked anyway, that she was never even certain what she was defending herself from. Up until this past year she'd had a Brownie troop, kept a scrapbook for the medical auxiliary, baked cookies regularly for whatever was going on at church. She didn't smoke, drink excessively, or cheat on her husband. Well, ex-husband. Susan picked up a book and thought how manageable those characters inside seemed to her—complex, yes, but manageable. Defending herself was an old story with no plot, murky characters— but, Susan suddenly stood up to her full 5'7"; she wasn't *un*friendly, certainly not to this beautiful male being standing beside her.

She queried, in a peculiarly low voice, "Do you want some Dr. Pepper before it boils?"

"No thanks, Susan. My favorite drink is Budweiser, which unfortunately the machine doesn't serve."

"The machine doesn't serve anything without a struggle."

She shifted her weight and looked at him directly for the first time. "But I do have some Budweiser in my apartment. The cans are probably frozen." He smiled without answering. "That might be just right for today."

"Does that mean I can have one of your frozen cans for my very own?" She nodded, and they headed toward the pool to scoop up her towel, lotion, and books. Out of the corner of her eye Susan surveyed the crowd. They seemed to be glancing in her direction with new respect. Well, Paul is one gorgeous hunk, and he might not even look younger than she. A younger man. She liked that idea. Judging from Robert, the season of her own birth had been a bad time for men. Maybe there were vintage problems. Some critic had said that Jane Austen corresponds to a white, dry wine; George

Eliot, to a rich port. Susan wondered what kind of wine she was. And what kind of man she'd ever wanted. There had been a nice sampling before Robert convinced her it was time to settle down.

"Gawd, it's hot today!" she suddenly exclaimed. "And if I take anything else off I'll be arrested." They both giggled a little nervously as they walked up the steps to her apartment.

"I've been to a topless bar before. The women there didn't look half as good as you."

"They certainly had more guts."

"If you hate the heat so much, why do you go out in the sun every day?" Paul questioned.

"To pick up men," she laughed loudly, and was embarrassed. "Any Texan in her right mind doesn't dare hate heat. After the year when my husband was stationed in Montana, I actually missed Texas. Summer even." She found she'd left the door unlocked and went inside first. "Besides, I have to read somewhere, and I get tired of this place and the library after a few hours."

"This is a nice place," Paul said, looking around the living room.

"Thanks. It's amazing what one can do with plants, baskets, and a few travel posters. I think of it as camping. Robyn loves the place and doesn't want to go back to Tyler in the fall."

"So Tyler's home." Not having a response, she ignored him.

"And besides, I don't go down there every day. If I did I'd look like all those *children*—and do Coppertone ads."

"You could do Coppertone ads, Susan." Paul took the can she handed him. "But I'll bet you'd rather read all those books you lug around. I've seen you on campus bumping into people and trees because you were half reading as you walked. Such dedication." He plopped himself onto the sofa and looked instantly comfortable. How could anybody look-instantly comfortable in a new place? she wondered.

Susan did not sit down. "The word is 'desperation,' not dedication, and school made more sense on my budget this summer than the south of France."

"You look like you could afford the south of France." He picked up one of the little brass animals on the end table. "Where is your husband?"

"I no longer have one of those. At least, I won't after September tenth. Look, I hate to leave, but Robyn will be wondering where I am. Help yourself to some frozen beer if you can find any while I get dressed." She darted to her bedroom before Paul had a chance to respond. She dressed in her prettiest terry cloth shift, marigold-colored, and the brown Italian sandals, scuffed and old. Reverse snobbery.

"Mmm-mm-m, lady, you look good even in clothes." They both laughed. He'd surprised her as she brushed her hair at the full-length mirror in the hall.

"If anybody could hear you, Paul, that wouldn't sound so good." But she obviously enjoyed the suggestion.

"I can take a frozen Bud with me." He got one as she tied her hair into a new ponytail. She took a long swallow in spite of the ice clunking around in the can. "Delicious."

"Are you going to let me go with you to get Robyn?" Susan waited too long to answer. The divorce thing was still new to the little girl. "I understand. But look. I'm even better with little girls than their mothers. All summer long I've wanted to take somebody special to that new French restaurant out on the Lufkin highway. Will you two go? Maybe this weekend?"

Somebody special, he'd said. How long had it been since Susan had felt like somebody special?

"That sounds just wonderful, Paul. We'd love to go."

The week flew by. Susan considered the pain of the last few years in a new way. After all, she'd been more relieved than hurt when Robert had finally moved out. Now she was saving twenty hours a week by living in Nacogdoches instead of commuting. Having made no decisions about what came after the degree, Susan realized that being out of the town she was born in was a good thing in itself, for reasons not yet clear to her. This week she read even more than she'd scheduled, took Robyn to two movies and three ice cream parlors. She had a date. A real date. She planned details of wine, music, perfume, frightfully feminine clothes . . .

When Friday came, Susan and Robyn were both ready when Paul arrived at seven o'clock sharp and Robyn, to Susan's surprise, answered the door and eagerly became acquainted with Paul. He acted interested in the rock collections and three butterflies Robyn treasured. Susan, dusting wine glasses, realized that it was going to be hard for her to pack in everything she wanted to do into one lifetime—a nice switch for a lady who had not too long ago winced at the idea of one more round of volunteer work or one more monotonous cocktail party with the same predictable people.

"You do have a way with younger ladies, Paul," said Susan as she handed him a glass. "I hope you like white wine."

"I have little sisters." He swirled the wine and held the glass to the light outside. "And sauerkraut juice would taste good in such company." Susan noted to herself that this fellow was smooth and she had better watch herself. Years ago, a coed at the University of Texas, she had known how to handle all types of men. Could she still? Or had Robert squelched all those instincts? She remembered the night he had proposed, how bored he'd seemed with the whole matter. "We might as well get married," he'd said, or something like that. He had fit the old family prescription for success—medical school, good family, hometown native—and she had been regularly risking pregnancy, so she married him. Even their honeymoon had been boring. Robert had read a James Bond novel the first three days on the way to Miami; then in Nassau he'd gotten sunburned. The best part of the whole boring ordeal, for Susan anyway, had been the beach.

Paul continued to enchant Robyn while Susan sipped her wine and puttered pointlessly in the kitchen. Visions of the last two years of her marriage had plagued her all summer. Screaming at Robert's cold, impenetrable countenance. Waiting for him until she cried herself to sleep before dawn. Watching him guzzle countless glasses of Scotch and finally pouring a few of her own. But Robyn had had an intact family for a long time; that was worth the price Susan had paid. Wasn't it? The little girl certainly was enjoying herself at the moment: giggling at Paul's stupid jokes, telling a few herself. They hardly noticed her.

Susan arranged the sofa pillows again, then went to the mirror in her bedroom to see if she could find any confidence there. Paul hadn't said anything about her hair. Did he like it better up in a ponytail? She went to the bathroom and checked her eye make-up again and drank several swallows of the wine. She was celebrating her liberation, she chided herself, and should feel more comfortable. What kind of man was Paul? Why was she going out with him? Drinking wine felt much better than facing all the questions. She finished the glass and went to the refrigerator for more.

"Hey, beautiful, we're getting hungry," said Paul.

"Then would you like to take a glass with you?" answered Susan, as she refilled her own glass. Paul had walked into the kitchen behind her and patted her. She was trying to decide if the pat was on her waist or lower. She had recoiled, almost, automatically, then poured his glass of wine. "Now. I'm ready when you two are."

Robyn whined, "I'm starved." But she was happy to be going, obviously. "Paul, do you like my new sundress?" She pirouetted and paraded a step or two.

"You're without a doubt the two prettiest ladies in East Texas. It's a good thing I get both of you in one package 'cause I could never choose."

Robyn continued chattering and decided to hold Paul's hand while Susan got her wrap. Remembering that a modeling instructor had once told her class not to wear anything close to the face if it were whiter than one's teeth, she decided to gargle. No, they could hear gargling in the small apartment.

Everyone chattered and soaked up the low western sunlight on the way to the car. Paul drove a new Pontiac coupe that he had recently cleaned. He didn't protest Robyn's sitting on the console for most of the twenty-mile drive, and he sang along with everything on the radio when he wasn't explaining about his degree in cinematography and his plans to go to Russia as soon as he finished his thesis. Susan's mind wandered to Robert, as usual, and the uncertain future.

Paul interrupted her thoughts with a hand on her thigh and a vague complaint: "Where have you been for the last ten miles?" Tonight, Susan decided, she would concentrate on the present.

"I've been working too hard. Thanks for rescuing me." He didn't answer. "Gosh, I'm hungry!" He was singing again, something old and awful, like calypso. Susan had avoided calypso ever since Nassau. Searching for conversation, she continued, "Texas has the most beautiful wildflowers I've ever seen. I used to stop and pick bouquets of Indian paintbrush and some blue and white things in the spring on my way here."

"Bluebonnets?" wondered Paul.

"No, that's against the law. Whatever it was, everybody got hay fever and I had to quit."

"Don't you ever break laws, Susan?"

"Well, not yet, but—"

Robyn interrupted, "She runs stop signs all the time." Everybody feigned horror, gasping as they arrived at The Country Frenchman.

Susan waited awkwardly for Paul to walk around the car and open the door. She looked in the mirror again. "If this is as good as I've heard, we're in for a treat," she said, as she took Paul's hand and lifted herself out of the car.

"And I'm ready for about six crêpes by now," answered Paul, as he corralled Robyn out of the parking lot. She'd spotted a nice rock, and Paul led her away and took them both down the path, well landscaped with railroad ties, green shrubs, and red geraniums.

"I wish my plants were that pretty. Do you know where I can find an old whiskey barrel to make a planter outside my apartment?" Susan asked Paul. "I want red, white and blue petunias spilling out."

And he answered, "Yes, my dear. But we'll have to do a lot of drinking before you plant the petunias. And the frost would kill them."

They had Bloody Marys before the tasty spinach salad and chicken crêpes. All three relished each bite and were feeling fine. This summer Susan had been cooking piles of food that nobody wanted. Also, she enjoyed having her chair held, and Paul remembered to stand when she excused herself to go to the ladies' room. She loved watching him pay attention to Robyn. Robert had paid little attention to either his wife or daughter in the past three or four years and occasionally reminded Susan that it was she who felt compelled to have a child, not he. Robert had never believed that Susan really was wearing her diaphragm the night Robyn was conceived. He had resented his wife's excitement about pregnancy and motherhood and had wandered off more and more on his own. With some satisfaction, Susan realized she could have another child if she wanted to. Robert couldn't stop her. She grinned at both her companions, who'd been chattering throughout the meal. And she had another glass of wine. On the way to the car she was humming, dreaming, almost flying.

"No wonder everybody recommended this place. It's worth the drive."

"I make good coffee, too, after I tuck beautiful ladies' daughters into bed," Paul promised.

"So who needs coffee? We still have half the bottle of wine at home."

"Mommy drinks more wine than she used to," said Robyn.

Everybody got sleepy on the drive back to Nacogdoches, but Susan was still humming as they entered the apartment. Robyn didn't object to bedtime at all, with a promise from Paul that he would read a story to her next time. Susan kissed Robyn on the forehead and handed her the old mangled rabbit.

"Tell Paul I might let him have one of my best seashells the next time he comes," the child mumbled sleepily.

Paul had already selected some jazz CD's she'd just bought, removed his tie, and sat down on the floor. He was singing again. Susan sat beside him.

He grabbed her affectionately by the shoulder and began. "Okay, tell me how you got here, Susan." Obviously he meant all of it. He meant Robert, a small-town doctor who often spent nights at the hospital because someone was having a baby, or a hemorrhage, or an attack of hypochondria. She skipped the part about his not coming home many times because of his nurse. Paul listened well. She even told him that being on her own again after all the years as a typical Southern housewife and Junior Leaguer just about scared the bloody hell out of her.

"When you're beautiful, brilliant, rich, and sensitive—what could you possibly worry about?"

"None of the above, Paul, just scared." She didn't know where to go from here. "How 'bout some more wine?"

"If you're not sure you wouldn't prefer coffee, Susan. In spite of what Robyn said, I get the feeling you're not much of a drinker."

He had heard what Robyn said. Maybe he even knew the comment had disturbed her. "Don't worry. Robyn's uncle is an alcoholic, pretty embarrassing at times, so she keeps tabs on everybody's intake." Susan sounded convincing, even to herself. "I go into a coma on the fourth can of beer in an afternoon, so I'd never stay awake long enough to do any serious damage. Besides, we're not driving."

"There are other kinds of damage, Susan, like the kind I might do to you." He chuckled as he retrieved the bottle of wine. Liquid courage. She laughed too.

"Rhapsody in Blue" didn't sound half bad on the new sound system. Susan was a little surprised when Paul stood after a few minutes of holding her hand and humming along with the record.

"Before I go, may I have this dance?" he asked.

"That last glass may have been just over my quota. Can you hold me upright?"

Susan had forgotten how much she loved to dance. And they danced as if they'd been practicing for years. Finally they collapsed wearily onto the sofa and wound up clutching at each other. Soon Paul was almost on top of her but shifted to her side and threw a couple of pillows onto the floor. He lowered one strap of her sundress and kissed her shoulder. Susan felt that she ought to do something, but couldn't think of what. So she giggled.

"Am I tickling you?"

"Yup."

Maybe that wasn't what he intended, for he started doing something that did not tickle. Susan resented his holding the booze so much better than she. He was talking coherently, touching her carefully, and she was leaning back on his arm and trying to relax. It got easier. In fact it got so nice that Paul lowered the other strap of the sundress, exposed her top half, and started kissing her neck while cupping her breast in his hand. Susan sat up.

"Lord, Paul." Suddenly she was at home in her mother's house, sixteen years old, and just caught by her big sister French kissing her steady boy-friend for the first time. A portrait of her bishop grandfather was staring at her. "Except for a couple of ridiculous college encounters, I've never even been touched by anyone but Robert." She felt disoriented and disturbingly sensual.

"I suspected that." His hand remained. "Why don't you let go a little and see what happens?"

"Paul, I've been a married woman. I know what happens." And she stood beside the sofa. Paul put his arms around her waist while still sitting on the sofa. She didn't move.

"Is what happens so bad?" Susan didn't answer. Her mind wasn't work-ing at all. "I can go home now of course." He stood, threw his tie around his neck, and kept smiling at her in that disconcerting way he had the after-noon out at the pool. Maybe she could worry about tomorrow, tomorrow. The old myth about husbands worshipping good women hadn't gotten her anywhere but to divorce court. Susan needed some new myths.

"You may kiss me just once before you leave."

And he did. "You feel excellent, Woman." And he was so good at kiss-ing. And suddenly, strangely, she was good at it too. She held his head be-tween her hands while she explored his mouth with her tongue, and she didn't protest at all when he unzipped her sundress, pulled it down to her waist, and dropped to his knees beside her. Soon their heads were on the pillows thrown on the floor. Paul didn't leave until the graying sky awakened Susan through the eastern eave of glass. Thank God Robyn had slept through the whole thing.

Maybe she felt rotten the next day because she hadn't had enough sleep. Maybe she yelled at Robyn because of the pressure of final exams. Maybe she took two baths and a shower because of the hot, sticky weather. And strangely, that night after reading another chapter of *Charlotte's Web*, kissing Robyn on the forehead, and holding her tightly for at least a minute, Susan still did not go to bed. She read thirty pages without seeing one paragraph, then called Robert for the first time all summer. A woman answered the phone, but it wasn't the clinic's answering service. Her ex-husband was on call all right. Susan was not. She unplugged the telephone, took four aspirin, and went to bed.

Two days later Paul knocked at the door, Susan answered, and he announced, "Your suntan will fade. I tried to call you last night—and the night before." Susan felt like crying and didn't know why.

"Come in, Paul." Both of them knew, without a word, that their one night together was destined to be just that. They sat awkwardly beside each other on the sofa. Susan kept drinking her lukewarm coffee but decided it would be better not to offer Paul a cup. "I guess I should explain a few things."

He attempted levity. "Friday night needs no explanations."

"I can't explain anyway. I don't even understand."

"Look. You're going to need a place to stay after your Monday night classes this fall. Shouldn't we *see* what happens?"

"I can't, Paul." She shifted her crossed legs and scooted out of the range of his after-shave. Robert had worn Aramis, too. Maybe she'd give up men entirely.

"Will you come over and let me fix your dinner tonight then? I have some steaks—"

"I can't." I don't know why." She groped for the precise words. "It doesn't fit, somehow . . . our lives."

"Susan, did what happened the other night mean anything at all to you?" He waited. "You know what they call it when—" She put her fingers to his mouth and stopped him.

Fighting tears and soaking up all the guilt which accompanied Paul's urgency, she slowly and deliberately answered, "Yes. It meant that I'd better concentrate on final exams and my child and my sanity." She waited for a response, but Paul just stared. He stood up and sat down again twice. Then he took her hand, held it to his cheek for a moment, left without a word.

Susan taught freshman composition at a busy, high-schoolish college that fall. The pay was lousy. She had a few stiff dates, too, and started eating frozen dinners. Robyn became busy with her own collections and catechisms.

About the time Paul was leaving for Moscow the following spring, Susan was marrying her attorney, whom she knew as well as she would ever know anybody, and settling into the old role with a new leading man. She never told her new husband about Paul, though she thought about him from time to time. In fact, she never told her husband much at all about that year she spent alone. Eventually she tried not to think about it herself. And to many people's eyes, she almost passed for happy.

THE GULL

SUSAN COLLIER

Every morning just as the sun broke through the traces of night, they came. Loud, flapping wings announced their arrival on the beach. They broke through her slumber, bad dreams mostly, to assure her that she was still alive.

Their calls soothed her and she would awaken early, padding softly across the squeaky hardwood floor of the beach-front house. What had once been an irritation, the calling of these sea gulls, now came as a welcoming sound.

Blessed with moments of solitude before the household came alive to beckon her attention, this had become her favorite time of the day. She sat down on the rickety steps, soaking in the healing caress of the early morning Galveston sun.

Clad in one of her husband's discarded shirts, she walked to the shore's edge, dipping her toes tentatively in the waters that danced to greet her. The soft, cotton fabric billowed against her thighs while the sand scratched at her bare feet. The music of the waves bid her good morning; the circling of the birds echoed the pronouncement.

First bowing low, she entertained them with a perfect pirouette, feeling stronger, feeling alive, as the sea gulls joined her in this strange salutation of a new day.

When the dance ended, they left, that is, all but one. The gull circled, cawing, crying out in pain. She reached up to clap her hands over her ears in an attempt to shut out the brutal sound. The bird circled again and plummeted in spirals, setting down hard on the white sand. Her heart pounded as she ran toward the injured creature.

The eyes were luminous white, burning through her soul. When she reached down to touch the bird, it flapped pathetically in self-protection as it tried to escape.

She picked up the gull when most of the fight was gone and cradled it to her breast. Without attention, it would die. Soft words, tender words, words of understanding, came whispering through her lips as she watched the pitiful beating of its heart, straining to leave the body that bound it.

"There, there," she soothed, running her fingertips over the broken wing. "I'll help you to mend, then set you free."

Entering the house, she found all was quiet except for the ticking of the clock in the kitchen. Searching through the utility room, she found an empty box and took the softest of the blankets, folding it against the bottom. When the bird had calmed, she would tend the injured wing.

Footsteps sounded from behind her. Automatically, she cringed. But on this morning, his voice came soft and low to her listening ears.

"What'd you find?"

She glanced up, watching his face change to an expression of sorrow. "A bird. Look, the wing's broken."

He knelt beside her, resting his weight on bent knees. His arm went around her and her heartbeat quickened, fighting against its cage.

"I'm sorry," he murmured and placed a kiss upon her bruised cheek.

"Breakfast?" she asked, not wanting to listen, for excuses would not heal.

He stood. "The bird will die."

"Without someone to care," she added.

Later, after his departure, the house became a safe haven once more. She busied herself by searching for bandages. Again, his shirt whispered of his presence as it breathed against her skin. Quickly working each button, she removed the suddenly constricting garment. The cool breeze from an open window sent shivers over her naked body.

Using her teeth, she tore the shirt into strips and carefully wrapped the broken wing. The bird let out a pitiful cry and she soothed. "It's not your spirit that is broken, pretty bird, it's your body. Your body will heal."

And in the afternoon, sensing his need, she took him to watch his friends. They soared high overhead, circling, ever circling, in an attempt to communicate. When moving, she noted that the gull watched carefully through burning eyes.

"Don't forget how to fly," she whispered.

As the sun kissed the day good-bye, her stomach drew into knots. Her goodwill, her judgment, her self-worth, kept tune with the ebbing of the sea. She dare not touch the bird, who seemed to read the language of her soul.

The slamming of a door, a footstep, then angry words, sent her running to the safety of their bedroom. But the door was no barrier against his private wrath. She felt her spirit detach, standing aside to watch the now-familiar happen.

With every passing day, the bird grew stronger as her own spirit diminished. Once, during a feeding, the bird was all too eager and pecked her finger, drawing blood. She watched the bright red liquid drip from her fingertip to the piece of fish. The gull saw also, taking greedily of her offering. When the fish was swallowed, she pleaded in silence with the bird. *Take it; take the blood of my spirit and all the bright tomorrows.*

She knew that all too soon, the bird would be strong enough to leave her. Her sudden feeling of joy died to be replaced with harsh truth. Before long, she would be alone once more.

Often now, as she took the gull to the shore, it struggled to fly, ever watching, ever learning from the others that beckoned him. But even after that first, experimental flight, the gull chose to return and watched her reaction through strange, achromatic eyes.

On the eve before the gull's departure, she dreamed. The music of the sea became angry, predicting a senseless death. The water turned a burnished red, speaking of brutality. A giant bird dipped its wing in rescue. And she knew her time was near.

The morning dawned cold and rainy like bitter tears. Hair soaked, clothes plastered against her once unbroken body, she set him free, pleading for him to remember her act of kindness. Once, she thought she saw him try to circle back but the wind carried him to loftier heights.

Sitting in the rocking chair beside the window, she listened to the pat-pat of rain against glass, marking time's passage. Only twice did the sky rumble a warning. She began to draw strength from her weakness.

His footsteps shuffled across the porch. Hinges groaned with the pushing open of the door. The master of her fate arrived to claim her.

Her fragile greeting drew heated words. *Fierce words*. His fist caught the side of her face. The pain came as a welcomed reminder that it was time to leave. Her spirit remembered the struggle of the gull and soared safely to the ceiling. Now there was only a shell to be destroyed, to be crushed beneath his cruel hands.

Shoving her into the kitchen proved to be his downfall. Her spirit danced, twirled, pirouetted, and bowed to the applause of the thunder. Her eyes sought protection and she reached out, fingertips curling around the cold, sharp metal of a knife.

Anger rose within her, growling through bloody lips, forcing her to go past the resistance of his skin and plunge deeply. He cried only once in contrast to her multitude of tears. And when enough blood had spilled, his heart stopped beating.

From the ceiling, her spirit returned. The rain stopped. Now the sea beckoned her presence with the crashing of waves. She stumbled toward the safety of the water, her life forces leaving drops of scarlet behind.

When the gulls came, they cried loudly for intercession. Her anguished moans mingled with the sounds of the circling birds as her heart fluttered in tempo with the flapping of their wings. But she was tired, so very tired. Somehow she knew if she lay down and closed her eyes, the bird of the night would come. The knowledge soothed her.

The tide came in to wash away the red liquid of her wounds, spreading it across the vast ocean. And as her life ebbed away, she saw him.

The giant white bird circled down to meet her on the cold, empty shore. It dipped its wing. She climbed aboard.

Speaking words of love, the bird reminded her, "It is not your spirit that is broken, only your body."

And in the center of his frame, she found a haven of rest as he soared toward the sun, taking her to new tomorrows.

THE GUY IN THE OLD JOKE

JERRY CRAVEN

One morning on our way from Port Arthur to Beaumont, William blundered by announcing to the guys in our carpool that he had never cut a single class. Snyder stared in disbelief. "Bull," Franklin said.

"How about in high school," Smitty asked. "You never pretended to be sick just to stay home?"

"Never. I got a citation on merit day for perfect attendance every year at Thomas Jefferson High School. I haven't missed a class since that time in the ninth grade when I got food poisoning in the cafeteria and had to go home during fourth period."

"No kidding?" Smitty said.

"Nobody can go through college without cutting at least one class," Snyder said. "Today you're going to cut your eight o'clock class."

"No, I'm not."

"Oh yes you are," Franklin said. "Huh, Smitty? Huh, Steve?"

"You leave me out of this," I said. "And you ought to lay off of him about that. He has a tough time with that eight o'clock." William gave me a grateful look.

"It's for your own moral good," Snyder said. "You would be some kind of freak if you never cut a class. I mean, how could you ever admit that to anyone after you got your degree?"

I got out of the car at the parking lot. Franklin, Smitty, and Snyder stayed in the car, holding William in place. He struggled some, then gave up. I was embarrassed, so I headed to the union.

During the day, Smitty told me they had held William in the car until eight thirty, then let him go. "And you know what that dumb turkey did? He went to class. Late. That dumb turkey."

Smitty laughed.

On the way home that day, William stared at Snyder in silence when asked how his early class went. That stare hushed their laughter.

"I always was ugly when I was a little kid," William said. Most of the time William talked, Snyder or Smitty would interrupt a bunch of times with some witty put-down that William never seemed to understand. But this time they just listened. "Even in grade school I was ugly. It was this big funny deal to be ugly. At recess, the girls would say, 'last one in line has to kiss William,' and always someone would say, 'ugh,' and they would bust a gut getting in line and laughing. They used to say all the time that I had cooties: 'Lookit William. He has cooties.' That's just how they would say it. And they would laugh. Sometimes they thought I couldn't hear, but sometimes they said it to my face, 'William, you're so ugly that you got cooties.' Some days I went to my room when I got home from school and cried because I was so ugly everybody laughed and thought I had cooties. One time my ma came in and asked me why I was crying, and I told her it was because I was so ugly, and you know what she said? She said, 'Don't worry, William. There are lots of people in the world uglier than you.'"

We drove the rest of the way to Port Arthur in silence. And the guys left William alone for a while.

William was twenty-six years old when he replaced Hyler in our car pool. Hyler had graduated at mid-term from Lamar University and moved on to bigger and better things, so we were left with a four-person car pool during the spring semester until William joined us. Snyder told me and Smitty and Franklin about William around seven-thirty one morning while we were on the way to get him for the first time. "He's kinda dense," Snyder said, "but he's a good old boy. Engineering major. A lot older than we are because he flunks everything he takes, almost. The next semester he takes the course over and fights his way to a *C*. He studies all the time, and it still takes him two shots at a course to pass. But he's okay."

I thought Snyder was putting me on, but he wasn't. William was more than kind of dense, and he did study all the time. I would see him in the library, by himself, sitting on the edge of a chair with his back straight as a board, his hands locked on an engineering text, his lips moving, and his eyes fixed on the page. It would make me tired just to look at him. His routine was to allow himself twenty minutes each day to relax in the student union, attend all his classes and labs with clock-like punctuality, and study in the library until time to drive home, which was five o'clock since someone always had a late lab. At home, William told us, he would eat, go jogging, visit with his mother (with whom he lived), and get to bed by eight so he could get up at five to hit the books.

Snyder, Franklin, and Smitty made William the butt of most of their jokes during the thirty-minute drive from Port Arthur to the Lamar campus in Beaumont. He never seemed to know the guys were ribbing him.

A week after making William late for class, the guys started in on him again. It began the morning they saw a couple making out in the parking lot.

I didn't see it, nor did William. We did see some kind of commotion at the other end of the parking lot, and Snyder, Franklin, and Smitty went to investigate. I headed toward the union, and William went to his eight o'clock. On the way home that afternoon, Snyder told us about it.

"No joke, Steve, you should have hung around this morning. You, too, William. You would have cut your eight o'clock to see this. Those guys we saw were hanging around, taking turns walking by a blue Buick so they could get a look at the couple doing the dirty deed in the back seat."

"Right there, in broad daylight?" William asked, astonished.

"Yeah," Snyder said. "That lucky slob. I mean, here we all are, all busting our asses to get to class, and he has this dirty leg to do the deed with him. They knew we were walking by, looking in at them, and they didn't give a damn."

"No kidding!" William rounded his eyes. "They were doing it, and they didn't care if you saw?"

"Oh, it got to them after a while," Smitty said, "because the guy got out of the back seat, into the front, started his car, and went to the parking lot across the highway. He was really cool about it—he got out, tucking in his shirt, got in the front, drove across to the other lot, and climbed in the back again to finish her off without an audience."

"Like dogs," I said, "in the middle of the street."

"Yeah," Snyder said. "But I'd have done the same thing. I mean, who gives a damn if some jerks see you do it? Come on, William, you woulda done it, too. Wouldn't you?"

"I don't know. Maybe."

"Maybe? Just maybe? 'Cause of all them turkeys looking in the window?"

"No. Because I don't know. I've never done it before."

He should never have said it. I cringed at what those three would do to him next.

"Bull," Smitty said.

"There ain't no such thing as a twenty-six-year-old virgin," Franklin said. "Of either sex. But especially not a man."

"I am."

"Yeah, yeah," Snyder said. "But then! He just might still own his cherry. Hey, William, how come you never told us this before?"

"You never asked." The answer came in all matter-of-fact innocence, and we laughed.

"You like being a virgin?" Smitty asked.

"No."

"Then why don't you grab you some chick and get on with it?"

"It isn't that easy. I don't have much time because of going to school, and if I don't study all the time, I flunk. I'm not lucky, like you guys, I got to work real hard to learn."

Any other time such an admission would have caused us to lapse into an uncomfortable silence. Good grades did come easy to us, and we all felt ill at ease in the presence of William's barely productive work. But his virginity was news so startling to us all that even I felt inclined to comment on it. "There must have been girls you liked?"

"Yeah. Lots of girls. But they never liked me."

"You want to lose your cherry, don't you?" Smitty asked.

"I guess so."

"Then," Snyder said, like he was talking to a child, "why not grab you a dirty leg and make your move?"

"I gotta study . . ."

"Bull," Smitty said. "Bull. That's just an excuse. Anybody has time for doing the dirty deed."

"Yeah." Franklin laughed. "Anybody. Even William."

"You guys lay off," Snyder said. "William's got a reason for staying a virgin. Ain't that right, William?"

"Yes. I do."

"What is it."

"You know. I never knew what to say to a girl. Remember that old joke about the guy who planned for days to lay a girl by painting her horse green so he could get in a long conversation with her about what made her horse green, then lead up to seducing her? Well, that's what I am, the guy in the old joke. I know I would say right off, 'green paint—let's go to bed,' and blow the whole thing. I never thought that joke was funny because I know it's real. It's about me."

"Bull," Smitty said. "It's just a joke. Anybody can blow his timing."

"Look, William," Franklin said, "there ain't a girl alive that can't be laid. All it takes is the right place and the right time and the right boy. And for half the girls, if the place and time are okay, it don't have to be the right boy."

That was too much for me. "You guys are so cool," I said, "talking about girls like they are all just fence posts with knotholes in them, put there for studs like you."

"What kind of crap is that?" Snyder asked.

"You talk like the guy in the parking lot acted—like dogs who'd just as soon do it in the street as anywhere so long as you found a bitch in heat."

"There's nothing wrong with a good lay," Snyder said. "It might not be as good or pure and all that crap as making love with somebody you care about. But it sure as hell is good. I look at it as two different things, actually, and both are important to any healthy, red-blooded American boy. You make love with somebody you care about. You screw a dirty leg. And William never even had a dirty leg."

"Look, William, it ain't all that tough," Smitty said. "I mean, all you gotta do is go into a bar and pick up a girl. They go there to be picked up and get laid."

"What do you say to them? I wouldn't know what to say."

"It don't matter much," Snyder said, "what kind of line you hand them. Everybody knows it all comes to the same thing, anyway. Just go up to some bar bitch and say, 'Hey, babe, what do you say to a little screw?'"

"Is that all? You just come right out with it?"

"Yeah, no joke," Smitty said. "I done that lots of times. Sometimes you score, sometimes you don't. It all depends."

"On what?"

"On whether she already has a lay for that night. Usually it works to be real direct like that. It does for me, anyway. And if she has a date already, she'll tell you."

William seemed to think about Smitty's advice. "But I would be too nervous to do that."

"Tell you what," Snyder said, "I'll take you to a bar tonight, if you want. I never went to this bar without getting laid. I'll be with you so you won't be so nervous, and I'll point out some chick that I know is there just to get picked up for a lay. And you can hustle her and lose your cherry. Okay?"

"I don't know. I'll think about it."

About ten o'clock that night, Snyder called me. As soon as I answered the phone, I knew he was going to tell me about William. Snyder's voice was barely under control from laughing. "That jerk. He did the damndest thing ever. You won't believe what he did in that bar."

"Snyder, I don't think I want to hear this." But I did, and he knew I did.

"He had to drink a couple of beers to get his courage up. I pointed out a real hard-looking babe sitting alone at another table and told him to put the hustle on her, and after those two beers, he tried it. I got to hand it to him for that. He did try. But that dumb jerk! He went up to her and said, 'Hello. My name is William. What do you say to a little screw?'" Snyder burst into laughter.

"Is that the truth, Snyder?" I asked, astonished.

"Gospel. That's just what he said: 'My name is William. What do you say to a little screw?' And you *know* what she said. You know it. She said . . ." Snyder laughed almost beyond control. "It was too good a set-up. I bet she waited years to hit someone with that line. She looked him up and down with that hard look bar girls cultivate and said, 'Hello, Little Screw.'" He laughed again.

"What did William do then?"

"But don't you think it's funny?" Snyder sounded offended.

"No. I don't think it's funny. What did William do, Snyder?"

"I think it's damned funny. Just today he said he was the guy in the old joke. Man, is that ever true."

"It wasn't a joke for him."

"Maybe not. But it was for a fact funny."

"What did he do, Snyder?"

"He just stood there for a few seconds, blinking at her. Then he left. Walked right out of the bar, stiff as a telephone pole. Soon as he turned his back to her, that old gal busted out laughing, and so did a bunch of other gals hanging around the bar. He never looked back."

We ended the conversation on a strained note. I asked Snyder not to spread it around, but I knew he would call Franklin and Smitty. They would appreciate the humor.

The next morning was my turn to drive. The guys had a good, loud laugh on the way to pick up William. I knew they would start in on him about the gal in the bar, and I didn't look forward to it, not one bit. But as soon as he got settled in the car, he started talking before anyone could bring up the incident.

"I want to tell you guys about yesterday. About asking a girl for a date. I never done that before. And there's something else I been thinking about. One time when I was a teenager I went to a church camp. There was about thirty of us, so we went on a bus. On the way, one of the guys said the girl beside him pretended to be asleep so he could feel her up. He told me to sit beside some girl on the way back and I could do the same thing. I asked him how he knew she pretended to sleep, and he said he felt her up and she didn't wake up or anything. And if she was asleep, that was okay, too, he said, because he got to feel her up anyway. So on the way back, I sat beside this girl I thought was really neat, and sure enough, before long she slumped over on my shoulder. She sure was pretty. But I didn't feel her up. I did something better. I let her sleep with her head on my shoulder, and I just looked at her. After a while she woke up and realized she had been sleeping on me, and she said how sorry she was. I told her not to be sorry, that I really enjoyed it. I tried to tell her what it meant to me to have a girl like her sleep on my shoulder, but she didn't let me finish. She just said, 'Oh?' real cold and turned to the window so I wouldn't talk anymore. Later I heard her telling another girl about how dog-tired she must have been because she even went to sleep with her head on *William's* shoulder."

No one said anything. Then William added, "They both laughed." I glanced at Smitty, Franklin, and Snyder. They seemed to be staring at something in their laps.

"Yesterday I asked a girl for a date." William resumed talking in a monotone. "A girl in my chemistry lab. She isn't real pretty, but she is real nice. Not the kind of girl you would find in a bar. She's the kind a red-blooded American boy would want to make love to—not a dirty leg. It was the first time I ever asked anyone for a date. She always said 'hello' to me, and I like her. So yesterday I went up to her and said, 'What are you doing Friday night?' I just wanted to take her to a movie or out to eat, you know, just to talk to her and be with her. She didn't even look me straight in the eye when she answered. All she said was, 'I'm busy,' and I stood there like a fool and didn't know what to say. So I said, 'Oh, I'm sorry,' and walked away. Later, I saw her talking to her lab partner and pointing at me and laughing about something. I guess that was pretty funny, too. The whole day was one goddamn big joke. Ain't that right?"

I looked at Snyder and saw his face flush and could tell the guys would leave William alone, for then, anyway.

That afternoon, I saw William in his usual place in the library, his knuckles white from clutching an open book, his eyes staring. I sat in a lounge chair off to one side. At first, he looked as he always did when he was struggling with trying to learn something, so I paid him little attention because of my own homework.

The next time I looked up, though, I knew something had to be wrong. William held his lips clamped tight, and his eyes seemed to bulge. He wasn't looking at the book—in fact, he didn't seem to be focusing on anything at all.

With a suddenness that startled me, William jumped to his feet. He wound up like a major league pitcher and threw his book across the library. I got a glimpse of saliva streaming down his chin. He overturned the desk and kicked it out of the way. Then he attacked the book cases, smashing his fists into them, jerking books from the shelves, kicking at those that fell to the floor. I was too startled to move. William hurled his body against a bookcase, knocking it against the one behind it, and the entire row fell like dominos.

"William," I said, going toward him. He stomped on a book, then turned to a display of magazines. Before campus security guards secured him, William had scattered and ripped hundreds of them. He didn't offer any resistance to the guys who arrested him, and they led him away without doing any talking.

When I got to the car at five, Snyder, Franklin, and Smitty were already there, and they were laughing about William and the bar girl. "No need to wait for William," I said, starting the car. "I'm going to tell you guys something, and you'll probably laugh. If you do, I'll stop and punch you in the mouth."

They grumbled some at that, but they listened, and when I told them what William had done in the library, they just sat there in silence. We got nearly to the mid-county airport before anyone else talked.

"It was that bitch in the bar done that to William," Franklin said.

"Yeah." Smitty nodded.

"Maybe," Snyder said. "Maybe not. I think it was that ugly gal in his chemistry class, the stupid scag. Seems like she'd have the brains to understand William meant no insult when he asked her if she was busy Saturday night. So what he said ain't a cool way to ask a girl out—so what? The bar bitch didn't know William from anybody, so it was okay to zap him. Besides, that's her job, to zap the bastards who go in there just to try to get into her pants. But the ugly girl in the chemistry lab—she knew William. Knew him enough to understand he wasn't out to do nasties to her."

"Yeah," Smitty said. "The bitch."

"I dunno," Franklin said. "I can't let that bar babe off the hook that easy. Any girl, dirty leg or goodie two-shoes, understands what a ball-busting answer that would be, to look at him like that and say, 'hello, little screw.' She pushed him over the edge, I think. Maybe the bitch in the lab set him up to be pushed over. But the bar bitch sure as hell stiff-armed him, and right where it hurts the most."

"Yeah," Smitty said.

"That makes sense," Snyder admitted. "Especially after what that church camp bitch done to him. And them mean little bitches in school, talking about his cooties. They drove William out of his tree, same as the rest of them."

"Yeah. The bitches."

"His mama," Franklin said. "What do you suppose she does to keep her apron strings tied around his neck?"

"Neck, hell. Balls. That bitch has him strung up so tight, he can't even breathe wrong without her jerking him around." Snyder laughed in a mean way, and I realized that these guys were dead serious. They hadn't indulged themselves in laughing at William since I threatened to punch them out.

"So," I said, lacing my voice with sarcasm, "in your book, you turkeys had nothing to do with what happened. Guys get off scott-free, and it's women that get dumped on. It was all the women in the world who made William go bananas in the library."

"Don't be stupid," Franklin said.

Snyder punched me on the shoulder. "You know what I'm saying, Steve, so quit playing Dumb Willie. I'm saying every bitch who ever jerked William around added some to what drove him over the edge today. Not guys. Girls, goddamnit."

"Yeah," Smitty said. "Yeah."

MID-LIFE CRISIS
(TO BE READ BY MEN ONLY)

JACK WELCH

I

Perhaps the problem would never have arisen if we had been in the habit of going out for lunch. Instead, to save money we sat inside Jerry's narrow office of the Up-Front Commercial Printing Company of Abilene, Texas, and watched bird-egg-blue paint drop onto Jerry's desk. I was eating a low-fat turkey sandwich with low-fat mayonnaise on a low-calorie, low-fat bun that kept shredding in my hands. Jerry was eating a green-spinach salad. We both had wives who were determined that we would live forever or at least until our children were adults.

Remembering that the preacher at our church had suggested we talk together about spiritual matters during depressing times, I said, "How's your spiritual life?"

Jerry's face told me the answer. He looked up with a piece of dark-green spinach the front of his mouth, a couple fake-bacon bits dropping off into his plastic container. His turquoise eyes told me, "Mind your own business, Pal."

I looked down at my shredded sandwich, then up at the ceiling as a flake of blue tumbled down into my lunch sack. "Well . . ." I said, "my own spiritual life hasn't been going great either . . . if you want to know." I picked up a crust of bread that had fallen on the generic white napkin on my polyester gray slacks and tossed it into my mouth.

"How's your father?" Jerry asked, looking down into the bowl and diverting the conversation.

"Oh, about the same. Although he came through the surgery all right, he's still hospitalized. He has a persistent fever. I'm going to see him on Saturday."

"Hummmmph," Jerry said. He sat slumped over his food, now mechanically feeding himself with a clear plastic fork. He reminded me of how my father now fed himself. Then I heard Jerry mumbling.

I leaned forward but said nothing, having learned my lesson once already. The words were the same words, over and over and over again, a kind of mantra. They slowly became louder, and as the crescendo increased, I could make them out. "Oh God! Oh God! Oh God! Oh God! Oh God! Oh God! Oh God! Oh God! Oh God!"

I reached into my right and closed the door quietly. "Jerry," I whispered.

He stopped speaking, but he didn't look up.

"Jerry. I'm sorry."

Humiliating tears streamed down his face and dropped like rain into his food. "What's wrong with me?" he croaked out.

His suffering silenced me. I watched as his carefully combed blond hair slowly dropped down over his creased forehead. He was a medium-sized man wearing a pale-blue shirt and dark blue trousers. He had played second-string football in high school. Now, like me, he was a combination editor-salesman with a sales territory here in Abilene and in the six surrounding counties. Our job was to service the accounts of our present customers and occasionally bring in new. Having worked here for fifteen or so years, we both know that we had risen as far as we were going to in this family-owned company and that we were making about as much money as the job could offer. We talked on the phones and met with customers and followed the orders through the printing process from eight in the morning to six or six-thirty at night. Our desks were never clear, but we were always being badgered to do more.

I noticed that around Jerry's eyes a fine skein of wrinkles spread out over his temple. After several minutes, Jerry told me something that had happened the preceding night.

Author's Note for Women Who Insist on Reading This Story. *(I am reasonably certain that some women are reading this story. No doubt you're curious or piqued that I've forbidden you to read. For those of you who think that I'm sexist, let me remind you that there are art exhibits for women only, poetry awards for women only, and even executive training sessions for women only. Fair is fair. If you have ever put up a poster for one of these female confabulations, you cannot quibble about one little story being aimed at men. This story is for men only, and especially the next section. If you must read this story—against my expressed intentions and advice concerning what I believe to be best for you—at least do me the honor of skipping Section II.*

II

"My wife, Pat," Jerry said, "was in bed reading *The Christian Woman Magazine*, and my two children (ages nine and fifteen) had been asleep for perhaps an hour. I'd stayed at my little second-hand desk in the corner of the bedroom trying to get caught up on the invoices which I'd brought home.

"So, it was midnight, and I was alone in the bathroom with its yellow bathtub and white and gold streaked fake marble sink. A two-wand florescent light was beaming down on me as I undressed. I was standing naked before the three-quarter-length mirror when I had the shock of my life. It was my chest. I stepped closer to the mirror to have a look. I've never been muscular, but I've always denied myself second-helpings and late night snacks so that I could stay thin, some people would say skinny. My chest had always had a kind of freshness about it, full and firm, but never rippling with muscles (even when I've done pushups and chinups). However, tonight my chest was different. It had sagged."

Author's Note: *I'm certain women will consider this part of the story to be funny. It must seem incongruous to all that you know about men. But this story is based upon my own true experience, close observations, and intimate conversations. It is true, but your amused face is a reproach to me and to yourself. I admonish you for disobeying my wishes and urge you to STOP READING AT ONCE! What follows is intimate masculinity and for male eyes only.*

"I took my hands and tried to push up the sagged muscles, but nothing worked. Then I tried stretching my hands and arms straight out in front and making little circles with them. The chest vibrated a little but still sagged. It was an old man's chest. For the first time in my life I had the image of myself as an old man."

Jerry stuffed his uneaten salad back into the brown bag on his desk which was covered with neat piles of letters, papers, invoices, and manuscripts in various stages of editing and proofreading. He then scooted down in his chair and put his feet up on the edge of the desk. He reminded me of my own teenage son when he wanted to resist my advice.

"Jerry," I said, "you're not old. I'm forty, you're forty-one. If we were running for president, people would consider us to be very young."

"Oh it's not just the chest thing," Jerry said, looking straight ahead. "It's the whole shootin' match. I've got a dead-end job, my boss couldn't care less if I dropped dead, my wife is all caught up in her new job, and the kids are totally consumed in their own little worlds." Jerry looked up at the ceiling. "Oh God! What happened to my dreams?"

Jerry made a great case for despair, and even though I was in total agreement, having confronted wrinkles in places I'd gladly reveal if I weren't sure women were still reading. "Jerry, in the morning did you look at your chest?"

Jerry kept his head down. "Naw."

"Go look at your chest."

"You mean now?"

"Yeah. Go to the rest room, unbutton your shirt, and look at your chest in the mirror."

While Jerry was gone, I finished off my lunch by spooning down a container of fat-free, sugar-free, salt-free tapioca. The sweet, starchy bubbles usually reminded me of better days when my wife had made tapioca for our little family in the evenings, and we would guess to see which one had the pecan hidden in the bottom. However, something that Jerry had said now reverberated in my memory. "What happened to my dreams?" he'd said. Now I wondered about my own aspirations. I had hoped to own my own printing business, but now that was impossible. I was never going to get enough money ahead to set up an enterprise like this. I couldn't even get enough money ahead to open a savings account. Like Jerry, I lived from paycheck to paycheck. "And it's not going to improve," I said aloud. "This is the best I'm going to have."

Jerry came back into his office, looking proud and happy.

"What did you see?" I asked.

"My old chest has come back. It's no longer sagging."

I nodded to acknowledge his happiness but held up an index finger of caution. "It's not sagging *now*," I said. "Tonight it will again."

Jerry sat down at his desk again, surveying the printing projects with which he would never catch up. His happiness at getting his chest back remained, but something else seemed to be troubling him. "You know, Larry, I didn't cry because of my chest only. That wasn't the whole ball of wax."

"I know."

"It's my life . . ."

"Yes."

"I keep wondering, is this what Jerry Wellborn's life has come to?"

"And I keep wondering, is this all there is going to be?" That thought continued to trouble me all that day and into the evening as I drove to the hospital to visit my father.

III

Abilene Baptist Hospital, where my father had been for the past two weeks, had been built on to so many times that the original shape of the eight-story, white-brick building had totally disappeared. I therefore had to follow signs to go down the right hallways and to the exact elevators in order to arrive at the proper section. Many sections of the hospital were now unused altogether or the sick rooms had been converted into office space. However, I tried to consider my relationship with my father. Somehow his being twenty-two years older than me had grown to mean less and less as we had both absorbed the decades.

I remembered an argument that my father and mother were having when I, myself, was a teenager like my own children. Because the ranch work that my father had loved was no longer paying off, he was driving to Snyder in order to work construction for a prison that was under construction there. The other construction workers were profane and big-time consumers of alcohol, and their company began to influence my father. I remember one phrase which he kept shouting at my mother, "My life has been a total waste!"

Thin and wasted, Dad was lying in his bed in the cardiac ward with his television tuned to a baseball 1 game. He wasn't moving, but I knew he was concentrating on the intricacies of the game.

"Hi, Dad, who's playin'?"

His head turned quickly toward me but his eyes somehow remained on the game. "Larry, son. It's the Rangers and the Cardinals. They have their hands full."

I nodded and sat down, watching the game. "What's gonna happen next, Dad?"

"Oh, the count is two and three so I predict a foul ball."

We both watched as the next pitch was fouled down the left field foul line. "You're great, Dad. You could almost always predict what was going to happen."

Dad lay smiling in his bed. His damaged mitral valve had left him gasping for months, and surgery had helped him some, but now the new complication of some unknown infection had left him without much hope. Doctors and specialists had tried everything from transfusions to antibiotics, but nothing had stopped the fever. His chest was healing up, but inside something was still very wrong. The color in his face was better than it had been in years, but he became daily weaker. In one sense he was growing younger, in another, he was simultaneously aging.

As the game progressed, I began to think of personal questions which I'd always wanted to ask my father and which I decided could wait no longer.

During a commercial which offered rebates on Crown Victoria Fords, I took the plunge. "Did, did you ever had a mid-life crisis?"

"A what?"

"You know, did you ever hate the idea of not succeeding even though you were middle aged? You know, a mid-life crisis."

My father turned his thin, still-muscled face my way and looked at me for the first time. "You plannin' on havin' one?"

"Well, I think I'm in the middle of one."

"Naw, I never had time for any such thing as that. I had to work."

"You don't remember tellin' me and Mom, 'My life has been a total waste'?"

Dad blinked hard at that revelation. He shut his eyes, as though resting them, then opened them again. "Yeah, I remember that. Your Old Man was nothin' but a fool, Larry."

"Naw. You felt like life had passed you by. Your dreams were never going to come true."

My father looked hard at me, then he stretched out his familiar, veined hand, still strong, and took my hand. Our clasp was hard and dry. "Now don't you start actin' foolish like me, Larry. You're a lot smarter than me. You've been to college."

"Dad, my dreams are never gonna come true either. I'm feeling . . . well, like I'm gonna die without ever having lived."

I saw my father's eyes well up with tears. In forty years of interaction, I'd never before witnessed this spectacle. What was there about this mid-life thing that could cause the two men who were closest to me to cry in a two-day period? "Now what did you tell me when I was talkin' so foolish that time, Larry?"

I thought solemnly back on that momentous argument. "I remember coming into the kitchen where you and Mom were. I remember sitting down at the yellow Formica table."

"Go on," Dad said, batting his eyes to keep the tears in.

"And I think I said that you had raised me and that therefore you weren't a failure."

"I remember that," Dad said, his voice somewhat raspy. "Now if you say that you're a failure, what will that do to me?"

I laughed. "All right, for your sake, I won't say I'm a failure, but how did you get through that crazy time when you were in your forties?"

"It wasn't easy," he said.

"Did you go chasin' after women?"

"Oh, I wouldn't say 'chasin' was the right word."

"Did you think of leavin' Mom?"

"No, not really."

Dad's answers made me fidget on the plastic chair where I was sitting. "Dad, you had all the symptoms of a mid-life crisis."

"I reckon I did. Now, I'd give anything to be able to have it all back again."

"You mean the crisis?"

"Naw, I mean the mid-life."

We turned our attention then back to the ball game. The Rangers were having trouble, but my father continued to give advice to each Ranger batter. When the game finished and the Rangers had lost, my father said, "The Rangers will have other games," Then he turned to me. "Larry, I'm not gonna be around much longer."

"Dad . . . don't . . ."

"No, I'm going on a long journey. I'll not be back, but I want you to come to me. Do you understand?"

I nodded my head.

116

"You know how to get there, Larry. I'll be waiting for you and your mother and your wife and your children. It's up to you to see to it that they all make it."

I wasn't able to say anything more to my father nor he to me. He seemed sleepy, so in a few minutes, I left.

As I was coming out of the hospital, I saw Jerry drive by in a new bright blue Chevy Lumina. Sitting in the front, nestled close, was a young, blonde woman.

IV

Third Author's Note to Women Readers: *Since you've come this far, I know I can't deter you. However, I've decided to disguise the main message of this section by using the code that men use in conversing with one another when women are present. I also request that all men maintain the code unbroken. Simply tell inquiring women that you, too, do not understand the words.*

The next day I wanted to avoid Jerry, but forced myself to look into his office first thing in the morning. I noticed that a rolled-up sleeping bag the color of army camouflage lying the corner. Ignoring it, I spoke to Jerry who sat at his desk with a proofreading pencil in his right hand. He was wearing khaki Dockers and a new unbuttoned red Rugby shirt. "Good morning. Everything all right today?"

"Great!" I said, forcing a smile over my lips but somehow not to my eyes. "You look . . . well, happier."

"I feel happier, too. I guess I'm just a buck again. Sit down." He pointed to the plastic chair I usually sat in without being asked.

"No, I just have a minute."

"I was at the hospital last night."

"And how's the old man?"

"Worse. We had a good talk."

Jerry's face remained aimed at me but his eyes glanced to the printed sheet with its light blue pencil marks. "My father doesn't think he's going to make it."

Jerry's eyes returned to me, but his jaunty smile was gone. ". . . That's too bad."

117

"He wanted me to be sure to come where he'll be."

Jerry frowned. "Where's that?"

"You know . . . heaven."

"Oh."

"Jerry, Dad had a mid-life crisis once."

Jerry leaned over his desk at his paper. "That so."

"He argued with my mother."

Jerry flicked his head to the right and then back.

"And he even chased tail."

"Me, I wouldn't know about this mid-life stuff."

I stepped back into the hall, raising my right hand to my mouth. "Jerry, is that your sleeping bag?" I nodded to the corner.

"Yeah."

"Goin' campin'?"

"Naw. I slept here last night if it's any of your business."

"Jerry, you aren't leaving your family are you?"

Jerry stood up. "My family left me a long time ago, and I've finally found somebody who cares for *my* needs. It feels great, if you want to know. You'd do yourself a favor to find some love yourself and stop trying to nib into everybody's business with your pretty little theories."

"You're the one who was cryin' in his salad."

"Well, I ain't cryin' today, and there's nothin' wrong with my mid-life either. If it feels good, do it. Get yourself a life, Man!" Jerry leaned forward and doubled up his hands, almost into a fist, but shot an imaginary marble at me. "Butterfingers," he said.

"And you're hunchin' across the line," I countered. "Who is she?"

"One of my customers' daughters. She's home from college and looking for a shooter."

I decided that Jerry was stuck in the middle of the right and that what I needed was a steelie.

"Jerry, my Dad last night said he'd give anything to have what we have."

Jerry looked a little less pugnacious and sat back down at the desk. At least I was going to be given my turn. "What's that?" he asked.

"Mid-life."

"What?"

"Our being alive and healthy even if we're drawing a new, smaller circle to play in."

"Hey," Jerry said. "I ain't playin' in no smaller circle. If anything, it's gonna be bigger, and I'll tell you what, it's keepers."

I left Jerry's office then, knowing that he had skunked me. But in this marble game we were playing, I would need some lays.

V

A few days after the meeting with Jerry, my worry about mid-life crises was distracted by the death of my father. Although he had told me about his coming death, I was nonetheless shocked. I went with my mother to choose a coffin, and we discussed the final suit for Dad to wear into the earth. I gave him my best necktie.

At the white-brick funeral parlor that evening, I took up my position outside the viewing room where I could greet, hug, laugh, and cry without violating the dignity of Dad's corpse. The room contained wing-back chairs, striped satin sofas, and paintings of bluebonnets growing near Texas ranch houses. Many cousins came, but only a few aunts and uncles were still well enough or alive enough to show up. When almost everyone had gone, Jerry Welborne arrived. He was wearing green golfing pants and a yellow shirt (unbuttoned to the sternum). A gold chain gleamed at his throat, just below his prominent Adam's apple. Jerry brought with him an immense, almost visible cloud of Obsession, the Calvin Klein cologne that I recognized from a fragrance-laced ad in the *New Yorker*, an ad that featured a nude model with the body of Apollo.

"Larry, I'm sorry, Buddy. I'm really sorry." He extended his hand to me and put the other hand on my shoulder. "All I can say is, 'Knuckles down and bonies tight.'"

I laughed, glad that I was in the lobby part of the funeral home. "Thanks for coming, Jerry," I said, a phrase I'd repeated perhaps fifty times that evening.

"That philosophy will get you through," he said.

"Well, I believe it. But why don't you follow it yourself?"

Jerry's eyes focused on the floor, and I felt that I'd just thrown a glass of water in his face. "I'm sorry. I just want you to have a great after-life," I said.

"After-life? What is this? After-life, mid-life. You have a conversion experience or somethin'? What I want is a good now-life. Will I go to hell for wantin' happiness?"

"We do belong to the same church, Jerry, and we're both Christians."

"So, why make a federal case of everything?"

"Jerry, you're about to divorce your wife, abandon your children, and go off with a young woman, possibly messing up her life. This is a federal case."

Jerry tilted his head to the left and raised his right shoulder.

"Didn't all that preaching, all that Bible reading mean anything to you? Ever?"

"Oh, I don't know. It meant something, but now—I guess I just don't care. I guess my life is so miserable that I've got to get some relief regardless of what God says." Then something seemed to light up inside Jerry, as though he'd detonated some internal, philosophical grenade. "You remember that sexual revolution that was goin' on when we were teenagers?"

I nodded.

"Well, I missed it. I was never a free spirit. I ignored the Age of Aquarius altogether. And I figure that in marriage, I paid for all my love and missed all that was free. It was a major mortgage, and I'm still paying. Well, I know that one of these days I'm gonna end up like your father in there." He pointed to the viewing room where a small cluster of women were gathered around my wife. "I don't intend to be the kind of guy who's lyin' on his death bed and thinkin' that he's only half lived. Know what I mean?"

I did know what he meant. Jerry had a knife to my throat and all I had to do to slit my own throat was gulp. "AIDS," I managed to say. "U.S. illegitimacy rate of about fifty percent."

Jerry nodded and kept on nodding his head and slightly grinning like James Dean in *Rebel without a Cause*. I confess that I envied Jerry. I wanted to get out of all my obligations and run free with him. I'd grown up in the chicken pen with him and had kept my wings clipped, but now they were grown out again, and I wanted to fly.

"It's like that Jerry Rubin guy said, 'If it feels good, Baby, do it!'"

I remembered seeing a book by that title years and years ago, and significantly I hadn't forgotten it. Then I remembered something else. "That Jerry Rubin, guy, he died not too long ago."

"That so?" James-Dean-Jerry-Wellborn said.

"Yeah. AIDS."

VI

I wish I could tell you that Jerry gave up the younger woman, stopped sleeping in his office, and went home to his wife and two children, but he did not. He divorced his wife, quit his job at Upfront Commercial Printing, left the church, and at forty-something, is the father of a little girl. He usually wears Levis and white sweat shirts pushed halfway up his arms. He couldn't keep up with the payments on the new Chevrolet, so he traded down to a ten-year-old Chevy pickup. He and his wife both work at Super Duper Markets. His first wife got the house and the other car and lives on child support payments.

And, I wish that I could say that I have no problem with my mid-life crisis, but quite honestly I still think I'm unappreciated, that I've dead-ended at my job, and that my body is heading full blast into old age. However, my father's death and our final conversation have made me afraid to risk my marbles on any new playground. My own problem seems to boil down what I'm going to use as a shooter. If I could find the right shooter, then I wouldn't mind a risk. In the meantime, I'm getting more and more wrinkled and sagging and gray.

Fourth Author's Note: *The remainder of this story is in the third person because poor Larry isn't able to articulate exactly what he is experiencing. In fact, his conscious life is in a state of denial about the brutal truth which he has come upon. So, I'll interpret his half-formed thoughts, providing just enough order to them so that they can be comprehended. Incidentally, I'm confident of Larry's dream in the following section because I had one like it while writing this story.*

One night Larry dreamed that he was looking at himself in his bathroom mirror one morning. He examined his chest and was alarmed that this *morning*, his chest muscles were still sagged, that the few hairs on his chest were mostly gray, and that the muscles in his face also looked sagged, producing elongated jowls. As he looked at himself in this dream, he grew noticeably older and no tugging and shoving could stop it. Larry awoke in a sweat and lay on his left side, away from his wife, staring out at the darkness alone. He remembered a passage in Job 33 concerning dreams: "In a dream, in a vision of the night, when deep sleep falls on men as they slumber in their beds, he may speak in their ears and terrify them with warnings to turn man from wrongdoing and keep him from pride, to preserve his soul from the pit, his life from perishing by the sword."

"What is the warning?" Larry asked himself, and for the remainder of the lonely night he wrestled that question until he came to an answer. Without articulating the realization, Larry intuited it all. "It's like death," he knew in his subconscious. He'd dare allow that realization to come to the surface. "I'm seeing death in my own body," he understood. "A mid-life crisis is in response to a somatic of one's own death. But what can I do about it? Who can help me?" That morning when Larry went into the bathroom to prepare for the day, he shaved without looking into the mirror.

VII

After the dream, Larry found himself thinking about other men's lives. He looked at his relatives whom he had known over his entire life. He looked at his fellow workers at the printing company. He watched the men at church, especially those who were a little older, who had been friends with him and Jerry. Every single one of them had had some kind of mid-life crisis without regard to race, social status, or religion. Some, he realized, were no longer with the congregation, having abandoned God along with their families. Some of these absent men had been preachers or deacons, and now they were gone, almost always seeking escape from the gnawing reality of death by taking up with younger women. "They must be trying to go back to an earlier period of their lives," Larry found himself thinking. "That's irrational, but maybe that's the only way that seemed open to them." There was something juvenile and sexual and pathetic about all this, and it was all so complex and psychological that Larry couldn't grasp it all.

Then he began to examine the men who were older than he who had not abandoned their families. What was their secret? Sometimes Larry would yearn to ask men about how they managed to survive their crisis, but he always went away without saying was most deeply on his heart. The problem was really too profound and troubling—the fear of death, the inevitability of death, the closeness of death—he didn't really have the nerve to face the real question himself, so he couldn't drift into the topic in any casual accidental way. Besides, his conversations with men usually revolved around sports, cars, the weather, and sometimes hunting. All these, he now felt, were distractions from his true quest.

As the months passed, Larry looked more and more haggard. His wife and fellow workers thought he was grieving over his father's passing, but Larry had accepted his father's death. He could not, however, accept his own. In desperation he began to pray.

One autumn evening, Larry was out walking on the broad, flat streets near his home in Radford Hills, a middle-middle neighborhood in northeastern Abilene. This sun was out of sight but still casting luminescent steaks of orange in the western sky, and far to the east a purple-black band was stealing over the West Texas plains. While Larry was strolling through the neighborhood in his navy blue walking shorts and tan sport shirt, Terry, a man from a few doors away, was standing in his yard. "Larry, you're out for your constitutional walk," he said. Terry was tall and paunchy, weighing about fifty pounds more than Larry and carrying all the extra weight around his waist.

Larry nodded. He loved walking in these dry, breezy evenings when the temperature trembled at about eight degrees. "Yeah," Larry said, even though he'd never use the term "constitutional" to describe what he was doing.

Terry was in his mid-forties, maybe pushing fifty. He taught at the local university, but when he spoke to people in the neighborhood who weren't at the university, he tended to slip into slang. "So if you're not going to bust gut, I'll walk along with you. Mind?"

Larry shook his head, indicating that he didn't mind. As they passed by the three-bedroom ranch houses, each one made of brick and each one with precisely the same amount of glass in front, Larry said, "We're all the same here, aren't we?"

"Oh yes, I suppose so," Terry said, his voice deep and resonant as a bull moose's. "But, we all come from so much less. This neighborhood, these ticky-tacky houses would seem like palaces to our moms, pops, and grandfolks.

Larry nodded. He remembered his own parents' tiny houses, and he thought about the outhouses owned by both sets of grandparents. He felt now as though Terry had just shouted "Fins!" to him.

"I'm just glad that we can walk in safety," Terry said, waving his right arm high into the air as though performing a feat of legerdemain. God is blessing us with peace, tonight."

Larry and Terry walked along in silence for a while. When they came to the section of their neighborhood that was given over to elegant patio homes which had almost no front lawns and the houses abutting closely together, Larry felt a need to break out of his self-imposed confinement.

"What do you think about mid-life crises?" he asked, glancing sideways at Terry and noticing that his hair was almost totally white.

"I believe in them," Terry said.

"Have you had one?"

"I think I did."

"How'd did you behave?"

"Well, to be a straight shooter with you, I'd have to say that I took up Taekwondo."

"Whoa!" Larry said. He stopped in the middle of the broad street, standing at the high point of the road's gradual arc. "Maybe you're playing in a square and I'm playing in a circle."

Terry walked on a few more feet and stopped. "No, I think we're playing by the same rules. Taekwondo involves families. We have Christian pep talks—yeah, it's cool. There's an emphasis on respect, control, and encouragement, but the Taekwondo idea—a humble cultivation of the self, joining mind and body—may be the most important factor."

"Tell me more," Larry said, walking on to where his neighbor stood. The brightest stars were just beginning to emerge where the great eastern hood of darkness loomed.

"Well, most sports stress only victory; TKD stresses a sort of right perfectionism, where humility must grow along with skill. And another thing, TKD helps join mind and body. People like me, with no athletic aptitude or experience, feel like the mind and body are barely connected. That's why we're clumsy. But in my case TKD was done by a fat man."

Larry looked down at Terry's rotund girth. He could see that Terry accepted himself and had gone on to develop who he was. There was something noble about that combination of acceptance and growth that appealed to Larry.

As they walked out of the neighborhood of elegant little houses with scarcely any room to breathe, Terry said, "If you can't come to terms with yourself, change the terms."

VIII

Larry changed the terms all right. He went back to college and finished up his bachelor's degree majoring in art and philosophy. He had always had an eye for color and words, so he started his own little graphics shop, and even though he hasn't yet made what he earned each month with his job at Upfront Publishing, he and his wife are continuing to bring up their children, continuing to love each other, and continuing to mature. Larry is now encouraging his wife to do something she's long wanted to do: earn a blackbelt in TKD.

Fifth Author's Note: *Quotations in the last section were adopted from Professor Chris Willerton's essay "What Taekwondo Means to Me As a Candidate for Black Belt" and from his corresponding poem "The Fat Man Does Taekwondo Forms." For all those women who have finished this story, I say, "For all the men who have ruined women's lives through uncreative responses to their mid-life crises, I apologize. You may do some woman a favor by passing the story one to a man because this story provides creative alternatives for the mid-life crisis that occurs in every man, the ruination of more long-time marriages than any other single cause." However, I beg of you, don't show it to another woman.*

DRAG

ERIC MUIRHEAD

Purple	*Violet*	*Monsignor*
Fuchsia	*Lavender*	*Mulberry (Morello)*
Mauve	*Lilac*	*Mignon*
Magenta	*Plum*	
Patriarch	*Heliotrope*	*Amethyst*
Prelate	*Hollyhock*	*Amaranth*
Gridelin	*Clematis*	*American Beauty*
Bokhara	*Redgrape*	*Damson*
	Jockey	
	Heather	
	Carmine (Animal Rouge)	

Animal rouge. Animal rouge. Yes, the lips were like that everywhere I looked.

And everywhere I looked in the ballroom a dervish of purples I could only array in vain to the litany of an order. I had never been called here before, was only just inside the door, chanting textbook purples maybe to keep my mouth from falling entirely agape. It was a wild, gorgeous scene—purples festooning the high walls of the club, and dependent in great folds from the ceiling, a congestion of shimmering, frenzied hangings engulfing the room, while below a buoyant and giddy legion of gowns swarmed the vast floor, pulsing and fluttering and swirling in a heat of purples flung like cool flame from the hot jazz of the speakers.

126

More specific. March. March.

Purple:	*Imperial*
	Royal
	Roman
	Pansy
	Phlox
	Dahlia
Violet:	*Parma*
	Cobalt
	Burgundy
	Hyacinth
	Hofmann's
	Petunia
Purple:	*Tyrian*
	Indian
	Prune
	Raisin
	Schoenfeld's
	Auricula

But the words failed, even in battalions, to hold any beachhead for my composure, just blown to oblivion as easily as clay birds in a skeet shoot by the twin barrels of drag and hedonism letting fly in satins and silk, and scents, that powered from the cloth, flooded the room. It seemed for sure that hounds released here on the trail of drag would only writhe back on themselves and gnash their own tails as prize, the escaping fox racing by them undaunted and free, the world his own, yet almost drowsy the fellow, even curling *à la mamelle* in the deep purples of the ceiling, draped buxom in their folds like swollen udders around the single galactic chandelier sparkling crystal in a thousand glittering shards of the rainbow and illuminating, if dreamily however, this heaviness of sex voyeuristically clothed and vibrant, *débauché*, to the point of sleep.

Was this sleep? A dream? I marshaled my lists yet again, in a desperate muster of mere names to resist this delirium of purple reaching a maelstrom of dance at the room's center, whirling in a mad heaven around some kind of strange, drunk requital bobbing in perfect happiness in the eye of it all I couldn't see, but beckoning me too—how could I help it?—to relent and give in and come to it too, ride wild to its heart on the eddies and flow and mating of these people. . . No, these were not people, but Bacchantes in the exile of the gods, attired for revel in every conceivable gown and swirl of exotic woman's *habit de soir*.

But these were not women.

"Cab!" I yelled over the music and my vertigo at the bartender. "Someone called." Cleopatra looked up at me from wiping the counter with a cloth of gold thread. She jangled all manner of gold bracelets and adornments, though the low cut of her lavender gown revealed inadequate use of the razor toward the cleft in her bosom. "Yes, honey," she replied in a low, sweety voice, and winked at me. Her wealth of black eyeliner tapered wonderfully from the rich impasto around the lids to a delicate, gently rising point beneath each temple, in a manner to squeeze the rather big-boned fullness of her friendly face toward at least the approximation of the gracious, long elegance of an Egyptian queen's countenance. "We can tell why you're here." (I looked down at my denim.) "Just park in front. You're the type that likes it in front anyway, aren't you?" (She winked again.) "I'll send the pair out to you in no time." I turned to go. "Oh, and honey," she continued, as I looked back from the door, "you be careful out there, you hear. They say the streets are dangerous out there. It makes you wonder why people can't learn just to have fun." She winked a third time, then turned to a tall dame in [damson?] stepping up to request a beer.

Back out the door the black swath of Travis Street was a relief. Dangerous or not, it was asphalt, hard sidewalks, reality. Under the streetlamps grey pools of light illumined weakly the late night, and the air was the malodor of refinery fumes drifting west in the dank, heavy atmosphere. Reality. I breathed it in full, and admired the scurry of a rat along the electrical line overhead. His instinct and precision in perfect habitat in this midnight silence he ruled, perfect pace, as he sprinted the length of the block in seconds and vanished utterly into his domain. King Rat. I tendered my allegiance, in a pact sealed by the sense of things defined and in a straight trajectory that he mapped upon the void.

For I felt in my domain too, defined and with a trajectory too, even enjoyed the clack of my shoes on the surface of the sidewalk as I returned to my cab, enjoyed the clean slam of the door, and the confident revs of the

engine as I started it up and moved 621 forward along the curb until opposite the door of the club. Everything clear and hard-edged again, straight.

The door opened in moments, and out came a bulky figure in purple
gown moving quickly to the cab. But lo and behold, the light that blinded
Saul with the roar of *Quo vadis?* could not have been a more sudden surprise than the vision that now dazzled and confounded me in her wake: a
tall, coiffured beauty in a bustier of radiant, *white* silk standing resplendent
and divine in the doorway. Where had she been in all that swarm of purple?
Pure grace was the sheen of her décolletage, hugging pertly the curves of
her bosom, and her low back revealed teasingly behind a waist-long tumble
of black hair as she turned to have a last word with someone in the club. She
wore chic, elbow-length white gloves, highlighting the nude allure of her
shoulders, and pearl earrings that glinted with just the tiniest cut of a diamond each in a pleasantly subtle downplay of the spangles that danced from
the little gold purse she carried. But nothing in her adornment could rival
the shimmering, sheer white of her dress, a radiance pure Renaissance,
married at her hips to the slenderest, perfect curvature of her body taper-
ing snugly down her length to the lustrous *punkt* of a pair of gold high heel
shoes.

Queen Bee. Where had you been in all that swarm of purple? Baffled, I
could only think her the conjury of some strange metamorphosis, magic as
foam-risen Venus delivered whole from the sea. Born at that door as if from
a chrysalis.

Her purple companion had long since entered the back seat of the cab
and slid across, announcing in a gruff, accented voice an address on Ave. K,
in the barrio east of downtown. Queen Bee now approached across the
walk as I watched, her long hair swishing lazily across her back from the
neat coiffure bound near the top in a bright gold band, and slipped into the
back with an easy swing of her body, rushing perfume ahead of her in a
flush of delicate musk that wrapped round me from behind and stopped
me right there in sudden, erotic arrest.

The back door closed with a light click. "Okay, we go now. Let's go," the
purple one pressed impatiently. But I was unable, simply staring in my mirror at her olive-complexioned face who sat behind me, inundating me with
a strange import of *déjà vu* and famishment from the nature of the perfume
she wore. I knew it somewhere. My fingers just walked around the wheel in
my captivated state.

"We go. We go."

"Yes, yes, of course," I finally muttered, and fumbled for the hard edge of the meter flag. Pleased at least to have an excuse to look back in order to slip into the one-way stream of Travis—though devoid of any traffic at this hour—I unhappily caught a good look at the big face of my purple passenger. She hadn't shaved nearly recent enough; I was appalled to see black stubble over her swarthy jaws, and her coiffure a mess of mangy ends sticking out this way and that. But peripherally I saw the beauty, gazing rapt at her consort in a mild, high bearing of her regal face that jarred and discomposed me in a rant of *wrong, this is all wrong. She's not . . . How can she be?*

I was driving north, and the one in purple was talking, in Spanish, which I couldn't understand, a manic, gravelly, haughty voice that seemed more appropriate for Pancho Villa or one of his *guerrilleros* boasting of victory than in a love journey home in the company of this queen who sat beside her.

She hadn't spoken. *Was she . . . ?* I kept asking myself. But how could she be?

She was a woman, I kept answering myself. She was a woman. And this was some kind of travesty, a mistake.

If not agitated enough, I was a complete prisoner of her perfume, gliding into my nostrils and soaking me with something I couldn't name, couldn't reach, teasing me, 'til the need was almost unbearable to just turn around, seize her bare shoulders and shout *please, please*, into that depth of her person so quiet, ineluctable, back there. Crazy, I gripped the wheel 'til my hands went sore.

You could even touch her, caress her, if . . .

That damn purple brute. She kept talking. Go back to Pancho Villa, why don't you, and the mountains and dust. Then suddenly I saw in my mirror that brute reach her hands across in a most unseemly and forward manner to feel up this prize she had no right to claim.

Only then did my white beauty speak. Almost in a whisper, mind you, but in her gentle Spanish it was clear she was protesting, trying to fend off the other. But not even her soft, pleading, tender tones could hide the suddenly brutal fact (for me) that she too (*damn*) was as drag as the other. The fox, fie on him! The voice had at some time broken in the past, and not even hormones, and all else that was perfect and graceful, alluring about her (those breasts? those hips? angel white at the door) could (*damn*, *damn*) deceive me longer.

Riling with rebuke, almost to tears with stupidity, I cursed my foolery in the name of His Highness, King Rat I'd seen, ruler alike of electrical lines and the fouled hopes of human folly. And renewed my fealty with a burst of speed and sarcasm that sent cab No. 621 hurtling through the lights on the straight trajectory of just another trip, precise and fast, to make a few bucks at the end and be on to the next one.

But damn them both, the scenario in the back seat worsened—I couldn't drive fast enough. She was crying out against the other, her perfume overwhelming me with something I couldn't name, compelling me with the need that I do something for her. And suddenly my repugnance was gnashing its own tail, desperate to help her but stupid, the compulsion becoming crazy again to turn and grab her bare shoulders behind me, shout *please*, *please*, from the crazy, wild indecision I was deep into the apparition maybe *she* was, all memory and familiar someway, inundating me like this with that perfume I couldn't name, a memory I couldn't grasp.

Her hairy mate pushed and probed relentlessly in the darkness back there, even giggled several times. Her voice in white rose in desperate appeal, carried now on the waves of her perfume insistent and deep to the heart of something *I* was, an apparition maybe I was, and suddenly it happened, crossing the empty streets of downtown, it came crying out of me: *Écusson*, the Shield, that was it, calling from a girl redolent with that perfume I had loved once, from the depths of a time wonderful and lost I had known once, from New Haven, Conn., Macy's where I'd found it, a timid first time at a perfume counter, and the Park Plaza Hotel where we'd christened it, in my first surrender, wild from a time young and lost that was suddenly remembered now. A past I'd forsaken, had failed, in a fresh rebuke that came up to slap me at this moment. And reeling from that memory something came clear to me: it was not that she was a man or a woman behind me, but someone beautiful and vulnerable, like the girl odorous of the same perfume I had known and loved before her, calling out to all of us in fealty to the King to renounce him, let the rat clatter into the trash heaps, be instead the keeper of the grail, the chalice, what it was she was holding out to me right now, if only we'd take it and say *yes*, *yes*, *yes* to what she was behind me, and now cried out for me to defend.

Purple, Fuchsia, Mauve, Magenta. . . . I was freed like a butterfly from the capture of my confusion. My anger came free as well, she suddenly screamed in a frenzy behind me and I rammed to the curb and yelled, "Stop! Stop it right now! Leave her alone!" staring brutally over my shoulder at the purple aggressor. Sheepishly she sat up, and slid back to her side of the seat.

I drove on, in the sudden silence of the cab lifted and free, fluttering like the butterfly I felt, in gay counterpoint to the high, solid towers of downtown Houston we passed—modeled powerfully at their base by the streetlamps and shadows of an empty city, in homage to the base of power they were for legions of executives now asleep at home. But I was not asleep, and my wings brushed stars the heights of which Shell One and the Exxon Building couldn't dream of reaching, in a tapestry of the air flooded in *Écusson* and possibilities, weaving me more and more into her who sat right behind me, ineluctable, real, and yes a woman.

The fox had found me. *I* was real. We were running together, through the fields, loose, wonderful, randy, *purple, fuchsia, mauve, magenta,* drowned to excess in purples and perfume as finally, a free man, I touched her running beside me, her shoulders, and said *please, please, I love you maybe . . . I . . .*

Damnit, one learns things.

Pancho Villa had paid me, grinning not so sheepishly now, and forced her way out of her side first, then her slow, graceful companion following in a slide across the back seat that rippled the air with soft sound of her silk and body, perfume to make me dizzy, to make me ache for her, who would not be mine after all. My hands gripped the wheel, I could think of nothing to say, only watch, as she swished up from the seat and stepped into the night. The other had already opened the front door of the little house, nestled behind a large white oak tree, and gone inside.

She closed the door of the cab with a light shove, and I watched her walk away, white silk whispering snug from her body, and her long black hair bobbing lightly upon her bare back, under that enormous tree and up to the porch. Then it was she turned and looked at me, silhouetted in chiaroscuro beneath a small lamp above the door, and I looked at her, and for a moment we were complete that way, for a long moment, before she turned and entered the house, closing the door behind her.

Exile of the gods. It recurred to me. And Cleopatra speaking to me over a bar rag of gold thread. The Bacchantes dancing through their mythic fields, the chalice still there for the offering. It seemed all true, as I lingered before that closed white door beneath its little lamp, the single light casting up into the night strange yet breathing shadows upon the overarching limbs of the great oak above. Her image still there, profound and quiet before her portal.

The goddess. Looking at me. And, incredibly, a man. I had seen her in a man.

I drove away, newly exiled myself, into the byways of the night. Dreaming, aroused, loose in the fields. Joining the fox.

A SOFT SPOT

BETTY WIESEPAPE

Mother put off telling us about the baby until the Sunday platter of pot roast was on its third trip around the dining table. Not that I blamed her. It was disgraceful—two old people like them doing you-know-what at their age. I knew something was up before Mother told us. I had seen the look that passed between my parents when Papa Bradley was praying. I was prepared for almost anything but "I'm pregnant."

The pot roast stopped in mid-air. No one moved. We just sat there with mashed potatoes growing cold on our plates and stared. Granny Hayes was the first to recover. Granny Hayes was old and shriveled like a prune, but she was stronger than she looked. She threw her fork on the table so hard that it made a dent in the wood and said, "God Amighty. I told you after the last one to get twin beds."

My father shifted uncomfortably, hunched his shoulders, and stared at a spot on the rug. Granny Hayes fastened a look of disgust on the top of his head. I could tell my father was unhappy. His neck and ears were bright red. What I couldn't tell was what he was unhappy about—Mother's announcement or Granny Hayes's comment about twin beds. Either way, I was glad. He deserved to be unhappy after what he'd done.

Papa Bradley said, "Lo, children are a heritage from the Lord, Mrs. Hayes. Happy is the man who has his quiver full of 'em," Papa Bradley spoke with a Southern drawl. Papa was a foot-washing Baptist from Alabama. He had a scripture for every occasion. Papa Bradley towered over Granny Hayes, but everything about him was softer.

Granny Hayes retrieved her fork and pointed it at Papa Bradley. "The man who wrote that scripture had a thousand wives and God *knows* how many children. He never so much as lifted a finger. If one of his wives had written Ecclesiastes it would be a different story. Isn't that right?" Granny

134

Hayes looked at me. I didn't answer. I couldn't. I was still in shock. I couldn't believe God was doing this to me. Not now. Not when everything else in my life was finally going right. Don't get me wrong. I had nothing against you-know-what, and the kids we already had were okay as long as they stayed out of my room, but enough was enough.

If I hadn't been so preoccupied with my own life that spring I might have figured out that Mother was pregnant before she announced it. All the signs were there—gagging in the bathroom, craving peanut butter and banana sandwiches, crying over Lisa and Bob's divorce on *As the World Turns*. Mother did all those things when she was pregnant with Danny. I should have known, but I was too busy to notice.

Twirler try-outs were the first week in April. I tried out and I won. Being selected BHS twirler was the most exciting thing that ever happened to me. The high school principal announced my name on the loud speaker. A photographer from the *Bingham Banner* came out and took my picture, and I was interviewed by a reporter from KKFI. The announcer called me Beth Brady instead of Beth Bradley all the way through the interview. I didn't mind, but Mother got upset. She said, "Someone in this family finally does something important, and that fool at the radio station can't get the last name right." Mother shut herself up in the bedroom and cried all afternoon. Mother always cried when she was pregnant. I should have known.

As soon as the new twirlers were announced, Sally Stahl's parents demanded a recount. I never could figure out why they thought she should have won. Sally dropped her baton four times during try-outs. I only dropped mine three. After that was settled, the twirlers' and cheerleaders' mothers got into an argument about the length of our skirts. With all that important stuff going on, I was as shocked as everyone else in the family when Mother announced on Mother's Day that she was pregnant.

"May I be excused?" I asked when I recovered.

"Is that all you're going to eat?" Mother asked.

Granny Hayes butted in before I could answer, "In my day children weren't allowed to waste food." I ignored Granny and pushed my chair from the table.

My father said, "Stay in your seat," and motioned for me to sit down. "Your mother's going to open her presents as soon as Granny Hayes finishes."

"I eat slow," Granny Hayes said and stared over her glasses and shook her fork at me. "It's good for the digestion." I folded my arms across my chest and stared back. In our family children weren't allowed to sass.

"What's wrong with our girl?" Papa Bradley asked.

"A bit spoiled if you asked me," Granny Hayes said. I wanted to tell Granny no one asked her. I wanted to tell her it was rude to butt in, but I just sat there with my arms folded and prayed she'd get indigestion. Granny finally finished eating. She lined her knife and fork up parallel on the edge of her plate, wiped a spot of gravy from her chin, and said, "All right. I'm finished. Let's get on with it."

Mother's presents were nothing to brag about—a hand print calendar with a blob of blue paint that covered all the Wednesdays in January, a bottle of Blue Waltz perfume wrapped in yellow tissue paper and tied with blue string, a cotton robe and a pair of Naturalizer house slippers. If I hadn't been mad at Mother for getting pregnant, I would have felt sorry for her when she unwrapped her gift from my father—a new stainless steel roasting pan.

Mother pretended it was just what she wanted, but I knew she was lying. I knew no woman in her right mind wants pots and pans for a present. Mother folded and smoothed the last piece of wrapping paper and thanked everyone for her presents, then she cupped her hand around her stomach and said, "Is there anything any of you would like to ask about the new baby?"

I wanted to ask a lot—Aren't you ashamed? Why did you do it? Now everyone in town will know what the two of you have been doing. Instead I said, "May I please be excused now? I have biology homework."

Before I slammed the door to my room I heard Granny Hayes say, "It could be worse. At least the two of you are married."

I fell face down on my bed and buried my head in the hollow of my pillow. I couldn't believe what was happening to me. My life was ruined unless I could come up with a solution. I counted on my fingers. Mother wouldn't start to show for a few more weeks. Maybe by the time she did I could convince her to move to Dallas and live with Aunt Dorothy. Mother wouldn't have to stay in Dallas long. Just until she had the baby and found someone to adopt it. If Mother wouldn't agree to go to Dallas, I'd go. I would miss being twirler, but anything was better than having everyone in Bingham gossiping about my family.

Not that I had anything against you-know-what. You-know-what was great for young people. At least I assumed it was by the way people who had done it talked. I lay across my bed and imagined Tony Curtis doing you-know-what with Janet Leigh. Then I imagined Tony Curtis doing you-know-what with me. I tried to imagine my parents doing you-know-what, but I couldn't. I couldn't even imagine them in bed with their clothes off.

Not at their ages. Mother was thirty-six and my father was thirty-seven. They had been riding in the car like old people for years—men in the front seat, women in the back. Like I said before, the thought of two old people like them doing you-know-what was repulsive.

A major disaster had occurred, but I went on with my life as if nothing had happened. I went to school, to band practice and to church, and I didn't mention Mother's pregnancy to anyone—except God. I talked to God about it a lot. I begged him not to let it happen. I had faith that a God who could cause a virgin birth had the power to reverse the process.

The more I prayed the bigger Mother's stomach got. I'm not sure when people outside our family started to notice. The beauty operator at Florine's Beauty Parlor was the first person who mentioned the baby to me. "Is your mother pregnant again?" Florine asked with her mouth full of bobby pins. I stared at the *Screen Play* magazine in my lap and prayed that no one heard her. She removed the bobby pins and said it again, "Is your mother going to have another baby?" I nodded. "Big families are nice if you can afford them. How many does this make now? Four or five?" I wanted to die right there in that chair.

A short time later I heard Mother tell Trudy about the baby over the telephone. Trudy was Mother's best friend. She was on a party line and was the biggest gossip in town. If Trudy knew Mother was pregnant, everyone in Bingham would know soon. Mother said something to Trudy that puzzled me. She said, "This baby was a surprise, but we'll make the best of it."

I didn't understand how Mother could be surprised. She was the one who told me girls who did you-know-what with boys got into trouble. Mother said something else to Trudy that didn't make sense to me. She said, "I guess I'll have to postpone enrolling in nursing school." I didn't know my Mother wanted to be a nurse. I didn't know she wanted to be anything but a mother. My father worked six weekends in a row after Mother announced she was pregnant. He said he needed the overtime—what with additional doctor bills and another mouth to feed.

"But we haven't been to a movie in two months," Mother said. "You should have thought about that before you went and got yourself pregnant," my father said.

"Before *I* got myself pregnant!" Mother screamed and shut herself up in the bedroom. My father slept on the couch that weekend.

I spent more and more time in my room with the door closed and the radio turned loud. My father said he didn't know how I could think with all that racket, but I could think. I thought a lot. I thought about quitting school. I thought about running away from home and getting a job. I was lying on my back, staring at the ceiling, and thinking when Mary Louise called.

"Beth, I've got the most terrific news," Mary Louise's voice bubbled from the telephone. "My mother's pregnant." I was sure Mary Louise had lost her mind—her parents were older than mine. I didn't say much. I just listened. I listened to Mary Louise talk on and on about turning their guest room into a nursery, about how she wanted a girl but her parents wanted a boy, about what they had decided to name the baby. For once I was glad when my father pointed to his watch and said it was time to get off the telephone. I said, "Mary Louise, we'll have to talk more tomorrow. I have something important to tell you."

Mary Louise failed to comprehend the disgrace of our situations, but after she told me her mother was pregnant, I had somebody I could talk to about the baby. The more Mary Louise talked about their baby, the more I remembered. I remembered how wrinkled and pink Danny was when my parents brought him home from the hospital. I remembered the fresh smell of baby powder, the feel of a soft warm body snuggled against mine, and the way the top of a baby's head sinks in over the soft spot. I remembered how I could put my hand on Danny's soft spot and feel it throb with each beat of his heart.

The more Mary Louise talked about their baby, the less I dreaded ours. I guess I was beginning to do what Mother said to Trudy—I was making the best of it. None of my friends made a big deal out of Mother wearing maternity clothes, and nobody at church stopped speaking to us. I even quit praying for God to reverse the pregnancy. I was pretty sure the answer was no. Besides, it was too late. Everyone in Bingham already knew my mother was going to have a baby.

I received some benefits from Mother's pregnancy that I hadn't antici-pated. Her stomach got big fast. Granny Hayes said that's what happens when a woman has too many babies. Her muscles get stretched out. Granny predicted Mother would be as big as a house by the end of the summer. Sure enough, by the end of summer Mother couldn't fit behind the steering wheel of our Buick. My father signed for me to get a hardship driver's license so I could drive the little kids to school. I was the first person in the Freshman class to get a driver's license.

My father was adjusting to the idea of a new baby, too. One night when Mother was dressing to go to a movie and fussing about the size of her stomach, she said, "Granny Hayes was right. I am as big as a house." My father grabbed her, pulled her close, and said, "You and the kid look beautiful to me." Then he kissed her. Right there in front of Granny Hayes. I decided that maybe thirty-six and thirty-seven wasn't as old as I thought. Name-the-baby became one of our favorite activities. We sat around the table after supper and discussed names. Mother wanted to name the baby Malcolm after her father, but my father disagreed. He said he'd been stuck with Albert all his life because one of his grandfathers was named Albert. My father said every child of his was going to have its own name.

I was in biology class when the principal sent a note to my teacher. The note instructed the teacher to dismiss me early because of a family emergency. I was to pick Sheryl and Danny up from elementary school and stay with them until my father returned. I knew something bad was wrong if Mother wasn't at home. I imagined all sorts of things. Maybe Granny Hayes had a stroke. Maybe Papa Bradley had another heart attack. Maybe it was time for the baby. I counted the weeks on my fingers. It was too early for the baby to come, much too early. Sheryl and Danny asked where Mother was at least a dozen times. I didn't know what to tell them. At six o'clock, I got out a pan, heated a can of tomato soup, and made peanut butter and banana sandwiches. I helped Sheryl with her arithmetic and made Danny take a bath.

When my father wasn't home by eight-thirty, I put them both to bed. I was sitting at the kitchen table, working on biology homework, when my father's car pulled into the drive. I waited for him to come inside. When he didn't I went to the back door and looked out. My father was leaning against the house with his hand over his face. He was crying. I'd never seen my father cry. I didn't know what to do. I put my arm around his neck and patted his shoulder, and when he stopped crying I asked if he wanted a peanut butter and banana sandwich. He shook his head, then he told me we weren't going to have a baby after all. Mother hemorrhaged, and the baby died.

My father said he was exhausted. He ate a bowl of tomato soup and went straight to bed. I went to bed too, but I couldn't sleep. I needed to talk to someone. I picked up the telephone receiver to call Mary Louise, and put it down. Mary Louise wouldn't understand. She had wanted their baby from the beginning. I had just found out I wanted ours. I lifted the receiver and dialed Papa Bradley's number. "Papa," I said when he answered, "does God always answer prayers?"

I went with my father to pick out the baby's casket. We chose a white one lined with blue satin. The casket was closed at the cemetery. I didn't see baby Malcolm. Yes, my father named the baby Malcolm after Mother's father. I guess Dad figured it didn't matter if the baby had a name of his own now. He'd never get to use it. My father said Mother would come home from the hospital in a couple of days. He told me when she did I shouldn't mention the baby. I didn't, but Mother cried anyway. I sat on the foot of her bed and tried to console her. "Don't cry. You can have another baby," I said.

Mother shook her head and said, "No. What happened was for the best. Deformed babies are more common at my age."

Mary Louise's mother had their baby. It was a boy. They named him Robert Harris Junior and called him Rob for short. Every time I saw Baby Rob I thought of Baby Malcolm. I wondered who Malcolm looked like and if he had a soft spot in the top of his head. My biology teacher said it was possible that he didn't. She said sometimes babies with birth defects don't. I didn't go over to Mary Louise's house much after Rob was born, and we finally drifted apart. I haven't seen Mary Louise since high school. Rob must be almost grown by now. I still think about Rob and Mary Louise from time to time. Whenever I'm home for the holidays, whenever our family gathers in the dining room and we bow our heads to pray, whenever I run my fingers over the dent in the top of my mother's oak table, then I remember.

HOW TO LISTEN TO COUNTRY MUSIC

LAURIE CHAMPION

There's a lot more to listening to country music than just going out and getting yourself a radio. I mean, if you really want to do it right. Anyone can pretend to like country music, when they only know one or two songs. These wanna-be country-western fans only recognize the songs that somehow make their way to stations that play popular tunes. Or maybe, by some weird fluke, they hear a Willie Nelson song on an elevator. That doesn't count.

To learn quickly, re-set all your car radio buttons to country stations. Dress in comfortable jeans, pull your hair back in a pony tail, and put on your bomber jacket. Then just sort of cruise around town punching around on the buttons. Try to figure out what songs are played most often and listen closely to the singers' names. If you want, you can get a six-pack, but don't drink too much—the songs won't make sense. Face it, lines like "I miss you already, and you're not even gone," "Let's quit before we start," "If your phone doesn't ring, it's me," "Is forever longer than always?" don't make a whole lot of sense even when you're sober.

Plus, you could get a DWI, but that's not all bad—it sort of goes along with country music lifestyle. You know, mama, trains, trucks, and prison. All that stuff, along with a little cheating and crying. You also meet a lot of country music fans in jail and can get a pretty quick education into the lifestyle. In fact, it's one of the fastest ways to learn first-hand what country music is all about.

It's best if you study country music before you fall in love. The lyrics won't make a bit of sense, but you can at least get a feel for the beat. Then you can sort of work your way backwards and learn the oldies. Hank Williams, Ernest Tubb, Bob Wills, Johnny Horton, Loretta Lynn, Patsy Cline—all the classics. That way, when newer artists refer to their forefathers, you

141

don't have to sit there like an imbecile—you'll know what they're talking about. Background is essential. You can't completely understand songs like "Achy-Breaky Heart," unless you know their predecessors—songs like "Your Cheating Heart."

Listening to this stuff takes a little getting used to. I mean, you'll hear some really strange lyrics that may sound a little weird at first. Maybe you'll hear something like "If I don't love you, grits ain't groceries," "Old King Kong was just a little monkey compared to my love for you," or "How come your dog don't bite nobody but me?" Don't panic—you get used to this stuff after a while.

You'll even get to where you can recognize recurring themes. For example, they sing about walking and shoes a lot. There's familiar lyrics like "I'm walking the floor over you" or "These boots were made for walking" and not so well-known lines like "My shoes keep walking back to you" or "I bought the shoes that just walked out on me." Then there's lines like "She can put her shoes under my bed any time" and "I wish I was walking out of your shoes tonight."

Anyway, ride around and punch the buttons a lot. But try to keep a low profile. You're not ready to go public yet. Shouldn't take more than a couple months 'til you start to get a grip on the songs. When you feel like you're starting to figure out what it's all about, get a "I Love Reba" bumper sticker and a Billy Ray Cyrus tee-shirt. This is a turning point, the place where your life starts to change. You'll get honked at, waved at, and even flipped off more often than ever before.

Next, you need to fall in love. That first-in-love feeling adds a little meaning to the songs. So you got to find someone to fall in love with. The best way to do this and increase your country music listening skills at the same time is to start going to country western bars. Pick a place with a name like *Cowboys* or *Billy Bob's*. Now you want to make sure you wear the right stuff. No lycra tights or skirts. You need to get you some Rocky Mountain jeans, the Calvin Klein of kicker denim. Then you need some Justin lace-up ropers. Preferably red or maybe black. Either way, make sure to get black laces.

Always get a matching belt. Trust me. If you just get the boots, you may never get around to buying the belt and it won't look right. Add a kicker blouse, one that buttons down the front and ties in the center, and you're ready to go. Don't get a hat. You'll look like a tourist or a beginner. You can only wear the hat once you're confident enough and after you get all the rules down real good. Well, you want to look good, of course. Curl your hair, paint your nails, all that stuff. And perfume, lots of perfume. Get some of those samples from the cosmetics counter at Foley's and stick them in your purse. Make sure to put lipstick on and always, always carry a comb and travel-sized hairspray.

Until you get used to country-western bars, it's best to go with a group of girls—that way you won't look so out of place. The first time, go real late, around eleven. That way a lot of people will be drunk, and they won't notice if you stick out. Just walk in like you've been there a million times. They'll easily mistake you for a pro, especially in those jeans.

First thing, get situated at your table. Sit next to the men's restroom, so there will be a steady stream of men walking past you. When the waitress takes your order, say, "Miller Longneck, please." Say it like you mean it. You might want to remind her not to bring you a Miller Lite. For some reason, waitresses confuse these two drinks a lot. Don't just drink the beer. You got to do this right, too. There's an art to drinking a beer. Whatever you do, don't pour it in the glass. Drink it out of the bottle. Squeeze a little lime in the bottle and around the rim, then sprinkle salt on it.

Observe the couples who sit near your table. Watch the girls and take tips from the ones who look natural. Notice what they do with their hands during conversation. Watch them fold cocktail napkins or touch their earrings. Look at them as they approach the dance floor. Note how the men usually walk behind the girls. Look at the way the girls stand alone on the dance floor for a second, waiting for their partners to arrange their arms. At first glance, it all looks so natural, but believe me, someone out there's doing some counting. Only the couples who are real good at it can dance and talk at the same time. Save all this for future reference—later, you will have to learn to country-western dance. Sorry, there's no way around it.

Take a cigarette out of your purse and light it with your friend's lighter. Never, never bring your own lighter. Sooner or later some cowboy will walk by; if he looks like your type, ask him for a light. He'll give you one; then he'll kind of hang around your table. "Wanta dance?" he'll eventually stutter. Say no. But you got to say it in real nice way. Believe me on this one. Sort of bat your eyes and flip your hair and say, "No, but thanks for asking. I just never really learned how to dance. Want to talk?" If he says, "Up yours. I just never really learned how to talk," you're out of luck. Most likely he's a smart ass who was potty-trained too early or something. Say, "Excuse me" and go to the restroom. Put fresh lipstick on. Buy some gum from the old lady sitting by the door, selling bar-hopping essentials. Tip her.

Return to your seat and wait for another cowboy to approach you. Ask him for a light. This time, say it this way: "Excuse me, do you have any matches?" He'll say "yes" or "no" and eventually get around to the dancing question. Answer accordingly, but change it a little to entertain yourself. Be a little more simple. It's getting later—people don't want to mess around. Just say, "No thanks. I can't dance. Want to talk?" If he *just* says, "I can't talk," you're in luck. He's got a sense of humor. If he smiles real big and adds, "but I think I can talk to *you*, darling," you're in double luck. He's also charming. Yeah. Go for this guy. Say, "Well, you're talking just fine. You can talk." Try to say it with a country accent. Don't say something real hip like "I bet you can really psychobabble."

* Warning: The music will be so loud, you'll barely be able to hear him. You cannot carry on a real conversation in these places.

Just nod and say "uh-huh" a lot. Smile and sort of act all fluttered. If he's your type, you'll really feel fluttered. If this is the case, try not to act *too* fluttered. Just sort of act like you don't care one way or another. You don't want to come across as desperate. Look up at the ceiling or watch people dance. Say, "Man, I sure do wish I could dance like them." Then look around, pretending you're staring at some of the other cowboys.

Now here's where all your studying of country tunes and singers comes in handy. Wait until the band plays a George Strait song. Say, "I sure do like George." He'll think you're on a first-name basis with these people. If he says, "Yeah, me too. You know, 'this really wasn't my chair after all,'" you are fortunate. This guy is into entertaining you, and apparently he's done some studying too. Laugh. Laugh and say, "That's funny, but I *meant* Jones. George Jones." He'll laugh. Maybe he'll quote George Jones. Maybe not.

* Note: If the guy sitting beside you is named George, pick another singer. He might think you're talking about him and feel uncomfortable.

If you get nervous, re-tie your boots. These boots really come in handy when you need something to do with your hands. Say, "Excuse me, my boot came untied." Then bend down and act like you're tying it. Don't look up and say something like, "Isn't that strange? I mean I was just sitting here, and my boot came untied." You know, the guilty dog barks. Try not to make a big deal out of it. Act like your boot really did come untied.

Immediately after you tie your boot, while your hands are still under the table, elbow your girlfriend's leg. Instantly sit up straight. If she doesn't react, nudge her again and wink at her. Hopefully, she'll understand that you're giving her the universal secret code. If not, she'll say, "Who's kicking me?" Quickly look at the table beside you. Pretend you don't know what's going on at your own table. Wait a few seconds and then make eye contact with her. This time, make sure she's looking you straight in the eyes. Nudge her again, clear your throat (ummmmm), then point your eyes to the women's restroom. Look at the cowboy, and say, "Excuse me." Now she'll get the message and follow you into the restroom.

Inside the restroom, tell her you think the guy standing beside you is kind of neat. She might be drunk and agree with you, or maybe she'll be a little ticked that the guy she danced with all night turned out to be married. Try to act like you understand. Then say, "Watch him . . . the guy beside me. See if you think he likes me." She'll say, "Okay." Actually, she'll say it like this: "God, okay, for Christ's sake."

Don't remind her that she came over and did laundry at your house for the last three weeks and borrowed your car the day before yesterday. Say, "Thanks, I need all the help I can get." Offer to let her use your lipstick, then when she asks if she looks all right, say, "Yeah. You look great." She will stand in front of the full-length mirror, bend her head way down between her knees, and run her fingers through her hair. Ask her what she's doing. "Fluffing my hair," she'll answer. Take notes. This is an important lesson. Stand beside her, and do the same to your hair. Gaze at her through your knees, cut your eyes, and ask yourself, "Is this what my life has come to?" Look at her and smile. Ignore the woman in the second stall who complains that her husband flirts too much. When your friend says, "They all flirt too much," laugh. Follow her out of the restroom, nonchalantly returning to your table.

Try not to get too drunk. Look at it like a first date. Drink water or Coke in-between the Millers. If the guy's last name is Miller, make a joke. If not, make a joke about something else. Don't talk about anything too serious. Remember, he can't hear you anyway.

If the band plays Garth Brooks, make up a story about something that once happened to you while you listened to Garth Brooks. Use your imagination. He's probably drunk by now, and there's a good chance he won't remember what you said. If he appears really drunk, just move your lips. Move your lips and smile a lot. And laugh.

145

Stay until the club closes. He'll walk you to your car. Give him your phone number, but don't, under any circumstances, kiss him. First kisses are important, and you want to make sure it's something he'll always remember. Keep up the cool act. Open your car door, start the car, and wave goodbye with your right hand.

On the way home, tell your girlfriends that you really like him. Say, "I really, really like him. I hope he calls me." Be thankful you gave him your correct phone number. Thank God you could even remember your phone number. Hope to God you *did* give him your correct number. Say, "What's my phone number?" out loud to your girlfriends. They'll look at you like you're crazy. Quote your number and ask them if it's right.

"Of course it is," one of them will say. "What's the matter with you?"

Breathe a sigh of relief and say, "I don't know. I think I'm a little tipsy." Giggle.

When he calls you, make light conversation. He *can* hear you, and he's probably sober. You are now accountable for what you say. Tell him you're busy Friday, but you'd be happy to go out with him Saturday night. Remember, you are not desperate. Pretend he's just one of many men you see on weekends.

On the first date, you get your chance to make the all-important first sober impression. Make mental lists of the things you'll talk about. Absolutely do not mention your dating history. Don't tell him your former boyfriend dumped you for his first ex-wife.

If the lyrics, "I wish I was a teddy bear, and I wish I hadn't have fallen in love with you" come over the radio, don't comment. Just laugh. He'll say the song doesn't make much sense. Agree with him, then laugh again.

Enjoy your dinner, then let him take you to a country-western club for a few drinks. Don't tell him you spend your weekends riding around town listening to country music. Pretend you're a regular at the bar scene. Act at home.

By the third date, you can go ahead and start falling in love with him. Always, always, keep your *real* goal in mind: understanding country music. It has little to do with the guy.

Go out with him on Friday and Saturday nights. Talk to him on the phone frequently. Learn how to two-step. Dance with him a lot. Remember, continue to listen carefully to the country lyrics. Keep up with the new songs and singers and listen for singers you don't recognize. Wait a couple months before you sleep with him, but wait much longer before you tell him you love him.

    * Note: No matter what else you do or don't do, *do not* tell him you love him for the first time while you're in a country bar. Make sure he's sober. Make sure you're sober. Make sure he can hear you. Don't laugh. Most likely, he'll say he loves you too. Believe him.

    Now you got things rolling. You're just a two-step away from knowing what country music is all about.

    * Note: "They ought to put warning labels on sad country songs."

    You're really in luck when he sends you flowers and cards and buys you country cassettes. Keep telling him you love him. Convince him. Convince yourself. He'll take you out and say witty lines and caress you and sing country songs to you. "I love you, and that's all I know," he'll sing. He'll dedicate country songs to you over the radio. Dedicate country songs to him. Dedicate "If I had only one friend left, I'd want it to be you." You can even fax dedications. Fax the d.j. a dedication for him every night. Every night for two weeks straight. Tell him you will *always* love him. Have Tammy Wynette sing "Stand by Your Man" for him. Don't cheat—stick to country tunes. Most likely, some man will call the d.j. and say, "Boy, he's a lucky man." Tell him other men think he's lucky.

    On his birthday, sing to him: "Happy birthday, Darling, I don't have anything to give you, but I'd like to take a few things away . . . doubt." On the six-month anniversary of the day you met him, buy him a Hank Williams C.D. boxed-collection. Hank Sr., of course. Wrap it. Quote Willie: "Pretty paper, pretty ribbon, of blue. Wrap your present to your darling from you."

    If he begins to act strange, forgets to call you or acts less anxious to go to country bars, assume it's your imagination. Blow it off when he tells you that he doesn't like the way you hold your cigarette, the way you fluff your hair, or your shade of lipstick. Presume his complaints are really job related—he's under a lot of stress at work.

    When he tells you he's moving to an apartment closer to his work, don't wonder why he doesn't suggest you move in with him. Assume he needs his personal space. Maybe he doesn't believe in living together before marriage. Maybe he doesn't believe in marriage. Never, never suspect that he doesn't believe in you. Remind yourself that you're only in it for the country music.

    Don't take it personally when he calls three weekends in a row and says that he's going out with the boys again. Remember, he was out with the boys when you met him. No, don't remember that. You'll start thinking about the night you met him, and you may get all wimpy. You'll suspect he'll be dancing with other women. Convince yourself that he won't even be thinking about lighting anyone else's cigarette.

When you're punching the buttons on his car stereo, and you notice a loop earring hanging over the volume control, jerk it off and hold it near his face. "What's this?" say loudly.

"An earring," he'll say.

Even though his sense of humor first attracted you to him, absolutely do not laugh. Whether or not he is really kidding is beside the point. Instead, keep a straight face and remain calm. In a straight-forward, informative tone, say, "Did I ever tell you I don't have pierced ears?"

"Uhhh. . . . I don't guess you did," he'll say.

"Isn't that weird. I mean everyone thinks it's strange that I don't have pierced ears." Put in the Hank Williams C.D. Punch the number for "Your Cheating Heart," then just sit back in silence. Believe me, the silence will torture him. Just sit there for a few songs, holding the earring. Pretend you're examining it. Hold it real close to your face, and ask him to turn the light on. Look at the C.D. case, and study the songs. Use the earring for a pointer, while you recite the titles out loud.

When he stops at the fourth red light, while "I'm So Lonesome I could Cry" plays, scream at him. Cuss him out. Lose control. Consider this a pivotal point in your country-music education.

He'll mumble something about ladies' night at some country bar. Wednesday. Yeah, it all starts fitting together. The night you usually have dinner with your mom or do laundry. Say, "I thought you just didn't want to meet my mom." He'll either nod or try to defend himself: "I get nervous."

Don't start pumping him. Don't ask him her name or how long he's been seeing her. Sing along with Hank: "If you've got the money, honey, I've got the time." Tell him to take you home. When he pulls in the driveway, he'll turn the car off. Ask him to turn the key on, so you can hear the music. Over Hank Williams, you'll find out all about the other girl. He'll explain how he thinks you both should date other people.

This is where it gets hard, but you got to do it. Remember your dignity. Agree with him. Say, "Well, yeah, I was thinking the same thing." Don't insist he see only you. Don't beg. Don't crawl. Don't, no matter what, become a whining character out of some country-western song.

A month later, when he calls you and says he's doing okay, hanging out with his friends, just say, "Yeah, well, that's funny. I'm going out with the girls a lot lately. Nothing like perfect timing. Perfect timing, that's what we got, isn't it?"

"Uh, huh," he'll say.

Don't admit you still love him. In fact, don't admit much of anything. Eventually, he'll say, "Well, I just called to see how you were doing these days."

Don't pretend you didn't hear him. Don't make a joke. Just say, "Oh, okay, I guess. Yeah, I'm doing all right." Wait a few seconds, then say, "Goodbye." But don't go out with the girls. Don't go out with anyone. Dress in some comfortable jeans, throw your hair back in a pony tail, and put on your bomber jacket. Then just sort of cruise around town, punching around on the buttons.

Fill your car up with gas. Treat yourself. Get full service, and ask the attendant to check your oil. Buy a six-pack of Miller Longnecks and cruise around. Sing with Wynonna: "How did you get to me?"

Crack your window and smoke a lot. After two beers and seven cigarettes, slip the Patsy Cline he bought you for Christmas in the cassette player.

When Patsy sings "Crazy for thinking that my love could hold you," light up another cigarette and drink some more beer. Whatever you do, don't cry. Do anything to keep from crying. Take Patsy out and turn the radio down real low. Sing to yourself: "Where there's a cloud don't mean there's rain. Tears in my eyes don't mean there's pain." Fidget with the cruise control. Reach under your car seat and feel for loose change. Find a quarter and sing: "Here's a quarter, call someone who cares." Re-tie your boots.

Take a couple deep breaths, then turn the radio back up.

* Warning: If you play the music too loudly, you'll bust your speakers.

If Merle Haggard starts belting out "Today I started loving you again," punch the button. Maybe George Jones sings "He stopped loving her today" on the next station. If so, punch the button again. When you hear "I can't help it if I'm still in love with you," cry. Cry and cry and cry.

Pull into a 7-11 parking lot and cry some more. Buy more Miller Longnecks. Don't forget the lime. If the checker asks you if you're okay, don't try to talk at first. Just nod. Keep nodding, while he rings you up. Take your change and say, "Thanks. Yeah, I'm okay. I'm just having a bad day." Don't, under any circumstances, cry while you stand inside the 7-11. Wait

149

until you get back in the car. Start the car and cry some more. Sing: "Funny Face, I love you. Funny Face, I need you." Light a cigarette, and start on another Miller Longneck.

Now you can drink too much—the songs will still make sense. The songs will always, always make perfect sense, and after all, that's your goal—to learn country music.

BLOOD RELATIONS

GREG GARRETT

Perry Franks used to tell anyone who asked that the only thing he got out of his first marriage was a lingering dose of the clap.

When he told Deborah that she was free to whore around however she pleased, Perry honestly thought that he was through with her forever. He said goodbye to the cotton fields of West Texas, left the acrid smell and clanging metal of the football weight room, and took a job managing an executive health club in San Antonio. He also left his graduate work in exercise physiology at Texas Tech, but all that seemed to matter at the time was putting some distance between himself and her.

Months went by. He found that sometimes he could go an entire day without thinking of her. And then the letter came. She would never have called him, of course. That would have meant telling directly, to his face. That would have been out of character. It had been, for example, mere accident that he had found out she—and consequently, he—had contracted a certain sexually transmitted disease somewhere. Only a check-up before a powerlifting meet had turned up the trouble. It could have killed him and she hadn't even bothered to warn him or explain. And he knew that he'd gotten it from her, despite her protests. He hadn't slept with anyone else.

"I took those vows too serious, I guess," he explained to Rip Walker at work. "I do that shit sometimes."

"What shit?" Walker asked.

"Serious shit." Perry said, and Rip nodded knowingly, despite the fact that he had probably never thought about serious shit in his life.

Perry pulled the letter out of his mailbox on top of a stack of bills and a flyer from Wal-Mart. When he first looked at the Lubbock return address, it didn't register; it was meaningless to him. It was like receiving a message from outer space, from the spiritual world. He had tried to hard to block Deborah from his mind that he had almost convinced himself that she had never existed.

Dear Perry, the letter said, *You have a son.*

In fact, there wasn't much more than that. She didn't sign it; it would have been unnecessary. She simply enclosed a Polaroid picture: a tiny ball of red topped by a dark cap of hair.

Which meant that he had to change his marriage refrain: He had gotten both a violent dose of the clap and an unwanted child.

"Can you believe this shit?" He and Kirk Martin were working out in mid-afternoon while the club was quiet, concentrating on chest and triceps. Kirk lay down on the weight bench, eyes closed. If he heard Perry he gave no indication of it.

Kirk grunted as Perry ease eased the bar of the rack and three hundred and fifteen pounds of iron forced its way down to this chest. He sucked in air as he readied himself. Perry talked on.

"What am I supposed to do about this? I don't want a kid. Why should I have to send her a ton of money for a kid I didn't ask for? Hell, how do I even know he's mine? She slept with every friend I had and half the Tech football team."

Kirk grunted, shut his eyes, and grimaced. The weights began to rise.

As Kirk locked out his arms at their fullest extension, Perry took hold of the bar and guided it back over onto the bench rack.

Kirk sat up. "You're in a world of hurt," he said as he wiped his face with a towel.

"Thanks for the update," Perry said. "Lie back down. I want to drop these weights on you."

"No thanks. It's your turn."

Perry lay down on the bench. Kirk lifted the bar off of the rack for him, and Perry filled his mind with rage, a technique he sometimes used to force the iron up just one more time, to coax his sore muscles into another repetition. His anger today was tightly focused; he hated Deb with every aching fiber of his body. He hated her, he hated himself for marrying her, and he hated this child he had never met and didn't want.

"Nice rep," Kirk said. "You pushed it right up."

"Perry, I just heard." The squeal belonged to Jana Powell, an aerobically-fit blonde twig who taught classes to overweight executive wives. "Congratulations about your baby."

Kirk Martin smirked. No secret where the leak was. Perry sat up, trying to think of a response with a vocabulary level Jana could comprehend.

"Well, thanks, Jana. But I'm not real excited about this thing here."

She looked at him dubiously, wary of one of his punch lines. "Parents are always glad for a healthy baby. What else could you want?"

"Some advance warning would have been nice."

Jana brightened. "So you could have been in the delivery room?"

"So I could have skipped the country." He pulled one of the forty-five pound plates off the bar; Kirk did the same on his side. Jana stared at them both with exasperation.

"I thought you were a better person than to shirk your responsibilities like this," she sputtered. "Don't you have any feelings for that little boy?"

"Sure I do," Perry said, as he and Kirk slid twenty-five-pound plates onto each side of the bar. "But I don't think you want to hear about them."

"Pretty cold, man," Kirk said, watching Jana stomp off the exercise floor. "Women today are looking for sensitivity. You've put off that piece of ass by a month or more."

"I like women with more meat on them," Perry grunted. "And more brain cells. How the hell am I supposed to have feelings for a kid I didn't even know about?"

"Nobody knows about them 'til they get here."

Perry rolled his eyes. "They don't know what they look like, yeah. Whether they're going to have Gramp's ears or Grandma's eyes. They don't know whether they're going to be a boy or girl. But, goddamnit, at least they know they're coming."

Perry pushed up his last rep without difficulty.

The anger faded, though, as the questions started. After all, this was anew experience for him. When he got home lat that night, the picture was where he had dropped it—on the dining room table—and, against his will he picked it up again and looked at it.

If he's really mine, how do I feel about that? What would it be like to be a father? To hold a baby in my arms?

His own father had been a remote, frosty man, and Perry had been the baby of the family. By the time he had graduated from high school, his father had been a gray-haired retiree, trimming the hedges and edging the yard with the same obsessive perfection he'd devoted to managing the plant all those years.

By the time he'd graduated from college, his father had been dead for almost two years.

They had never had an intimate conversation, never played catch in the backyard, never gone fishing together. On his deathbed, Perry's father had waved off any expressions of concern. His last words to Perry were, "Study hard. A man needs a college degree to get a good job these days."

What would it be like to be a father?

He looked at himself in the mirror. Blonde hair, mustache, blue eyes. Just under six feet, just under two hundred, hard as iron, handsome as all get out. Still young. Free.

Free.

That was the important thing, wasn't it? He had gotten out of that marriage and now he could do anything. Anything. If he didn't like this job, he could pack up, find another. If he wanted to move in with a girl, or have one move in with him, he could do it. If he wanted to buy a car, or sell it, or drive it off a cliff, everything was up to him.

And all of that could change. Recognizing that he had a son would only open him up to more emotional upheaval, a lifetime of responsibility, a permanent link to that bloodthirsty bitch in Lubbock.

But the questions would not go away.

He sent a tentative letter, making no promises, simply asking for details. Her reply was leisurely; she was in no immediate need of money, she said, because she and Richard Hamilton were living together. Hamilton, Perry remembered vaguely, was an attractive middle-aged sociology professor, a compulsive womanizer. He smiled wryly. They deserved each other.

The boy's name was Brian Richard Franks. He was now eight months old, sitting up, crawling some. The picture showed a chunky kid with a finger in his mouth, his head almost half the size of his body. A few days earlier, Perry would have called this baby ugly. Hell, he would have called any baby ugly.

Now he smiled. He thought he could see a trace of himself in that face. "Good looking kid," he muttered.

He continued to think. To wonder. And when the chance to take a long weekend came up, Perry decided to travel back to Lubbock for a few days. "Just to see the place," he said. Deb would probably be out of town, visiting her parents. He wouldn't make any special effort to see the kid. It would probably never happen.

He put it off. When he hit town on Friday afternoon he went by the stadium and chatted with some of the coaches he'd known, then called up Christy Parker, an old girlfriend. They would up drinking the night away in a side booth at a bar just off the highway, and he woke up the next morning back at her place, a third-floor apartment over a hardware store, with a jackhammer hangover.

He rolled out of bed and winced as his feet hit the cold wood floor. It was nearly ten-thirty, but Christy was still passed out, so he padded silently over to the table where the phone was. Pulling the phone directory from underneath a stack of papers, he looked through the book to see where Deb was living these days.

"What are you doing?" Christy said sleepily. "Come back to bed."

"Just a second." He found Hamilton, glanced at the address, didn't write it down.

But he remembered it. The next day, on the way back up to the airport, he stopped his rented Taurus in front of the white frame house just off-campus where Hamilton lived. Deb's car sat in the driveway.

He thought that driving on would probably be the wisest thing to do. Instead, after a moment that seemed endless, the engine idling and Stevie Ray Vaughn singing from his speakers, something about it flooding down in Texas, he got out and rang the doorbell.

Hamilton answered. He was a slender, handsome man in his forties, best known for his wardrobe, fresh from the pages of *Gentleman's Quarterly*, and for his dry wit. He was not famous, however, for any skill in physical confrontation, and when he recognized Perry he took a noticeable step backward.

Although Perry savored the moment, he had no real reason to intimidate Richard Hamilton. "Afternoon," he said, and introduced himself, although it obviously was unnecessary. "I was in town and I wondered if I could see Bryan."

Hamilton relaxed. He even smiled. "Sure," he said. "Come on in. I think Deb put him down for a nap, but—"

"That's okay," Perry said. "Don't wake him up. I just want to take a look at him."

Deborah walked out of the living room. It was the first time he had seen her in a year and a half and it surprised him how little he felt. He felt numb, nothing toward her; she could have been a total stranger, except that he would probably have been more curious about a stranger. He wondered if it was the same for her.

Apparently not. "Jesus Christ," she said, and her jaw dropped for a moment. "What are you doing here?"

Hamilton calmed her with a shushing hand. "He came to see Bryan. I told him it was all right."

Deb peered at him in the poor light of the hallway. "You look different," she said.

"Must be the moustache," he said. He glanced down the hall. "Can I go in?"

"Quietly," she said. "He just went to sleep."

The boy lay in a crib, under a Mickey Mouse blanket. He was so tiny, Perry thought. *Look at those fists.* And his head was still the biggest part of him. He looked totally defenseless.

He crouched down beside the crib, a few inches from Bryan's face. It wasn't until he got this close that he could hear the boy breathing, feel the delicate force of that breath.

Then Bryan sneezed—in his sleep—and Perry started in surprise. He caught himself, sheepishly, and looked back at the door, where Deb was standing. He got up, brushed himself off for some reason, and made for the door.

"Nice-looking boy," he said. "Thanks for letting me take a look."

He drove to the airport, thoughts careening through his brain. Seeing Deb hadn't been hard at all, and he wondered about that. *Funny. You can sleep next to someone, knowing everything about her, how she walks, talks, moans. And all those experiences don't mean anything once it's over.*

He also thought about the boy. From Lubbock to Dallas. From Dallas to San Antonio. And for some time after.

Bryan was two when he first came to spend some time with Perry. Deb and Hamilton were now married, which brought a smile to Perry's face. The two of them could provide a steady living for Lubbock's private detectives. Anyway, Deb had agreed to let Bryan come for two months.

Perry flew to Lubbock and brought the boy back with him. It was the first time that the two had really been alone together; they had spoken a few times on the telephone (or, rather, Perry had spoken while Bryan listed or babbled), but Perry was unsure of what to do or say on the phone.

He needn't have worried. Once the initial excitement of being on an airplane wore off, Bryan fell asleep leaning against his shoulder, and Perry protectively covered him with his own jacket.

That's a beautiful boy you have there," the middle-aged woman across the aisle said, leaning over to get a good view.

"Thanks," Perry said. "He is, isn't he?" He took the boy's hand, and the sleeping Bryan instinctively grasped onto his fingers.

"Yes," Perry said to himself, looking down, "he really is."

Perry lived in a three bedroom house off Bandera Road in a hilly, quiet suburb of San Antonio. He had always reserved one bedroom for weights and a bench, but the other had been unused. To prepare for Bryan he had moved a stack of boxes to the garage and had ordered a child's bed and dresser, but they were late in being delivered, so that first night Perry fixed Bryan a bed on the couch.

It was only six-thirty, and Perry began to wonder what children do, what kind of routine Bryan had. "What do you usually do at night?"

"Sleep," Bryan said.

"I mean before you go to sleep. Do you and your mommy do things at night before you go to bed?"

"Television," Bryan said. "And playtime." It sounded like "pwaytime." Perry smiled and bent forward to hear more, but Bryan was more interested in the powerlifting trophies on the bookcase shelves, huge wood and metal trophies with tiny golden weightlifters perched atop them.

"I got those for picking up heavy things, lifting weights," Perry said, trying to steer Bryan's attention to the question of night-time habits. "What else do you do at home?"

"Bathtime," he answered absently. He went over to one of the lower shelves and tried to pick up a trophy

Perry hadn't thought of child-proofing the house. He leapt to his feet. "No no no," he said, pulling the trophy away from him and relocating the lowest ones on the top shelves. "These are very important."

"I want to play with Superman," Bryan stammered.

"Superman?"

Bryan flexed his tiny biceps like the figures atop the trophies.

157

"No," Perry told him. "These aren't toys. They're prizes. I won them for being strong."

"I'm strong too," Bryan argued.

During his life, Perry had handled crying lovers, whining dogs, complaining customers. But his usual feeling of detached calm did not seem to apply to this little boy with the earnest look on his fact. Perry found himself giving in.

"Can you ask nicely to see the big trophy?"

"Please can I see the Superman?" Bryan responded. He smiled expectantly at Perry.

"I guess so." He lifted the trophy and placed it on the floor. Bryan ran his hand over the tiny plastic figure and looked up.

"Thank you, Daddy," he said brightly, and he turned his attention back to the trophy.

Perry realized what Bryan had said. The implications were frightening and life-long, but he was not afraid; instead, it was as though someone had just switched on a sun lamp inside his chest.

"You're welcome," he said. He tousled Bryan's dark hair, letting his hand rest there for a moment. "My pleasure."

Perry put Bryan to bed at 8:30, after a bath and a story about bunnies told as much by Bryan as by Perry, and the boy was asleep the moment he hit the couch. Perry sat down in the recliner, picked up the new *Sports Illustrated,* and opened it midway. He couldn't read though. Whenever he glanced over at Bryan he got worrisome thoughts. *What if he rolls over in the night and falls off of the couch? He'd hit his head on the coffee table.* So he moved the coffee table. Then he thought, *What if he falls on the floor?* So he picked Bryan up and carried him in to his waterbed.

Perry hardly slept at all that first night. Instead, he lay awake next to Bryan, eyes open, ears alert for the tiny noises, the breathing, the sniffling that Bryan made, sensing the tiny sleeping movements that were transmitted to him through the mattress.

When Perry walked into the club the next day holding Bryan's hand, Rip Walker began to laugh. He had known that Perry was bringing his son to stay with him, but he had never seriously thought about seeing Perry with the child in tow. The whole situation struck him a highly incongruous.

"Ladies and gentlemen, the father of the year has just entered the club," Rip announced to the sparse weekend turnout over the P.A. system. Perry blushed but held on to Bryan's hand.

"Don't be afraid of this man," he told Bryan confidentially, "even if he does look like a scary monster."

An older member in a maroon designer jogging suit stopped to survey the scene. Children were usually not to be found on the premises.

"Where'd you get the boy, Perry?"

"Sir, this is my son, Bryan. Bryan, this is Mr. Gutierrez."

"Pleased to meet you, Bryan." Gutierrez bent over and offered his hand. Bryan hid behind Perry's leg, merely peeking around at the man.

"He's a handsome boy." Gutierrez gave up and stood up straight. "I didn't know you were married."

"Used to be."

Gutierrez laughed. "Best way to be. You can enjoy the kids without having to listen to the wife. Good evening, gentlemen.

Rip shrugged as the door swung shut behind him. "Hadn't thought of it that way, but maybe he's right. Bryan's kind of a cute kid, but from the way you talk about his mom—"

Bryan blinked, as though he had just remembered something. "My mom? I want my mom."

"What do you mean?" Perry demanded, his feelings stung. They had spent the day shopping for clothes, picking out toys. Bryan watched *Sesame Street*, and they had bought Bert and Ernie dolls, a Sesame Street playhouse, a Big Bird cookie jar, and a comforter with Cookie Monster on it. They had shared a chocolate chip cookie and a Coke in the mall and had laughed together as they began to get comfortable with each other.

"I miss my mom," Bryan said.

Rip gave Perry a commiserating smile. "You're on your own with this one, Pop."

"Thanks a lot, pal." He picked Bryan up and set him on top of the front desk. "This man's real name is Ripley," Perry said. "Can you say that name, Ripley?"

"Wipley."

"Close enough," Perry said. "Isn't that a funny name? Ripley?"

"That's a funny name," Bryan agreed, giggling.

"Tell the kid not to expect any Christmas presents from me this year," Rip said. "Why don't you guys go someplace and do family things?"

"All right," Perry said. "Just let me check the books. You got anything working?"

"Got a guest who came to join and two renewals in the can. Eighteen hundred bucks. Not a bad Sunday."

"Okay, Rip," Bryan nodded approvingly. "You can keep your job. I think me and the kid are going in for a swim. Does that sound good?"

"I like swimming," Bryan said.

"Bet the kid sinks like a rock," Rip said, reaching for his wallet.

"He's two and a half," Perry said. "Give him time." He took Bryan's hand and the two climbed upstairs to the locker room to change.

After a few weeks, they fell into their own routine; Perry was supposed to work ten to ten, so he left Bryan in a daycare center after breakfast, and arranged for a babysitter to bring him back to the house in the evening, feed him, and put him to bed. Perry would slip out of the club early if things seemed to be running themselves, and if he got home in time he would give Bryan his bath, let him play with his toys for half an hour, and then read him one of the books they had picked out at the mall. Bryan had developed a liking for the Berenstein Bears, so most nights Perry found himself reading some moralizing tale like *The Berenstein Bears and Too Much Junk Food.* That was okay with him; maybe Bryan would take home some good habits in the fall.

"I can't believe the way you've changed this summer," his girlfriend, Carmen, said one night as they watched the Cubs and the Cardinals on ESPN and Bryan played in the other room before bed. She had just given him a Father's Day card which Bryan had signed with his mark, something that looked like a drunken amoeba.

"You don't like the way I've changed?" He looked at her. She was dark with raven hair and dimples when she smiled, which she was doing now.

"No, no, Perry. I think you are *muy simpático.* Much nicer than the first time I met you. When I saw you walking through the health club you looked too arrogant."

"Hell yes, I'm *simpático,*" he growled. "And I'll show you just how *simpático* as soon as *el bambino es*—how do you say 'in bed'?"

"*En cama.*"

"*El bambino es en cama.*"

"Very good," she said, applauding lightly. "I'd like to be *en cama* myself. Isn't it about time—"

Carmen's question was drowned in the clank and clatter of falling iron from the weight room, and almost immediately, Bryan's wail of pain.

Perry leapt from the couch. "Holy shit," he said. "What was he doing in there?"

Bryan was lying on the floor next to the weight rack. He had somehow tipped the iron bar off the rack, and as it fell, the heavy bar had opened a huge gash on his forehead. His face and the carpet beneath him were already covered with blood.

Bryan was crying very loudly, and Perry took this as a positive sign.

"*Dios Mio,*" Carmen breathed from the doorway. "Get him into the bathroom."

Perry scooped him up and hurried to the sink. They tried to stop the flow of blood to see how bad the cut was, but the blood continued to come, and Perry felt himself go empty inside as he looked down at the crimson washcloth. He applied pressure to the wound, which made Bryan yell even louder.

"We've got to get him to a doctor," he said. "I want you to drive."

"I can hold him—" Carmen began, but Perry was adamant.

"I want to hold him. You drive. When Arnie Scott was working out this morning, he said it was because he was on E.R. tonight. Let's take him to the hospital."

Carmen drove Perry's Saab competently and quickly, occasionally sneaking a glance at Perry and Bryan. The boy had stopped crying, and the silence now was bone-chilling. Perry talked to him, made him answer questions.

"What were you doing in that room." he asked. "Why were you messing around with those things?"

"I was being strong," Bryan said quietly.

"Like your daddy?" Carmen asked.

Bryan nodded.

Perry moved the blood-soaked washcloth to check the wound. Still bleeding. The emergency room sign glowed just ahead and Carmen downshifted as they entered the parking lot.

A crisp white uniform stepped in front of Perry as he tried to walk through the swinging doors back to where Arnie must be.

"I'm sorry, sir, but I'll need you to fill out these admittance forms," the uniform told him.

He stepped right through her; at least, he walked through the space she just occupied. "Get Arnie Scott. My boy is hurt bad."

161

Dr. Scott heard Perry's voice. He stepped out of a curtained alcove and assured the nurse, "It's all right, Ellen. Send him on back. The admitting nurse pursed her lips disapprovingly, but Perry carried the boy into the cubicle another nurse indicated.

Scott stepped in and pulled the curtain behind him. He removed the compress. "Whew. That's quite a knock. Looks like he's lost a lot of blood. Know what type he is?

Perry shook his head. He didn't. "Mine's O Positive, I think."

"We'll need to take a little from him and type it."

"Take more blood?"

"Just a little medical irony." The nurse drew a sample expertly from his arm before Bryan could even realize a new pain had been added to the equation.

"I'll give mine if he needs it," Perry said. He crowded closer. "What do you think?"

Dr. Scott began to sponge around the wound."Got to see what it looks like before I can say anything. Hmm. Stitches, definitely. Probably a bunch. How'd it happen?"

"He got into the weight room and tipped the bar over," Perry said. "Is he okay?"

"Give me a second," Scott repeated.

Perry clenched his fists until the nails dug into his palms. He could pick up a quarter-ton of steel; he could break every bone in a man's body; he could hit a softball into a different area code. But right now he couldn't do a damn thing; he was as helpless as Bryan.

Scott had cleaned the wound enough to make some conclusions.

"Big lump," he said. "Gonna be there a couple of days. Stitches will have to stay in for a week. Keep him from scratching, and bring him in, and we'll check them after that."

Perry unclenched his fists. Corpses don't scratch, nor do doctors want them brought back. "He's all right?"

"He got a good bang on the head. I'd like to hold him overnight to make sure there's no concussion. But he should be up and around and getting back into things in no time. Karen, I'm going to need some local and my stitch-em-up stuff." The nurse left, and Dr. Scott looked over at Perry, whose canary yellow polo shirt was still yellow only in spots. "Jesus, you look like something out of a horror movie," he said. "You okay?"

162

Perry nodded. "I was just scared, that's all. Just scared."

Scott nodded and bent back to his work, taking the hypo from the returning nurse. "I know," he sighed. "I've got two of the little monsters myself."

Bryan had been asleep for a little over an hour. They had moved him upstairs into an empty semi-private room, and now he lay in one bed while Perry sat on the other, watching. He had sent Carmen home, promising to call her if he needed anything. He hoped he wouldn't. Arnie Scott had said he would check in around midnight, and Perry wanted to stay awake until he was sure Bryan was out of danger.

He checked his watch; both hands were straight up. Soon after, the door eased open and Dr. Scott peered in. He went over to Bryan and woke him gently. After examining the boy's half-opened eyes, he nodded to himself and let Bryan roll over.

"He's fine," Scott whispered. "Or will be, after he gets a little rest. Can I talk to you outside for a second?"

"Sure," Perry said. "You by any chance happen to run across a clean shirt somewhere?"

The two slipped out into the empty corridor. "Not hardly. I don't know where to find something you wouldn't just burst out of, unless I put you in a gown. Just wanted to tell you something you might need to know for future reference."

Perry nodded. "I know," he said. "I was rude. I didn't go through proper channels. I was just—"

Dr. Scott waived his hand disparagingly. "Forget that. You had every right to be scared, and I'm not going to stand on ceremony when lives are at stake. I just needed to pass on some information."

Perry nodded. "Okay. Thanks."

"You need to get your blood typed some time. I'll do it, if you like, but your blood type can't possibly be O Positive. It doesn't match Bryan's."

"Doesn't match." Perry felt suddenly short of breath, as through he'd taken a helmet to the gut. He looked down at Bryan's blood on his shirt.

"No. So you should get it typed for certain. Just in case, God forbid, you wind up in here someday."

"Oh," was all he could say. His mind was elsewhere.

His blood had been typed. Twice. Once in high school biology class. And once just over three years ago. The doctor who prescribed steroids for his shoulder rehab had done it, had written it into Perry's file while he was sitting right there across the desk from him.

Bryan's blood type didn't match his. But that was impossible.

"Thanks," he heard himself saying. "I'll have to get it done one of these days."

You better get some rest," Scott told him. "You look awful. Bryan will be back on his feet, and you're going to have to keep up with him, Dad."

"Right," he said. "Thanks, Arnie. I'll see you later."

He opened the door and went back inside. Bryan had gone back to sleep. Perry walked slowly over to the boy, stood looking down at him, suddenly seeing all the similarities he had imagined melting away like ice cream on August sidewalk. *How could I have been so stupid? How could I have believed her? The bitch. She must be laughing up a storm.*

Bryan stirred beneath him, and without meaning to, Perry let his hand drop to the boy's cheek. The pressure woke the lightly sleeping child, and he opened his eyes.

"Daddy," he said, groggily. "Daddy. I hurt my head."

"I know," Perry said. "It's all right. I'm here." Bryan reached up and took his hand. "Close your eyes. I'm right here. Everything's going to be all right."

Bryan went back to sleep, his hand still closed on Perry's fingers.

Perry pulled up a chair with his foot and sat down quietly.

It's all right," he said. "I'm right here."

TO MAKE TALK

VIOLETTE NEWTON

My friend, when we come to Port Arthur and go work at refinery, we rent a house with good ground for garden, and we plant okra, pepper, onion, all what we have back home on bayou, only now we got money too. My wife, Essie, she get high heel and lipstick, and we city folk now.

We have old Ford to come here, but after while buy new Chevrolet, two seat, four door, and we go back home to see kinfolk and sport new car. Everbody say we rich and not forget where we come from, it in our blood. And we say, when we cross border, our blood feel good, we know where we are when we see moss hang in tree and people sit by ditch with crawfish pole.

We got screen front porch and back now, and our relative come visit in two car, spend weekend. In ice chest, they bring fish to make courtbouillon, and sometimes all the men go crab and come back and make big gumbo, and we laugh and laugh, and play card and it just like we home and the bayou run down middle of Sixteen Street. We ain't got no oak tree, no moss, no, but when we together, we home.

One time when they come, they say is something happen, a girl die, and nobody is find out why for awhile, and sheriff ride round and round, trying find Spider. She is been seeing Spider and he ain't no good. That is the Naquin girl, that one name Isabel, with the long black hair and big eyes, you know, yes? Not the prettiest girl on the bayou but almost. She good girl, Isabel, too good to be fool round with no count man she meet in Arceneaux grocery. She make excuse to get thing at store, and he always happen be there when she come. Everybody call him Spider cause he say one time in school play, he play part of someone name Spider, so it don't mean nothing, is just nickname. He buy Isabel creme soda and he drink beer, and they pass time a day laughing and everybody see it. On the bayou, man don't play round with girl. He serious or he going know why.

You know, Isabel mama dead and buried long time in graveyard with big tomb Naquin keep whitewash and nice all the time. He raise that girl up straight, and some day she go marry with some fine boy roundabouts. When he out hoeing in cane, she keep house for him, cooking and cleaning and minding her business. She do it real good 'til lately. Then she been pulling bedspread up on her daddy pillow, not even sun the two pillow, just spread them over, and she half do the plate and cup in dishpan and hardly sweep floor. Cause she off running round looking for Spider. It been scandal, yes, and everbody got something to talk about now, not just how bad is mosquito.

Well, Naquin worry and tell her behave, stay home, and why she ain't seeing that nice Broussard boy, he like her so good. And he tell her if he find her doing something bad, he beat her half to death. But she just laugh and say ain't she cook his dinner, drip his coffee, wash his clothes. She ain't doing nothing wrong unless having a little old fun is wrong.

This go on and everybody is expect something happen. But nothing do. Cause Spider go away and nobody ain't see him no more. But Isabel don't seem blue, she just skittish as before, just like she know he coming back. And her poor daddy almost crazy.

Well, all this is told on front porch in Port Arthur, and it just like we back home on the bayou. They tell how Isabel show up one day with ring she say come out of popcorn box Spider buy her in grocery store before he left, and she ain't never wear it until now. And Etoile Guidry, she ask why she wear it now, and Isabel laugh and toss head and say for fun, to make talk. Etoile told this, and everyone on the bayou say what a sassy girl Isabel turn out to be, what would her poor mama say, could she know. And everybody say if her mama live, she ain't never act this way but behave and by now be marry with Clovis Broussard.

And Isabel is keep going on to church like she ain't doing nothing wrong, and everybody is wondering if she ain't. She really something, that girl, with her black eyes looking out at everybody like she watching them watching her and getting a big laugh herself. And then it happen! One morning Naquin is got up to go to work and Isabel still sleeping, not up with coffee drip. He mad, a man is got to have demitasse at five o'clock, and there is that girl fast asleep in her big four post bed. So to keep peace, he decide he don't need coffee but come back later when it time for breakfast. He go hoe, and an hour or two later, come back. He see she drip the coffee, the pot on table and one cup she drink out, but no breakfast. So he go, mad, to her door, and there is Isabel, all dress in her clothes, lying cross bed, and bed all muss up like she fight it. She lying on her face.

He call, "Isabel! Why you lie down? Why you don't be fixing something t' eat?" And she ain't answer. And he call, "Isabel! You get up this minute and come here!" But she ain't breathe but lie still. Just think, there is this poor man what raise that girl himself and she give him trouble last few month, and now no breakfast this morning and he come in hungry and find her lying there. He reach out to touch and she already cool. He cry, yes, he scream! He call her name and she ain't move. So poor Naquin run out the house and call loud and pretty soon somebody hear and some people come and in no time crowd come, and the sheriff, and he get the doc. And doc say she dead for sure, and she been poison.

How you like that, yes? Sure, you guess who done it, Spider is who, that what everybody say. Nobody ain't seen him around, but that don't mean he ain't around. So posse get ready and start looking, going in pirogue down bayou and on horseback and all over where Spider could be. But nobody ain't turn up no Spider. Somebody say he done been to California three week. Well, the women come bring thing to eat for all the cousin, aunt, and uncle who come. They find that Miss Isabel ain't kept her daddy house very clean. So they sweep and dust and put clean bedclothes on the bedsteads, all the time shaking their head at this fine come-to-pass, while Naquin sit on front gallery rocking and fanning and crying. Naquin's cousin, Marie Boudreaux, she bet she know what Isabel find wrong with herself and when she tell Spider, he give her something. But some women ain't so sure, and some say yes it so, and all the time, they dusting and mopping and fixing. Poor Naquin, he fit to be tied, crying and carrying on. He come in and sit down by table, and when he see coffee cup and drip pot, he cry and cry.

"That the last thing my baby have," he say, "and I come fussing cause she ain't fix my something t' eat! Oh, if I only know!"

Marie say, "What you crying for, S. J.? You know nobody bring shame on family like that girl. Ain't nobody from here do what she do!"

He start up to hit her. "Ain't no proof of shame!" he say.

"Well, everybody know it."

"Ain't no proof!"

About that time Esther Mae Arceneaux come in with plate fried chicken and put on table. Marie pick up Isabel's cup and the drip pot and go toward table where they wash dishes, and in comes doc saying where is that drip pot, he want to examine it. He bring glass bottle to pour the coffee in and there not much left in the pot, just enough for one cup after Isabel had hers. Everybody come watch doc pour that coffee out that pot, and there something floating in the black coffee. Everybody get real still and the doc take stick out of bag, all wrap and sterilize, and stir round and bring up what it is.

"It look like spider," he say. One man say it look like black widow, he sure. Everybody real quiet, ain't say nothing.

"That what kill my baby?" Naquin ask and doc say it so. Marie say Mr. Spider come put it there, it be his mark. But Esther Mae say, "Ain't no murderer going leave a way for sheriff to know who he is. Anybody know that. Isabel ain't wash that pot clean, and if she keep her mind on her business, she see that black widow in pot and not drip on him. Besides, Spider is way to California . . . he going try for movie."

Marie stare at her and say, "Humph," and twist herself out on gallery, her head in air. Naquin cry and cry, saying he accuse Isabel unjust.

Well, all the people in that kitchen stand around looking at that bottle doc putting in his bag, ain't nobody say nothing. That whole crowd been talking about that girl saying awfullest thing, but nobody say nothing now, nobody not look at nobody else, all just stand there first time in their life with nothing to say.

Isabel have biggest funeral in long time with lot of flower. Everybody go, and to be sure, some most likely thinking, poor Spider, he not know it happen. Cause right soon after, somebody say, "That Spider, he good looking boy going be movie star! He just a little old handsome flirt. I remember how cute he be, hanging round grocery store. I bet he promise Isabel to get her in movie too. Just think. Boy from here going be in movie!"

Anyway, we sit around in rocking chair and on swing in screen porch in Port Arthur and listen when this story be told. It like we back home, it so real. I tell you, when we all together, we home. And if you ever make a pass by Port Arthur on Sixteen Street, you get down and come in. We make you cup fresh drip—we let you see the pot clean—and we tell you some more story, yes.

KEEPING THE MYTH ALIVE

CHARLIE MCMURTRY

I was thirteen the first time I saw Wayne. He emerged from the early morning darkness, sitting on a horse as black as the night. Dad had a day's work planned and had called the foreman of a neighboring ranch to see if he could send someone to help us. The foreman, a friend of Dad's, said he'd send a man, and the cowboy would meet us on the road somewhere. Dad slowed the pickup to a stop, and we got out as the cowboy got off his horse. By the pickup lights I couldn't see much of him.

"My name's Wayne Petit," he said to Dad, as they exchanged names and shook hands. I kind of stood back, in the edge of the darkness, wishing I could see better and thinking of the strangeness of this early morning meeting in the middle of the road.

"Been waiting long?" Dad asked.

"No," Wayne said. "Damn mosquitoes were about to carry me off though."

Dad looked at the darkness surrounding us and then at the cowboy and the horse again.

"It was pretty dark coming across that pasture, wasn't it?" Dad questioned. We could barely see the barn light at Wayne's, high on a hill, a good three or four miles away.

"Damn right it was," Wayne chuckled, glancing at the tiny speck of light, "and this black son-of-a-pooch was wanting to throw me off. It was so damn dark I could barely see his head."

We loaded the black horse into the trailer, climbed into the pickup and headed on up the road.

I got a better look at this cowboy in the dim cab light, and he looked to be in his twenties. I'd been going with Dad a long time, and this was the first young cowboy I'd seen in a while. Dad was sixty-two that year, and most of the neighboring ranchers were near his age. I was always the youngest around any cow-working.

Wayne was slim, broad-shouldered, and muscular. He wore a sleeveless shirt, which was kind of strange for a cowboy, a felt hat, though it was summertime, a pair of shotgun-style leggings with big, silver dollar-sized conchos down each leg, and a pair of spurs that jingled as loud as Dad's. He pulled a sack of tobacco from his shirt pocket, rolled a cigarette, found a match that he struck with his thumbnail, and lit his smoke. Then he looked at me through a long stream of smoke and stuck the match in the side of his mouth. God, I thought, he looks exactly like a cowboy ought to look.

"You have a name?" he asked, with a big, old friendly smile on his face. He cocked one leg over a knee and spun the big rowel on his spur.

"John" I replied. I was looking at him, thinking about him riding that bronc across four miles of pitch-dark pasture. That took real nerve.

"Well, John," Wayne said, "you can call me Hotshot." My heart nearly skipped a beat and then began to race. Dad's head jerked around suddenly.

"You're Hotshot Petit?" Dad asked.

"Yeah," Wayne laughed, "someone at the Waggoner Ranch gave me that nickname when I was a kid, and I've been trying to live up to it ever since."

I couldn't believe my luck. I'd heard the men tell stories about a young, extremely wild and reckless cowboy called Hotshot, who worked for Waggoner's. They claimed there wasn't anyone wilder or crazier than this man, and he was sitting in the pickup next to me. It was said that he could ride anything with hair on it, and rope and do everything better than anyone had seen it done before. He was a living legend.

"Well, I'll be damned," Dad said. "Well, that's good. Yeah, nicknames have a way of sticking to ya." Even Dad was a little impressed, though, of course, he tried not to sound like it, and, of course, Hotshot paid it no mind.

"I guess they do," Hotshot said, "anyway, I quit that outfit about a month ago and came to work for Cowans. I haven't had time to get around and meet anybody yet."

"You will today," Dad said, "and we're glad to have you. We could use some more young hands around here."

Dad resumed his normal, strictly-business tone, and they talked on a minute or two about the weather, cattle prices, horses, and so on. It was just getting acquainted kind of conversation, and I was only half-listening. The light was getting better, and I was taking in every inch of this man.

Hotshot looked at me again. I guess he could feel my eyes on him.

"Yeah, I started drawing pay from Waggoner's when I was about your age," he said, looking me right in the eye. "You wanting to be a cowpuncher too?"

Hotshot was talking to me but Dad answered.

"Hell, he doesn't know what he wants to be," Dad said,"but he's going to get lots of practice at cowboying and ranching while he makes up his mind."

Hotshot laughed at Dad's remark and winked at me. "Why, ya look like ya got the makin's of a damn good hand to me," Hotshot said.

"I'm learning," I said, grinning. I couldn't think of anything else to say. I'd never met a legend before.

"Hotshot," Dad said, "you'll probably find things on these smaller ranches a little tame compared to the big outfits, but most of us still do things the cowboy way. I do everything I possibly can on horseback. I figure the good Lord gave a horse four legs and me only two for a reason."

"Sounds plenty good to me," Hotshot said, chuckling. "I've damn sure got a bunch of 'em to ride." He looked at me again.

"Hell, you're old enough to ride a few broncs, John," Hotshot added. "I started riding 'em when I was younger than you are. Maybe you can come by and give me a hand sometime?"

Dad didn't say anything to that, so I did.

"Well, I don't know much about bronc riding, but I'd be glad to come help," I said. I really didn't know much about young horses, but there wasn't anyone who wanted to learn any more than I did.

"You're not going to learn any younger," Hotshot said. He winked at me again, and laughed that easy way that I was already beginning to like.

"Well, here we are," Dad said, slowing the pickup. "It's time to go to work."

We had reached our ranch, but I remember wishing we'd had another hour's drive at least. I wanted to talk to Hotshot some more, but around one of Dad's workings, I really had to be on my toes. Dad expected me to know as much as possible, as soon as possible, and he wasn't long on patience. He'd chew my butt out if I didn't pay attention to the work, and that day he chewed on it plenty because I couldn't keep my eyes off Hotshot.

Several times during the day, I'd be in my usual sulk after I'd got a butt chewing for something, and Hotshot would ride up beside me laughing and grinning. I'd never thought there was anything funny about butt chewings until he came along.

"Hey, Honcho," he'd say, grinning from ear to ear, "do ya know what ya did wrong just then?" I didn't know what Honcho meant, but I sure liked the way it sounded, and he was talking to me.

I'd shake my head no, so he'd explain. Sometimes he could even make a joke out of it, so I'd laugh too.

One time, after I really did screw up royally, he looked at me, shaking his head. "Honcho," he said, looking solemn for just an instant, "you got the makin's, but you're going to have to get your head out of your butt, or your Daddy's not going to let you live to see twenty."

We both just roared with laughter. Cowboying had never been this much fun. And I wasn't the only one to benefit from Hotshot's presence. The other men, including Dad, took to him instantly, and he to them. Cow-workings were not necessarily solemn affairs, but the work demanded a serious attitude. Hotshot's easy laughter and his constant banter with me and the others changed the tone. Even Dad laughed more than I'd ever heard him laugh before. The hard, hot workday fairly flew by.

Late that afternoon, Hotshot rode up beside me, while we were sitting around the roundup. He sat there, looking like he and that black horse were glued together, just looking me over good.

"So Honcho, ya think ya want to be a cowboy, do ya?" he asked. He was dead serious.

"Yeah, I do. I like it, sometimes," I answered.

"Well I've got some bad news for ya," Hotshot said. "Your Dad's not gonna let you have time to be a cowboy. He wants you to go from boy to cowman right away. I've seen it happen before."

"I know he wants me to be something," I said. "I'm just not sure what."

"That's where I'm gonna help-ya out," Hotshot said. "Do ya know what the difference between a cowboy and a cowman is?"

I wasn't sure, but it seemed like cowmen were old and cowboys were young, but I knew there was more to it. There were a few older men around who Dad claimed were "old, worn-out cowboys who never amounted to much, never owned anything but a saddle," and unless that was all I wanted to be, he said, then I'd better learn to think, study cows, and pay attention constantly.

"I don't know for sure," I said, "but I think that Dad's a cowman and you're a cowboy."

"You're right as rain about that," Hotshot said. "I may or may not be a cowman someday, but right now I'm a cowboy, and that's all I intend to be."

"So what's the difference?" I asked.

"Well, it's pretty hard to explain," he said, "but I'll give it a shot."

About then I had to ride off a ways. Dad was looking at me pretty hard, but I didn't go so far but what I could still hear Hotshot.

"Honcho, it's all in the way ya look at things," Hotshot said, "and how ya feel about 'em."

"What do you mean?" I asked.

"A cowman like your Dad looks at these cows, this work, everything, as a way of making a living," Hotshot said. "It's serious business to him, and he figures the sooner you get serious about this stuff, the more likely you are to be a cowman yourself someday."

I nodded my head, thinking, listening. "And a cowboy?" I asked.

"But to a cowboy Hotshot said, "punching cows, riding horses is a living. A cowboy don't give a damn who owns 'em, as long as he can have some fun doing what he does best and draw a little pay for doing it, and neither should you, not now, and there's not a damn thing wrong with looking at it that way. Leave that serious, worrying about everything crap to the old-timers. You savvy?"

He rode off a ways then, probably to let me think about what he'd said. It made sense. I liked to do things with cows; I liked to be around 'em; I liked to work 'em; but I didn't like to think about 'em all the time, like Dad wanted me to. I rode over closer to Hotshot again.

"Hotshot, I think that I understand," I said. "So what do I do now?"

"Ya go right on doing what you're doing," Hotshot said. "Ya watch, listen, pay attention, and learn, but ya quit worrying about doing everything right. Hell, butt chewin' never hurt anybody. I've had plenty of 'em. Laugh once in a while. It's a hell of a lot more fun."

That all sounded pretty good, but I hadn't forgot about Dad's part in this yet.

"But what about Dad and his wanting me to be a cowman?" I asked.

"That'll all come in time, Honcho. Trust me. Many a good cowman was a hell of a good cowboy first," Hotshot said, and he paused for just a second, "like your Dad."

That stunned me. Dad had always been an old-timer to me. "Dad, a cowboy like you?" I asked, unbelieving.

"Damn sure was," Hotshot said. "I'd heard of him long before I met him today, from other old-timers. But he's forgot about the fun of them old days where you're concerned.

I was still having trouble thinking of Dad and Hotshot as the same thing, but Hotshot himself said it was so.

"Then it ought to be all right for me to be a cowboy first," I said, thinking, getting excited.

"That's what I'm tellin' ya. You're catching on," Hotshot said, "and if ya really want to be a cowboy, I'll help ya."

"You mean it?" I asked.

"Ya damn right, I mean it," he said. "Me and you gotta be *compadres*. We're the only ones around here under fifty. We've gotta stick together."

I didn't have the slightest idea what *compadres* meant. But if Hotshot said it, and we were going to be, then it had to be good. I was all for it.

"What do ya say, Honcho?" he asked. "We got a deal?"

"I say damn right. We got a deal." Lord, I felt so good I could just squeal.

He grinned at me real big then and rolled himself a cigarette.

"Now we'd both better spread apart a little more," Hotshot said, "and start paying attention, or we'll be needing another job tomorrow." He winked at me again and rode off.

I couldn't remember ever feeling as good as I felt right then. Something was different; I could feel it.

When we finished the work that day, we hauled Hotshot home and met his wife and baby. I hated to go off and leave him, but I knew that he'd be coming to help us regularly from then on. I guess that I was pretty quiet on the way home. I couldn't quit thinking about Hotshot and the things he'd said. Dad looked different too. I kept glancing at him, trying to imagine him and Hotshot as the same thing, and I wanted to keep it all to myself, sort of a secret that I could play with over and over in my mind.

"What's on your mind?" Dad asked.

"Hotshot," I said. I wasn't going to turn loose of much.

"He's something, isn't he?" Dad said. "He's ever bit as good as any cowpuncher I've ever seen, and I've seen a bunch."

"I like him," I said.

"Yeah, you two seemed to hit it off," Dad said. "I noticed you all talking, maybe a little too much."

"He told me things," I explained.

"What kind of things?" Dad asked.

"Things about cowboys and cowboying," I said. "You know, just things that a cowboy needs to know."

"Did he talk about cowboys that he's been with and the things they've done?" Dad asked.

"Mostly about the ones he's heard about," I said, "and some about the way cowboys do things."

"That's damn good, son," Dad said. "That's the mark of a sure enough good hand. A good cowboy, or cowman either for that matter, always talks about the good ones he's known or worked with, not himself. Hotshot will be a damn good one for you to learn from. You remember that."

I gave Dad a good, long, hard thirteen-year-old's look then.

"Okay, I sure will," I said.

That night, I got Mom's scissors and cut the sleeves out of my work shirts. I put a rope string on my saddle and decided to carry a rope, even though I didn't know how to use one. I told Dad that I wanted to buy a felt hat, and before I went to bed, I went out to the barn and practiced saying things like Hotshot said them. I even tried to walk like he did. I was determined to remember everything, especially how Honcho sounded a whole lot like a cowboy's nickname.

COCONINO ESCARPMENT

GRANT SISK

Cowboy Bob sidles his horse up to the edge of the Coconino Escarpment and peers over the edge of the bluff where a herd of cattle they were chasing has just plunged. Cowboy Bob looks down into the bottom—about three hundred feet below—and takes in the scene. Two hundred and fifteen cows are piled there, quietly assuming the ambient temperature. Roughly four-hundred-thousand pounds of Grade A beef. He curses quietly. Cuthbert, his horse, whinnies and stamps one of his hooves. Yes, thinks Cowboy Bob, it's better we go now, and assemble the others.

Cowboy Bob rides slowly back to camp, contemplatively braiding the fringe on his black leather chaps, and thinking about what the other cowboys will say. Mr. Frazer, Cowboy Bob's employer, will not be pleased, nor will Olaf, the foreman. Olaf personally raised the herd, winnowing out the bad blood and culling the weak until it was the envy of every cattle rancher within 200 miles.

Cowboy Bob rides into camp to find he is the last to arrive. He dismounts, unsaddles Cuthbert, and slowly approaches the campfire where the others are in repose. It is early evening and already there is a chill in the autumn air. Mike, one of the cowboys, speaks first.

"Here he is finally—Bob, what in hell have you done t'yer chaps? You look like one a them faggots down there to New York City or somethin'."

"Did you find the herd?" Olaf asks. Olaf is concerned. Cowboy Bob takes a deep breath, looks at each in turn and says, "No."

The cook brings Cowboy Bob a plate of red beans and sourdough bread. Coffee hisses over a primus stove.

"We didn't see hide ner hair of 'em neither," says Melrose, the other cowboy. "I been lookin' all day. I'm startin' ta think mebbe the Goverrment come in here with one them Stealth-like hellachoppers and swooped 'em off to do secret tests on 'em."

"I looked all day too," Mike asserts, beans and tobacco juice streaming down his chin. "But I don't know nothin' about no secret 'hellachoppers'."

"I stayed in camp, calling and ringing the cowbell," Olaf says mournfully. "All day. They never came."

Cowboy Bob thinks it highly unlikely they ever will. He looks at each in turn.

"I rode all day, northeast along the top of the Coconino Escarpment as you requested. I never saw them," Cowboy Bob says convincingly. He eats slowly and with great care. He does not spill.

"Well, we done cuvert this whole valley end ta end," Mike says, looking at Olaf. "What you say, Chief?"

"I guess there ain't no need to keep watch tonight," Olaf says, looking at Cowboy Bob. "There's nothing to watch over. Tomorrow we'll ride farther west. Maybe they're in the next valley." Olaf spreads his groundsheet out, throws a couple of blankets on top, looks at the surrounding countryside, and rings the cowbell, twice. Almost all of the men strain their ears to listen, as if expecting the dumb brutes to answer. Olaf sighs and climbs under a blanket. The rest sit up a little longer. Mike fiddles with his pocket knife and eventually cuts himself. Melrose and the cook play checkers, stopping every so often to take sips from a silver flask. The game continues until they get mad at each other. They eventually wander off to their respective bedrolls, leaving Cowboy Bob to his thoughts.

Cowboy Bob leans back against his saddle and looks out into the night. Past the circle of firelight, the colors fade from red-orange to neon blue. Frost has begun to form on the leaves of the bushes and the cactus spines. Steam rises off the bigger, dark colored rocks. His breath begins to steam. Cowboy Bob rolls a cigarette, but it is big and lumpy. Rolling cigarettes is something he will have to work on, he decides. He lights it and blows a puff toward the Coconino Escarpment.

The next day breaks cold, but clear. The cook serves bacon and more sourdough rolls. It will be a day of searching. Cowboy Bob chews the stringy bacon and ruminates. He is thinking of when he was in the business world.

Those days, though only months removed, hide in his memory like the events of a past incarnation, shadowy and vague. Melrose comes and sits beside Cowboy Bob, carefully angling his plate so he does not spill its contents. He fails.

"Don't worry none 'bout them cows, Bob," he says. "They'll turn up over yonder in one a those valleys we ain't checked yet. They're all probly wanderin' round askin' each other 'Where'd they go?' and bein' stupid. Like cows tend to do."

Cowboy Bob knows that Melrose has always liked him, though he thinks Melrose is not sure why. Neither is Cowboy Bob. He flicks some dust off his black shirt and squints into the morning sun. Olaf calls out for everyone to saddle up and head for the next valley, due west. They all ride together for an hour or so, talking idly about where they would go if they were lost cows. Cowboy Bob knows where they would go if they were lost cows being chased by him. The air is crisp and scented with the smell of cedar, dust, and a strong organic horse odor.

When they reach the valley, Olaf reins in next to Cowboy Bob and tells him to search along to the northeast again. It is the roughest country, and Olaf knows this. He also knows that it was Cowboy Bob who let the herd slip off in the first place. Cowboy Bob nods his head once and adjusts his black bolero. He thinks of Clint Eastwood in *A Fist Full of Dollars* and makes a mental note to get a serape. Maybe one made from a Navajo blanket. As he rides away from the others, Cowboy Bob wishes he could make Cuthbert and himself thin out and stretch to the top of the screen, like Clint Eastwood.

When Cowboy Bob is out of sight of the others, he rides around slowly, looking for a good place to stop. After fifteen minutes he finds the kind of place he is looking for. He looks around, once, and then dismounts. He loosens the cinch on Cuthbert's saddle and ties the reins to a post oak. Then he unrolls a blanket and sits on it. He rolls a cigarette—this one a little less lumpy—takes a pack of playing cards out of his shirt pocket, and begins a hand of Solitaire. Hours pass. Occasionally, Cowboy Bob will look up from his game, back toward the Coconino Escarpment, as if looking for the herd. Cowboy Bob thinks about the others, riding around in big, lazy circles, looking for something they will never find.

At the camp that night, ten miles farther from the previous night's, an air of annoyed persecution settles over all the men, including Cowboy Bob. Solitaire always leaves him depressed. The others still want to know where the cattle are. Olaf has been crying now and the cook looks around suspiciously, though at no one in particular. Mike starts playing with his knife, but evidently is struck by a thought, puts it away, and looks at his cut. Melrose takes a pint bottle of whiskey out of one of his saddle bags and passes it around. Cowboy Bob goes out among the rocks. Cowboy Bob thinks about the herd, lying at the base of the cliff, carcasses stiffened, eyes clouded in death. He rubs his hand across his eyes and down the side of his face, feeling his three-day beard. Cowboy Bob used to shave every day, wear expensive suits and Italian shoes. He used to go by the name of Lawrence Bascombe. Now he works for room and board, plus seventy-five dollars a week spending money. He is content this way.

Cowboy Bob takes his wallet out and fishes a business card from it. He doesn't remember whose card it is, and does not read it. He carries it to remind himself of how he hated Fort Worth. On the back of the card is scribbled "John. Lunch sometime. Mobile phone #691-5537." It may have been a client's. The corners of the card are rounded off because of late Cowboy Bob has been using it to clean between his teeth.

Cowboy Bob dozes off and has a dream. He dreams he is downtown in some huge city, riding down a major street. As far as he can see are skyscrapers that go to the horizon and beyond. Off in the distance he can just make out the outline of a mountain. It is the noon rush and everywhere he looks, people are laughing and pointing at him. As he rides he hears someone playing the same three chords on a guitar, slightly out of tune. He is on a horse he's never seen, and as they travel it begins to go lame, slightly at first, then worse and worse until it stops in the middle of an intersection and refuses to go any farther.

Cowboy Bob takes his revolver out of the holster, cocks it and places it at the back of the horse's skull, right between its ears. He pulls the trigger and as the gun bucks in his hand, he tries to jump clear of the falling animal, but one of his boots gets hung up in a stirrup and the horse falls on him, pinning him to the pavement.

Ants begin to crawl out from under manhole covers and sewage drains. As they trickle across the ground towards him, Cowboy Bob looks up, and realizing he'll never make it to the mountain, begins to cry. He wakes up.

There are tears frozen in small rivulets down both his cheeks. Cowboy Bob sits up straighter and wipes them off. His joints are stiff and he thinks he should go to sleep, but he's afraid he'll dream.

Cowboy Bob returns to camp to find Olaf kneeling by the fire, slowly feeding small sticks into it, and fanning it with his hat. A thick, white smoke rises lazily, but stays close to the ground. Mike and Melrose wake up coughing and swearing. Olaf goes to his bedroll to try to sleep. He does not ring the cowbell. Cowboy Bob sits by the fire for the rest of the night, watching it slowly fade to ash but doing nothing to replenish it. This is his nature and he accepts it.

He is still thinking about the herd, but now his thoughts run more to the abstract. In the random occurrence of that plunge, he thinks he detects the presence of a twisted logic. He is confident that eventually he will overtake it, or it will overtake him. He thinks about the city where he once worked, the cars, buses, sidewalks, and the glass buildings that seemed to force their way up through the pavement. He thinks about the people and the dead herd. He sees very little difference. His thoughts fade away to sleep.

Olaf nudges him with his boot. It is full morning.

"Coming with us today?"

"Yes. Of course," he says, getting up. Cowboy Bob dusts himself off with one hand and holds a stick in the other. "Where are we going?"

Olaf looks up at the sky and grimaces. "West. They must be farther west than I thought. You sure you checked out the Coconino Escarpment? You sure you looked real hard?"

"I looked for them all day, you know that. I was the last one back to camp. They're probably out there, just over the next hill."

"I hope so," Olaf returns, "I miss the herd."

Cowboy Bob looks away from the startling blue of Olaf's eyes. They remind Cowboy Bob of his grandmother's. He doesn't look back until Olaf is gone. Mike and Melrose are cinching their saddles down, looking their horses over and not saying anything.

Melrose looks fearfully overhead as a black helicopter, flying high and fast, darts its shadow across the camp.

A MATTER OF TIME

A. C. GREENE

It was like all the maps strangers drew for you. It wasn't right.

The thin, blue line the old man at the store had drawn across the back of the envelope wavered off to the right. The road wavered off to the left. Where was he supposed to waver to? Something had been left out.

"Cross the creek about a hundred yards below the old rock pen . . ." he'd said. What was below? Was it below *this* or *this*?

But this couldn't be the wrong road. It was the only road. If it was the wrong road it was bound to be the right road, too.

So he wavered left with the road and put the map down on the front seat of the car.

The road was rough and getting rougher. It climbed over ridges and backbones on the rolling, hilly country just for the joy of climbing them, then dropped right back down into the swells and draws it had climbed out of.

What made him maddest was he should know this country. He was sure that sometime in his fifty years he had been out here. He was no newcomer. He had been born in this region. But this stretch had him whipped.

There were no landmarks to follow except the hills away off in the west. But they were too far to gauge your distance by. They seemed to be on your left whether you were going north, northeast or northwest. It didn't matter.

He bumped across a cattle guard the old man hadn't mentioned either and found himself in a wide pasture which he could look across for miles without a thing to break the vision.

After he had driven through the cattle guard he went for several miles, or several minutes at least, and stopped. He got out of the car and went out and stood on a front fender to look around. Then he saw a house. It stood off to the left. It was the first sign of life he'd turned up in the past thirty minutes.

He drove toward it and the house would disappear as he went through a draw, but the road was definitely going toward the house. He finally came out into a pleasant sort of little valley in the endless sea of landscape he had been traveling. There were willow trees around the back of the house which meant there was a spring.

The house was stone, the kind of a house that had been built when this was frontier country.

He opened the yard gate and went to the front porch. He knocked quickly on the door-facing; there was no screen and the door stood open. Nobody answered his knock so he called out, "Anybody home?" Nobody answered that, either.

He looked into the house because he couldn't imagine anyone going off and leaving the door wide open like that. When he did, he discovered the old woman sitting right there in the rocking chair. He jumped, it scared him so.

He could tell he had awakened her when he called; either that or she was deaf and just hadn't heard him.

"Hello," he said.

Her lips moved before he heard her say anything.

"Come in." It was dry, soft, yet with a harsh edge to it.

"Pardon me, ma'am," he said. "I didn't know you were asleep or I wouldn't have hollered and waked you up." He felt awkward.

She looked at him very closely before she spoke again, and she said, "You caught me."

"Pardon?"

"Nappin'. I was takin' a nap."

He smiled and stepped through the doorway. She was seated right by it. She should have heard him knock. She must read lips, because if the knocking hadn't waked her, she was bound to be stone deaf. That was all. He spoke loudly and distinctly.

"I'm looking for some people named Abercrombie," he said.

"Who?" She seemed to hear well enough.

"Abercrombie."

She thought it over for a long time.

"They used to be some Abercrombies hereabouts, but I ain't seen an Abercrombie for quite a spell."

"I believe they're still around here," he said, "but I can't seem to find them."

"Used to be it was Gus lived down on th' Pine place," she continued as if she hadn't heard him. "Lived on th' Pine place and ran a little short herd. Wasn't no good. Gus ner th' herd neither one. I ain't seen ner heard of Gus Abercrombie since about th' time Hinton was a baby."

"I don't think I'm looking for Gus Abercrombie," he said. "Is there another house around here close where I might find out?"

She looked at him again in her curious way and shook her head. "Naw. Less you wanta ride half th' day west to th' Starbuck ranch. You call that close, it's over ther't Peace Mountain."

Peace Mountain? Good Lord, that was the landmark that was too far away for him to use. He know good and well there were other ranches around here besides the Starbuck ranch, wherever that was.

Maybe somebody else in the family could tell him. This old granny wasn't to be depended on.

"Ma'am, any of your family around here?"

She looked at him when asked and shook her head.

"I got two sons livin' in Rock Hole."

Rock Hole? He'd never heard of the place.

"But don't you have anybody working the place for you?"

She surely didn't live alone out here. He had seen a woodpile out in the back, and it looked like there was a little vegetable garden to one side of the house. Somebody was here. She couldn't do the work.

"Yes," she finally replied, "I've got a lazy grandson here, but he's th' out'enist no-good boy they ever was."

She leaned forward in her chair and put her hand to her mouth.

"Santher," she called, "oh, Santher . . . you come in here."

"Who are you calling?"

"I'm callin' Santher, my grandson. He stays off yonder beyond th' spring so's he can't hear me."

"Santher? Your grandson's named Santher?"

"Yes," she said, "I named him myself when he was borned. His mother died. Santher Williams."

The visitor went slowly toward the door, backing.

"I believe I know now how to find the Abercrombie place," he said softly. "It just came to me. I think I know."

She looked at him and suddenly she smiled and lifted one hand as if to stay him for a moment.

"Don't go," she said, "You don't know how lonesome it gets out here waiting. I just don't seem to see nobody anymore. You're th' first one that's been by in such a spell, such a blessed long spell."

But he had run out of the door and was going across the yard, not looking back. He got into the car, spun the wheels and whirled off in a cloud of dust and rock, back up the road the way he had come.

He topped the ridge out of the green valley and drove recklessly down the rock path until he was completely out of sight of the house. Away in the west he could see Peace Mountain.

He finally came to the cattle-guard, jolting across onto the gravel road, and stopped the car. He got out and looked closely at the road. Thank God. There were tire marks, automobile tire prints. Not his, either. Someone else had been here sometime.

He wiped his forehead and took out a pack of cigarettes. His hands shook as he lighted one with a beautiful silver lighter engraved "Santher Williams IV."

REDEMPTION

MARLA COOPER

Cooney McGraw stood up from where he squatted in the field. Squinting against the sun, he looked his brother L. D. right in the eye. He couldn't match his brother's height, but his build was heavier, more muscular. "I ain't gonna do it," he said with the edge of a dare. He did not blink.

L. D. said, "The damn water's full of ants. I can't drink it I tell you! Now go get me some more!"

"I called you good and loud when I got back here with this bucket. It's your own damn fault you didn't get it 'fore the ants did." Cooney was sick and tired of being told what to do. "I *ain't* going, I tell ya."

Since their pa, Ballard McGraw, had been picked up by the law for bootlegging whiskey, the two boys had been running the farm. That wasn't an easy task on days like this when weeds had to be chopped in the cotton field. A couple of kids could get mighty thirsty working in the sun on a hot August morning. Cooney, the 14-year-old, had gone back to the house and drawn a bucket of water. He'd hauled it the half mile or so to the field where he and his brother L. D., his *older* brother at 16, worked. That's the way things were done in the late 1930s on a family farm on the Staked Plains.

L. D.'s eyes flashed as he said, "I'm warning you, ya' little brat. That water ain't fit to drink and I'm thirsty. Now turn your butt around and git!" With that, he kicked the pail over. Water and ants flooded one lucky cotton plant.

"Suit yourself L. D. I done had my drink. Reckon you'll have to find yours someplace else."

"I won't be finding it." L. D. took a step toward Cooney and pushed him at the shoulders. "*You're* going after it!"

Fear raced through Cooney's head. Hate, the kind of hate only a little brother can have, won out over his fear. Before he knew it, his meaty right hand had doubled into a club. Hell bent, it caught L. D. in the gut.

Only slightly did L. D. crumple. Cooney caught the look of utter surprise in his brother's eyes. Furrowed brows and fury weren't far behind.

Cooney's innards knotted up. Suddenly he knew beyond any doubt that he was in serious trouble. It might have come too soon, but the time to take a stand was upon him. Time for *him* to be the one to say how things were going to happen.

L. D. lunged for him and together they fell over the cotton into the mud and the dust. They struggled, rolling back and forth between the rows, each trying to hold enough control to deliver a good solid wollop.

Cooney kneed L. D. in the groin. He huffed and released his hold long enough for Cooney to jump up. He was standing, arms positioned and ready to fight fair when L. D. recovered.

L. D. stood with steely eyes and said, "You chicken shit. That ain't no way to fight. I'm gonna whup your ass the way a *man* would." L. D. raised his arms and in the briefest of moments jabbed at Cooney's face with his strong right. Cooney dodged, but the fist grazed its mark leaving an ugly tear near his eye. It poured blood. Thrown off his center for just a bit, Cooney recovered and ducked in time to avoid the second slug from his brother's wicked right.

Hoping for an opening to his belly, Cooney danced in front of L.D. When it came, his left shot out. The punch was solid. L. D. went down. Cooney jumped in the middle of him, punching again and again at his face, at his gut.

Years of little brother frustrations rumbled out of Cooney. The summer's weight gain kept him on top of his skinny brother. L. D. landed a few good ones, one on Cooney's jaw; but he never again managed to come up on top. Blood from the cut on Cooney's face splotched both their overalls. L. D. bled from the nose and his lip.

When Cooney felt the fight go out of L. D., he rocked back on his heels. That's when he saw it. The pouch of tobacco that had fallen from L. D.'s shirt. And the box of matches.

His breathing was too ragged to say a word. He only looked at L. D. There in the middle of a dusty cotton field, the brothers swapped a powerful look.

And all the power belonged to Cooney, the *little* brother.

He got off L. D., pulled a blue bandanna from his back pocket and said, "Now. I'm going to the house. And I won't be coming back with no water." He daubed the rag to the cut on his head and looked at it. He turned away from L. D. Though it hurt, his swelling jaw pulled into a tight grin as he started for home.

The half-mile seemed like it had lost a bit to Cooney. Before he went in the house, he drew another bucket from the well and washed his face. The racket brought his ma to the back door. Letha McGraw hollered out to him, "L. D., is that you and Cooney? What're you boys doing back so soon?"

When Cooney stepped in from the heat of the day, his mama got a good look at him. She gasped. Blood and dust covered his clothes. Spots of mud clung here and there. Jonah, his five-year-old brother, gaped up at him.

She said, "Lord, child, what happened to you?" Then her brow wrinkled as she thought of where he was supposed to have been and with whom. She said, "Where's L. D.?"

"I'm right here, Mama." L. D. came through the front door and stood against the door jam holding his side.

He must have seen me out back, thought Cooney.

Cooney looked rough but, L. D. looked like he'd been run over by the cows! Caked blood hid most of his face. His leg showed through holes in his overalls. Splotches were beginning to darken on his arms below the sleeves of his shirt. One eye looked as if it could swell shut, the white in the other had a bloody spot.

"L. D.!" Letha rushed to him and cried, "Criminy sakes, boys, what's happened here?" She spun on her heel and fixed Cooney with a stern look. "You got some explainin' to do."

"Ma, he ain't so bad off as he looks," Cooney began. He walked from the kitchen toward his brother taunting, "You ain't hurt, are ya' L. D.? You can't be beat up by your *little* brother, can ya' L. D.?" Out the corner of his eye he caught a quick movement coming from the direction of his ma.

Thwack! His sore jaw began to throb again. The slap his ma delivered stung, but there was more of Cooney hurting than just his jaw. He looked at his mom as if she had betrayed the deepest secret he had. But before she could say one word, Cooney pushed past both of them. He left the screen door whining as he took the porch in one downward leap.

He heard his ma saying, "Let's get you cleaned up and you tell me . . ." The door slammed.

Cooney had long since given up tears. Still, hurt and anger led him to the cow pasture east of the house. He'd just go see what Frances, L. D.'s yearling calf, was up to. It took a damn animal to put up with L. D. Most humans had better sense.

As he stumbled through the yard, Cooney thought of the way things had been and how they would be from now on. *Even if Mama does stick up for L. D., I'm not taking any more shit off him! Pa ought to be here, not holed up in the jail. He wouldn't let L. D. get away with this crap. Just let that butt try to push me around! I'll whup his ass AGAIN. I hurt him. I know I did. What if Mama knew about him smoking. She'd have his hide for sure!*

He found Frances near the windmill, not far from the tank.She always recognized Cooney and made some little movement. Even if it wasn't the hoopla she'd throw for L. D., Cooney hoped she felt *something* for him. *Hell, just 'cause L. D.'s the one that nursed her along don't mean I can't be her friend too.* Today though, Frances seemed agitated. All the cows did. And there was something . . . something in the still summer air.

Cooney started to get a bad feeling. In his mind, a picture of cigarettes and matches and possibilities all fell into place. He ran south as hard as he could, 'til the house and barn were out of his line of sight. There, to the west, was a dirty smudge hanging just above the cotton field. *Smoke!*

Cooney ran back to the house and burst through the door. L. D. lay on the sofa. His mom sat in the big chair nursing his baby sister, Vossie. Jonah played at her feet.

"L. D.! There's a fire in the cotton field!" Cooney yelled between gasping breaths.

L. D. shot from the divan to the porch. He ran back for his shoes, issuing orders the whole way. "Grab some blankets, Cooney! Ma, keep the little ones in the house! We sure as hell don't need no babies underfoot now!"

"Mind your tongue young man!" came the automatic reply. Then she added, "You boys be careful, hear?"

Cooney knew it was times like this that made his ma anxious about him and L. D. taking charge of the farm. He pulled two of Letha's best quilts from the cedar chest in the front room and followed L. D. out the door. They ran west down the road toward the cotton field. As they ran, Cooney noticed L. D. holding his side where he had beat him earlier.

When they got to the field, the fire had not yet spread so far and wide the two boys couldn't handle it. If the wind stayed down, they'd have a chance.

But the wind never stays down for long on the Staked Plains in West Texas. Just as the last of the flames disappeared under the furrows of the hurled quilts, an ugly gust of wind blew life back into the enemy. Seemed like every dying ember on every plant had reignited. A tidal wave of heat washed over them. The boys were at it again with double the effort. Smoke and flying ash blew into Cooney's face. With each slap of the quilt he lost hairs on his arm.

The boys cussed and hollered, gritted their teeth and continued together to fight. With the wind's encouragement, the flames chewed down the rows of ripe cotton as if they were braids of firecrackers. Though they swatted at every fiery tongue and kicked dirt on the bits of burning debris that fell to the ground, they were losing the fight.

Cooney's arms ached, not only from the constant motion of slapping at the flames, but also from the morning's fist fight. L. D. caught his eye. His brother's face was set with determination. Cooney took some comfort knowing that whatever L. D. set his mind to, usually came out okay.

Over the crackling of the fire, L. D. hollered, "I'm going for the tractor. You keep on holding it back!"

The fire was only half a dozen rows from the field of hay the boys had yet to tie into shocks. The stubble left on the ground was like dried tender. Cooney slapped harder and harder at the flames. He knew that once that stubble and the hay drying on the ground caught fire, there'd be no stopping it. The fire would burn plumb to the house and the whole place, his ma, Jonah and little Vossie, would all go up in smoke.

The wind died for a bit. Cooney hoped he might make some progress. His eyes burned and his nose was full of smoke. He backed through yet another row of cotton, the dried bolls ready for harvesting tore at his overalls pleading for help. All alone with the angry licking flames, Cooney prayed for his brother's quick return.

Too soon he was forced to abandon his post. He ran south to the road. Cooney McGraw could only stand and watch as the fire wiped out a whole season's worth of cotton.

At last he heard something. But it wasn't the tractor chugging toward the field. Unmistakably, he heard the approach of his dad's old truck. He looked up to see the vehicle slowly coming down the road. With his arm sticking out the window, L. D. led Frances beside the truck. He slowed as he approached the cotton and turned onto the dried stubble of the hay field.

What in the world? Cooney thought. He wadded up what was left of the quilt and ran to the truck. He got there just as L. D. got out.

L. D. explained, "I couldn't get the damn tractor started. We're gonna have to drag Frances."

"What the hell are you talking about, L. D.?" Cooney hollered over the noise of the truck.

"I read it in a book about cowboys and fires on the prairie.

We need a firebreak. That's what the tractor was for, but the damned thing won't start. But Frances here, she'll make us a swell firebreak." He stroked the calf's neck and kissed her nose. That's when Cooney saw the tears streaming down his tough old brother's blackened face.

L. D. said, "Now I'm gonna drive the truck and you're gonna have to push it, little brother, with everything you got left in ya'. Here. Take Frances and follow me."

L. D. got back in the truck and drove a short distance down the field until he was almost directly in line of the fire's edge. Cooney had to run Frances just to keep up with him. The truck stopped, stirring up little bits of hay. L. D. jumped out and ran back to the bumper. He grabbed a length of rope waiting in the bed of the truck. A sledge hammer lay nearby. He threw one end of the rope to Cooney and said, "Here, leave about a foot then tie her leg good and solid to the bumper. Like I'm doing."

Cooney hadn't yet figured out what L. D. had in mind but did as he'd been told. Frances moved anxiously back and forth, fearing the fire. She stayed only because L. D.'s reassuring voice soothed her.

Finally the tying was done. The truck chugged and shivered with anticipation. L. D. took a deep breath and looked over the wild-eyed calf and the rope one more time. Cooney saw him bend toward Frances's ear and whisper something, but he couldn't make out what.

The gleam of sunshine on metal caught Cooney's eye. He barely had time to look away before he heard the sickening thud of the sledge hammer on Frances' head.

When Cooney looked again, L. D. had his Bowie knife sunk to the hilt in Frances' throat as she lay on her side. He slit the underside of the calf clear to her tail. L. D.'s eyes were dry as dust. He stood and said, "Now Cooney, you push like you ain't never pushed before!" He ran back to the front of the truck.

Looking down at the grisly mess that used to be Frances, his shoes coated with her blood, Cooney understood. It would take L. D.'s most prized possession to stop the fire. Cooney was awed. *How could he have done it? He loved that calf!*

Suddenly Frances' bashed-in head and spilled guts jerked forward. The smell of blood hit his nose. Shaking himself out of the shock, he pushed against the tailgate of the truck with all the strength he had left. The ropes stretched out the slack and gradually the calf's carcass began to inch forward.

A shiny puddle dragged out five yards, then ten in the August sun. Cooney had seen cows butchered before but always the gruesome task had some order to it. The way Frances' front legs were spread out kept the slit open to the ground. Her entrails caught on the stiff stalks of cut hay, coating them with wet gooey animal juice.

They dragged Frances like that the fifty yards or so that her wetness lasted. It was enough. The fire had burned much of the cotton, right up to the line between the cotton field and the hay. But the fire died when it tasted the trail Frances left.

Cooney hollered up to L. D., "That'll do it! Hey! That's enough now!" It was plain that a line stood between the fire and the house.

The truck stopped. Cooney ran to the cab. His big brother lay slumped exhausted over the wheel.

There wasn't much Cooney felt like saying. L. D. didn't look much in the mood to hear anything anyway. Love, the kind of love only a little brother can have, filled the void between them. A gentle breeze blew away the last of the smoke and ash. Cooney said, "Reckon I'll go back over the fire line and make sure this wind ain't stirrin' nothin' up."

L. D. grunted.

As Cooney walked away from his brother a second time that day, he thought of the terrible sacrifice L. D. had made to keep the farm safe. He wondered what secret his brother had whispered to Frances before he'd hit her.

Cooney ran over the fire line, checking every spot that might start again. He kicked a little dirt here and there. The fire had definitely died. So he turned toward home and ran even faster. When he got there, he drew a bucket of water, but was careful not to make any noise.

He walked slowly back to the field, thinking over the whole afternoon. *Man, that was some fire. What's Ma gonna say about the cotton?* But mostly he thought about L. D. and his calf. *Why Frances? How come he didn't just bring some water? I never seen a man hang on like that.*

When Cooney got back to the field, L. D. stood at the downturned tailgate of the truck finishing the job on Frances. He'd skinned her and was busy cutting the carcass into quarters. Cooney set the bucket next to him. L. D. barely noticed. "What'd you tell her, L. D.?"

191

His big brother gazed at him for a long time. He chuckled and said, "Shit, Cooney." L. D. looked over toward the house. "That don't matter." Smiling in the saddest way ever, he shook his head and took a long slow drink of water. Wiping his mouth with the back of his hand, he said, "Reckon we oughta go tell Mama it's gonna be barbecue for supper."

How We Got a New Screen Door

KATHY MILLER

Mama noticed the screen door right before supper. I'd been out trying to get Buford to leave the chickens alone (he's fond of catching them and then trying to figure out where the ears are which is kinda weird but he's only six so I guess it's all right), and I heard her let out a scream that could have woke the dead, or at the very least stirred some real old people. I came running from the barn with Buford in tow cause I figured that she'd seen what we'd done to the dog and was gonna whip us. See, me and Buford had been bored earlier that day and decided to see what would happen if you dip a hound in Mama's dye vat. The dog was kinda blue now (in more ways than one—we couldn't get him to eat and he spent the afternoon lying around with a glum look on his face) but we'd been careful about keeping him away from the furniture, so I figured she couldn't get too mad. Well, we get to the house and she's standing there with the kitchen screen wide open staring at it like it was some kinda cancerous mole on her arm. I thought the hound had smeared his big blue body all over it and she was gonna pitch a fit.

"Well. What do you think?" she asked in the same way that she had said, "Uncle Zeke passed away while reading a Minute Rice box" the night before my very first funeral. There was awe in her voice and emotion that I couldn't recognize.

"Think 'bout what Mama?"

"'Bout the screen door." Me and Buford looked at it real hard trying to see what she was talking about. I didn't see no blue dye on it, so she wasn't talking about the dog. There were lots of holes in the netting from all the times Buford passed toothpicks through it. Buford figured if you could pass anything through a closed door it meant you had superhuman powers. I didn't have the heart to tell him that the netting was made of little holes that anyone could pass toothpicks through. He eventually figured it out on his own, but by that time he'd made some mighty big holes (Daddy liked the extra large toothpicks on account of the rot givin' him a lot of space between his teeth) that stood out like pimples on a pig's butt. When I told Buford he might get whipped, he decided to make all the holes bigger, so that no one would notice. It was a long process (I figured there must be a billion holes), so he had only about a quarter of it finished the day Mama noticed the door.

"Is there a new hole in the screen?" I asked figuring that it would be better to get Buford in trouble than to find that I was being yelled at for something I'd forgotten I'd done.

"No, look real hard. You gotta open your mind up to see it." I tried but I just didn't see nothing. There were scratches and little bits of residue left from the neighborhood watch sticker that had once hung there (Daddy had stuck it on the inside of the door not realizing it wouldn't do any good if people on the outside couldn't see it). There was a couple of dark blotches from all the times Buford had leaned his greasy forehead against the door to see if he could open it without using his hands. Other than that I couldn't see what she was making all the fuss about.

"I'm sorry Mama, but I don't know what you're talking about."

She then looked toward Buford who shrugged and began to silently count the holes in the screen. She let out a sigh and then said, "Don't you see? The Lord Jesus's face is on our screen door!" Mama pointed at a shadow that extended from the end of the screen portion down to the wooden half of the door. It had a funny shape to it that didn't seem to be made by any trees or furniture nearby. I s'pose that to some it looks like the Lord Jesus in profile (there was a line that could be hair and a strange hump that might be a nose). To me it looked more like a bunch of asparagus, but I wasn't about to tell Mama that. Like a cloud it had a real vague shape that anyone could see just about anything in. "We're blessed boys. We have been blessed with a sign from the good Lord. Let today be the most important day of your lives."

I didn't know how to respond. Mama was getting tears in her eyes, and I was afraid she was gonna start reading us the Bible or something. Finally I said, "Are we gonna eat supper Mama? Buford and me are really hungry." She stared at me like I was speaking a foreign language and got a sad look on her face.

"Don't you boys realize how important this is?" Our lives are gonna change forever because of this screen door." I'm afraid I just didn't see that. I mean, it's not like we won the lotto or something. Rather than voicing my disbelief that the world as we knew it was going topsy turvy, I let Buford do the talking.

"Why?"

"Because anytime Jesus shows up in your house it means you're special."

"Why?"

"Well, because Jesus doesn't just show up for anyone so I reckon when he does it means it's pretty special."

"Why?"

"Because He's Christ. He has so many people to worry about that to pay so much attention to one family must mean we have a special mission and are worth all his trouble."

"Why?"

"Well we go to church and pray and always say grace before every meal . . ."

"Why?"

"Buford, are you capable of saying anything other than 'why'? Because Christ Child or no Christ Child, I am beginning to lose my patience."

"Why?"

We all went inside and I started setting the table while Buford tried to balance on his head without leaning against the wall. I think he thought if he looked at the door upside down he might be able to see what Mama saw. Instead, he turned a nasty shade of purple and got a nose bleed. By the time the table was set and Mama had finished garnishing the pork chops, we heard the front door slam close and Daddy scream, "I'm so hungry I could eat this damn blue dog!"

We all scrambled to our seats and waited for Daddy to make his grand entrance. Without her saying nothing, we knew Mama was waiting for Daddy to take notice of the door. He took his seat at the head of the table and began scraping food onto his plate. Once his trough was full, he began the holy ceremony of the first bite of the evening moving from the plate into his mouth. Mama couldn't wait any longer; she looked like she was about to burst.

"Henry do you notice anything different around here?" Daddy wasn't one for supper chit chat, but he loved Mama and was willing to sacrifice valuable eating time in order to make her happy. He surveyed the room for a moment and then turned to me and gave me a private wink.

"Son, why is the dog blue?"

"He fell into the vat, Sir. Me and Buford had to fish him out."

"And just why was the vat full of blue dye?"

"I don't know."

"If you want me to believe your story, you better come up with a better reason than that. I'd hate to start off my evening by punishing you."

"Yes, sir," He looked eagerly toward Mama to see if that had satisfied her. She shook her head and stared at him in a way that said, "How can you be so insensitive as to not notice something that's so important to me?" He surveyed the room again.

"Buford, why is there kleenex stuck up your nose?"

"Nothbleeth."

"That's a damn good reason." Once again he turned to Mama for approval and met her glare. For the third time he looked around the room like someone playing the championship round of "I spy." "You want to give me some sort of clue, so I don't end up making your eyeballs jump out of your head?" She continued staring at him with the pained look of a woman reevaluating her choice for eternal partnership. I couldn't stand it anymore. If Mama wasn't gonna play fair, I was gonna help him out.

"It has to do with the screen door, Daddy." With he smirk of a man about to finally eat his dinner, he turned toward the door and studied it inch by inch.

"Is it all them dang holes in the screen?" Buford and I shook our heads and Mama let out a rush of air that sounded like a steam engine. Daddy looked like he was starting to sweat. "Did someone repaint it?" I started feeling kinda bad for him. After a day out bargaining for seed, he was being forced to guess the last possible thing anyone would suspect about their screen door. I began to mouth "Baby Jesus" hoping that Mama wouldn't notice, and Daddy could say it like he thought it up.

Daddy stared at my mouth and began to mimic the motions of my lips. Finally he blurted out, "Maybe cheeses!" I let out a low moan and Buford began to giggle. Mama slammed her napkin onto the table and narrowed her glare until she looked vaguely like a badger.

"For your information Henry, the screen door has the image of the Christ Child on it."

Daddy turned toward the door again and stared intently at the pale shadow that Mama so adamantly insisted was Jesus. After a considerable silence he muttered, "Well I'll be darned. Will you look at that." He pushed back his chair and approached the door in a slow even stride that reminded me of a wedding. When he reached it, he dropped his knees and began to follow the outline with his hands. Mama joined him, and the two of them just stared at that shadow like it was a newborn baby or something.

For the rest of the evening they conducted a series of experiments. They blocked off all the light in the room and then approached the door with just a candle. The shadow was still there. They turned on every light in the house and put three lamps directly in front of the door. The shadow was still there. They wet the door with water, gravy, and 409. The shadow was still there. They even tried adding another coat of paint to the door just to see if it was something they could cover up. The shadow was still there. If you ask me it was kind of creepy.

Me and Buford went up to bed once it became obvious that the thing on the door was there to stay. I was feeling kinda queer about the whole thing and really wanted someone to talk to who wasn't gonna start flying off the handle about what a miracle this whole dang thing was. Buford wasn't one for talking but he was always a great listener.

"Hey Buford you wanna hear something strange?"

"Why?"

"Well, 'cause I wanna tell you." He didn't respond, which meant he was either listening or asleep. I decided he was listening. "I don't see it. I mean I see a shadow, but I honestly don't see Jesus. It just looks like a dark blob to me. Or asparagus. Nothing more." I paused hoping he would take that moment to say something. He didn't. "Do you think that means that Mama's making a lot more of this than there really is, or are only certain blessed people who are really good and never dye their dogs allowed to see it?" I really began to get scared about the whole thing. What if not seeing it meant you were going to hell? "It seems to me that the way Jesus looks in paintings and stuff is the way that we want him to look. I mean, he may not even be human and he most certainly isn't some young looking guy with a beard. So if he don't really look like that, why would he show up looking that way on our screen door?" My brain started hurting from thinking so hard, "Buford, can you hear me?" No response, not even an asthmatic whistle. "Buford, I ain't been talking to the wall this whole time have I?" More silence, followed by two tears that appeared at the corners of my eyes. "Damn you, Buford! Why can't I have me a brother that talks? Instead I got this damn weirdo who chases after chickens." I lay down and pulled the covers up to my neck. My hands began to play with the frayed ends of the blanket in hopes of that familiar movement making all this weirdness go away. I stared into the darkness for a long time trying to make sense of the shapes all them little particles of air make. Finally my eyes began to feel heavy, and ideas began to dart across my brain like ping pong balls. Just as I was about to catch hold of my first dream of the night, I heard a quiet sound beside me.

"Don't worry. I can't see it neither."

I don't remember dreaming much that night. When I woke up, I heard a lot of voices downstairs. I tiptoed to the landing and saw about twenty people including the minister and his wife standing in the kitchen and talking non-stop. In the center of the crowd were Mama and Daddy beaming like they'd just won a prize for most creative kitchen decor.

For that entire day there was non-stop traffic in our kitchen. I don't know how word about the screen door got around so fast, but there were people from two counties away taking photos and rifling through our silverware drawers. Mama made sure no one touched the door and that not a soul was allowed to walk through it. She even borrowed some of them fancy velvet ropes from the bank and fenced the door off so that you couldn't get closer than three feet. Me and Buford were forced to put on our Sunday best and stand around the kitchen like altar boys. That wasn't nearly as bad as having to talk to all the people.

"You must be a very special little boy to live in a house with the Christ Child," said one blue-haired lady just inches from my face. Her breath smelled like Mr. Smith's mentholated cough drops.

"It ain't the actual Christ Child, Ma'am, it's just an image." She looked a little ticked off at my statement and decided to turn to Buford for polite conversation.

"And what about you little man, you must be very excited about your screen door!"

"Why?"

"Well, because Jesus is on it."

"Why?"

"Well, we don't know why which is why it's such a miracle."

"Why?"

198

For the entire week we were subjected to hundreds of strangers who thought we were saints because of a stupid blob on our screen door. People were starting to make pilgrimages to San Antonio from as far away as Canada just to see the faint outline of a bunch of asparagus. Mama and Daddy were celebrities now. And Buford and me? Well, we kind of faded to the basement of everybody's mind. Mama only uttered two phrases to us: "Don't use that door, you know you can go around" and "it may be all right to chew with your mouth open when it's just me and Daddy, but I think you can learn some table manners now that Jesus is here." Daddy was just as bad. He treated me and Buford like we was unattended children in a museum. Every time we did something we got a lecture about "responsibility" and "discipline." Not only was dying the dog blue out of the question, but we couldn't so much as fart without being told it was improper behavior in the House of the Lord. I got dang tired of having to watch everything I did just because the Christ Child was emblazoned on our back door. It was easier to avoid the house altogether than to hang around and only get attention when I was doing something wrong. While I was hiding and looking for a chance to leave for good, Buford was making a plan.

One night after a week of masses and news interviews, Buford crept out of bed with two pieces of coal and a dirty kleenex. Rather than chasing after him, I let him go about his business figuring a good Buford performance would liven up the place. When he returned a half hour later, he was empty handed with a big grin across his toothless face. As tempting as it was, I decided to stay in bed and greet whatever he'd done in the morning with everyone else. I figured if I was really surprised to see what he had done, I couldn't get in trouble for it.

Mama started screaming around seven A.M. At first I thought the thing on the door had disappeared altogether. That was enough to get me to throw on some pants and run downstairs. When I got down there, Mama was standing at the screen door with Daddy and a very upset Buford. I'm not real sure what they were saying to him because the moment I saw the door I stopped listening. Someone who will remain nameless had snuck down in the night and added their own touches to the shadow on the door. I think the original intent may have been to just change the shadow by making the nose bigger and the beard big and wavy like Santa Claus's. Unfortunately, Buford had a problem with something called perception. See, when he looked at something, he usually saw it backwards like it was in a mirror. So when he de-

199

cided to give the thing on the door a real big nose, he didn't do it by putting it on top of the old nose—he put it on the opposite side of the head. Same with the beard and what I think may have been a wart. If you just looked at one side of the thing, you saw what Mama saw; if you looked at the other side, you saw something that looked like Karl Malden. If you looked at the whole thing straight on, it looked like some sort of warped Mickey Mouse whose ears were low and misshaped and who had some sort of thrush on his neck. You just had to laugh at it.

"Son, if you insist on that inappropriate laughter I suggest you go back upstairs." Daddy glared at me until I thought he might burn a hole straight through me. I quickly shut up and looked down at my feet. He turned his attention back to Buford.

"Buford, do you know what 'desecration' means?" Buford shook his head and I felt a snicker escape me. I don't think Buford even knew what "know" meant. "It means to destroy a holy object. It's a bad thing son. A *real bad* thing." Buford nodded his head and began to trace the outline of the new shadow with his finger. He looked like a puppy who didn't understand why he was being punished since peeing on a new rug was a great show of affection. "Why'd you do it boy?" Buford shrugged his shoulders. "Didn't you know it was wrong? Haven't we raised you to understand when something's wrong?" Buford nodded in response to the second question and continued mapping out his version of the shadow's shape. "Can't you answer me boy? Use your voice! Tell me why you did this to something so important to your mother." Buford finished connecting the lines of the shadow and then turned to meet Mama's eyes while he answered Daddy's question.

"I don't know."

Mama looked away from him and stared back at the shadow. Her eyes filled up with something strange, like the cloud that had been Jesus had also revealed itself as a choo choo train. She glanced up at Daddy and then quietly said, "I think you boys oughta leave for a while. Why don't you find something to do until supper."

We spent the day in the barn playing like we lived in a haunted house. One of Buford's favorite things in the whole world was to be scared. I figured that we oughta do something fun for him on account of Mama being so upset. I would hide and be the ghost and then Buford would walk in all scared and nervous 'cause he knew I was there but he didn't know where.

After a while, we switched parts, but Buford was so nervous about upsetting Mama that he kept farting and giving away where he was hiding. I pretended that I was surprised when he popped out, though, 'cause I would hate to disappoint him.

We went back to the house around 6:00 and made sure we went through the front door so that no one would get mad. Daddy and Mama were sitting in the kitchen waiting with supper on the table. Neither said a word to us as we sat down. Matter of fact, the whole meal was so quiet that I could hear every little noise Buford made when he chewed.

Me and Buford noticed it 'bout the time the pumpkin cobbler started being passed around. The screen door was brand new without a single hole, scratch, or image of the Christ Child on it. We kept quiet about it but I was sure grateful. I didn't know if the door was replaced to protect it or to forget about it, but either way it was gone from staring us in the face everyday.

That night as I was fading off to sleep Buford crawled into bed beside me. His breathing was so loud and heavy that for a moment I thought he was some sort of lecher coming to aid me in my sinful future. He tapped me on the shoulder repeatedly until the haziness of sleep left me.

"What?"

"Do chickens have ears?"

"Buford, why the hell are you asking me that?"

"Tell me! Do chickens have ears?"

"Of course they do!"

"But you can't see them so how do you know?"

"Because a chicken acts like it can hear."

"Oh." He was quiet for a moment, contemplating this troublesome fact of the hearing abilities of chickens. "Can things exist without us seeing them?"

"Of course they can Buford. You fart all the time and we never see it. We just smell it." He fell into silence again. I could almost hear the wheels churning in his head. Just as I was about to fall asleep I felt him tapping me again. "What?"

"We don't need to see the screen door."

"What?"

"We don't need to see the screen door. We can see him without it."

"Him who Buford?"

"The asparagus man."

"Go to bed Buford. You're starting to babble." And he did. In a matter of second, he pattered across the room, let out a few quiet farts, and climbed into his bed.

TICKET TO FREEDOM

JOHN R. POSEY

"Boy, you act like you been here before," announced my father at the dinner table. "And that ain't good." He shook his head in frustration like he knew that I would someday pay a heavy price for that character trait.

"What you mean Pop?" I asked, knowing that this conversation was going to lead to a point of no return. It always did when he started speaking in that cryptic fashion like he was an old, African griot slapping one of life's lessons upside my thick head as part of my rites-of-passage to black manhood.

I slapped two chicken legs on my plate, waiting for him to take me on this journey to only he knew where. I knew one thing for certain; I was the passenger and he was driving this train and we weren't stopping until he dropped his size eleven's on the brake.

"It ain't good for a young, black man to be so wise. It scares white folks," he advised as he reached for the bowl of collard greens and piled four, gigantic spoonfuls next to the mound of corn bread on his plate. "And scared white folks is bad for your health."

"Huh?"

"Son, I've watched you look white folks square in the eyes. You walk around huffin' and puffin' like you and they equal." He splashed hot sauce on his greens, heaped a stack in his mouth and let out an ear-shattering belch. "You sportin' that wild Afro and talkin' like them young fools at CORE and SNCC. That scares me son, 'cause white folks ain't got no problems takin' an uppity nigger on that final journey to meet his maker."

Another tremor roared from the bowels of his vast midsection. "This is Dallas. And some things ain't gonna ever change in the Big D," he offered with the resignation of a man beaten down by life.

"Billie Dahhden. Say excuse me," scolded my mother in her chicken-fried voice. "Raght now. I mean it."

She plunked her hand on a plush, round hip and whipped her neck and gave Pop that "I'm-pissed-off-and-you-better-get-your-house-in-order" look that makes a smart black man change his ways.

Momma Darden was a petite woman, with smooth, muted brown skin, cat eyes, and caramel-colored hair. Her legs bent in opposite directions—no doubt inherited in the genetic sweepstakes. Lillie Mae was a proud woman with a regal air that filled a room when she graced it with her presence. Momma taught me that style was a matter of mindset, rather than money.

"You settin' a bad example for that boy and ah don't like it." She pushed her glasses up her slender nose. "Ah'm tryin' to raise him to be a gentlemen. Ah don't want him actin' like he don't have no home trainin' just cause you don't know no better."

"I'm sorry baby," Pop mumbled as he ducked his head to avoid another frontal assault from Momma. "Scuse me Son," slipped out between Pop piling another mound of greens in his mouth.

Pop and Momma had been married for eighteen uneventful years. I wondered if they ever really were in love or just got tired of searching for the ideal partner and settled on each other—warts and all. Over time, they developed a quiet love, based on mutual respect and trust. Nothing fancy, but solid. I should be so lucky.

Pop learned from experience that Momma could kick your butt with her razor-sharp tongue. When Lillie Mae Darden's mouth went to work, it was like watching a surgeon performing an operation. Momma could talk about you so bad all you wanted to do was find a hole, crawl into it, and heap dirt on yourself. Nobody messed with momma, unless they wanted their feelings hurt.

Lillie Mae was a piece of work. She escaped from a hard scrabble life in Lubbock, Texas. Times were tough for black folks in Lubbock back then. Schools were bad. Good jobs were scarce as hen's teeth. Everything was segregated. And blacks served as little more than indentured servants for white folks as their nannies, janitors, butlers, maids, porters, cooks, and sharecroppers.

Momma liked to say that "slavery is alive and well in Lubbock. I don't care what Mr. Lincoln did. They only lets black folks have a taste of freedom on Juneteenth. Then they snatch it back at the first hint of midnight."

204

Life was even tougher for Momma since she was a bastard, a half breed. It seems the county sheriff infected Grandmomma's essence one night after she cleaned the jail's toilets. Oh, they gave Grandmomma her day in court. Then the grand jury threw the case out. Something about "two adults and mutual consent." Justice is a capricious beast in West Texas.

Black folks laughed at Momma and called her all kinds of half-breed names. There's no doubt in my mind why Momma was so color conscious. "Black is a state of mind not a shade of color," she drummed into me whenever people made fun of my cream colored skin.

Lubbock white folks avoided her like she carried the plague in her bosom. She might as well have been a ghost because people looked right past her. Lillie Mae Darden was a living reminder of the double standards of justice that existed between black and white folks. But people don't discuss those things in the "genteel South." It's not proper.

When Momma graduated from high school, she packed up her meager belongings, headed for Dallas, married Pop, and never looked back. Lillie Mae built up a nice little seamstress business making clothes for the rich, white ladies in Highland Park. She made enough money to get me a private tutor to compensate for the inferior education of the public schools. Ms. Lillie was a retired principal and smart as they come. I learned more in three hours a week from her than from all my teachers combined.

Whenever somebody challenged Momma, she jumped on them like they had stolen something. The only thing Lillie Mae Darden was afraid of—outside of the Almighty—was going back to Lubbock, Texas. Momma wouldn't even go back for Grandmomma's funeral. Just sent flowers. Everybody in the family begged her, but she was stubborn as a mule about it.

I don't blame her. Lubbock left nothing but shattered glass in the windows of her mind. The Klan killed her oldest brother, Willie. He had gone off to Howard and gotten his law degree, and his life looked bright as the sun in full force.

When Uncle Willie came back home, he was different. Living in the North had changed his perspective and heightened his expectations.

At first nobody thought anything unusual about Uncle Willie spending time at the library reading all those law books until he decided to sue the Board of Education to integrate the schools. Why did he want to do that? White folks didn't take too kindly to educated black folks challenging their system of laws.

One day, on his way to the courthouse reality snatched him by the back of the shirt. When it turned him loose, the black folks in Lubbock understood the consequences of speaking up for equality. I believe that's what the think tank intellectuals call an object lesson.

That was in 1945. Momma was eight. She never forgave my Grandmomma for staying in Lubbock. Things like that have a way of sticking in your mind—kinda like white on rice.

Pop always followed his mysterious statements with more confusion. He'd take a draw on his cigarette, swirl the smoke in his lungs and ask me, "Didn't you learn anything in your first life?" Then he'd wait for my answer while he was quietly killing us both with his bad habit.

What was I supposed to say? I was thirteen and the most challenging thing that crossed my mind was how to get Freda Jones on her daddy's couch. Like most teenagers I couldn't remember what I did last week. And he's asking me to recall a previous first life? Please.

But I wasn't going to bring it to him like that because Pop cast a big shadow in my world. We're talking huge. Pop just walking into a room put fear into most people. He had hands as large as Virginia hams. When we horseplayed and he clutched my peanut head, it felt like someone had covered it with a salad bowl. He could blot out the sun with his huge body.

After dinner and a couple of shots of Gordon's Gin, he would take me into the living room to finish our one-sided, man-to-man talk. He'd put his hand on my shoulder and tell me to sit on the cold, plastic-covered couch that Lillie Mae only let the children sit on during holidays.

Pop rambled on about how, at birth, I wore the look of someone who had graced this earth at another point in time. Wisdom dominated my cherubic, bronze face and steel forged my heavyset eyes. "I saw the sadness in your face—you wore the look of a man who had witnessed great tragedy and injustice. You must have been black in that life too," he added taking a long pull on the gin.

He told me the nurses nicknamed me "little man" because I only weighed five pounds at birth. I was two months premature. The doctors didn't think I'd survive the night. Guess I was too evil to die. He said he knew then that I would always have a special way with women. Pop swore, through his tobacco-stained teeth, that he saw a couple of them stick their phone numbers in my diaper bag. If lying was a profession, Pop would have made a hell of a lawyer. I guess that's why he drove a cab in South Dallas. Looking back through the prism of time, I think Pop was trying, in his uniquely convoluted fashion, to get me to understand what it meant to be a strong, black man in a society that penalizes you for your skin color.

Pop's lying aside, I come from proud stock on his side also. We can only trace my family back five generations to a sugar plantation in Louisiana. But judging from the stories my great aunt's told me, it's not hard to imagine my ancestors being from the great Yoruba tribes that dominated the plains of Africa and refused to bend to the oppression of slavery on South's plantations.

Grandpa Darden carried on the family tradition in compelling fashion. He was an octoroon. Blood was blended with more white than black. He could have passed like his sister did, but chose to exist in the world of living color.

Grandpa died two months before I was born. From all accounts, he sounds like one part Malcolm X and one part Adam Clayton Powell. All the elders in my family say that I'm the spitting image of him because of my fiery spirit.

As family legend has it, the year was 1920 when destiny changed his life. Grandpa was walking with his family along the broad boulevard leading to Fair Park during the State Fair. Black folks weren't welcome on the grounds in those days.

A white man, riding in his buggy, flashed by Grandpa and cursed him for blocking his path. Grandpa told him where he could put his buggy. He thrashed Grandpa with his horsewhip. Being a strong black man,or a damned fool, depending on who you ask, Grandpa pulled out his .22, shot him in the chest, and left him staining the ground.

Imagine shooting a white man in Dallas in 1920? Grandpa gathered the Darden clan and caught the first thing smoking due north. The freedom ride ended on the east side of Cleveland. Pop came back to Dallas after serving in World War II.

Grandpa set a civil rights standard for the family. He headed the local NAACP Branch for 29 years. We were taught not to take anything from white folks. "Look 'em in the eye and don't back down," was the family motto. Momma used to say "You just as good as they are." I believed what she told me. I'm still waiting for them to come around to my way of thinking.

❖   ❖   ❖

"Momma. I don't wanna go to no all-white, Catholic school," I argued and slammed my acceptance letter from Saint Phillip's on the kitchen table.

"Those white people don't want me there. And I don't want to go." I poured a glass of milk and sucked it down to quench my anger. "I want to go to Lincoln."

It was an official looking envelope with a red crest at the top of the page like the ones the Christians used during the crusade. The words Saint Phillip's were in bold letters underneath. The motto *We mold boys into men* was in italics at the bottom of the page. The letter was very direct and cold, like it was written by a man who had pledged a life of celibacy. A life without knowin' a woman's love will take the emotion out of a man, I guess.

> Dear Mr. and Mrs. Darden:
>
> The Board of Trustees of Saint Phillip's Academy is pleased to inform you that your son Stephen has been accepted for the incoming class of 1969. We look forward to his matriculation and have every reason to believe that he will uphold the high academic and moral standards of this institution. If you have any questions, please don't hesitate to call me.
>
> Sincerely,
>
> Father John J. O'Conner
> Principal

I stalked around the room waiting for Momma's inevitable response. She had been oddly silent during my tantrum, sewing together a quilt for the Van Patton family. I should've known that was the quiet before the storm.

Momma slammed her fist on the table knocking the colorful fabric and needles across the room. "Sit down young man! Raht now," she demanded as her gray-green eyes narrowed to two, beady dots. "'Fore you do. Please pick up my material from off the floor."

I stooped down and collected the fabric up and put it in her basket. As I walked over to the table and moved the *Dallas Post Tribune* and cereal bowl over to the counter, the headline caught my attention, "Blacks Boycott Downtown Diner." Hundreds of young blacks circled the store with their picket signs singing "We Shall Overcome."

Momma touched my hand to salve the pain of her harsh words. Momma's soft, finely manicured hands smelled like cocoa butter. "Honey. I wants you to go to that school so you can have the opportunity to do things your father and me can only dream about."

"Momma, nobody black ever went to that school," I heatedly protested. "Why do I have to go?"

"Baby, things is changin' all over the United States because of Dr. King," smiled Momma as she leaned back in her chair and pushed the sleeves up on her blue sweater. "Black people can eat where they want and go to schools with white children."

"Momma. They can pass all the laws they want. White folks ain't gonna accept us as their equals." My eyes bounced off of hers. "Why you think we were slaves for over three hundred years? Besides, things are changing cause black folks are burning down cities and listenin' to what Malcolm X preached. He's the prophet for young people, Momma. They're tired of all this praying."

"That may be," she replied coyly setting the trap as she cupped my arm. "But they ain't burnin' down nothin' in Dallas."

"That's cause all the black preachers have been bought and paid for by the Citizen's Council."

"Say that again boy," Momma challenged indignantly. "What you know about that kinda thing?"

"It's true Momma," I countered with attitude. "Everybody knows it."

"Then men from the Citizen's Council is some of my best customers," Momma yelled. Her eyes were glaring with anger. "If it wasn't for them, you wouldn't have this ticket to freedom," Momma said as she violently shook the admission letter in my face. "They done more for us than our own people."

"Momma. Wasn't it you that said don't trust white folks that want to give you something for nothing?" I challenged. My heart hung in the balance. I had never taken Lillie Mae on, but I could tell that my words cut deeply. No one had ever questioned her loyalty to the white men who ran Dallas.

Momma slowly dragged over to the stove and poured a cup of chickory-laced coffee into the scarred brown cup. She turned around and looked right through me. I pulled eyes away from her to avoid her intense gaze. I just knew Momma knew what I was thinking. And she knew I knew. And I knew that she didn't give a good damn that I knew. Lillie Mae was tryin' to will me into going to that school. But I wasn't buying her freedom ticket argument, if I could help it.

"How you know 'til you tried? Or are you jes plain old scared?" she hissed across the table.

Momma had played her trump card. She knew that a Darden couldn't back down from a challenge.

"I'm not scared of them white boys," I said in an angry whisper.

Momma smiled and slowly moved her lips. "Then what's your problem honey?" She lifted the letter and fanned it back and forth in my face. "This is your ticket to freedom. Are you going to cash it in? Or do you want to spend the rest of yo' life drivin' a cab like yo' daddy?"

I squirmed in the chair trying to find the right words to deflect Momma's attack. I watched the birds hunting for worms in the grass. The cool wind brushed the tree limbs against the house. I was silent for a long time. I knew Momma was sizing me up for the kill.

"Momma. All my friends are going to Lincoln," I weakly shot back. "I don't know anybody at that stupid school."

"Honey, you can make new friends," she laughed. "'Sides, you'll find out that they really ain't your friends, only acquaintances." Momma pulled the needle through the taffeta fabric and propped her elbows on the table. "Let somethin' bad happen to you and see how quick they scatter for cover. Like roaches when the light goes on." Then Momma said softly, "Will you go for me?"

After I heard Lillie Mae say that, I tried to draw a mental picture of the school and the sea of white faces that would flood the halls every day. And wearing a necktie every day. Could I make friends with white boys, I wondered? How would I act when they called me *nigger*, which they surely would? Damn her. I turned toward the refrigerator and nodded my head weakly. I suddenly felt older than the banks of the Nile.

"Hey nigger," shouted the red-headed boy. "Why don't you go back to the jungle with the rest of the monkeys?"

A banana landed at my feet as I walked toward my locker. So this is what freedom was like?

"I don't like you people," snarled Moose Burnett, the huge guard on the football team, as he knocked the books from under my arms. Moose wore a crew cut that was so short you could see what he was thinking. His red letter sweater, with the big gray "P" perched over his chest, was bursting, barely concealing his powerful arms. "Why should I have to block for a nigger. You ain't smart enough to learn the plays. Why don't you go back to South Dallas and be with your own kind."

A crowd quickly gathered as I carefully stooped down to pick up my books. Watching Moose out of one eye, I stood up and looked at him. "And why don't you kiss the raw part of my black ass you fat pig?"

Moose descended on me. I moved to the left and gave him a push. He crashed into the lockers. He charged me and tried to tackle me waist high. I smashed my algebra book into his broad, flat nose. He fell and I kicked him hard in the ribs once, then a second time for good measure. Moose groaned.

I began to laugh hysterically. Moose got up holding his ribs. "If you don't block for me, I'ma kick your ass again."

Moose limped off to his next class.

Molly Flaherty's face was covered with freckles that highlighted her strawberry blonde hair and ended long past her shoulders. The golden orb of morning bounced off her freshly scrubbed face. Molly's hair was pulled back in a neat ponytail. She had a ready smile that brought joy to everyone.

Molly went out of her way to speak to me every morning on the school bus that we shared with the girls who attended our sister school, Sacred Heart. She was one of those rare people who didn't see a color when she looked in your face.

One clear, November morning, Molly plopped down in the seat next to me. Her leg felt warm and vibrant. I had never been this close to a white female. Her hair smelled of lilacs. My stomach turned flips as I thought about how many black men had met an untimely end for less.

"You played a wonderful game on Saturday. How many touchdowns did you score?" She asked and elbowed me playfully. Molly winked, oblivious to the cold stares that knifed into her back. My heart hummed like an airplane motor.

Lord, what was this white girl up to, I wondered? The silence was ear-splitting. It grew louder and louder until it filled the bus. I looked past her reflection gleaming in the window and counted the tops of the elm trees guarding the elegant homes along majestic Swiss Avenue.

"Three," I mumbled.

Someone got up and offered her his seat. She waved him away. "Three? Wow, that's fantastic." She moved a little closer and asked me if I wanted to be her date for homecoming.

The bus slammed to a stop.

The driver, Barney, was a gruff old man about sixty who had stuttered and stammered his way through life. I had once heard him say that he was originally from Mount Pleasant in East Texas. He wore Dickey jeans and T-shirts with a pocket over his heart. A can of Red Man always peeked out of his shirt pocket. Tobacco juice stained the floor mat under his eelskin boots.

Barney had never called me *nigger* before, at least not to my face. But he said it in his fierce, gray eyes every morning when I walked past him to my seat. There was a fierceness borne of a tradition that reached back to his parent's parents. The hate was drawn on his eyelids and formed an invisible shield, like the white robe I'm sure he wore on his night rides terrorizing decent, black folds.

"G...G...G...Get in the f...front of the...the b...b...bus," he ordered as he pulled me by my sleeve.

"What did I do?" I asked as I got up and walked with him. I decided there was no sense in confronting him. When I got to the front, all the seats were taken. I turned to him. "Where do you want me to sit?" I asked.

He jerked open the front door. "I...I...d...d...don't wantchu...t...t...to..s...sit anywhere. G...get y...your b...black ass off m..m..m...my b..bus," and shoved me down the stairs.

"Mr. Darden, please hand me your demerit card," demanded Father O'Rourke, the stern-faced vice principal. His wrinkled skin looked like a well-worn ballet. He was an ex-boxer who had some moderate success in New York's tough CYO tournaments. Father kept a pair of boxing gloves hanging in his office to convert the hardheaded to the ways of Saint Phillip's. A real tough guy in the John Wayne tradition.

I reached into my wallet and handed him my card. He snatched it and deftly punched two holes through the numbers four and five. Bingo.

"Mr. Darden, it appears you will be my guest for Jug this Saturday morning," he sneered. "Please make sure you bring your dictionary." He turned. I hesitated. Now was the time to stop him.

Jug was Saint Phillip's way of instilling fear and ensuring conformance to their rigid code of conduct. Once you got your fifth demerit, you were Father O'Rourke's guest for a day of memorizing a page of the dictionary, sanding desks, and doing any other odd jobs that needed to be done.

"Er . . . excuse me Father O'Rourke," I asked, "What did I do?"

"Look on your locker," he told me and abruptly headed for his office. He turned and said sharply, "You'll be painting it on Saturday."

I ran down the hall and slid around the corner. I stared at my locker for a long time. I pushed back my anger. The noise and the people no longer mattered as the words *Nigger, Coon, Darkie, Jungle Bunny,* and *Tar Baby* screamed at me. I twisted the lock and the latches clicked. I yanked the door open quietly and dropped my English book in the locker.

Father Fahey was my Latin teacher. A crinkly, orange shock of hair served as sort of a barricade protecting the broad, empty space on his head that cast a shadow on his glassy eyes. Years of tossing down cheap bourbon had sucked the life out of his cheeks and carved dark circles in his face. He eased around the classroom with short painful steps, like he had a permanent case of hemorrhoids.

He ran his classroom like a marine drill instructor—which he had been. Conjugating verbs was our daily military exercise. Failure to complete an assignment earned the offender a stern backhand upside the meaty part of the head and fifty sit-ups. The wonders of a Catholic education.

Father Fahey was a small man, with an even smaller mind. He made it clear to me that he didn't like black people from day one. However low his opinion of me was as a person, his expectations for my performance were even lower.

"Calvin, I don't expect much from you," he told me. "My experience with Negro students, in the North, is that they don't do well in Latin. It's not your fault. You people don't excel academically," he pontificated before the entire class. Everyone exploded into laughter.

213

Embarrassed, I slid deep into my seat until shoulders were level with the desk top. A fly landed on my lip. The thought of what Momma would do to me if I smacked this arrogant white man helped me slam my mouth shut before I could tell him where he could stick his opinion. It was eerie. Suddenly I felt my grandfather's hand stroking my shoulder and holding me back. As I turned my head, I swear I heard him say, "Not now. It'll be okay."

Damn if it was okay.

It was a windy, May morning. This was the final week of the semester. Track season was ending on Monday. The fresh bluebonnets were sprinkled around the base of the broad-shouldered cedar tree outside the classroom. The housing projects loomed large off in West Dallas. I stared out the window at the small airplane that buzzed in and out of the clouds headed toward Love Field.

Father Fahey handed me my weekly test back. The grade eighty-four, in red, jumped off the page. I checked his corrections carefully. Once. Then a second time. My calculations showed I scored a ninety-five. This was the third time he had made an "error."

Momma had been into visit with Father Fahey about this problem on two other occasions: once with Pop and once by herself. He reassured Momma that it was an honest mistake. Lillie Mae was a normally skeptical person, but each time his flimsy excuses left her appeased. Momma wanted me in this school so bad she could taste it. She was living her dreams through my eyes. I guess she wanted white folks to accept her through my accomplishments.

I raised my hand and asked if I could come up to his desk. Putting my paper gently on the desk, I politely asked, "Father, could you please review my score? I think my grade should be a 95, not an 84."

The gold cross swung carelessly about his neck. His head shot up from his grading book. Anger clouds formed in his sallow eyes and he was so still—like he was frozen in time. Father Fahey turned living color red. I guess you'd call it crimson. He slammed his pencil against the desk and fragments shot across the room. One hit me in the eye.

"How dare you challenge me, *nigger*," he shouted. "You shouldn't even be in this school." He pointed to my desk and ordered me to, "Sit your black ass down."

I clutched my eye and felt my morning meal of two scrambled eggs and bacon climbing up my throat. I could see Father Fahey, through my tears and snot, from the corner of my other eye. I brushed my sleeve across my runny nose. No one can talk like that to me, not even a priest, I thought. My eyes turned directly on his. Steel met glass. The window panes shattered under the intensity of my gaze. Anger surged through me like lightning.

I can't remember what happened first, but it was the way he looked at me that set me off. Maybe it was everything that had happened since I began this long journey to freedom. The locker. Jug. Moose. The bus driver. White people. Sell-out ministers. Racism.

Grandpa's spirit flashed before me, dark on darkness. I thought I heard him say, "Okay, now." My head was pounding. I shifted my weight and began to run blindly in Father's direction. My mouth was open far wider than I imagine possible. I never heard sounds like those that came out of my mouth. He tried to shield himself from my vicious punches and kicks. I looked into his eyes one last time.

"Who's the *nigger* now?" I shouted clutching his throat with the rage of a man gone mad.

"Who?"

"I am," he murmured. "I am," he cried and then he fainted.

The ghost was exorcised.

I spent the afternoon sitting uncomfortably in the supply closet, surrounded by mountains of textbooks, rulers, pens, and paper, waiting for the board of advisors to determine my future. The room was dark. Darker than any room that I had ever been in. I could hear the second hand sweeping, sweeping, sweeping its eternal journey. If only I could turn back the hands of time and erase this nine-month nightmare that had descended upon my head like a swarm of locusts, devouring everything in sight. This had been no ticket to freedom Momma. It was more like a passport to hell.

An uneasy tension gripped my stomach so hard that I doubled over in pain. I suspect it was the anticipation of a man who is about to be executed. My only question was how was I going to die? There was a familiarity about this experience. Maybe Pop was right. Maybe I had traveled this path before. As Crispus Attucks. Or Nat Turner. Or John Brown. Or Garvey. Or Paul Robeson.

Someone turned the handle of the door. When he entered, a sudden light burst into the room. It scalded my eyes. This stranger was tall and thin and his white collar rode tightly on his red, chapped neck. His jaw was set. The small, black eyes told me everything I needed to know. He handed me an envelope and ordered me to clean out my locker. The rest of his speech I did not hear. I folded my hands, shifted my head down and said a little prayer of thanks.

The school bus shook violently to a halt at Sacred Heart. The drab, red bricks served as an appropriate backdrop for the tight-lipped nuns, shrouded in their white and black costumes, guarding the horde of giggling, bubble gum-chewing girls. Among the phalanx of plaid uniforms, I spotted a shimmering, blonde ponytail bobbing back and forth through the crowd. Molly Flaherty scurried to the front of the line.

She leaped on the bus. Molly's brilliant blue eyes blinked off and on like turn signals. Her face full of distress creased her even, polished forehead. "what happened?" Molly asked as she dropped down next me, her cheeks stained from sobbing.

I noticed the panicked look on her face. "What happened?" she demanded. Molly shook me hard, "Please tell me," she pleaded.

"Got expelled," I admitted quietly. Someone yelled out, "nigger lover," but it bounced off Molly harmlessly into the afternoon breeze.

"Why?"

"It's . . . it's," I stumbled out. "sorta . . uh complicated."

I explained the incident as best I could to this sweet girl who didn't see a color, but simply judged me as a human being. I showed her the letter and watched Molly closely as she read it several times. She seemed to deliberate over every word searching for any subtle implications. Molly carefully folded it and expressed her sympathy and disgust at the hate and viciousness of her people toward blacks. I told her not to worry, god just didn't make me to be a pioneer. To be a pioneer, you have to be an early settler I explained. And I didn't have the meek personality that the job description called for.

A sheet of lightening discharged and severed my words into one thousand shreds of sound. Thunder boomed across the low, gray clouds; I rested my head against the window and watched the wet pellets bouncing crazily off the ground. It was something about rain that comforted me. The steady

216

beat of the raindrops hypnotized me and made me relax. Maybe I enjoyed the rain because the clouds protected me from the rest of the world.

I reached for the smeared, crumpled envelope buried in my jacket pocket. I watched a squadron of crows buzz over the even row of trees. Beyond the angry sky, I could barely see an orange ball of light that helped shed the revelation that I lived in a land that was not my own. I smiled at Molly, let the window down, and cast my letter to the wind. It was spring. A time for new beginnings.

LOOKING FOR SHADOWS

LIANNE ELIZABETH MERCER

"Wind's from the east." Gran listens. "They'll be comin'."

She rocks on the braided rug, taps the dishpan in her lap with a worn paring knife, spears an apple. "When I was a green girl, when the chimbleys had fallen into piles, old Leila told how one year from corn shocks to lilacs her and her ma and pa got drifted shut by snow in their sod hut."

Not fifteen minutes ago, when I stirred the fire, I heard the howling of dogs a hundred years beneath the cornfields. Gran peels and cores an apple, spews pieces into the crusted pie plate I hold, raises her head, sniffs. "Buffalo chip smoke."

All I smell is apple. I snitch a crunchy chunk.

Gran says, "They're lookin' for their shadows, slippin' in by the bald place where there was a gate 'til Henry's cow knocked it down."

"Who's looking? Who's slipping in?"

"Maybe Leila's ma or pa. Maybe Leila herself." Gran hollers like when she slops Frannie and Maybelle. "That you, Leila?"

I jump, spill apples, remember Leila stitched the sampler now crooked in a patch of sunlight on the wall.

"Or anyone who's lost, child," Gran says while I scoop apples from my lap, drop them onto the thick crust. "The only shadow they got is their home place. When the wind is cruel, they come to remember where they were, so they can find out where they're goin'. You know yourself when fuzzy rainbows ring your eyes picking noonday corn, you look for your shadow between the rows to get your bearings."

She hands me a long peeling for wishing, and I wish Joel Armstrong would kiss me tonight. He's been lifting up the phone on the party line to talk. Sometimes he just breathes. This morning, just before he put the phone down, he whispered, "Carrie? I'll come at sundown."

I pitch the peeling into the fire. It hisses.

"Never mind if you feel 'em around you, child. They mean no harm."

"I'm not going to tell Joel they're here. He might not kiss me."

"So many folks wandering," Gran says, "so many needing food. Leila herself showed me how to put the spices just right." She cuts the last apple and sets the dishpan on the floor. She watches me stir in sugar, sprinkle cinnamon and cloves, add butter, carve a curving C-into-J in the top crust, lay it on top, cut off the extra, pinch top and bottom together. I set the pie into the oven.

While Gran dozes, I eat the pieces of raw crust and wash up. When I'm through, the sun's left Leila's sampler straight in the shadows. I put another log on the fire. Flames crackle and dance. In the chimney, the wind whispers. In the loft, Joel waits.

I take the bubbling pie from the oven. The smell fills the room.

Gran wakes up. "Bring me a piece, child. Have one yourself. And set out another. Use the plates I won at the fair. The ones with the pansies."

I slice three pieces, lift them out, steaming. I take her hers. Go back for mine. "Who's the third piece for?"

"Maybe Leila." She rocks. "Maybe whoever's trying to get found." She chews and stares into the fire. Logs pop. Light flickers on her cheeks. They look soft and unwrinkled.

"Thanks, Gran." I slide both pieces onto one plate and slip out the door. I feel the wind on my shoulders and smell rain. Lightning plays in the clouds off to the east. But stars still shine overhead as I hurry to the barn.

ROBERT FLYNN

Harold was on his way to a high school football game. He hadn't missed an Edison Tech game in the fifteen years he had been out of high school; hadn't missed a kickoff or a warmup although sometimes he had to leave the pet store early or take a day off. Harold was loyal to his school and had once pledged his best limb for a football uniform. He didn't ask to be a star; he just wanted to wear the uniform of his school, to be on the same team with Jackie Starbuck, the old mail carrier. "Starbuck delivers the mail for Edison Tech." Harold could still remember the caption below a photograph of Starbuck hurtling into the end zone.

It was worth a broken leg to Harold to wear the same uniform as Jackie Starbuck, but after two weeks of practice the coach asked him to give the uniform to someone who could contribute to the team. Unable to play, Harold supported the team as vice president of the Light Bulbs and still wore the polyester maroon and black leisure suit that had been the uniform, without the hat that lighted during halftime activities.

Harold stopped for a traffic light and was straightening his jacket when he was startled by a misshapen head that appeared in the passenger window. The head was attached to a body covered with metal braces as far as Harold could see. Harold quickly looked away.

He was astonished when the man with the misshapen head tried to get into his car. Harold did not pick up hitchhikers; it was a promise he had made his dying mother. He would have driven away except that the light was red. The cripple made such a rattle and clatter with his braces that Harold feared he was tearing the paint and trim from the car. He leaned over and opened the door. "I don't pick up hitchhikers," he explained, avoiding a glance at the small, gnome-like cripple who with much ripping and clanging scrabbled into the seat beside him.

Harold hated embarrassing situations. He hated them so much that he avoided football players, pretty girls, minorities, and those who made manly noises when they urinated. "I promised my mother," he said. The light turned green; the car behind him honked. Reluctantly, Harold closed the door and drove across the intersection.

"Edison Tech Stadium," the gnome said.

"Are you going to the game?" It never occurred to Harold that a cripple might go to a football game.

"Yes."

"Did you go to Richland?" Harold asked, annoyed that he was giving a ride to one of the snobs from Richland that beat Edison Tech year after year because they had more coaches, better equipment, and six twirlers.

"No."

Harold's heart sank. It had never occurred to him that a cripple might go to his school. "Edison Tech?"

"I'm a sports writer."

Harold was so relieved he forgot to be astonished that a cripple could get a job in sports, or know enough to write about a game.

It was still early when they reached the stadium. Harold would have time to find a parking place and get to his seat without missing the team warmup. "I'll drop you off at the gate," he said magnanimously.

"Too far."

Harold was a generous person even when it was not in his best interest. His was the vote that elected Gerald Thornton president of the Light Bulbs because Harold had refused to vote for himself. But he was not going to be pushed around by a cripple. "I'll drop you in front of the gate."

"You'll have to carry me to the elevator."

Harold turned to look at the cripple. The man looked even worse than he had thought, a wad of dough that had rolled through a box of paper clips. Harold realized he was staring and looked away.

"You'll have to carry me to the elevator to the press box."

That was too much. If the cripple had driven himself he would have had to walk even farther. Harold thought of something. "Show me your press card." Harold was benevolent, but not stupid.

He stopped the car in front of the gate and examined the press pass. It looked genuine. He thought of something else. "There is no elevator to the press box." Edison Tech couldn't afford one.

"You'll have to carry me."

Robert Flynn

"To the top of the stadium?"

"You look strong enough."

No one had ever thought him strong before and for a moment Harold caught a glimpse of himself as Jackie Starbuck—carrying the cripple to the press box, posing for pictures of himself with the cripple on his back, and allowing himself to be interviewed about those glorious days he had carried the mail for Edison Tech. "It's not a question of strength," Harold said. He didn't know if he could carry the cripple or not.

The cripple laid a doughy hand on Harold's arm. It looked something between the pudgy hand of a child and the webbed foot of a toad. Harold recoiled. "You think I'm grotesque."

Harold was not liberal enough to lie. "You can't be a sports writer; you're a cripple."

"I got a press card."

"How do you usually get to the press box?"

The cripple's face broke open to reveal a row of misshapen teeth. A sound like a sob escaped the curled lips. "First game. Was going to catch a cab. Pay driver to carry me. Saw your purple and black suit." The metal braces rattled.

It was a test and Harold understood tests. Some paper had hired the gnome and given him an assignment they knew he couldn't do. A coach had told Harold to tackle Starbuck in the open field and he could keep the uniform. Nobody could tackle Starbuck in the open or alone. Harold had gotten his feet tangled and had fallen without touching Starbuck. Everyone laughed so hard the coach gave him another chance. That's when he offered God his best limb but he did no better. The third time, Starbuck felt sorry for him and instead of feinting, ran over Harold, dislocating his hip. Harold had hoped the coach would fulfill God's part of the bargain although he didn't actually break his leg, but the coach had ordered one of the players to follow the ambulance to the hospital and pick up the uniform.

Harold determined the gnome would have his chance. He cut the engine, got out and waited for the cripple to extricate himself from the car. "How do we do it?" he asked.

"Bend over." Harold bent over. "Lower." Harold squatted, bent his back and the cripple climbed on, slipping the fleshy but formless hands around his neck and digging the metal braces into his legs and ribs. "You'll have to carry these," he said, hitting Harold in the head with the crutches.

222

After two tries, Harold was able to rise without toppling to one side and he staggered toward the gate. An attendant accosted him. "You're going to have to move that car."

"Press," Harold gasped, his voice strangled by the arms around his throat.

"Okay, but the guy on your back has to have a ticket."

Harold lurched through the gate. He didn't want to be rude but he had to get rid of his burden before he collapsed. He staggered to the stadium steps and sat down to rest his back and catch his breath. He looked up. There were three steep flights of steps to go.

By the time he reached the second flight of steps he was elbowed, cursed, and shoved by Richland fans pushing their way to their seats. Stainless steel dug into his muscles and snagged his maroon and black leisure suit. By the third flight he had learned to let the momentum of the mass carry him to the top. While the others stood for the national anthem he staggered to the press box, dumped the gnome on one of the high stools and collapsed on the floor, gasping for breath, his muscles aching. "I had to carry him up here." The sports writers seemed not to hear, their attention turned to the kickoff.

In fifteen years he had never missed a kickoff. He wanted to get up but could not. He lay on the floor, trying to ease his cramped muscles. He listened to the game over the loudspeaker for a while before trying to stand. Once on his feet he braced himself against the back wall and tried to straighten his back.

"You have to take me to the toilet."

"What? Why can't they take you?" he asked, gesturing at the oversized ex-jocks who were smoking, drinking coffee, and laughing over an obscene joke.

"They're watching the game," the gnome said.

The only toilets were under the stadium. "How will you get back?"

"You'll have to carry me."

Once he had pledged a broken leg to play in a game. Now he was going to have to pledge a broken back for the gnome to pass his test.

The first quarter had ended by the time Harold had gotten the cripple to the restroom and into one of the metal stalls. He leaned against the wall to catch his breath, catching the attention of others who were in the toilet, and a cop who looked simple, bored, and humorless.

"No loitering," said the cop.

"Crippled sports writer," he explained. "In there. I had to carry him."

Inside the stall the cripple was trying to stand, banging and scraping the braces against the metal sides of the stall.

"That don't sound like no sports writer," said a man making a manly noise at the urinal. "Sounds like a crab in a metal bucket."

"One of them drum majors's beating his drum in there," said another.

The door slowly opened and with more crashing and rattling of metal, the cripple slowly emerged. "Bend over," he said.

Harold kneeled on the floor, let the cripple crawl on his back, took the crutches and tried to stand, stumbling for the door that opened before him. He plowed through three high school boys who were trying to enter, tottered up the steps, unloaded his burden, and fell on the floor to gasp. "You got a press pass?" one of the writers asked.

"I carried him," he explained, pointing at the cripple.

"You're not carrying him now are you?"

Harold reeled from the press box bumping into the simple, bored and humorless policeman. "No alcohol in the stadium," the cop said.

Harold leaned against the top rail of the stadium and faced the cop. "Cripple," he gasped. "Toilet. All the way up."

"If I have to speak to you again, out you go."

Harold would have explained further but Richland fans were yelling "dim bulb" and "glow worm." He set out to park his car, find a seat and enjoy the game. When he reached the gate the attendant said his car had been towed to the police pound because it was blocking traffic. "I was carrying a crippled sports writer to the press box," Harold said.

"You said you were a sports writer."

"No, no," Harold said. "The cripple—"

"If you ain't a sports writer, where's your ticket?"

Harold took a deep breath. He disliked having to explain to slow people. "I came to move my car and buy a ticket."

"Hey," the attendant yelled at the policeman who must have followed Harold. "This guy said he was a sports writer and he ain't a sports writer and he ain't got a ticket."

The policeman sighed and shook his head, saddened by the depravity of mankind and his painful duty. "You got a press pass?" "No. I carried a sports wri—"

"Let's see your ticket."

"I came down here to buy a ticket. And move my car."

"He was leaving," the attendant said. "Look at that suit. He's from Edison Tech and he was leaving because they're losing again."

"Okay," the cop said. "Get in the squad car."

The man was too simple to talk to, but Harold knew when he explained to the cop's superior that he was trying to help a cripple, he would not only get an apology, they would return his car without a fee. He had been embarrassed and he had missed the kickoff and perhaps the first half of the game, but he had helped a cripple and he would be vindicated.

At the station he was pointed to a chair and the simple cop reappeared with his superior who looked stupid. "Drunk and disorderly, parking in a restricted area, attending a performance without a ticket."

"What?" Harold said, his voice shriller than he wished. "The newspaper made a crippled sports writer cover the game. I took him to the stadium and carried him to the press box." The cops were staring and he didn't like what he saw in their eyes. "Because there's not an elevator."

"That makes my butt want to dip snuff," said the simple cop. "Taking advantage of a cripple like that to beat your own school out of the price of a ticket. I didn't know they made scum that low."

"What school was it?" asked the stupid cop.

"Edison Tech. Look at that suit; what else could it be."

"I played for Richland," said the stupid cop. "Edison Tech was the dirtiest team I ever played against. Some sleazebag named Jackie Starbuck broke my leg with a cheap shot. You ever hear of Starbuck?'

Harold was in a fix but he could not deny his hero. "We were on the same team." For two weeks, he whispered to himself.

"Okay, creep, you can pay fifty dollars and walk or you can wait in the lockup for the judge."

"What about my car?"

"In the police pound. That'll cost you another fifty."

"How will I get there?"

"Take a cab."

"If I take a cab I won't have enough money for the car."

"Listen scumbag, it's time you learned something they don't teach at Edison Tech. Crime don't pay."

"You make a living out of it," Harold muttered.

"Whattidyousay?" growled the stupid cop.

"Will you take a check for the fine?"

They looked at each other. "Let's do it," said the stupid cop, the one from Richland High. "Maybe it'll be hot and we can throw him in the slammer. I'd like to see this little shit again."

Outside the station, Harold consulted his wallet. He had enough to get his car from the pound, but not enough to catch a cab. He went back inside and asked directions to the pound. He came out, propelled by slander. It was going to cost him a hundred dollars for the first game he had missed in fifteen years. For trying to help a poor cripple earn a living. And the cripple was still in the press box with no way to get down, no ride to the newspaper to deliver his story.

It was three miles to the pound and he would have to hurry to get there before it closed. He paced himself, running, walking, running; he hadn't been a Boy Scout for nothing. The pound was in an industrial area of the city with few lights and dark rows of warehouses. He accidentally kicked a can that clattered across the pavement and banged on a metal-sided warehouse. He ran and in his fright he took a wrong turn.

He looked for a friendly light, a human being. He saw nothing but dark streets, overhanging trees, and a rare dim bulb outside a locked warehouse door. Not knowing what to do he kept moving; it was the wrong direction but it was a direction. There must be a security guard. But what to yell? Help? No, they would call the police and he would have to explain that he was looking for the car pound. Rape? Worse. Fire? "Chew tobacco, chew tobacco, spit it on the wall," he yelled. "Richland, Richland can't play ball. Yea maroon, yea black, yea Edison Tech, stab 'em in the back. Yea black, yea maroon, yea Edison Tech, light up the room."

"Go sleep it off, buddy, or I'm calling the cops," someone yelled before slamming a door.

"I was helping a cripple and the police towed my car." It was no use. No one would listen. His rambling brought him to the end of the street where he could see the floodlights of the police pound. He had come on the wrong side and had to run around the high wire fence, but he was in time. The pound operator refused to accept a check but for cash Harold received his keys, three forms to sign, and a slur on his parentage.

It no longer mattered. He had his car and he was on his way to the stadium. Snobbish Richland graduates, officious gate attendants, stupid police, hateful pound operators could not stop him. He drove to the stadium, parked, and ran to the gate as victorious Richland fans yelled. "Turn out the lights."

He ran up the steps of the stadium as the loudspeaker counted down the last minute. He burst into the press box to find no gnome. The announcer was the only person left. "Where is the cripple?" he cried.

"Gone. Everybody's gone. This game was over a long time ago."

"How did he get down the steps?"

"A couple of guys carried him."

It took two of them. Harold smiled. "How long ago?"

"Not long."

Harold raced down the steps. He had circled the stadium once and was on his second round when he spotted the cripple outside the gate in what was probably a sitting position.

"Sorry I'm late," he said.

"I called a cab."

"You'll have to pay for the ride, for the cabbie to carry you."

"Expense account."

Was that the end of it? A hundred bucks, insults, risking his life in the warehouse district, and the cripple went home in a cab? "You're going with me," Harold said.

"I can take care of myself."

Harold had explained himself for the last time. He bent over as before. "Get on."

"I'm taking a cab."

Harold got up and tried to lift the gnome who struck at him with the metal crutches. Harold took the crutches and threw them aside. With the steel braces pounding his back and the cripple's toad-like arms squeezing his neck, he picked him up and struggled toward his car.

"Help," the cripple yelled. "Help, I'm being kidnaped."

Harold looked around, fearing he would have to explain to the simple cop but he was nowhere in sight and the fans who heard the cripple seemed embarrassed and looked away. Harold dumped the gnome in the car and closed the door. Rattling and clattering, the cripple opened the door. Harold pushed him back in and closed the door again. "If you don't stay in the car I'm going to go off and leave your crutches." Harold fixed the yellow, floating eyes with his own until the cripple nodded.

Harold turned away, and quickly looked back. The gnome had not tried to escape. He took a few steps and looked back again. The gnome was ignoring him. He ran to the crutches, snatched them, threw them in the back seat and jumped in beside the cripple who seemed defeated.

"First, we're going to the newspaper office."

"I phoned in my story."

"They took it? They took your story?" Harold's eyes burned with triumph. "I'll take you home. Where do you live?" It was a long way and in a bad part of town but the gnome had passed the test. It was Harold's biggest victory. "I want to explain why I wasn't there to carry you down from the press box."

"I am not dependent on you."

"The police impounded my car because it was parked in the gate and they arrested me when I went to buy a ticket. It cost me a hundred bucks. I had to run three miles to get my car. It was the first game I've missed in fifteen years."

"You're lucky. Edison Tech was embarrassing."

"Don't say bad things about my school. And don't write them either."

"They were pitiful."

"I'm trying to help you."

"I don't ever want to see that suit again."

"The police thought I was some kind of freak for helping you. And for supporting Edison Tech," he admitted. "But I'm a very loyal person."

The gnome's house was a small cottage on a run-down street.

"Your folks live here?"

"They're dead."

Harold got the cripple on his back and lurched to the door.

"I'll be over tomorrow to mow your lawn."

"I have a lawn service."

"I'll bring a hammer and nails and straighten that gutter for you."

The gnome braced himself against the door. "I can't pay."

"I'll take you to games," Harold said. "I'll get you there and you can write the story."

"I don't want to be dependent."

"I don't want a pass or anything. I'll pay my own way," Harold said. "I've never been part of anything."

"Thursday night. Junior high game," the gnome said and then scrabbled his way inside the house.

Harold waited for a moment, listening to the cripple banging the wall to turn on a light and clattering across the room. It was a heavy burden he had taken upon himself. It meant he would miss some Edison Tech games. It meant buying another suit because it wouldn't be fair to wear maroon and black to all the games. Maybe they could wear the same kind of clothes. So people would know they were a team. He'd have to get the car seats recovered. It didn't matter, he was a contributor.

OIL

JUDY BRAND

Facing the mirror without looking at it, he fingered the bow tie while his past reeled by in fast forward. Forming the first loop, his fingers continued as his mind paused to remember walks with his dad through the oil fields in happier times.

"Son," his dad had said, "you'll never have a problem with people. As gentle and friendly as you are, dealing with the public will be easy for you."

And it has been, he thought.

After years of practice, the bow tie materialized without a mirrored glimpse from its maker. In the good old days, elegant evenings and gala balls had nurtured his talent for tying. A valuable tool, he recently realized.

While wrapping the knot, his memory reeled forward, stopping briefly on those teenage summers spent roughnecking on offshore rigs. His dad had created a strenuous climb up the ladder from the lowest rung, never thinking one could fall.

"Son, I know I'm working you hard, but pressure builds character."

Tugging at the second loop, he completed the tie. Glancing in the mirror, he smiled, never dreaming his tying talent could be beneficial to his career.

His thoughts pressed on, pausing at his father's death bed in 1984, almost ten years ago.

"Son, your hard work paid off. The oil company has prospered under your guidance. I'm relieved to go knowing you'll be taken care of by that black gold you've devoted your life to. You know, Son, oil in Texas is better than cash in the bank."

Finished, he turned from the mirror. Dad left at the right time, when oil bubbled like champagne. Slipping on the familiar tuxedo jacket, masked with a smile, he entered the restaurant, and took his place as maitre d'.

230

RUNNING BEFORE RED SKIES

TERRY ZUMWALT

Stepping onto the bobbing fiberglass deck of the twenty-two-foot sailboat, Mark Mason felt the week's worries blow away, even though the early morning air was still.

Only on Saturdays could he forget he was the new kid in school and apparently the only one not smoking dope at lunch. He'd forget he desperately needed a college scholarship because if the peace initiative didn't hold, he could end up One-A and be dropping bombs over North Vietnam by this time next year. He'd forget that not one student spoke to him all week.

"Red sky at mornin', Marky," his father called from the old shrimper's dock.

"I know, Dad, sailors take warning. I'll be careful and be in before any squalls."

"They can sneak up on you—keep an eye open. I've got a few more sermon notes to make, so call me at the church when you get in and I'll come get you."

"It may be late."

"As long as the weather's good," his father slammed the yellow Volkswagen Beetle's door and drove off.

The aluminum mast stabbed at a clear blue sky. The first breeze broke the crystallized morning air. The sun felt warm and in minutes Mark would discard his windbreaker. The gentle breeze would become a steady wind that would blow until dusk. Thursday's cool front changed wind direction enough to present a new sailing challenge, although the Gulf of Mexico always challenged him.

Mark stowed his sack of snacks below and pulled out the bags of sails. After slipping the battens into their pockets, he snapped the dacron sail onto the jib stay.

The blast of a car horn and the crunch of sea shells beneath tires made him look up. Don Pine's rusted out '69 maroon Mustang screeched to a stop, scattering sand and shells.

"Hey, Casey."

"Mark. My name's Mark."

"Oh, yeah. Can you do me a favor? Are you going to Corpus today?"

"Wasn't planning to. I'm headed to open water."

Mark studied the school stud. Stringy blond hair serpentined across his shoulders and Mark wondered how that hair got past the vice-principal who enforced the dress code every Monday.

"I'll pay you to take Karen to Corpus. She'll need about an hour ashore." Don jutted his thumb toward Karen Cooke, who huddled in the passenger side of the car. Although a freshman cheerleader, she seemed sweet and shy, lowering her gaze whenever Mark tried to make eye contact.

Mark hesitated. Pushing back thoughts that these were popular kids, why did they want him to take her? Why didn't one of their own crowd drive her?

"Fifty bucks, man. Fifty bucks—and you're going anyway, right?"

Mark threw caution to the wind. He'd miss fighting the gulf waves, but Karen's company would make up for any lost fun. The only girl he'd ever had on board was his eleven-year-old sister. Who knows, maybe he'd gain a friend.

"Call my Dad at the church and tell him I've changed plans."

"Sure, groovy. And Mark, no questions—keep your mouth shut after you're back. Okay?"

Karen got out of the car. She wore little white shorts and a red and white striped blouse. She wasn't smiling her usual sweet smile now.

She glared at Don. "Why can't you take me?"

"I'm going to Port."

"I don't see how a surfing contest can get you three hundred dollars."

"A bet here, a bet there—a first place win and before low tide, I'll have *five* hundred." He brushed a kiss across her cheek. "I'll call you when I get home."

Scooting behind the wheel, he burnt rubber on the shell parking lot, leaving Karen standing there, beach bag in hand. She stared after his car until the only remaining sound was screaming gulls and the ping of the halyards against the mast.

Mark threaded the mainsail onto the boom. Karen stood on the dock looking like she might cry. He tugged the lines holding the boat to the dock to draw the stern to the old tire that served as a bumper. He held out his hand to her. Her fingers felt like ice. She extended a long tanned leg across the green water and stepped on board.

"I've never been on a sailboat before, just a ski boat."

"Good," he said feeling very self-conscious, even though he was a senior and she a lowly freshman. "Sit here on the port side," he indicated a flotation cushion on the molded fiberglass seat. "You know how to swim?"

"Does this turn over a lot?"

"Nah, she has a four foot draw, fixed keel with a real heavy ballast. I've grounded her, but never turned her over."

He noticed the girl gripped the hull tightly as she stared at the cloudy green water.

"I'll bet this water's pretty cold," she said, "it being October and all. Don's pool thermometer was 87 yesterday but the water felt freezing."

"You want me to stow your stuff?" he asked.

"Let me get my magazine and suntan lotion."

She dug around in the purple and orange beach bag, extracted what she wanted, then handed it to him. He went below and when he came back up with her life vest she was slathering Hawaiian Tropic on those long legs. For a minute, the smell of coconut oil overpowered the tang of salt and sea. She caught him staring.

He shoved the vest toward her. "You don't have to wear it unless the weather gets bad."

She slipped her arms through the holes and pulled the black straps tight across her chest. "I don't mind."

"There's a head below, a toilet, just follow the instructions on the lid. And help yourself to the Dr. Pepper in the 'fridge."

"You have a kitchen?"

"A couple a' burners, a sink, and a 'fridge. The table makes into a double bed, sorta like a mobile home. Go look around, if you want."

"Maybe later," she said. "You could spend all weekend and have great parties if you wanted."

If I had any friends, and if my parents would let me, he thought. In his two months at Sam Houston High he hadn't met anyone who would value the snapping of the sails or who would think the boat good for anything

233

other than a floating bedroom. The girl weren't exactly flocking to his side. With mousey brown hair and wire-rimmed glasses, he didn't exactly qualify for tall, dark. and handsome—something like smart and plain would be more like it. He hoisted the mainsail and jib.

"I'll be moving fast . . ."

She smiled for the first time. "Are you asking me to stay out of your way?"

He nodded. "This is the boom, it's gonna swing toward your head sometimes; watch out for it—don't ever forget it's there, because if it hits you, it'll hurt, or worse, knock you into the water. And this kind of boat doesn't stop on a dime. To circle around and pick you up might take a half hour."

He released the stern line, then walked forward to release the bow lines. Kicking the dock, the nose swung starboard and he rushed back to grab the tiller and trim the jib. The wind caught, heeling the sloop.

Karen gasped.

"It's okay," Mark said as he trimmed the mainsail. "Boats have yaw, pitch, and roll." He indicated the movements with his right hand. "It takes a while to get used to it."

He loved the precarious balance, bending his knees to absorb the roll of waves, the crash of the bow into a trough, the crab of the hull sliding up onto a wave. The sheets filled and they began to clip along.

"How long will it take us to get to Corpus?"

Mark shrugged. "Depends on the wind, two hours of running before the wind, one hour of reaching across the wind, or five miserable hours of tacking into the wind."

"I don't know what you said, but it doesn't sound very reliable."

He tried to suppress his grin. "That's what makes it fun—man against himself, man against nature, and all that. It's like life, sometimes fast, sometimes slow, always unpredictable."

She stared blankly at the slowly passing shoreline, not appearing to see the treeless savannah or the gray cranes that stood on one leg.

He thought, *I guess it seems boring to a hot chick like you who runs with the fast crowd. Obviously my version of fast isn't fast enough for you.* She appeared so sad and forlorn, he wondered why anyone would think of her as fun. Suddenly the day stretched before him long and miserable. Why had he let Don Pine use him? He knew—the money and the girl. The greedy thought of increasing his college fund by sailing, although he'd probably never see a dime, and the idea of spending the day with a popular girl who smelled like coconuts and pineapple.

"I have to tack under the bridge, to enter the channel, so the boom's gonna swing." He warned.

Her fearful brown eyes met his.

"Switch seats with me." She moved cautiously, sliding her white-knuckled hand along the cabin edge. "Whenever I say 'ready to come about,' watch the boom and expect it to shift to the other side."

He tacked. The sails filled with air, he tightened the lines and cleated them off.

"That wasn't bad," she said.

"Be careful," he warned, "you'll get addicted."

"Are you addicted?"

"If that means I'd rather be here than anywhere else, I'm addicted."

"It doesn't seem real harmful."

The wind whipped his bangs off his forehead "Just bleached hair and frequent sunburn or, in the winter, freezing nose and fingers."

"You sail in the winter?"

"Sure. New Englanders laugh at what Texans call winter; they'd say it's spring or fall."

"Did you move from New England?"

He laughed, "No, this is an East Texas twang, rather than your South Texas accent."

"If you didn't have an ocean, where did you sail?"

"Vacations at Lake Texoma. My folks gave me an option: I could stay in Mt. Pleasant my senior year, or move here with them and they'd buy me a used sailboat or a car."

"Easy choice?" she asked.

"Easy choice," he said nodding, but on a couple of lonely Friday nights he'd had his doubts. "You want to hold the tiller?"

"Not really."

A lone seagull floated above the sail, then screamed, diving for the rear of the boat until about six feet off the water. When it realized they had no food, it flapped wings and disappeared.

"The salt and humidity makes my hair stringy and limp." She said, "I can't wait to move away from here."

Although her thick brown hair lay in a pony tail down her back, curly tendrils danced in the wind around her oval face. It looked pretty good to him. Mark stared under the jib to the horizon.

"Where would you go?"

"Austin or someplace less humid." She tugged at her life vest. "How do you know where we're going?"

"That red marker," he pointed, "tells me I'm returning to a port, that green marker indicates we're headed to sea. Some boats have radios, all sorts of fancy navigation equipment, and weather radar. We just have charts and markers. But I've sailed to Corpus enough I don't need the charts anymore."

"Don's little sister said you take your sister to Corpus every Saturday."

"Not every Saturday, just when there's a good kid movie. She likes those Lovebug movies. She calls Dad's car Herby. Ready to come about?"

"Change seats again?"

Mark nodded and loosened the line from the cleat. He shoved the tiller and held it with his knee while he hauled the jib sheet. The wind caught and the boat surged forward heeling at a forty-five degree angle. Karen gasped and braced her feet against the opposite seat.

"Don't worry, this is good. We'll make great time on this leg of the channel. See, the bend up there? We'll be slower on that leg."

When he glanced at her face, she looked pale, almost green, beneath her tan. "It's okay," he tried to reassure her. "This isn't dangerous at all." But he loosened the lines to lessen the boat's angle to the water.

"I don't feel so . . ." Suddenly she barfed over the side.

Anxiety flowed through him. He looked behind, the channel was still clear, so he pushed the tiller over and headed into the wind, leting the sails flap impotently. Grabbing the lightweight anchor, he shoved it overboard, knowing it wouldn't hit bottom, but it would drag and slow them down. She gagged again. He went below deck and wet a rag with the distilled water he'd brought in a jug. Grabbing a cup of ice and a Dr. Pepper, he went up top, where she coughed dry heaves.

"Karen, here's a wet wash cloth."

She turned and looked at him with pitiable eyes as she took the cloth.

"We can go back," he offered.

"No," she said quickly, "I've got to do this today."

He went below and popped the table down making it into a bed. When he came back up, she still looked green around the gills. "You can lie down if you want, but it's better to stay in the fresh air. Up top you don't feel the rocking movement as much as below."

"I'm okay, really. I feel much better now."

"Hey, look!" He pointed toward the bow. "Porpoises!"

She smiled shyly, "I think I just ralphed on their heads."

Mark burst out laughing and the shiny sea creatures disappeared under the water. When he came back to the tiller he offered again, "We can turn around."

She shook her head no, "I'm not sea sick, I'm just getting over a touch of flu or something."

Mark pulled anchor, tightened the jib lines, and swung the bow. The wind grabbed the two white triangles.

"Am I on the right side?"

Mark adjusted imaginary glasses, "Not only are you on the right side, you're on the correct side."

"You must have Mr. Whittingham for English. You should do that imitation for Senior Follies."

He knew he'd never be invited to participate. He'd quickly learned that the athletic teams were Sam Houston High's keepers of tradition and only an athlete could penetrate their holy territory . . . in South Texas, sailing didn't quite constitute a team sport. And at five-foot-nine, one hundred and forty pounds, he wasn't anxious to butt heads with the six-two, two-twenty pounders, and he was no Pete Maravich or Pete Rose.

A loaded oil tanker leaving port approached them. "They're carrying a lot of oil to sit that heavy in the water. Makes you wonder about the energy crisis, doesn't it?"

"I don't think about stuff like that," Karen admitted. "My mom says girls who are too brainy aren't very popular."

"So she thinks being popular is more important than being smart?"

"She knows lots of smart people who are poor, but every popular person she knows is rich."

Mark laughed. "That's pretty weird logic."

"She just wants what's best for me. She says even when you're old, if you're rich, you can buy beauty."

Mark contrasted his parents' life views with Karen's. His parents harped about inner beauty and being rich in spirit and not doing things just because "everybody's doin' it." Sometimes he got tired of their philosophies.

"What's your dad say about that?" he asked.

"My parents never married. I guess you could say I was a love child before it was popular to have love children. My mom would have named me Astral Plane or something like that, if she'd known it was going to be in. She wanted to go to Haight-Ashbury so bad . . . but never had the money. I think she just wanted to go some place where she could be 'with it.' That's why she married Cal. He's on the school board, you know, a real mucky-muck. Short, fat, and bald, but rich and very respected in the community. Very 'happenin' with the old crowd."

"She must be proud you're a cheerleader."

"It's all she thinks about."

Mark loosened the boom, "On this leg we'll be a little slower." He laughed. "I know . . . you could walk there faster. I've heard it before, but we're making great time."

"I wish we had some Jefferson Airplane or Led Zeppelin."

"Really?" Mark asked. "I'd rather hear the swish of the bow cutting the water, the zippered clicks of the jib winch."

"Silence drives Don crazy."

Mark couldn't help but wonder why she hung around Don. Of course, Don's father owned the funeral home in town and he had a lot of money. But it was a known fact that he smoked a bong and popped lots of reds. He bragged about it when he was sober . . . almost as much as he bragged about sexual conquests. "I need to water the pipe," was his last period battle cry.

Mark wondered if Karen did drugs and sex. He didn't think he should think of her like that, so he decided to talk about something else, but he couldn't think of anything to say. She obviously wasn't worrying about carrying the conversation. He wanted to ask where she was going, but he decided it wasn't any of his business. Oblivious to everything around her, she flipped another page of her *Seventeen Magazine*.

He fantasized about meeting her in the halls and sharing a laugh, going with her to the victory dance after the game, and sitting next to her in church . . . but she obviously wasn't having the same thoughts. *I'm just a taxi to her.*

Finally the span of the bridge and the skyline of the city came into view. The sun dropped noon rays and they shattered on water in a magnificent spray light that obscured the T-head marina from immediate view.

"It's so beautiful."

Karen looked up. "I've never seen the city from this angle before."
"Most people don't."
"What'll you do while I'm gone?" she asked as they neared the docks.
"Eat lunch, fish off the jetties."
"Watch girls?"
He laughed, "Probably. Can you hold the tiller here?"
He shoved the teak wood handle into her palm before she could protest.
Then he ran forward and dropped the jib and mainsail. The momentum
carried them forward. He ran back to steer the craft to the end of a pier.
A Chicano kid ran up holding out his hands. "Toss me the line."
Mark hurled the rope. After the kid caught it, he stuck out his leg to
cushion the impact. The kid tied him off.
"Thanks, man."
"No problem," the kid said over his shoulder as he walked off.
"I'll need a taxi," Karen said.
Mark pointed to the pay phone. "We're at the T-head by the jet airplane."
As she walked off, he pulled out a balogna sandwich. When she came
back it was half eaten. He asked if she wanted one. She shook her head no
and kept pacing back and forth.
A blue Chevy Impala with the light on the roof and the sign on the door
pulled up. She looked panicked.
"I've never been in a cab alone. Will you wait here for me?"
"Want me to go with you?
She shook her head no as she got in.
Mark watched until the cab turned the corner. He pulled out his rod and
joined the Chicano kid on the jetty. After a brief conversation about the
best bait, they fished in silence.
Far across the bay, cumulus clouds that looked like exploded kernels of
popcorn appeared on the horizon. Scattered thunderstorms would develop
all afternoon. One more month of hurricane season.
He thought of Karen and wished he could say something or do something that would make her like him. But a chick like her didn't need a guy
like him for a friend. . . . She had plenty of friends. His dad would say, live
fast, burn out quicker. But sometimes Mark wondered if his dad was right.
After an hour and forty-five minutes Mark was watching every car that
pulled onto the T-head. Where could she be? All sorts of crazy things popped
into his head. What if she'd gone to buy dope and wanted him to transport

it? He pictured Jack Lord turning to James McArthur and saying, "Book him, Danno."

Finally a cab rounded the corner. The door opened and Karen stepped out. Dark circles ringed her eyes and her lips and face were deathly pale. She looked far worse than when she up-chucked.

"Are you all right, Karen?"

"Just take me home, please," she whispered.

As quickly as possible, he set sail. The channel was busy and although he had right away, he tried to give larger ships clear steerage.

She said, "I think I'll lie down."

When he glanced into the cabin, she was curled into a fetal position. She looked dead. He took a second look and saw her rapid shallow breathing. Then he saw big tears roll down her cheeks. He felt so helpless and confused. He didn't know what to do for her. But Don's words, "No questions—keep your mouth shut," rang in his ears. What had he agreed to?

Then he noticed a red stain seeping onto her white shorts.

"Oh, Jesus!" he cried out in an invocation rather than a curse.

Her eyes flew open.

"Karen, you're bleeding."

She sat up and her face flushed a little. "The doctor said I would."

"What did they do to you?"

"An abortion. I had an abortion."

Mark knew the word from the nightly news. Roe vs. Wade. Pregnancy termination.

"You were going to have a baby?"

"And now I'm not."

He'd never thought about it. Abortion was something adults did. To end a pregnancy required surgery, didn't it? To have surgery, you went to the hospital, didn't you?

An almost irrational anger welled up in Mark. "That little slime, Don Pine, did this to you and made you face the consequences all alone?"

"I've really made a mess of everything."

Mark wished he could tell her it wasn't true, but it was.

"Are you okay?"

She trembled and her teeth chattered. He didn't even have a blanket to give her. He tossed her his windbreaker.

"No. It was awful. The doctor said it wouldn't hurt, but it did. It was supposed to be the nicest clinic in Corpus, but there weren't even walls, just curtains, and I could hear everything happening to the other women." She covered her face with her hands. "I can hear it still."

The sails luffed. Mark wondered if he should drop anchor and do something. He felt so useless. He wanted to kill Don Pine for being such a selfish son-of-a-gun, but he knew it wouldn't do any good. Once a jerk, always a jerk, especially when there were no consequences. Mark would make sure the bozo paid now. And as far as he was concerned, fifty dollars after knocking up a girl and sending her off alone, while cavorting around the beach with other chicks, was not suffering serious consequences.

Nearby, a flash of lightning, quickly followed by a crack of thunder, split the air. Mark tightened the sails and flew toward home. He pulled down the cabin cover, knowing they'd sail through a squall. A squall bright with lightning and deafening with thunder, but lasting only an hour or two then disappearing from memory forever. Life's squalls, like Karen's, would remain forever. The flare of lightning and boom of thunder might fade, but the damage done would be hard to repair.

The first drop of cold rain stung his cheek. He pulled a slicker from under the seat and slipped it over his head. No matter how well he sailed, it would be a long trip home. He wished he could take away Karen's suffering. He thought about his parents and felt grateful that they were his parents. They might not have the Pines' money, or the Cookes' free spirit, but they loved him and did what they thought was best for him.

At times the big wind-whipped drops obscured his vision. But finally the clouds moved inland, taking the rain with them. Steam rose off the water. He pulled off the slicker and threw it into a heap on the deck. A sigh of relief exploded from deep within his chest when the bridge came into view. Home!

He lifted the cabin cover, then docked the sloop.

Woozily, Karen came up the steps and dropped onto the fiberglass seat.

"Now that I've done this, he might still break up with me," she said. "He did the same thing to Monica last spring. I should have listened to her, but I thought I was different."

Mark didn't marvel at her stupidity too long. He remembered a certain Jane Elmore who had almost done him in with her wild flirtations and lies his sophomore year. Emotions did strange things to your head.

241

He sat next to Karen and put his arm around her. He didn't say any-thing, because he didn't know what to say. They sat there a long time ab-sorbing each other's warmth, her head on his shoulder.

"Rain's comin' again."

Her eyes flew open. "Don't leave me." She clung to his arm like it was a life preserver.

"I've got to go call my dad to come get us, I'll be right back."

She began to cry again. "He'll wanna know what happened—he'll think I'm a slut and I guess I am."

"You don't know my dad yet," Mark said with pride. He'd seen his dad react to situations far worse than this.

"You promise, he won't tell my parents."

"I promise, *he* won't tell, but after talking to him you might."

"Mark . . ."

He stopped. "Yeah?"

"Thanks for being here."

"You're welcome, Karen." He knew that on Monday morning when she was back with her old friends, she'd probably ignore him—or wish she could. In an hour, she wouldn't be his problem anymore. He'd eventually forget this happened, but she never would. She paid a high price for her popular-ity. He didn't think it was worth it.

He walked off toward every sailor's delight—the red sky at night, and the pay phone.

At One Stride Comes the Dark

JAN EPTON SEALE

Whenever Mavis tried to tell her mother how she was dedicating her life to bareback riding, her mother stopped what she was doing, put her hands on her hips, and looked straight at her. "Mavis, we are not white trash. I don't want to hear another word about the circus."

Urgency was barreling down on Mavis. She had chosen light pink and purple for her costume, and had several times managed to put her hair in a bun high on the back of her head, borrowing a little wreath of plastic flowers from her mother's tray to put around it. If she didn't start practicing right away, she might as well give up on the idea. Later, her legs might get spotted and jiggly, or she might forget how necessary it was to love the horses.

The captions under the circus pictures in the *Locksville Leader* stressed that the performers were constantly practicing. That was why, the summer she was eight, Mavis brought up the subject of Dixie right after supper the first night. And to soften Root up, she asked him right *before* supper why his name was Root.

Mavis knew why her name was Mavis. Her mother had told her. "When I was carrying you, I was simply mad for that square red can of Mavis talcum powder." Mavis also knew that Root was short for Rupert, but she was willing to be dumb each time she asked.

As for Dixie, Root's black and white mare, Mavis would have to work up to the big question of riding her alone. Tonight she would ask Root to tell her Dixie's story again. Very soon, if he didn't offer to take her behind him, she would ask. Later, at just the right moment, she would ask to ride Dixie alone.

The other three summers that she had come to the Panhandle, Aunt Regina had insisted she ride behind Root. That had been okay; she would take any practice at all for her coming role in the Locksville Community Circus.

Her mother didn't think it was a good idea for the circus to be composed of hometown people. "Mr. Trewell should leave the funny business to Charlie Chaplin and stick to selling groceries," she said. About other mothers who sold cotton candy, she said, "They are making a spectacle of themselves."

Mavis had once ventured to say hello to Mrs. Lumpkins, who played the piano at church but also directed a trained dog act in one of the side rings. Mavis could swear, from personal experience, that Mrs. Lumpkins was not white trash, nor was she making a spectacle of herself.

They would let you be part-time, like Mrs. Lumpkins, but Mavis was planning to make the circus a vocation. If people could dedicate their lives to Jesus in the Baptist church, she could dedicate hers to the circus. When she got to high school, like Root was now, she would ask her mother if she could live at the livestock show grounds where the circus stayed. Her mother would probably like that.

If Mavis didn't get to do bareback riding, she would be a trapeze artist. During the winter, she worked out on her backyard trapeze, acknowledging the crowd when she balanced no-hands on the bar, or hung by one leg, or hung by her toes (though her hair got leaves in it when she did that). But this was only in case they had too many people in the bareback riding act. Horses were her first choice.

When Mavis asked about Root's name, he said, "Because I'm a big overgrown carrot."

"No, *really*!" Mavis begged.

"Short for rutabaga," Root said. He liked to squeak the swing idly as he waited for supper, dragging his heels, not going nearly as high as Mavis thought he should.

"You're kidding me." Mavis twirled in front of Root until her skirt billowed. He would play along with her.

"Is it 'cause you wear boots?" she asked, running up close to his freshwashed face when he moved forward, inadvertently spitting on him a little in the throes of rhyming.

Root reached out and grabbed her—exactly what she wanted—and trapping her between his legs, dug his heels into the boards and lifted her high in a wide swoop of the swing. "Little city critter on a buckin' bronc!" he said. She screamed and held on to his hard thighs.

When Aunt Regina heard Mavis, she came to the screen, a bowl of peas in one hand grasped by a yellow hot pad. Aunt Regina was a tall strong woman who had never had a husband. Or a permanent or a manicure. Aunt Regina did not mind how often Mavis fingered the veins on the back of her hands or rippled the skin on her freckled arms. She had let Mavis teach her how to play Old Maids. Then she had taught Mavis dominoes. When they were too tired to play anymore, she let Mavis rest her head on her bosom when they sat in the swing together for a while before bedtime.

Aunt Regina and Root, her younger brother by twenty-five years, lived alone in the house, though the hands came in every day for lunch and supper, and some of the other six brothers and sisters were always driving out from town or flying in from across the country to stir the bills around on the roll-top desk in the den. Mavis's mother was one of those, but she didn't like to come visit them at the homestead. She said it made her sad, thinking of Mavis' grandparents, Rupert Senior and Dora, who'd been gone since before Mavis was born. So when she brought Mavis in the summer to stay, she went away that same afternoon. Mavis tried to look sad when her mother left.

"Rupert Junior," Aunt Regina said, "put her down right now! You'll have her so worked up her dinner won't digest properly."

Root grinned and stopped abruptly, opening his legs, lifting her down with gawky young hands already wide and red from farm work. After Aunt Regina went on to deliver her peas to the long dining table, Mavis climbed into Root's lap and whispered, "I'm going to marry you, Root." He had such pretty white teeth, and a horse.

Root would never say no to her marriage proposal, just "You're already my niece, Miss Mavis-Davis."

The first summer, when Mavis was five, Aunt Regina invited her to come to the farm for two weeks, and Mavis heard her mother tell Aunt Regina in a whiny voice over the phone that she hoped Mavis wouldn't be an extra care. Mavis made a note to find out what an extra care was and not be it. She didn't want to do anything that would keep her mother from letting her be in the circus.

Mavis's mother hung up the phone and acted cheerier than she had in a while. She told Mavis that Mavis was going to Aunt Regina's, for "my rest cure." Her mother didn't sleep any that afternoon, and did not make Mavis go to bed early before her company came. She started right away packing Mavis's clothes—cool little shorts and swirly skirts and sleeveless tops. She packed all her summer clothes and two tubes of toothpaste. "We never want to appear cheap," her mother said, when Mavis told her she could use Aunt Regina's.

Three years in a row, when Mavis finished her mother's rest cure with Aunt Regina, she went to her father in Kansas City. He called her Brownie for the tan she'd gotten at Aunt Regina's. He was supposed to have her for the remainder of the summer.

For about a week they did city things and then he left her with the maid in the apartment to watch television and drink red sodas. The maid plaited Mavis's hair in a French braid fresh every day but after a while, that got tiresome. Finally, the week before school started, she went back to her mother in Texas. All this took a lot of phone calls and car trips, and as Mavis got older, bus and train rides with her name and destination pinned to her blouse. Mavis watched the frowns on the grownups' faces as they copied down schedules and drew circles over meeting places on road maps. She agreed with her mother: these arrangements for her required so much of everyone's valuable time and money.

All except Aunt Regina's. Each summer Aunt Regina made up some excuse to keep Mavis a little longer. As Mavis got bigger, Aunt Regina pointed out that Mavis could swat flies and peel apples and crank the ice cream freezer. And in return, Aunt Regina paid her a penny for every two dead flies, and she didn't mind the extra time Mavis took to peel a whole apple with one long curlicue, and she let Mavis lick the dash.

It seemed like Aunt Regina had a space for her, and Aunt Regina re-did the space every summer so that it was bigger than the summer before. This summer, when Mavis was eight, Aunt Regina said she just *had* to have Mavis the *entire* summer. Mavis was *too* much company and *too* much help to do without.

This summer had started out to be the best one yet for being in love with Root. It began when she got to ride in Mr. Williams' camper, along with his niece and nephew, all the way out to the Panhandle. Aunt Regina had found out Mr. Williams was coming to central Texas and had arranged for her to ride out with him. When Aunt Regina called to propose it, her mother had said, "Oh, what a load that will take off my shoulders." Aunt Regina sent Root along to watch over Mavis.

Every time they stopped, Root came around back and poked his head in. "You all right?" he'd ask. "You want a cold drink, Miss Mavis-Davis?"

Sometimes she'd say she wanted out and lean down and fall into Root's waiting hands. They felt like soft clamps, warm and firm under her arms. He'd set her gently on the ground and she'd trot off to the bathroom. When she came back, she'd put her foot on the bumper and he'd make a little seat for her behind with one hand and boost her up, then give her the Dr. Pepper he'd bought her.

"Thanks, Snoot," she'd say, or Hoot or Shoot, making up a new name for him each stop. She liked to see Root's hair with the little crest in front and a part on the side, not pasted down to his brow by his hat like when he ran the harvester all day.

On this first night of the first whole summer she would spend with them, they sat on the porch after supper, after the floor was swept and the wet tea towels Mavis had used to dry the dishes were spread over the backs of the breakfast chairs to dry.

Mavis cleared her throat. "Root, tell me the story of Dixie." She would ask for nothing but the story tonight.

"Miss Mavis-Davis, you know that story as well as the nose on your face," Root said, waggling his long leg on the banister as he rested his back against a post.

"But I've forgotten some of it." She was sitting cross-legged on the porch floor in front of him.

Root sighed and flicked his toothpick into a bush. "Dixie was born out on the open range in Utah. Her mamma and daddy were from a wild herd of mustangs that was running all over. The man we bought her from says he cut her from her mother's side as a foal." Mavis once winced at this cutting but not anymore. It only meant that Dixie had been separated from her mother by riding between them.

"He ran her into a brush corral, then snubbed her up to a tree three days before she quit kicking. She was a feisty little devil."

"Rupert, watch your language," Aunt Regina murmured from her rocker without looking up from her embroidery.

"Well, she was," he said, pausing.

"Go on! Go on!" Mavis begged.

"The man will always fear the horse"—Mavis chimed in to finish with him—"if the horse doesn't fear the man."

247

参

Root laughed. "Mavis, *you* tell *me* the rest of the story."

"So then he fed her sugar until she took the bit and he led her around and finally could climb on her and to this very day she loves a sugar lump best."

"That's right," Root said.

"And she's a mustang paint," Mavis finished.

Two days passed and Mavis could not figure out for the life of her why Root had not asked her to ride Dixie with him. The third evening, she asked the whole thing: Could she ride Dixie by herself? In a way, she hated to give up riding behind Root, remembering other summers how she hugged him around his middle and could feel the warm muscles of his back against her cheek. Still, she must practice alone. An article in the paper said a girl only thirteen had gone on the high wire with her family of acrobats. That was just five years away.

Root laughed. "If Dixie had tires instead of legs, I'd ride her more. She probably won't even let *me* ride her," he said. "I bet I haven't ridden her twice all year." Root had just finished his junior year in high school in town. He and his friend John Don had been riding around a lot in the second-hand pickup Aunt Regina had bought him.

All Mavis could do now was go with Root to the corral in the evenings to feed Dixie her grain. When she felt Dixie's nibbling lips on her palm, a tingling began in her feet and crept slowly up the insides of her legs.

After Dixie finished the grain Root ladled out for her, Mavis watched her take long draughts from the trough, the mare first checking lightly with her muzzle for scum.

Finally, Root would say, "Now you can pet the mustang in 'er," and Mavis would scratch and rub the beautiful prominent bone of Dixie's nose and lay her face against Dixie's strange huge piebald head. Mavis could not think what to do with her longing.

She began to beg and beg so that one afternoon, when a soaking shower in the morning had kept the hands out of the fields for the rest of the day, Root put a bridle on Dixie and led her around the corral. At first Dixie chewed the bit and shook her head and leapt sideways, but after a while, she calmed and eventually took the saddle blanket and saddle.

John Don and Mavis watched while Root climbed on Dixie and rode her around the corral and then out into the field. She plodded along indifferently, like the oldest horse in the world, about dead from old age. "No prob. Your turn," Root said, dismounting.

While John Don held the reins, Root helped Mavis put her foot in the stirrup and swing up. She felt the saddle spreading her legs wide. It hadn't been that way when she rode behind Root. It had seemed more circus-y when she could feel Dixie's solid warm rump moving up and down.

Dixie's eyes flared and she shied momentarily, then seemed to settle in her mind that the person atop her was the same one who'd been coming nightly with Root to feed her. Root led her around the corral once, then took his hands away and let Mavis guide her. "So far, so good," he said, more to John Don than Mavis, it seemed.

Next he opened the gate to the inner yard encircling the house and said, "You can ride her around here a little."

Dixie plodded through the gate slowly and Mavis gave her a little goose with the heels of her sandals. At this, Dixie tossed her head and pranced forward a step or two into the yard. She began to dance sideways, first one way and then the other. Mavis looked back at Root.

"Rein her up a little," he called. She pulled sharply on the reins. Dixie half-reared.

"I said a little!" Root called. She heard Root and John Don laugh.

She loosened the reins and Dixie acted as though nothing had happened. Mavis led her across the lawn and began a path around the fence. Dixie was steady, picking up her feet and placing them almost daintily in the lawn grass.

When she thought she was farthest from Root and John Don, Mavis pulled Dixie to a halt.

"What's the matter?" Root called.

Mavis pretended not to hear. She had work to do.

"Give 'er a little spur," John Don called.

Letting the reins go slack, Mavis shook her feet from the stirrups and shucked off her sandals. Dixie put her head down and began eating Aunt Regina's gerbera daisies. Mavis raised her feet and carefully planted them one behind the other on the saddle. Then she stood up.

There was a moment when she was taller than anything else around except the apricot tree. She felt the wind puff out her shorts and fill up her top. It was wonderful, so wonderful. Though she had dreamed it many times, this was her first real time to be a bareback rider. She threw her hands up and out and heard the crowd clapping. Her picture was in the paper. She was captain of the bareback riding team.

In asking for the applause, she forgot she was holding a rein in each hand. When Dixie felt the jerk of the bit, she raised her head from the daisies. That drew her attention to the fact that something had changed atop her. She slung her head and bolted, taking off across Aunt Regina's bachelor buttons and pinks.

The sudden move flung Mavis into the air in a kind of half somersault. For a moment she wondered if she had planned to do this trick anyway. But she came to rest on her back in a pile of duck squat.

"Goddamnit, girl!" Root sprinted across the drive and entered the yard, catching Dixie as she dashed through the gate. John Don came chuckling and took Dixie's reins.

Root sprinted across the grass to Mavis. "What the hell's the matter with you?" he shouted. "You don't stand up on a horse."

By now she could feel the knot growing on the back of her head and the duck squat soaking her blouse. Root reached down and lifted her up and for an instant she was back at a filling station with Root reaching up into the truck for her. Except this time his hands squeezed her too tight and she couldn't breathe. He set her ajar on her feet, swearing softly as he felt the duck squat between his fingers.

She began to cry. "Go to the house," he commanded. "Now you've got to be doctored like a damned baby. I shoulda' known better."

"Oh Rupert Junior!" John Don called in a high voice over his shoulder as he led Dixie toward the barn. "Your sister's gonna' tan your hide."

In the time before supper, Mavis lay on Aunt Regina's bed with Campho-Phenique on her hands where the reins had cut. "I know you didn't mean to, Dixie," she whispered over and over until she dozed.

Aunt Regina called supper and Mavis hobbled out slowly from the bedroom. Root tousled her hair and held her chair. "The rodeo queen!" he announced. Mavis smiled wanly and took a sip of milk.

When Root had filled his plate, he checked that his sister was occupied in the kitchen. Then he got right into the story for the hands. "Dixie's takin' it real slow and steady around the fence in the yard and the next thing we know she's on the far side of the house and they're stopped." He stuffed a roll in his mouth, chewed twice, took a swallow of tea, and looked at John Don. "We thought Dixie had gone into one of her mustang fits, didn't we, John Don?" John Don nodded, his cheeks puffed with steak.

"But no, it wasn't old Dixie this time, no sirree. It was Mavis here. She stood right up on that horse's back and threw her arms out like she was about to cut the wheat on both sides of 'er."

A ripple of laughter turned into guffaws. Root felt his audience and was winding up to embellish the story when

Aunt Regina entered with a refill on rolls. He looked quickly at Mavis. "Isn't that about the way it was, Miss Mavis-Davis?"

Mavis's eyes filled with tears. She tried to sit them out, but they splashed down her front. Finally, she let out a sob and, springing from her chair, stumbled toward the porch.

Aunt Regina looked from Root to John Don and back. "Brother, can't you just leave her be? She's hurting enough."

Root took a bite of meat. "I 'spect her backside hurts more'n her feelings right now." And that brought on another spate of laughter while Aunt Regina took Mavis's plate to her on the porch, saying to her that it was cooler and nicer out there anyway, but be sure to come in if the mosquitos get bad.

Alone again, Mavis sat looking at the flies on her food, studying how a girl could start out in the morning going to marry a nice boy with white teeth and by that night hate his guts. The next day Root tried to make up with Mavis by popping the elastic on the back of her halter.

She drew back. "Don't you ever, ever do that again!" It was what the boys did to a girl when they discovered she was wearing her first bra. She stomped her foot. "Don't you know that's the *worst* thing a boy could do to a girl?"

Root looked at John Don. "The worst, huh?" They laughed. And from there things just went down.

Days now, days on end, with nothing to do but play alone or help Aunt Regina. Mornings, she gathered eggs, sometimes stroking Biddie, Aunt Regina's favorite Rock Island layer. When Biddie was sitting on the nest and started to cluck, there was no way she could keep from laying. Mavis raised Biddie's tail to see the egg emerge.

Midmorning Mavis shelled peas, making up a game of speed, or counting each motion. She was good at telling whether to open the pod and run her thumb down the inside to release the moist peas into the steel bowl, or to snap the immature pod into sections. The shelled ones were the older ones, big people who got their way. The snapped ones were babies, with no say-so about when they were picked.

Noons saw the table laden with cabbage, roast, potatoes, squash. Evenings, Aunt Regina would call, "Mavis, honey, come be my legs," and Mavis would trot between the kitchen and dining room, laying out the leftovers—cornbread, cold dabs of vegetables, apple cobbler brought from under the tea towel.

After supper, there was putting away every last dish, sweeping out the kitchen, setting the mouse traps. And finally, to the porch, where she practiced the tight-rope on the railing with Aunt Regina's umbrella until she became shaky and jumped down to sit beside Aunt Regina on the glider and watch the stars burn silver holes in the sky.

Root never touched her now, never engaged her in their silly conversations. He didn't even invite her to go with him in the twilight to feed Dixie. And she was too proud to beg.

One afternoon Root came in early from the field. He bathed and put on fresh jeans that Aunt Regina had ironed nice creases down the legs of. He stood in front of the mirror for a long time combing his hair, making it arch over his white forehead.

Mavis could stand it no longer. She went to Aunt Regina who was setting out peach preserves on the supper table. "Where is Root going?"

"Socializing," Aunt Regina said. "Boys that age like to socialize."

Mavis could not think what that meant. And Root was out the door, leaving behind a sweet smell that reminded her of her mother's boyfriends.

After they had done the dishes, Aunt Regina said she had a headache and believed she would go lie on the day bed with a wet washrag on her forehead.

Mavis went outside and strained to see the black and white spots of Dixie's sides in the corral twilight. The horse was not there. Maybe Root had fed her early. Or maybe he'd totally forgotten her and she was waiting at the gate. Mavis crossed over to the corral but Dixie was nowhere around. She found a feed bucket and turned it upside down to stand on in order to reach the latch on the grain bin. Opening the door, she plunged her hands into the grain. She would touch Dixie's food.

Her motion made the kernels pour down on her, burying her arms up to her shoulders. She climbed up into the little room and sank, half-covered, in the seedy deep. Drawing slow circles, she waded about a while. Then she climbed on a board nailed against the wall and jumped off, landing prettily in the safety net of grain. When she did it again, she acknowledged the crowd far below her. The third time, she did a flip. Maybe, after all, she would be best as a trapeze artist.

Now the kernels filtered into her clothes, eating at the waist of her shorts, filling her panties, making her pockets heavy. She started to sneeze. It was getting dark and Aunt Regina might come looking for her.

As Mavis extricated herself, she heard a scratching noise off to the left. There had been talk at the dinner table of rats this season twice the size of prairie dogs. She jumped wide, banged the door of the bin, and ran for the house, grain trickling out of her clothes.

The next day at noon, she was making a nice pyramid of sliced tomatoes on a pink platter Aunt Regina had let her choose when Root came into the dining room.

"Not yet, Brother," Aunt Regina called from the kitchen. "Y'all wait on the porch. It's cooler and we're running behind today."

Root's face was dark and unsmiling. "I'm here to talk to Mavis," he said. He had never spoken her name like that.

She laid down her knife. "What?"

He stretched across the doorway to the kitchen, resting one hand on the door frame, leaning his face into his sleeve, not entering this women's domain but not letting anyone escape from it either.

Mavis looked at the dark sweat stain circling his underarm. It made her ashamed to remember she had once liked the smell. He had on the same shirt he had gone socializing in, except now it was wrinkled and the tail hung out.

"You ready for that horse of mine to die?" he said.

"Brother!" Aunt Regina turned, still stirring her gravy.

Mavis swallowed. "Die? What do you mean?"

"You out there at the grain bin last night?"

Mavis picked up her knife and resumed the slicing. "So what if I was?"

"Yes or no?" He looked around as if he might spit, then seemed to remember he was inside. He was acting crazy.

"Yes," Mavis said slowly. "I wanted to feed Dixie. You were gone. I thought she was hungry."

"You left the grain bin unlatched," Root said. He paused to see if she might admit it. "Dixie came back in the corral during the night and ate herself sick to death."

Aunt Regina poured the gravy in a bowl. "Oh surely not, Brother." Mavis took her cue from Aunt Regina. "No big deal, Root the Snoot."

He went on. "You can't let a horse eat their fill of grain and then drink all the water they want. Now she's bloated. She's down out there in the pasture—can't even stand up. Probably dead by tomorrow."

Mavis's eyes filled with tears. She rubbed them with one hand and the tomato juice stung. She dropped her knife and ran from the room.

"Oh Brother," Aunt Regina said, "she's just a child. As for Dixie, it's happened to other horses and they made it through. Must you be so harsh?"

"Probably killed my horse," Root said and turned to go. "You women don't understand nothing."

Mavis lay curled all night beside Aunt Regina, praying, praying for Dixie until she fell asleep exhausted, only to awaken in the pre-dawn with a cold start. She eased off the bed and went out to the porch, sitting down on the top step, pulling her knees against her body under her nightgown. She strained to see out into the darkness.

When things started turning rosy in the morning light, she saw Root walking toward the house.

When he came upon her, his frown deepened. "What you doing up?" He smelled like cigarettes.

"You know," she said, not moving.

Root propped his foot on the step. "You ought to be wondering about Dixie." He spat into the yard.

"I am."

Root popped his knuckles one by one. When he had finished, he said, "Well, little girl . . ."

Mavis looked up quickly. "Don't call me that!"

"You must not want to know about Dixie very bad."

She looked out from between her fingers. "I do and I don't."

There was a long silence. "She's gone," Root said solemnly, "gone as she can be."

Mavis lowered her head and pressed her eyes into her bony knees. She draped her arms over her head and began to moan.

Root sat down beside her. "You ought to have been more careful, little Miss Mavis-Davis."

"Don't call me that either!" she blubbered.

"Well, it's true," Root said, "and you deserve to be called anything I call you."

"I'm sorry." She began rocking. "I'm sorry, I'm sorry, I'm sor- "

Root rose. "Okay, but just don't ever let it happen again."

She lifted her head. Snot streamed across her lips. "Happen again? How could it happen again?"

A smile, crooked and slow, came to Root's face. "I said she's gone. So where did you think—horse heaven?"

Mavis fisted her eyes. "I-I don't know."

Root took her by the shoulders. "Let this be a lesson, little girl. Lately you've gotten real high-handed and I had to take you down a notch." He gave her a shake. "I said Dixie's gone, but I didn't say where."

Mavis jerked from his grip. "What—?"

He stood back, hands on his hips. "She's gone . . . down to the other end of the pasture." He spat over his shoulder. "She's no dummy. She sure ain't coming back up this way for your poison any time soon."

Mavis gathered her feet under her and stood. She moved slowly backwards across the porch to the door, never taking her eyes off Root. He shoved his hat back and put his thumbs in his front pockets. At the moment she opened the door to go back in to the warmth of Aunt Regina's snoring side, he grinned.

She took a deep breath. "You're not Root, you're rot," she said and went in.

THE HISTORICAL MONUMENT

GUIDA JACKSON

Across the road and down about a half a mile off in the bottoms was an old place you could hardly see for the scrub brush and weeds. And the trumpet vines had taken over the front porch so you'd think the screen door wouldn't even open. I didn't remember ever seeing anybody about the place, it'd been vacant that long. I'd like to've forgotten it was even there, so I could hardly believe it when I heard somebody was moving in.

It fell into Lula Bob Murphy's hands when she found it on the delinquent tax rolls in the county clerk's office. All you have to do to claim an abandoned place, it turns out, is pay the back taxes. But nobody could figure out why anybody would want this place, much less a handsome looking single woman who didn't even come from around here. Lula Bob Murphy was her real name, the name Beaufort said she used when she paid the seven thousand dollars in back taxes up in Conroe, but I knew her as Margot LeBaron.

She grew up out near Vega, she told me later, but she wasn't ever part of the well-off wheat farmer crowd. Her daddy was dead and her mother worked in the tomato greenhouse, along with her aunt and her cousin. The only other jobs in Vega were at the gravel pit or the grain elevator. There was a DOE office there for a year or so, but they didn't hire any locals. They folded up and left after it looked like the farmers would shoot anybody that got serious about burying nuclear waste in Oldham or Deaf Smith County, Reagan or no. Margot, or Lula Bob she was then, said she used to get up every morning and look off out at that sandy haze boiling in from New Mexico and listen to the wires twanging in the wind and said she'd be goddogged if she was going to spend her life in any tomato plant in Vega, Texas. She always knew she was going to amount to something, because her daddy, name of Bob, had counted on her to leave them all in the shade,

256

and to her, shade meant trees, not standing on the north side of the grain elevator.

So she went off to West Texas State in Canyon and got a business degree and took off for Houston. She hit there about the time that petroleum engineers were out looking for work as waiters and people with degrees like hers were collecting cans out of dumpsters, just about. Not the best time to go into business for yourself, but Margot never considered working for anybody else for very long. I never asked how she accumulated the seven thousand, but it took more than four years to do it, and by then she'd realized that life in the city is too much of a hassle. Vega's safety and slow pace were two advantages over Houston that she'd discovered. But her mom had died by then and wasn't any reason to go back; besides, she figured there must be some place that had Vega's safety and Houston's trees. So she scouted around until she found the place outside Winton Corners, here on the edge of the Big Thicket. You may not have pizza, she says to me later, but at least you've got trees.

She probably investigated me before she showed up and offered me a job. Just drove that big van right up into my yard with the dogs going crazy and jumping up against it, rolled down the window and offered me a job over all that barking, no questions asked. But Margot didn't do anything by halves. She knew I'd had a little trouble with the law. Nothing serious—a few routine poaching charges is all. "My daddy always said you could trust a man who admits to being a little dishonest," she says. She knew about my pirogue and she knew that I was open to propositions. But the thing that amazed me was, she even knew about the summer some of us boys decided to make it rich by selling Bibles to Iowa farmers and in the process sold ourselves to some of their wives. "I hear you covered yourself with manna from heaven that summer," is how she put it.

Now who could resist that kind of flattery. Margot has also got a dangerous grin that makes you conscious that you've had the same shirt on for two to three weeks and that your breath probably smells like buzzard shit. The grin was as hard to resist as the flattery. So was the kind of money she offered, even though I purely wasn't looking for steady employment. If you don't want to work, don't hire out, is what my daddy always told me. Steady employment doesn't run in the Fancher family. We've lived off the land, cutting timber and hunting squirrels and deer and running trot and frog gigging for about as many generations as there's been folks in Montgomery

County. We've never been taken in by the lures of a regular paycheck, except for an uncle that went off to become a roustabout over at Beaumont. But like I say, Margot's offer was hard to resist. Except for the accident-prone incidents that I didn't know about yet.

The best part was the hours. I didn't have to start until sundown and I could go home as soon as I'd delivered the last customer back down the river to a place called Kingwood, on the northeastern edge of Houston. Because Margot had devised the ultimate plan for staying clear of the law: I would take one of her girls downstream to Houston for recruiting purposes and then transport the customers by pirogue back to the house—unless it was raining, and then I'd use the van and go around by the road and hit the Eastex Freeway just before Humble. So there was never a crowd of cars around the place to give it away, and never any local customers to brag around the domino boards at Winton Corners where the deputy might hear. Margot furnished the house and the business know-how, and everybody else involved, which included me and the cook, got an equal share of the profits. It was a pure juicy set-up.

And the girls—lawddog, talk about sweet meat! Those were seven of the flashiest bimbos ever assembled under one roof, and not a one of them local. Not much of a wonder. Winton Corners doesn't have any girls much left, pretty or ugly. But Margot's first rule was that nobody could have any kin in Winton Corners, or anywhere else in Montgomery County. So she ended up with girls better looking than any woman I'd ever seen outside of television. I can't stress that enough. Even the fat one was pretty enough. Margot explained about Fat Alicia after she caught me checking her out, listening to the friction when she walked.

"Some johns only get the hots for fat ass," she says. Says, "We got something for everybody here." And I'd say she was right. Besides Fat Alicia, there was Flame, the bad-tempered Cajun who was just bow-legged enough to make it interesting. Her actual name was Renée or something French but she'd dyed her hair red and changed her name to Flame, because she grew up in Houma, Louisiana, as the only daughter of a prominent Pentecostal preacher who ran an exterminating business, and she didn't want word of her present occupation to leak out to the congregation or the termite customers back home. Flame made periodic trips to the liposuction clinic in Baytown that she claimed were torture, so she purely hated skinny women. Buddying up with Fat Alicia made her feel like she didn't need to go back to the clinic so often and get sucked out. Otherwise, I don't think she cared for Alicia very much, any more than the rest of us did. We all just tolerated both of them, after we got to know them.

There were the Gonzales twins, Alma *y* Corazon, who called themselves *Las Calientes* and who always worked together. Alma called Corazon "*Cita*," meaning little sister or something, because she was thirty minutes younger. God knows how they earned their fee, which was three times the price of one. Margot always told me there were no free samples, that the only way to find out how they earned that fee was to pay for it. But being a product of the Depression, I hate to part with that much money for anything that doesn't have four wheels and a tailgate. Anyway, I'm not sure I'm up to that much excitement. I was leery of those two at first, because they jabbered to each other *en español* and you always figured they were plotting something. And because their daddy'd been one of the original *El Paso pachucos* and their grandmother was Crystal City's leading *curandera*. I don't know how far as the crow flies a *curandera* can zap you with a spell, but who wants to chance finding out by getting crosswise of the Gonzales twins.

We had your token blonde, Katrina, the oldest of our girls. Katrina was a monument to the cosmetic surgery industry and the underwriter of her beauty shop down in Houston. She went in for leopard-looking outfits and wore nail-studded belts and neck collars. Katrina managed to be the center of attention whenever we took her to town. More than that, she was a flat-out spectacle. You just couldn't tone her down, although Margot sometimes tried, in public.

Passion Flower, our rash oriental, had taken to the streets after her rich boyfriend filed Chapter Seven and she hit him with a priceless vase and took off in his Porsche. The cops nailed her with the car and she did a little time—not much. Not enough to take the bloom off the vine, for damn sure. Her name was Naomi when she came aboard, and she was only one-fourth Japanese. But Margot said it was that fourth that she was hiring. So Passion Flower dyed her hair jet black and learned a few tricks about painting her eyes to make them slanty, and she billed herself as the mistress of massage. You've heard about your inscrutable orientals, but Passion Flower wasn't one of them. She grew up in Tulia where she claimed there's a lake, but if there is, she didn't have both oars in it. She had that same Panhandle twang that Margot had that didn't fit with the image Margot was trying to create.

She got Passion Flower a mess of oriental pornos and shut her up in her bedroom with the VCR and told her to watch and don't come out until she'd got the technique and the speech down pat. When Passion Flower came out of that room after six straight hours of watching oriental jig jig, Margot says, well, have you learned anything? Let me hear you act oriental, she says. Passion Flower does a mini-grind and says, "Hi there, sailor—want your ashes hauled by a by-God pure-dee China doll?" Margot threw up her hands and told Passion Flower just to keep her mouth shut and act like she couldn't speak English.

I saved our black girl Makeisha until last because she turned out to be both the best and the worst. At first she was my favorite because of her looks. It wasn't just that she was the most beautiful of the bunch—although she was—but she had a way of looking that said, you're going up on the rack and you're not coming down until I've cleaned your spark plugs, drained your crankcase, rotated your tires, and given your shocks the test of their lives. She may not have delivered but the look alone was worth the price, and you'd be surprised how many visiting preachers specified a black girl. Preachers must know something, I figure.

Makeisha was twelve shades lighter than her aunt Precious, the cook, and she treated Precious like hog spit to boot, because Precious was older and talked country and wasn't as refined as everybody else. But Precious was the queen jewel and she knew it. Wasn't any working girl going to try to put her down. Precious used to tell Makeisha, "The whole bunch in this house be changed out like old tires except me and it don't make a bootful of piss difference. You be able to make étouffée like me," she says, "you maybe be worth something someday. Until then," she says, "stay out of my kitchen or I'll part them corn rows with a cleaver."

Otherwise, it was a happy little family that all pitched in to get the place ready for business. To avoid suspicion, Margot didn't change the looks of the outside of the house, and I brought in all but the heaviest materials for the inside on my john boat. The girls supplied the labor, once we'd had a fellow come in and strip off about a hundred layers of paint. He turned up some beautiful wood on the floors and fireplaces and railings, and Margot decided she had a better house than she bargained for. How much better caused us some problems later on, fact is. The plumbing fixtures were so out of date that the girls called them "quaint and charming" and ended up painting them pink and orchid, what Flame called "designer hues," so that saved a passel on costs. The kitchen had an old gas stove that stood up on bowlegs with a tall oven up on the side that Precious wouldn't let them haul away, but Margot got her a new dishwasher and refrigerator and a separate freezer. We needed major groceries because we were so far from Houston that an evening's entertainment had to include one of Precious's famous meals.

While I was helping Margot hang new drapes, she told me how she happened to get into the business. Mostly out of curiosity, after she'd saved up a nest egg, she'd answered an ad for "business opportunity" and it turned out Alicia and the Gonzales twins had put the ad in because the streets had got so dangerous and they were tired of getting beat up. But for sure they weren't looking for a woman, and Margot for sure wasn't looking for any business managing prostitutes. But they all took to one another and Margot wanted to know how they got into that line of work.

Fat Alicia's story really got to her. Alicia's old man was the coach of the football team and the history teacher at someplace up around Tahoka, and her mom was big in the Baptist church and the garden club. Alicia got herself knocked up when she was fifteen, only she didn't do it quiet—the whole town knew, and her folks couldn't take the mortification. Her dad slapped her around and threw her out and told her he never wanted to see her again. Once or twice she tried to contact them after that, to see if they'd softened up any, but their reputation was more important than anything else, and far as they were concerned, she was dead meat. She'd been out on the streets ever since and had been turning tricks the whole time except for times in various charity hospitals for work-related injuries, including a broken jaw once. Ten years on the streets on top of her daddy's genes hadn't improved her disposition any. It had turned Alicia permanently mean, but Margot could overlook a lot.

Margot said the Gonzales twins had a worse story, only they'd left home much earlier because that *pachuco* daddy did pretty much whatever he felt like whenever he got a snootful of *tequilas dobles*. Margot said she asked those girls were there any more out there on the streets like them and they said just about all of them. A bunch of small town girls, just trying to survive, not all that different from Margot except that all of a sudden she felt very fortunate.

Margot went on home but she couldn't get those girls out of her mind, and she knew she was just going to have to do something to help them if she was to ever get any peace with herself. That's when she got the idea for the house in the woods. It turned out to be a good investment, because business was brisk from the first night we opened.

Margot thought we needed some extra razz for the grand opening so, even taking into account the possible noise level that might alert the local citizens up at the Corners, she hired a five-piece band that she'd heard at the Blue Moon in Houston's Montrose area. Called themselves Lenny Marks' Lean Machine. Since I'd wore myself out getting ready for the opening, Margot got me in on the party as a little reward. The band made a pretty good sound so that you couldn't hardly set still. Corazon even got me up trying to teach me the Lambada that she'd picked up watching cable.

Part of the band's fee they took out in trade, with Lenny having the first pick. He chose Katrina, I guess because she was the flashiest and because he didn't have any better taste. Later he told me he always picked the oldest ones because experience counts the most in those situations.

Katrina didn't have any better sense than to get serious over the jerk, and on her day off she used to go into town and give him what he would've paid good money for otherwise. Fatal mistake. She might've thought she was in love, kept telling anybody who'd listen that she was, but Margot said Katrina fell for Lenny because of his celebrity status.

Every Tuesday, Margot hired me to take the girls up to Houston for a visit to the beauty shop to touch up roots and whatall. It was hard enough to keep them satisfied off out in the country as it was. Usually the girls couldn't wait to get started, but this particular Tuesday Katrina surprised us by refusing even to get out of bed. She needed a bleach job bad, but the Gonzales twins talked Margot into leaving her alone. She'd just got word that the famous band leader Lenny Marks had got married during a Quaalude binge after a gig down in Corpus, and she was dragging ass. So Margot took Precious along in her place to pick out a side of beef for the freezer. That was our worst mistake. We should've never left Katrina alone.

We got home after dark, but there wasn't a light on anywhere, our first clue that something bad was wrong. And we could smell the gas before we even got the door open. Damned if Katrina hadn't dressed up in a red lace nightgown and laid herself out in the front room and expired right there of gas from Precious's oven. She'd raided everybody's jewelry box and she was wearing every necklace and bracelet in the place, including a locket that had Makeisha's picture in it. Katrina had her photogenic side up and you could just see how she'd thought it all out for the benefit of the newspaper photographer. It was just like her to try to make a good impression on the reporters and the coroner.

Only of course, Margot couldn't call the coroner or anybody else. That would tip off the law and spoil our whole operation. Katrina never give that a thought, I ganny. Or maybe she did. Maybe she meant to bring us all down.

We all stood around—soon as we'd aired out the place—and said nice things about Katrina, with her all the time lying right there covered over with a sheet that nobody ever used again. She was a good friend, Passion Flower said, and she knew how to attract a crowd in a cemetery. Not exactly the right thing to say under the circumstances. Makeisha remembered the time Katrina lent her her last pair of net stockings and said Katrina could keep the locket, because she would feel creepy ever wearing it again. The Gonzalez twins said Katrina knew more about S&M than anybody else, and that her passing would be a great loss to the industry. Fat Alicia and Flame stood in the back and refrained from saying anything bad, which was about all you could expect out of those sorry floozies. Precious said Katrina never failed to compliment her beignets of a Sunday morning, and I recalled how Katrina had managed to attract a crowd even that time Princess Di was in town. Then it was Margot's turn and she looked around and saw that we expected her to wrap it up. She bowed her head and cleared her throat and said, "Well Lord, here comes our blonde."

Although Katrina'd never been anybody's buddy, the Gonzales twins had known her the longest and they said they thought her real name was Betty Clyde Manning or something starting with an M. Alma said Katrina never told anybody where she was from, because if anything was to ever happen to her, it sure as hell wouldn't be the kind of thing anybody in her hometown would want to hear. Or maybe they'd love to hear it, probably would, but she wouldn't want to give them the satisfaction. Corazon said it would be a shame to tell Lenny Marks and make him feel guilty for marrying somebody else—even though we all knew that's what Katrina meant to happen. But it wasn't going to. Katrina had just run out of chances to grab the spotlight and just finished attracting her last crowd. I wondered if she'd ever thought about that.

Margot asked me to go up to my place and get the shovel, but I had to remind her that on every side, her house was choked up by trees and thick undergrowth. There was no question of digging a grave through that mess of roots, and besides, I flat-dab draw the line at burying people. Margot said that with all that silicone, Katrina would bob to the surface if we tried to sink her in the river, so she did the only logical thing: she told Precious to empty the freezer. The next morning she sent me up to Houston for another freezer and an electrician to put in extra wiring on the back porch. It is amazing how fast you can get an electrician to come out all this way if money is no object.

The new freezer was installed in the kitchen, while what became known as the K freezer was moved to the screen porch. After that, nobody took morning coffee on the back porch and nobody but Precious ever even looked out that direction. The whole bunch was uneasy sleeping under the roof with the K freezer just gently pinging along out there.

During the day, just to get out of the house, four of the girls took to sun bathing down by the river out on the little dock I'd repaired. It was the only place besides the road that wasn't covered by trees, where they could catch a few rays. I generally pulled my boat out of the water about thirty yards away, closer up to my place, and turned it upside down when I wasn't using it, to keep it from filling up with rainwater.

I found out about the sun bathing the hard way when I went down figuring to get in a little fishing and came upon one of the girls spread eagle face down on my pirogue. You couldn't tell which one it was because she had a towel over her head and the rest of her was jay bird naked. Coming upon a sight like that unawares came near to giving me a heart attack, and I said "Jesus Keerist!" and turned around and beat it back to the house. I heard Flame cackling and she says, "Jesus Christ won't help you a bit this time, Cleon," so I guessed it was Flame I saw. There was some calling back and forth and more laughing from the other girls down on the pier. I didn't figure I could ever go back over there and be the butt of them laughing.

All my life these have been my woods and my river. My great-grandaddy came from Tennessee down here after the Civil War. He built a place with his own hands on this very spot—only my great-grandmother, who smoked a pipe upside down—you figure it—burned it to the ground three different times. Later my grandpa and some others tried clearing forty acres for a dab of cotton, but he couldn't get any help and the brush all grew up faster than he could weed it out. My daddy cut timber off the place, made a nice living. Built this place here on the foundation of the old home place. My momma raised twelve children on this place but only four of them lived to be grown because of smallpox and diphtheria. She died, too, and then the three girls, my sisters, went west to be raised by their Aunt Minnie and Uncle Floyd. Poppa and I batched it together up until he died almost twenty years ago. By that time I was pretty much set in a certain way of doing things, and all these years I've come and went whenever I took a notion. So now I'd be damned if I was going to be a prisoner in my own house, afraid if I went out I'd find bare butts splattered out all over the place every time it come a sunny day. I'd sooner blow the whistle on the whole operation and go back to the way it was before Margot showed up.

Margot's naturally sensitive about things. She must've read my mind when she heard about what happened. When I didn't go down for lunch that day, like I'd been doing for a good spell, Margot came up bringing me a plateful of chicken fried steak and a piece of Precious's chocolate meringue pie. I would've cleaned up the place if I'd known she'd be coming inside, which she never did before. She gave me that grin and came right on in and sat down at the table with me, but I couldn't eat a bite with her watching. She said she really came to apologize for the girls acting like that and it wouldn't happen again, them exposing themselves and embarrassing me to death. I commenced to feel sorry for the girls being stuck inside all the time with that freezer puttin' away out back, never getting to sun bathe anymore on account of me, so we worked out a compromise. When I got ready to go outside of a sunny day when they were apt to be sun bathing, I'd get out on the porch and bang on my iron skillet first, and the girls would disappear, so I could come and go and not worry about running into bare ass. Margot gave her word on it.

The timing of that little incident was uncanny. It happened that that signal that we'd just worked out saved our necks about a week later.

There's a lady name of LaWanda Tolliver in Winton Corners that was a member of the Montgomery County Historical Society that met one month up in Conroe and the next month in Montgomery and the next in Magnolia and the next in Splendora and so on. Never in Winton Corners, since LaWanda was the only member so they couldn't have a real chapter here. Probably she thought the other members looked down their noses at her because she was from little old Winton Corners, although she's the widow of Junior Tolliver who run Tolliver Feed and Grain for years and years and was known by everybody for miles.

Anyway, unbeknown to us, she'd been poking around in old records trying to find her a house in Winton Corners old enough to be declared a

265

historical monument and give her some reflected glory. And the first we found out Margot's house was it was when a car full of women came past my house one sunny morning headed for Margot's. Lucky I saw them, although I naturally would, since nobody ever comes by that I don't see. I rushed out in my skivvies and banged on the skillet and LaWanda gave me a eat dirt look. I got the straight of what happened from Margot later.

The Historical Society ladies all got out and followed LaWanda up onto Margot's front porch. Must've been five or six of them with their patent leather purses and matching shoes and their little notebooks. Precious opened the door just a crack and like to of stunned the pee out of old LaWanda because she thought she'd brought all her high-toned ladies to stand on the porch of a black woman. But on the hope that she was mistaken, she asked if Miss Murphy was in and Precious only says, "It's Ms. Murphy." She asked LaWanda to state her business and the old girl sputtered about it being a historical house and the committee had come to examine it, and Precious says, "Are you asking to come in? Do you want me to put all the chickens up first?" LaWanda says, "Oh no!" and the ladies commenced backing away and sort of tested the porch columns and went on chipping about how they'd seen enough to verify it was an old house, all right, and a few weeks later, on a cloudy day when the girls happened not to be outside, a man came and nailed a plaque on the front of the house. All that rat-tatting like to of scared the pants off the girls, if they happened to be wearing any. That was the next to last time LaWanda Tolliver caused us trouble.

All this time Flame, who didn't have the sense God gave a mule to know when she was well off, had just been waiting to find some weakness in Margot's set-up so she could weasel in on a bigger piece of the take. Having the K freezer humming out there on the back porch definitely qualified as a weakness. So one morning she went in and laid out an ultimatum that either Margot cut her in for an extra share of the profit—to make up for all the mental aggravation living under the roof with a frozen whore was causing— or she was going into Winton Corners and tell the deputy what we kept in the K freezer.

Flame should've known better. Nobody shakes down Margot, especially some no-count sorry Cajun. Margot would've sent Flame packing on those bowlegs of hers if she could have—but she knew what that Cajun would've done next. So Margot did the next logical thing. She told Flame she'd have to think about it, and she went straight upstairs and sicked old Fat Alicia on her.

"If you don't want your coonass buddy to queer the best deal you'll ever get, you'd better stick to her like sweat on a mule," Margot told her.

So anytime she wasn't horizontal, Fat Alicia didn't let Flame out of her sight. She'd pop her head in the bathroom while Flame was taking a shower and she'd come up from behind and read over Flame's shoulder while she was writing those phony letters home to Houma. She even took to looking in on her during working hours and that just tore the rag with old Flame. She got so mad that after the johns went home one night, she got to screaming and throwing things and calling her best friend names I wouldn't use on Saddam Hussein. She must've landed some punches on old fatso, because Alicia started throwing them back, and the woman had a right like a ball peen hammer. She coldcocked that Cajun, dropped her with one pop, and Flame's head landed against the andiron by the front room fireplace with a crack that you could hear all the way to Winton Corners. We never knew whether it was the fist or the fall that broke her neck. But you guessed it: Margot sent me back to Houston the next morning for the electrician and another freezer, henceforth known as the F freezer.

Flame hadn't enjoyed the popularity even of Katrina. I doubt if anybody could've thought of anything good to say about her, so we dismissed the idea of a ceremony. Margot felt bad about not being able to notify her next of kin, but we all knew that Pentecostal preacher didn't really want to know his daughter died in a whorehouse brawl. Better to let him hang onto whatever bazoola she'd been feeding him and just wonder what ever happened than to know for sure. Besides, notifying Flame's parents, even if we could find their name in her stuff, would've implicated Fat Alicia, and as it was she was already pretty well wiped by what she'd done. You can't imagine how much a fat woman can drink when she puts her mind to it. The woman was always drifty anyway, and after a few drinks there wasn't any reasoning with her whatsoever. She wasn't worth a damn servicing customers after that, either. And the bar bill would've paid for a year's worth of nights with the Gonzales twins.

Finally one morning Alicia staggered out drunker'n a hooty owl and hollered for me to take her into Houston. "I got to find a priest and go to confession!" She was blubbering and slathering all over the place, big old sloppy cow with mascara dribbling down those fat cheeks.

I'd been on the verge of setting out on a quiet morning of trap setting just to calm my nerves. The steady job had commenced to eat into my social life, too, and I figured on later on pitching horseshoes with the boys and catching up on the news. But this thing with Fat Alicia looked like a major emergency. If you've ever been in the path of a hurricane spawning off tornados in every direction, you got an idea of the destruction a drunk Fat Alicia could've caused. Come to think of it, I believe there was a hurricane through here one time name of Alicia. So I says, "Oh no siree." I says, "If I was to take you to town, both our tails would be in a crack." I got her by the arm and tried to hustle her back over into the house, which was like trying to haul a tractor out of the mud with one hand. Margot and Passion Flower came out on the porch just as Fat Alicia broke away and flung me back like I was no more than a piece of fatback. Then she lurched off saying she'd just have to walk up to Winton Corners.

There wasn't any danger of finding a priest in Winton Corners, because if you wanted to start a fire, you couldn't find two Catholics to rub together in the whole of South Montgomery County, but there wasn't any use to try to explain that to Fat Alicia in her pie-eyed condition. I picked myself up and said, "Better stop her, Miss Margot. She's going to find a priest and tell him what she done." Margot, who wasn't wearing much, told Passion Flower to get the van and go after her. Passion Flower is the one I referred to as being rash and something of a dim flickering bulb herself.

Passion Flower ran in and got the keys to the van and a long piece of rope out of Katrina's late S&M equipment that I guess she planned on lassoing her with, and came barreling that van backwards out the drive, figuring that surely Alicia must be well on down the road by then. But old blubber-butt was weaving sideways more than she was going forward, even staggering around backwards some, and so she was smack in the path of that van. But the sound was more like splat or twock.

It took a commercial sized freezer this time, known as the Big A instead of the Fat A freezer, out of respect. The thing was so big, Precious could hardly squeeze past it to throw out the slop, and she was threatening to quit if Margot didn't move those things out of her path.

For three days Margot rummaged around in Alicia's stuff looking for a clue about which specific town around Tahoka she came from and what was her real name. But again, we knew that high school coach'd had ten years to try to find her if he'd wanted to. It was Corazon who finally convinced us to give it up. "Nothing is going to make her feel better now. She is history and the rest of us got to look out for ourselves."

By now the whole house was pretty demoralized, even Margot. Nobody wanted to stay in the house with all those freezers chugging away on the back porch, and Margot tried to talk me into staying down there of a night for moral support. But I wasn't too keen on the place, either. Once or twice I swallowed my misgivings and invited her up to my place, being about halfway scared she might take me up on it. But she didn't feel like she ought to leave the girls unattended at that point, although she thanked me for the compliment. She says to me, says, "Daddy always said while you're waiting for opportunity to knock at the door, you might ought to settle for convenience scratching on the window screen."

After that sometimes when I was down on the bank she'd come down and we'd talk. She felt like she had to make it up for not taking me up on my invitation which, like I say, it was just as well. She got to reminiscing about growing up outside of Vega, about standing out beside the road waiting for the school bus to take her into Hereford and the sand and sleet both stinging her legs at the same time, and about one time standing waiting in a red ant bed and getting stung all over and liking to have died. And I told her about the brush arbor revivals I had to go to when I was a kid, not only having to go, but even having to help build them in the first place every time they took a notion to get in a visiting revival preacher, which I always thought was the height of cruelty. I told her about being made to get up at the front and confess my sins so I could be saved, only I kept my real sins to myself and made up some better ones to tell. I told her about the time when I was little that a colored man was accused of setting eyes on a white woman and how they dragged him around from the back of a car with him screaming bloody murder until he died, and how after all these years I can still hear how that scream sounded. And she says, "Life is still mighty cheap, though, after all this time." Margot took losing those girls, sorry as they were, pretty hard. And she couldn't for the life of her figure out what she was going to do with all them freezers that just kept stacking up.

One morning I happened to go up to the Corners for some Red Man and everything was draped with red, white and blue bunting and there was TV vans and people milling around. And here come LaWanda Tolliver twittering over and she says, "Oh, Cleon, would you mind stopping by and telling that colored neighbor of yours that our future congressman plans to stop by our historical monument home?" I didn't know what the hell she was talking about because it'd escaped my attention that it was near election time.

269

Now, I purely couldn't imagine this particular candidate deciding to make a visit to Margot's in broad daylight, since he'd been our guest on several occasions in the dark of night.

I hurried on back about fifteen minutes ahead of them to tell Margot, so we could decide what to do. She sent the girls to their rooms and said there wasn't much else we *could* do. "He needn't worry about meeting up with anybody he knows, though," she says. "The only ones he knows are in the freezer."

So in a little while here comes the candidate and some other people and LaWanda and Weldon dressed up in a by-God coat and tie that I didn't even know he owned—Weldon is what passes for mayor of Winton Corner—driving up in a long black car that I swear almost wouldn't make it around the curves. And in behind them came like about ten cars and vans of news people, and behind that come every by-God pickup and automobile in South Montgomery County, all threading up this little narrow road. Then it came to me that this candidate didn't have a clue in hades about where the hell he was fixing to end up because he'd always come by way of the river on my pirogue.

But I figured he might would remember me, so before he could get out, I stepped up to the window and says, "Hey there, Congressman (which he never got to be, by the way), nice day for a ride on the river. You want to take a trip on my long john?" LaWanda was glaring knives at me and Weldon tried to push me aside so he could open the guy's door. The candidate commenced looking from me to the house and you could see the lights finally dawn.

The man reacted fast, I'll give him that. He looked at his watch and he says, "Is this the right time? Why didn't anybody tell me we were running so late?" And he shut the car door without setting a foot on the ground and apologized to Weldon and LaWanda and says he's got a speech to make somewheres else. I doubt he was afraid of losing too many votes at Margot's anyway.

All this string of cars was behind him, remember, and there wasn't any way to turn around on the road because there's bar ditches full of swamp water on each side, so the only thing to do was come on down and go up into Margot's drive and back out and turn around. Either that, or back all the way to the crossroad. So that whole string of cars had to decide whether to creep forward or just try and back up. Some of them did one thing and some another, but it was a mess around there, stirring up clouds of road dirt for a good half hour until they all got cleared out. LaWanda Tolliver quit causing trouble after that, and it was a good thing, because Margot'd had about all the trouble she needed.

But nobody kicks Margot when she's down, and that's what Makeisha did. Makeisha had gotten to be the most outspoken about what a stinking rat trap this was, how you couldn't walk outside without sinking in an alligator bog or being banged back into the house by the sound of my iron skillet, and how there was a lot more to life than just money, night life and shopping being two of them, and one other being if you wanted a little snort of crack—that Margot didn't allow—you could get high without somebody making a federal case out of it. And then there was the biggie: the indignity of sharing the same roof with three frozen hookers in those damn ice boxes that hummed and buzzed and chugged the livelong day and night without letup. The sound of all them freezers was driving them all bonkers till they were about ready for the nut house. To say nothing about the scrape they'd be in trying to explain all those corpses to the law if they ever were to get raided. She claimed she was so on edge that she was grinding her teeth down to the nub, and she had paid a fortune for her caps. She obviously hadn't caught Margot's vision of what she was trying to build out here.

Makeisha never was a team player. On the nights when it was her turn to go into town with me to hustle, I always felt uneasy turning my back on her, like maybe she'd stick a shiv in my back or push me overboard. So I wasn't surprised when one morning Margot got up and found the night's take cleaned out and Makeisha and the van gone. That girl knew Margot was in no position to send the law looking for her.

But Margot wasn't as put out as I would've expected when she came up to ask me to come on down and stand by; she looked pert and fresh-faced with her brown curls done up with a little pink ribbon like she might be going out to pick daisies. Except that the flush of her cheeks alerted me that she'd spotted game: she had that same bristly excitement my squirrel dogs get when they're onto something. "My daddy always said, if you can't get rich, get even," she says, with a wicked grin.

We went on back to the house and she called in Precious and went straight for the jugular. "You want to tell me where Makeisha went, or you want to spend tonight back at the Star of Hope?"

Precious didn't have to think about that one. Anyway, there was no need for family loyalty, the way Makeisha had been walking all over her from day one. "She probably be staying over in New Orleans, uh huh, down in the Quarter. I know that's where she's like to go, because I heard her calling over there last night," Precious says, like she'd been waiting for this chance for the last twenty years.

It was no trouble to call the phone company and get the number Makeisha had called, which Precious recognized as belonging to a place called the Temple of Diana in New Orleans. For a country girl, Precious knew an awful lot about the dives in the French Quarter, but we let it pass.

I took Margot into town to rent a big dolly and a fork-lift truck, which she drove back to the house while I parked my pickup at my place then hurried down on foot to help out. The hardest part was getting the freezers out to the fork-lift, but those girls are tougher than they look, and all of us together even managed to get old Big A aboard. Then we all climbed in the truck and headed out, stopping on the freeway feeder only long enough to buy a better set of wheels for the girls to make the trip in. The Gonzales twins whined for something sporty this time, but Margot said we couldn't manage without a van. She never even considered trying to get the old one back from Makeisha.

We were in Beaumont in four hours' time, me and Margot in the truck and Corazon driving the others in the new van. Passion Flower had given up driving for good after the accident with Fat Alicia. It took longer than it should because we had to stop a couple of times and tie down the freezers when the load shifted. I was afraid to drive too fast and get a ticket, although I figured Margot knew every judge for miles around. But I knew her better than to think she'd ever blackmail a customer, so I kept it down to sixty-five on the Interstate.

It was taking so long that I commenced to worry about the thaw factor and asked Margot did she think we ought to stop and get a couple of portable generators. But she said, "It's not like we have to worry about botulism."

With Precious's directions, we still made it to Makeisha's doorstep before the sun came up. I paid a couple of strung out junkies to help us unload. Makeisha must've been stunned out of her garters when she looked out the window that morning at those three freezers on her front stoop. We didn't stick around to find out how Makeisha got rid of them before she had to explain to the cops how come one of those stiffs was wearing a locket with her picture.

On the way home, after we'd turned in the truck and got through horsing and laughing and having a good meal on the road, Margot got sober and began to tally up her losses. With only three girls and Precious left, the ranks had thinned too much to make a pleasure palace profitable. Then it hit us all that we'd reached the end of a grand experiment and there wasn't any good excuse to stay together any more.

But the safety of the operation in the woods had ruined the whoring business for the girls. They couldn't see going back to hustling out on South Main, suffering through raids and jailtime or else payoffs to sleazy cops, getting stiffed by some junkie for the whole night's take—maybe even shot to boot. So Passion Flower would probably go back to being Naomi Smallwood from Tulia and eventually migrate down to Lubbock and wait tables at a truck stop on the Slayton highway, maybe eventually move in with the driver of an eighteen wheeler who doesn't even own his own rig and blows his nose by holding one side and snorting out the other.

The Gonzales twins would ride the bus back to El Paso and marry somebody from the barrio who would keep them pregnant and who'd stay out all night on paydays and then come home drunk and beat hell out of them. They'd end up making *migas* for breakfast and *menudo* for supper, even though they both purely swore they never intended to even own a frying pan. They'd grind all the pork by hand for all those hundreds of Christmas tamales, and they'd kill theirselves putting together every *Cinco de Mayo* and then hang back and never get any of the credit. They'd each have a kid a year and when their old man run off or got cut up over in Juarez, they'd get by on milk from the WIC and food stamps. When the last kid got old enough for Headstart, they'd try, even though by now they'd ballooned out to about one-eighty apiece, and get themselves a job at the check-out at Wal-Mart, and wouldn't anybody ever know about all the wasted talent.

Precious would go back to the deep Piney Woods where some relative in a tar paper shack would take her in in exchange for drudgery for the rest of her life, washing clothes on a rub board and hanging them on a broke down fence to dry, shoveling the crap out from under the outhouse and spreading down the fresh lime, and bleaching out flour sacks to make herself something new to wear once in a while.

I would go back to laying out trot lines and watching cable movies, which wasn't ever going to cut it again for your X-rated sex, not after being so close to the real thing. I would outlive the dogs and eventually break down and join the domino players at the Corners and probably die of emphysema. It was the life I'd always aspired to, but it didn't look so hot anymore.

Margot, on the other hand, wasn't ever going to go back to the tomato plant in Vega and all of us knew it. She sat over on the co-pilot side of the van and stared out at the trees whizzing by with their Spanish moss drooping almost to the ground. Margot loved those trees just as much as she hated the bare prairie. I'd never been on the plains, but right then I hated them too, or was scared of them, which is what Margot was, scared they'd grind her down till she couldn't keep trying any more. I could imagine the grit getting in your teeth and blowing into your eyes 'til you couldn't keep them open. I could hear those fierce blue northers come whipping in and hear that lonesome whine of the wind blowing under the edge of a corrugated iron roof or whistling through the crack under the door. Not the same sound at all as the rustle that builds up when the wind catches the tops of the trees out here in the woods. I could imagine those strung out July days, when that sun flashes across the plains in one shot at dawn with nothing to hold it back the livelong day, frying every living thing in sight and not giving way to night until almost ten o'clock. I could see the tumbleweeds stuck along the barbed wire fence and I felt the numb monotony of that flat dusty land that Margot'd tried so hard to escape before it got the best of her. And I knew, if it was me, I'd throw myself under the first train that come along rather than go back. Also I knew how much I would miss Margot if she was to do anything like that.

Then Precious cleared her throat and says, "I got something to say." We all perked up because we needed a word.

"I didn't have a daddy to tell me things like Margot," she said, "but my momma be worth about a hundred sorry old men—excuse me, Cleon," she says. "She had to bring up so many children we all lost count, and they wasn't no government aid in those times. We picked cotton for a penny a bale and we dug crawdads and gathered dandelions for poke salad and, if she found one, Momma could make a rabbit last for three days, um hum! We learned to survive from Momma. And Momma always said, if the sky look dark, it probably only be a flock of crows full of mulberries, and the best thing to do is duck your head and keep moving, and it'd all soon pass. Anyway, I never before lived in a monument."

Margot took it in and seemed to come to after a minute. When Margot came to, the air crackled and got ionized like before a lightning storm. The color of the light even seemed to change and take on a blue-white quality, and sound traveled better through it. It was like all the particles of pollution were swept away, getting ready for the storm.

She said, "There's one thing I didn't learn in business school that I had to learn by experience: they spend a lot of time in board rooms figuring out ways to get around the law, just out of pure-dee greed. Where I worked, business ethics turned out to be a conflict in terms. There must be lots of businesses operating outside of the law, not just the one we've been in." It never occurred to me until then how much it had bothered Margot that, even though she'd been doing something good for the girls, what she was doing was against the law. Margot's the kind would of wanted her daddy to be proud of her if he was alive.

When I thought about it, it seemed like the laws are made by one bunch of people to keep some other bunch besides themselves in line, so they word the laws so that they only apply to the other guys. I knew the fellows that made the laws never give a thought about what put young girls like Alma and Corazon out on the streets to survive.

Alma said where she was from the laws were all made by gringos to control the chicanos, but Passion Flower said where she came from it was just SOB's made the laws. "Men," she said, laughing and reaching up to pat me on the back. And Precious muttered something about honky men, and they all chimed in and commenced bitching about who'd done them wrong, and it sounded like they were dumping on me. No by-God law I ever heard about ever seemed to work in my favor, and I was getting flat-out by-God steamed and halfway of a mind to get out and be shed of the whole goddamn rotten bunch. They were getting completely out of hand. I think I may've commenced snorting and steaming out loud over this ungrateful bunch I'd like to have got into serious trouble for the first time in my life on account of.

Margot put her hand on my shoulder and patted it like she was gentling a horse. Everybody got quiet, like they'd just caught on they'd gone too far and needed to rein in. They'd been dazzled by all that ionized air that Margot's coming to had caused. She started talking low and smooth, pretending she was talking to them, saying how probably what they all meant was that they thought rich folks made the rules and poor folks were the only ones who didn't have much choice about following them. Everybody was quick to say, yeah, that was what they really meant to say.

That satisfied me more or less. I took a deep breath and everybody else did too. It's terrible to be mad at your own clan and like it or not, these women seem to've adopted me as part of theirs. Well what the hell, come to think of it, if I still got any relatives living anywhere, hasn't any of them bothered to get in touch since before my daddy died, so this bunch was as good as any, probably a whole lot better than most.

Now that the climate wasn't so hostile anymore, Margot's creative juices were flowing again. We were coming up on the house, and it looked sad and dark, like a big mausoleum: a monument to our failed project. I turned off the ignition and we all sat there looking at it. It was growing dark back here in the woods where dusk comes on real early, soon as the sun drops behind the pines. It's a sort of melancholy time deep in the woods, anyway, a little after the birds quit chirping and before the frogs and crickets commence singing. It's too dead quiet, like if something don't happen quick, the whole thing is going to die.

"You know," Margot said, "to look at this place out here in the Wetlands all by itself, you wouldn't even know it was in the United States. A place like this would have no place to hide up in Vega." We didn't catch her drift so we waited for her to go on. "Before we came along and rescued it, nobody in the world cared anything about it or even remembered it existed. And besides us, there's still nobody who cares—maybe not even Old Lady Tolliver, since she knows colored people live here." We all laughed a little and agreed. I could see what Margot was getting at. The house matched the people that lived there, a bunch that nobody cared much about, that everybody else'd give up on and forgot all about. Maybe she was trying to justify that she'd been operating outside of the law, but she was also making sense to the others. Maybe they needed to feel okay about the whole thing, too. I didn't even mind it, myself.

"So it seems to me that it'd be a crime to abandon it," Margot went on, turning to me. "Cleon, you and Precious are historical monuments yourself, living off the land, in harmony with it. I just figured out why Vega was so unbearable: we'd plowed up rangeland, grazing land, that should never have been touched. We caused our own misery."

She reached back to touch Precious. "Can you two teach me to live without money?"

276

I said, "You mean trot fishing and bird hunting?"

Precious said, "Cooking rabbit stew?"

"Whatever it takes. I want to become a historical monument to subsistence living. Can the woods support me?"

The rest chimed in. "All of us?"

I remembered that it used to support my whole family. My other family. I looked around at Precious's broad, strong face, caught her look of consent, and said, "Like as not."

WAITING FOR RAIN

JAMES HOGGARD

The morning sky bleeds as the neighborhood's cadre of joggers and walkers drones by, the soles of their shoes whispering like gossip over asphalt. Standing on her front porch across the street, a woman in an orchid housedress watches the spray coming off the rotary sprinkler clicking in her yard. A rolled newspaper—its grey tint matching her hair—lies tucked under her arm. The last of the joggers passes, a small bearded man without a shirt, the length of his feet slapping the street's surface flatly. A breeze brings the smell of moisture over to me as I glance at the thinness of cloudcover. There seems to be no chance for rain, although the sailor's saw— "red sky at morning"—teases me into hoping we might have a shower by dusk. Drought is desiccating this region.

In the octagonal planter, pink and blue larkspur petals quiver at the edge of the sand-colored stalks gone to seed. Not much green is left in the yard, though there is a sizable, amoeba-shaped patch around the tiny pine we've struggled for three years to keep growing. The soil, where weeds have been pulled, is still dark from last night's heavy watering; but the fescue I sowed last week shows no sign of sprouting. Birds have even quit gathering there.

As I watch the woman gaze at her sprinkler, the electric night-lamp goes off. I forgot to turn the coffee on. I need to get back in, need to do calisthenics to loosen my back, need to take the trash out and bring a cup of honeyed coffee-milk to my wife who finds it hard to rise early—"or even at all," she has said. Her heartbeat's arrhythmically arrhythmic.

Much of the lawn has turned to straw. Crickets whistle. A mockingbird sings like a sparrow, then chortles like a grackle before sailing off into a high-pitched trill that ends with a comical sputter. Cicadas begin whirring. During the last week they left their brown shells hanging by claws on the fruitless mulberry leaves. Yesterday my son brought a batch in to scare my daughter, both of them here for their summer visit. As long as Damon kept them more than an arm's length from her, Gaddi wasn't bothered. She even pointed out that some of the hulls, stacked, looked as if the cicadas had been mating. Damon swore he hadn't tampered with them. "Sure," Gaddi said, mocking him, "sure."

❖   ❖   ❖

With my old Boy Scout hunting knife I dig up crabgrass and Johnson grass. The long ivory tubers seem to be independent of the first stage of roots: claws tangled in topsoil. For two hot days I have been digging them out and have filled two trash cans and a plastic garbage sack. My next door neighbor, a retired Air Force colonel, tells me that weeding is futile unless, like him, you use Chemlawn. The other next door neighbor, a psychiatrist and Cuban emigre, gave up trying to nurture his thinning Bermuda; he paid to have his yard tilled and reseeded. But more weeds than grass are germinating in the sandy loam he purchased. Scratching nape with the knife's dull blade, I decide to keep trying.

Last month, while pulling out another load of weeds, I cramped up so much I walked stiff-legged for a week To relieve the pain, I got my wife to walk on me while, paralytic and prone: I sprawled on the burnt-gold carpet in the den. This time, though, I'm not getting so stiff. The knife works better than the V-tipped weeder.

Stabbing the clayey earth and ripping through it, I notice that I'm also not having after-images as much as in years past. In another house across town, I saw little, after working in the yard, except illusions of weeds and strawy grass. Once even a friend's face suddenly became a tumble of clover, goatheads, and grassburrs. That was disconcerting. She was going through grief, but it's hard to look sympathetic when your friend has stickers for eyes and a tangle of weeds for a face. In time, though, both of our fits passed. They usually do.

Dirt, which has gotten into my leather gloves, feels gritty. Specks of dark soil freckle my forearms. Sweat drips down my face and enlarges the stain on my shirt. I used to call this process driving out the poison. Happily, terms of corruption don't seem to apply any more, at least not as often as they did. Or so I like to think. Leaning back on one arm, I mop my face with my shirt. My son comes out and asks if I want a glass of iced tea.

"Sure," I tell him.

Smiling, he says he already has it with him and pulls the glass from behind his back. I foolishly ask if he wants to stay and help me.

"It's too hot," he says, drawing back.

"Be good for you," I tease him.

"I'd rather work on stamps."

"If you change your mind, come back out."

"How much longer are you going to be?" he cautiously asks.

"Nineteen hours," I lie to leave him free.

"No way," he says. "Want some more tea?"

"Maybe later," I tell him.

As he walks back to the house, I see my daughter watching us from the door. I wonder if she's dressed yet. The waxleaf ligustrum keeps me from seeing what she has on. I do notice, though, that she hasn't brushed her hair. She says she doesn't have to get dressed at home so she shouldn't have to fix up here, or do anything that's not her idea. Sometimes, though, she'll hit tennis balls with us, or go shopping, if Mary or I ask, but she prefers to spend her days watching game shows and soaps.

The dog gets between us. My two children have been taken to the planetarium by my father. My wife is lying on the carpet in the den. Acting as if I'm relaxing, I stretch out beside her, but our Samoyed wants us to romp. But we won't. We'll just wait for my wife's mother to finish the thirteen-hour drive to see us. Uncertain, however, that she's actually coming today—she is, after all, erratic—I kiss Mary behind the ear. "That tickles," she complains.

The dog again noses between us. Thinking about a woman I saw test-munching grapes at the grocery store, I get up and pour myself a glass of water. I ask Mary if she'd like something, too. "No," she says, then, sitting up, welcomes the dog back into her arms. I sit down at the dining table and open the new copy of my alumni magazine. My parents lent me theirs. Somehow I've been dropped from the mailing list. Flipping to the back, I see that my classmates haven't reported doing anything, not even dying. The surrounding classes, however, have some new bank presidents, births, and marriages. I feel on edge.

Before long Mary goes upstairs. I know there'll be a crisis if I follow her up, and there is, though it's a moderately civilized spat: charges about my moodiness, about the fact that that's a sign of repression. I suggest there's another point of trouble: her disinclination to be a spur-of-the-moment voluptuary. With more than a dash of pepper in her voice, she disagrees; and the argument's over. Sounds of the children returning are now with us.

Before long the four of us are back downstairs watching television, then having supper. Mary and I talk some more, this time about the coming presidential election. No one seems to have good things to say about our candidate.

After I wash dishes we have coffee together. Damon has ridden off on his bicycle—"Already learning to tomcat," Mary says, sounding aggravated—or maybe amused: I don't know which. "Just let the sun go down and he's off."

"He might find something interesting," I say, defending him. She smiles indulgently at me. Gaddi has slipped away upstairs, perhaps to draw or maybe just pout.

Mary tries calling her mother to make sure she's left, but there's no answer. I try calling myself, then we go upstairs and stop at the entrance to our bedroom. Mary has plans to read: tales of our time's compatriots back in the 14th century: buboes, chancres, and a lust for magic. Although we're affectionate in the doorway, I keep quiet about some fantasies I'm having: a sybaritic life with her. She tells me she loves me, and I say I love her, too.

"Do you really?" she asks.

"Sure," I say, clasping my hands behind her waist. "We wouldn't be doing this if I didn't."

"You don't hate me—think I'm horrible and unresponsive?"

"No."

She pulls away and goes into our chamber. Thinking I ought to gather up my daughter and watch TV with her, I go toward my study. I do, though, first ask Gaddi if she'd like to come with me: we could draw or read together. Scarcely glancing up, she says, "No."

When I finally come downstairs for a drink, I see that my son has returned from prowling.

"Guess what?" he says, then tells me he's just discovered that one of his stamp-collecting buddies is a member of our church. He seems glad about the fact and unmindful of the vicious fights he's put up about having to go.

I squeeze his shoulder.

"Can I go now?" Damon asks, pulling away from my hand.

A friend, who's leaving tomorrow to visit his family in the East, comes for dinner. He's tall and red-headed, and his eleven-year marriage has recently been annulled. I congratulate him on his sect's enthusiasm for illusion, but he won't take the bait—possibly because the state says he still has fifteen months of payments left: his non-bride's half-share of the retirement funds he and an insurance company accumulated.

For supper I barbecue spareribs and Mary prepares spaghetti squash, green salad, then lemon meringue pie for dessert. After eating, we retire to the den where we watch a program on that French-American-Scotch-Irish writer of crocodilian extract: Brother Bill. John says he hasn't yet really worked Faulkner into his studies of Plato, Heidegger, Nietzsche, and Derrida. I tell him he should: the South's weird-talking folks are closer than he thinks to Odysseus and Priam, Isis and Arjuna. He says I ought to hire out to write blurbs; I say I have then switch the TV back to convention coverage. Mary keeps getting up and leaving to take care of something in the kitchen. I ask her what she's feeding in there—a ferret?

She says she's going to turn the sprinkler on in the front yard. When she comes back she waters the plants in the living room then sits down on the sofa beside me. Soon, though, she gets up to put the dog out. Before long the children come back from the show. They went with the paper's Fine Arts editor who they and I used to live next door to. They scarf down their pie. Mary rises again, this time to load the dishwasher.

During the weather report, John suddenly asks what we think about Structuralism. Noticing that Mary is smiling, I tell him there are only two kinds of people: good ones and bad ones, that the good ones are those still capable of having their hearts broken. He says that's interesting, and I remind him I haven't answered his question. "But why don't we have a drink?"

Mary declines but John and I have Irishes on rocks. As the evening passes I have several more. The children go to bed about the same time the weatherman says we'll have more clouds but probably no rain in spite of the hurricane moving toward the coast. Galveston's going to get creamed.

Their last week with us, we take Damon and Gaddi to Santa Fe; and Mary's mother comes with us. She and the children quickly spend all their money. Suckers for adventure, we also take them to their first opera. High on the grace of mountain air, they sit (for awhile) on the edges of their seats during a fine production of *Elektra*. Gaddi says the huge waves of blood painted on the raked floor of the stage look like gigantic smashed strawberries. She also says that when she gets more money she's moving out here and she and Damon are going to build a mansion. Damon says he'd rather have one for himself. Laughing, Gaddi accuses him of having bad manners. Whispering to them to hush, I tell them intermission will be here soon.

At the airport, Mary looks worn as we kiss and hug the kids then tell them goodbye. Their arms wave like flags until they disappear into the tunnel.

As Mary and I walk toward a window to watch the plane taxi off, I see a woman releasing a little boy to a flight attendant. The kid has a paper heart pinned to his shirt; he's clutching an unwrapped stick of gum. When the pretty attendant takes his free hand, he grins. Looking lovely in her grief, his mother starts crying.

Home now, Mary and I rearrange two of the upstairs rooms so a larger sense of space now prevails in our chamber. Feeling hyperactive and lunatic, I find myself anxious to tell the kids about it, but I hold off calling them. I don't have the stomach to tell them there's something else that's different from the way they remember it. No. That's not true. I just don't want to hear them say they don't care.

ABOUT THE AUTHORS

Nancy Bell, a native of Pittsburg, Texas, received a B.A. in English from East Texas State University. *Jack and Jill* and *The Dallas Morning News* have published her nonfiction, and *Concho River Review* and other literary journals have included her fiction. Bell, an active member of Austin Writers League, often returns to her East Texas childhood for material. The author of "Oladean's Diary" is working on a book of short stories set among the Texas coastal pines.

Judy Brand, a fourth generation Texan, studied art at The University of California, at Berkeley, before graduating from the Glassell School of Art in Houston. Now living in Sugar Land, Brand creates visual art, exhibiting in Houston galleries. Brand has become similarly devoted to her word art. "Oil" is her first published work of fiction.

Born in Wyoming, **Pat Carr** writes on an Arkansas farm when not teaching college in Kentucky. Nevertheless, she is a Texas author. Carr lived in South Houston before graduating summa sum laude from Rice. After obtaining a Ph.D. from Tulane, she taught at Rice, then Texas Southern and the University of Texas at El Paso. Her short fiction has appeared in such collections as *Yale Review*, *Best American Short Stories*, *Her Work: Stories by Texas Women*, and in *Common Bonds: Stories by and About Modern Texas Women*. Her "Indian Burial" won the 1977 Texas Institute of Letters Award for the short story. Carr's novella *Bluebird* appeared in the 1993 SMU Press anthology, *Careless Weeds*. Her ten books include a collection of Civil War stories, *Our Brother's War*, and a novel, *The Grass Creek Chronicle*.

Laurie Champion's work has appeared in such publications as *New Texas '93*, *North Texas Review*, *Southern Literary Journal*, and *American Literature*. The author of "How to Listen to County Music" has lived in a variety of locales in Texas and in the U.S. (she graduated from Princeton High School in Texas). Today, she lives in Alpine near the Big Bend. Champion is an assistant professor of composition and literature at Sul Ross State University where she also teaches creative writing.

Richard Clinton, a graduate of Rider University in New Jersey, lives in Houston. After thirty-five years in the business world, he is pursuing a career in literature. Clinton studied creative writing with Texas author/teacher Christopher Woods, and he has begun a collection a short stories. Although he has published a number of nonfictional works, "A Night for Mystery" is Clinton's first short story to appear in print.

Mississippi native **Susan Collier** lived in Houston before moving with her family to Fritch, a small town north of Amarillo on the shores of Lake Meredith. Her story "The Gull," set in Galveston, dates back to her Texas coast self. A member of Romance Writers of America and Romance Writers of the Texas Panhandle, Collier has studied creative writing at Amarillo College. Her first book, which has the working title of *Time Heals*, has just been purchased by Leisure and is tentatively scheduled for release later this year.

Marla Cooper, from Odessa, Texas, graduated from Stephen F. Austin State University. Her nonfiction has been published in *The Chapbook, Good Old Days,* and *The Dallas Times Herald*. Marla Cooper's Depression-era West Texas story, "Fate's Acquittal," received second place in last year's *Texas Short Fiction* contest. The author of this year's "A Man's Gotta Do" lives in Carrollton, where she is working toward a collection of short stories.

Jerry Craven, a Corpus Christi native who now lives in Amarillo, has published his poetry, fiction, and drama in such places as *Concho River Review, RE: Arts and Letters, Texas Short Fiction*, Issac Asimov's *Science Fiction Magazine, Analog,* and *The Texas Anthology*. Craven, an editor of anthologies and a co-editor of language textbooks, also writes a column for the *Amarillo Daily News*. His books of poetry include *The Last Running, My Own Choric Song,* and *Oleander Wine*. Craven is a professor at West Texas A&M University, where he teaches literature and conducts workshops in creative writing. The author of "The Guy in the Old Joke" is an editor of the WTA&M Press Series.

Along with being a poet, short story writer, visual artist, and a high-school art teacher, **Carol Cullar** is editor of the Maverick Press of Eagle Pass, Texas. Cullar graduated from Hardin-Simmons University and Instituto

286

Allende, San Miguel de Allende, Mexico. One can find her writing in such publications as *Southwestern American Literature*, *New Texas '93*, *Grasslands Review*, *Texas in Poetry*, and *Concho River Review*. Her poetry chapbooks are *Haiku*, *The Hunger*, *Life & Death, Mostly*, and *Inexplicable Burnings*. Cullar lives near the Rio Grande in the small community of Quemado.

Robert Flynn, a Chillicothe native, knew wartime Vietnam as a news correspondent. Today, the San Antonio author is Novelist in Residence at Trinity University. Flynn's five novels—*North to Yesterday*, *In the House of the Lord*, *The Sounds of Rescue, the Signs of Hope*, *Wanderer Springs*, and his most recent, *The Last Klick*—have found national recognition. *The New York Times* selected Flynn's *North to Yesterday* as one of the best American books in its publication year. His other books include *Seasonal Rain*, a short story collection, and *A Personal War in Vietnam*, a nonfictional narrative. He also co-edited *When I Was Just Your Age*, a collection of interviews of famous Texans for an adolescent readership. His short story, "The Savior of the Bees," was anthologized by editor Don Graham in *South by Southwest*. Flynn's short story collection, *Living with the Hyenas*, is scheduled for release by TCU Press this fall.

Greg Garrett was born in Oklahoma and has lived throughout the South and Southwest. He received his Ph.D. in English from Oklahoma State University, where he studied with Gordon Weaver. The author of "Blood Relations" now lives with his son Jake in Waco. An award-winning professor at Baylor University, Garrett has had his short fiction appear in the *South Dakota Review*, *High Plains Review*, *Grain*, and *Writers' Forum* as well as in a number of other Canadian and American magazines and journals. In 1993, Greg Garrett won the Pirate's Alley Faulkner Prize for Fiction for his novella *Minuet*.

Among other things, **A. C. Greene** is a sixth-generation Texan. He is also the author of *A Personal Country*, *The Last Captive*, *The 50 Best Books on Texas*, and *The Santa Clause Bank Robbery*—to mention only four of his twenty books. Greene has worked as a bookstore owner, newspaperman, television editorialist, and college professor. His honors include a Dobie-Paisano Fellowship and a Texas Institute of Letters presidency. A native of

Abilene and for decades a resident of Dallas, Greene and his wife, Judy, presently reside in Salado. Although this volume's "A Matter of Time" was written in 1954, some fifteen years before *A Personal Country*, readers can enjoy in this narrative A. C. Greene's now much admired treatment of West Texas themes. In 1994, UNT Press released his *900 Miles on the Butterfield Trail*, which won the T. R. Fehrenbach Award from the Texas Historical Commission. Greene is finishing a book about his Texas ancestry.

James Hoggard, the author of nine books, has degrees from Southern Methodist University (B.A.) and the University of Kansas (M.A.). In 1990, Hoggard won the Texas Institute of Letters Award for the Short Story. The Wichita Falls author has been a former N.E.A. Fellow, and he is presently President of the Texas Institute of Letters. Hoggard has penned a nonfictional book, *Elevator Man*, and a novel, *Trotter Ross*. His poetry and prose have been anthologized in *Texas Stories and Poems*, *Travois*, *The New Breed*, and *New and Experimental Literature*. The 1993 anthology, *New Growth 2*, contains his story "The Scapegoat." Recently, Northwestern University Press published Hoggard's collection of translations, *Chronicle of My Worst Years*. Hoggard has been a professor at Midwestern State University since 1966.

Guida Jackson, an author of fiction, nonfiction, and plays, grew up in Amarillo and received a B.A. in journalism from Texas Tech. After raising four children, she returned to school for an M.A. in third world literature and a Ph.D. in comparative literature. Among Jackson's book-length publications is the 1979 novel, *Passing Through*, published by Simon and Schuster. Her short story, "The Evil Eye," appeared in *New Growth* and "The Umbilical Cord" was selected for inclusion in *New Texas '91*. Jackson, who lives in the Woodlands, edits *Touchstone*, a prestigious Texas literary journal. In addition, Jackson has a comprehensive reference work, *Encyclopedia of Literary Epic*, scheduled for release next year. "The Historical Monument," Jackson's story in *Texas Short Fiction II*, is only one story of several that she has started with the same opening sentence.

James Ward Lee, a former President of the Texas Folklore Society, is Executive Director of the Center for Texas Studies at the University of North Texas. Lee is known for his scholarly articles, editorial work, historical studies, personal essays, and his short fiction. His writings have appeared in a variety of publications, including *Concho River Review, Southwestern Historical Quarterly*, and in the annual volumes of the *Texas Folklore Society*. Lee founded the Southwest Writers Series and co-edited *Southwestern American Literature* and *The Texas Tradition*. Critics consider Lee's 1987 *Classics of Texas Fiction* to be the definitive study on Texas novels. His 1993 collection of humorous essays, *Texas, My Texas*, has been widely appreciated.

Joy-Ellis McLemore, a Longview native, has had her essays, stories, and poems included in a diversity of publications. She has taught college English for twenty-one years in five different states. McLemore is now a faculty member of the Department of Humanities of the University of Texas at Tyler. Her story in *Texas Short Fiction II*, "The Seduction," is set in the East Texas she knows so well.

Charlie McMurtry is a Ph.D. candidate and a teaching fellow at the University of North Texas. The author of "Keeping the Myth Alive" has had his work appear in *Concho River Review, Grasslands Review*, and *Texas College English*. Living with his family in Wichita Falls, McMurtry routinely makes the long commute to Denton to instruct freshmen and sophomores in literature and composition.

Lianne Elizabeth Mercer's poetry has appeared in *RiverSedge, Concho River Review*, and *Negative Capability*. Her short story, "Waiting for Shadows," was anthologized in *New Texas '93*, and "The Legacy" was included in *Common Bonds*. Mercer, a psychiatric nurse, has taught both writing and nursing courses. In 1994, she moved from San Antonio to Fredericksburg, where she is closing in on a book-length collection of short fiction.

Kathryn M. Miller recently graduated with a degree in English and theater from Trinity University in San Antonio. Besides studying theater and creative writing, she has worked with emotionally disturbed children. "How We Got A New Screen Door" is Miller's first published short story.

Talibah Folami Modupe, a businesswoman and writer, graduated from South Oak Cliff High School before receiving her B.S. from North Texas

State University. Modupe has published three books of short stories: *Talibah, Can We Talk? Let's Be Frank*, and *The Grapevine Still Alive & Workin!* Modupe has participated in a number of community programs, including The North Texas Society of Legal Aid and The I Have a Dream Foundation of Dallas. Another collection of short stories is forthcoming, and the author of "Inmate 93274" has a novel scheduled for release later this year.

Eric Muirhead, currently a Houstonian but originally a Dallasite, received a B.A. in psychology from Yale. He then endured a few "incredibly unhappy years in med school." After receiving an M.A. in English from Rice, the author of "Drag" made a living as a poetry-writing cab driver in the greater Houston area. Muirhead administrated a school for the children of an engineering company on an island off the coast of Borneo before returning to America on a sailboat. Muirhead now teaches creative writing at San Jacinto College in Pasadena, Texas. His work-in-progress is a collection of short stories based on his taxi-driving years.

A Pulitzer Prize nominee, **Violette Newton** has published ten books of poetry, including her Texas Poet Laureate collection, *The Proxy*. Among her other titles are *The Scandal and Other Poems* and *The Shamrock Cross*. Her poetry has been anthologized in the yearbooks of the Poetry Society of Texas as well as in *Travois, Texas Stories and Poems*, and in *New Texas '92*. Newton's short stories have appeared in *Stone Drum* and *Fiction and Poetry by Texas Women*. Readers can discern Newton's poetic gifts in this book's "To Make Talk," a prose piece told in Cajun dialect. The poet and short story writer has long lived in Beaumont.

John R. Posey, a graduate in history from Dartmouth College, can claim among his business-world credits the directorship of a Texas chamber of commerce and a managerial position with Mayor Harold Washington's administration in Chicago. Among his literary accomplishments, Posey was a national semi-finalist for the Beeking Foundation Novel-in-Progress Competition for his book *Charlatans*, and is currently working on his first play, a comedy entitled *411*. His work has appeared in such publications as *Our Texas Magazine, The Fort Worth Star-Telegram, The Houston Post, The Dallas Morning News, Texas Short Fiction*, and *Minority Business News USA*. Posey is a free-lance writer, a Fort Worth business consultant, and Editor of *African-American Literary Review*, a key regional publication.

Native Texan **Clay Reynolds** holds a B.A. from the University of Texas, M.A. from Trinity University. His doctorate is from the University of Tulsa. Among many publications, Reynolds has produced three novels: *The Vigil*, *Agatite*, and *Franklin's Crossing*. *Franklin's Crossing* was selected for the Violet Crown Award in 1992 and was nominated for a Pulitzer Prize in that year. *Agatite* was reissued under the title *Rage*. He is a member of the Texas Institute of Letters and recently he taught as Writer in Residence at Villanova. Recipient of an N.E.A. Fellowship, Reynold's short stories have been anthologized in *New Growth* and *New Growth 2*. The author of "Right Field Blues" lives with his wife and two children in Denton, Texas, where he is completing a history of the Southwest Exposition and Livestock Show of Fort Worth. Reynolds also coaches youth league baseball.

Paul Ruffin has a B.S. and an M.A. from Mississippi State University and a Ph.D. from the University of Southern Mississippi. He is Director of Creative Writing at Sam Houston State University and Editor and Director of *The Texas Review*, one of the state's foremost literary journals. His prose and poetry have appeared in such publications as *Texas Prize Stories and Poems*, *Contemporary Southern Fiction*, *Best of the West*, *Texas Stories and Poems*, and *New Growth 2*. Ruffin has authored, co-authored, edited, or co-edited twelve books, among them, two notable anthologies, *The Texas Anthology* and *That's What I Like About the South*. In 1993, SMU Press released Ruffin's critically acclaimed short story collection, *The Man Who Would Be God*.

Before receiving her B.A. from the University of Louisville and an M.A. from the University of North Texas, **Jan Epton Seale** graduated from Waxahachie High. The author and creative writing teacher has been the recipient of an N.E.A. Fellowship, participated in seven P.E.N. fiction projects, and has taught in the Artists-In-Education Program. Her prose and poetry can be found in such collections as *Quartet*, *Southwest*, *Common Bonds*, *New Texas '91*, and *This Place of Memory*. In 1992, TCU Press released Seale's well-received short fiction collection, *Airlift*. In 1993, editor Mark Busby published Seale's "Cockscomb" in *New Growth 2*. Seale is the author of two books of poetry, *Bonds* and *Sharing the House*. A collection of essays about the Valley, *Homeland*, is scheduled for release in Spring 1995. Seale lives with her family in McAllen in the Rio Grande Valley.

Grant Sisk, the author of "Coconino Escarpment," has lived all over the state. A native of Garland, Sisk graduated from Abilene Christian University. His work has been published in *Texas Books in Review*, *Western American Literature*, *Heritage*, *Literary History of the American West*, and *Review of Texas Books*. Sisk, a fifth-generation Texan, is working on a novel and a collection of short stories.

Lin Sutherland, who speaks Spanish and Portuguese, teaches creative writing at the University of Texas. She also freelances as a travel writer/ photographer for national magazines. Her nonfiction has appeared in a variety of publications, among them *Field and Stream* and *Texas Monthly*. Sutherland has also written a life history and a mystery novel, and her professional credits include the 1991 President's Award in Nonfiction. Sutherland has a piece in the anthology, *The Little Fishing Book*, forthcoming from Atlantic Monthly Press. The Austin author dedicates "The September Babies Birthday Party," her story in this collection, to her late father, Thomas Sutherland.

Jack Welch received his bachelor's degree in English from West Virginia University, his master's in creative writing from the University of Iowa, and a doctorate in English from Carnegie-Mellon University. Since 1984, he has taught at Abilene Christian University. Among Jack Welch's publications are three novels, one county history, four produced film scripts, one produced opera libretto, and a long list of essays and short stories. The prolific writer and longtime educator has poetry forthcoming in *Echoes* and a short story in *Mesquite*.

Betty Wiesepape, a Ph.D. candidate at the University of Texas at Dallas, lives in Richardson. As the daughter of a Texas highway contractor and the wife of a petroleum engineer, Wiesepape knows the sundry lands and cultures of our state. The author of "A Soft Spot" is the 1993 winner of the Texas Creative Writing Teacher's Graduate Fiction Award, and her work placed Third in the 1994 Pine Grove Press Literary Competition. Weisepape's nonfiction article, "The Manuscript Club of Wichita Falls," appeared in the May, 1994, issue of the *Southwestern Historical Quarterly*. Weisepape's fiction can be found in such publications as *New Texas '93*, *Just a Moment*, *Texas Short Fiction*, and *RiverSedge*.

Terry McKinley Zumwalt, a native of Uvalde (she remembers John Nance Garner from her childhood), holds a B.A. in humanities from the University of Texas at Austin and an M.A. in communications from Regent University in Virginia. She now lives in Corsicana. Her story, "Desert Flight," received first place in last year's Texas Short Fiction contest. In 1994, Zumwalt resigned a film arts teaching position at Texas Christian University to work full-time on a novel. Besides writing, Zumwalt, who soloed at age seventeen, maintains an interest in aviation. The author of "Running Before Red Sails" is also developing a new interest in sailing.